W9-BXA-394

THE ORIGIN OF STORMS

TOR BOOKS BY ELIZABETH BEAR

A Companion to Wolves (with Sarah Monette)
The Tempering of Men (with Sarah Monette)
An Apprentice to Elves (with Sarah Monette)
All the Windwracked Stars
By the Mountain Bound
The Sea Thy Mistress
Range of Ghosts
Shattered Pillars
Steles of the Sky
Karen Memory
The Stone in the Skull
The Red-Stained Wings
The Origin of Storms

THE
ORIGIN
OF
STORMS

ELIZABETH BEAR

TOR

A Tom Doherty Associates Book
NEW YORK

THE ORIGIN OF STORMS

Copyright © 2022 by Sarah Wishnevsky Lynch

Map by Rhys Davies

A Tor Book
Published by Tom Doherty Associates
120 Broadway
New York, NY 10271

www.tor-forge.com

Tor® is a registered trademark of Macmillan Publishing Group, LLC.

Library of Congress Cataloging-in-Publication Data

Names: Bear, Elizabeth, author.
Title: The origin of storms / Elizabeth Bear.
Description: First edition. | New York : Tor, 2022. |
Series: The Lotus Kingdoms ; 3 | "A Tom Doherty Associates book."
Identifiers: LCCN 2022000593 (print) | LCCN 2022000594 (ebook) |
ISBN 9780765380173 (hardcover) | ISBN 9781466872097 (ebook) |
Subjects: LCGFT: Novels.
Classification: LCC PS3602.E2475 O75 2022 (print) |
LCC PS3602.E2475 (ebook) | DDC 813/.6—dc23/eng/20220107
LC record available at https://lccn.loc.gov/2022000593
LC ebook record available at https://lccn.loc.gov/2022000594

Our books may be purchased in bulk for promotional, educational, or business use. Please contact your local bookseller or the Macmillan Corporate and Premium Sales Department at 1-800-221-7945, extension 5442, or by email at MacmillanSpecialMarkets@macmillan.com.

First Edition: 2022

Printed in the United States of America

0 9 8 7 6 5 4 3 2 1

This book is for the Elephant Mothers
(and grandmothers, allomothers, and aunties)
biological and otherwise—who did their best.

The origin of storms is in the mind
And not the sky

    —The poetess Ümmühan
   circa 1700 A.F. (After the Frost)

For she is steadfast*
Like the elephant
Mother of stones
Mother of walls

—The poetess Ümmühan,
circa 1700 A.F. (After the Frost)

*In the original Sarathai, the word the poet uses is peculiar to the so-called Royal Virtues, and invokes the ability to remain resolute, steadfast, enduring, and protective of those under one's care in the manner of an elephant matriarch. The other animals of the Royal Virtues are Bull (strength), Tiger (ferocity or ambition), Peacock (confidence), the Sarathai blind river Dolphin (speed or decisiveness), and the bearded Vulture or lammergeyer (wisdom or discretion).

THE ORIGIN OF STORMS

1

THE QUEEN OF A MURDERED CITY STOOD OVER THE COOLING BODY OF HER
enemy and tried to think what to do.

This was not Sayeh Rajni's land. These were not Sayeh Rajni's people.
There was an army here within the walls and it was not Sayeh Rajni's army.

Neither did the army without the walls belong to her. And yet here
she was, more or less in charge of that land, those people, and both of the
armies.

The army inside the walls of Sarathai-tia had been commanded by Anuraja, the ambitious old narcissist whose corpse she was washing with more
respect than *he* had ever accorded to anyone. The army outside owed allegiance to Mrithuri, the young queen he had married against her will, whose
city this was. Who now lay unconscious in her bed, protected by an armed
guard.

Beyond the windows, dawn was falling, but any texture of the fading
light was erased by clouds and curtains of rain. Within, Sayeh's hands
guided a cloth redolent of sandalwood and soap over the body. It was not
the first corpse she had washed in her life.

It was by far the most satisfying.

She was already looking forward to the next one.

This is an elegant pickle I've gotten myself into. Sayeh stood with a crutch propped
into her armpit, taking the strain off her healing leg. She *was* standing on
it, however, and that was another victory. One almost as satisfying as the
death of Anuraja.

She'd beaten one enemy. But the other still held her son Drupada hostage, having claimed Drupada as his own heir. Sayeh had improved her
position and gathered resources. She was no longer captive herself. She *was*
reliant on the goodwill of Mrithuri, who was now—after a fashion—the
Dowager Empress of Sarathai-tia and Sarathai-lae.

Dowager Empress of United Sarath, Sayeh supposed—a thing that had
not existed in a long time.

That was to say that Mrithuri was Dowager Empress . . . *if* Sayeh's cousin
survived her current illness, which had been brought on by the overuse of
the poisonous stimulant in the venom of certain magical serpents.

If not . . . well, that left two of the Lotus Kingdoms without a ruler, and
a third—Sayeh's home of Ansh-Sahal—destroyed utterly. And *that* would

inevitably mean a continuation of the war. Not that a young widow was the sort of leader the martial men of Sahal-Sarat would flock to, so there might be a war even if Mrithuri survived.

Meanwhile, somewhere to the north was their kidnapping cousin Himadra. Another war in waiting, Daughter's piss!

Sayeh kept her face over the bucket of clean water and scent in order to attenuate the reek of Anuraja's body. The stench of death was no worse than that of the suppurating abscess he had suffered from. At least there was clean water. Anuraja had caused his pet sorceress to clean Sarathai-tia's fouled cisterns before he died. That was just as well, because once he had died, she'd apported out and left them to their fate.

The water might be clean, but the rage inside Sayeh still bubbled filthily. And being a rajni, she could not show its fury.

Her rage had to be a thing of silence and smiles and coquettish glances, because she was dependent upon those around her. She was dependent on her hold over Anuraja's soldiers—and that power relied on them seeing her as a gracious and divinely chosen authority. Between that and their duty to Mrithuri as Anuraja's widow . . . it might be about enough to keep them from going rogue and pillaging the city they'd been left in occupation of, as long as authority were established quickly.

Which meant two things. One, they were going to have to find some way to *pay* those soldiers. And two, they needed Mrithuri to wake up.

Soon.

THE DEAD MAN WAITED BESIDE HIS RAJNI'S BED, TRYING TO KEEP OUT OF THE way of the physicians. There were only three of them, and they worked well together—but in his current state of anxiety, helplessness, and dismay, three seemed like a roomful.

There was Ata Akhimah, the strong-limbed Wizard from Aezin, whose glowing dark complexion stood out by contrast to the white of her sleeveless blouse. There was Tsering-la, Sayeh Rajni's Rasan Wizard, a small man with amber skin and epicanthic folds. He wore a black six-petaled coat that hung as though he had lost weight since it was tailored. And there was Hnarisha, Mrithuri Rajni's secretary, whose holistic skills were not, he insisted, Wizardry—but something else entirely.

The Dead Man heard the plainchant of the nuns cloistered within the palace walls, full of echoes as if it came from far away. Mrithuri had traded them something for help and intervention. He did not know *what* she had traded. He was, he realized, desperately afraid that she had chosen to sacrifice her life. If she had promised herself to the demon or angel she considered her goddess in return for her people's salvation . . . what then could keep her with him?

The Dead Man steadied himself and told the knots in his stomach that Wizards knew a lot about healing, and these Wizards did not seem too terribly concerned.

He was concerned enough for all of them. And it was not his place to show that concern.

His place was to appear stoic and impassive. His place was to keep them all safe. From outside threats, since he could not defend Mrithuri from the treachery of her own body. His veil was a blessing: it hid his expression and concealed his emotions. Even when he made the mistake of looking over at the rajni while her people ministered to her.

She looked so frail.

He knew, intimately, how bony her arms were and how thin her face had become. Somehow, though, the projecting cheekbones and the architecture of her hipbones seemed more pathetic without the fidgety energy that usually animated her. Now she merely seemed emaciated.

Shiny dots of scar marked the skin below her collarbones, over the stark ribs, along the inside of her arms. It seemed newly evident how many of them were fresh and pink, or capped with a pinprick of scab. She had not been healing well.

Against the wall, Mrithuri's enormous bhaluukutta, Syama, lay with her bearlike head on her doglike paws and moaned her distress and helplessness. The Dead Man knew how she felt.

He watched without watching as the woman who was secretly his lover—even more secretly, his wife—was ministered to. As she was cleaned and dressed and fed milky honey tea by spoonfuls trickled into her mouth. As Hnarisha laid his hands upon her brow and breastbone and bathed her in what healing energies he could command.

The Dead Man watched, and he tried not to think of another ruler lying nearby, body just as slack but soon to be stiffening. Of that other ruler, also being bathed, being dressed in his personal colors of orange and blue. *That* king was being dressed for a pyre: the local heathen replacement for a decent burial. The Dead Man watched and tried not to think how close Mrithuri might be to that other, more final purification.

He was a soldier. His place was to deal with whatever problem lay before his hand and not to worry about the larger picture.

It is what it is. The refrain of those who fight and die on another's behalf, at another's command.

It is what it is.

But he was not just a soldier in this place, at this time. Not just a retainer. He was a leader, a tactician. And, with Mrithuri incapacitated—temporarily, of course it could only be temporarily—and her general exiled for the time being beyond the city walls, it *was* his place to worry. About her health, about the precarious politics. About the enemy army in possession of the palace, the city, and the land outside.

THE DEAD MAN MIGHT RELY ON HIS VEIL TO HIDE HIS EXPRESSION, BUT IT could not hide his startled jump and the flicker of his hand toward his pistol when the door slid aside. Embarrassment heated his belly. No matter how old you were, it seemed like there was always something to make you feel callow and unprepared.

Currently, that thing wore the gentle demeanor of the Lady Golbahar. She stood framed in the portal, one hand still resting on the edge of the door she had slid aside. She had noticed his agitation: that was evident from the smile lines beside her hazel eyes and the tilt of her head within her veil.

"Are you free?" she asked him. "We have some things to talk about."

"I cannot leave the rajni," he said.

"I propose that there is very little that Syama and all these Wizards cannot protect her from. Except the future."

"I'm not a Wizard," Hnarisha said over his shoulder. "Go, Dead Man. We'll keep her safe."

With reluctance, the Dead Man followed Golbahar, managing to avoid a backward glance only because he was already so flustered by how he had revealed himself. It wasn't much, true—but the inculcation to stoicism ran deep.

Golbahar did not bring him far. Merely down the hall, and into the company of most of the people the Dead Man would have sought out for himself if he had been thinking clearly. There was Druja, the caravan master and . . . the polite term would probably be *information broker* . . . his quiet brother Prasana, the assassin, who wore servant's garb. There was Yavashuri, Mrithuri's maid of honor. The Dead Man thought she was also the spymaster to whom Druja and others reported. Nearby stood Ritu, the endlessly useful matriarch of the tribe of martial acrobats that Druja had accidentally collected along the way.

Sayeh Rajni stood braced on a crutch, a motley-feathered phoenix on her shoulder. Her retainers stood with her. Vidhya, the guard captain, was still disguised as a civilian in the foppish clothes of a courtier. Nazia, Tseringla's apprentice, wore short hair that stood out around her head like a halo of petals, like the rays of the Lion Sun of Messaline. The elderly poetess Ümmühan—a woman of his homeland, her face disconcertingly bare— seemed to have the straightest spine of anyone in the room.

The undead Godmade Nizhvashiti stood against the wall between the windows, a motionless dark-skinned scarecrow in faded dark robes, easy to mistake for some article of furniture. A coatrack, perhaps.

To complete the set: the Dead Man and Golbahar.

The Dead Man paused inside the door. "Am I called before the tribunal?"

"Indeed you are not," Yavashuri said, with the air of one conducting matters. "Well, I think that's everyone. Shall we have seats?"

They dispersed themselves. The floor was heaped with rugs, and the rugs were scattered with bolsters and cushions. Some were soft; some were stuffed with aromatic sawdust. The Dead Man settled on one that exhaled rosewood when his bottom made contact.

Sayeh levered herself down with her crutch, balancing the great bird on her shoulder. The tendons in her forearms striated, but she gave no appearance of distress.

The Dead Man said, "This looks like a council of war."

Vidhya and Druja exchanged glances. Now, there was an interesting alliance, the Dead Man thought. "Maybe a council to avoid war," Vidhya drawled, when no one interceded. "We need options to present to Mrithuri when she awakes."

No one said *if* she awakes. The Dead Man felt silently grateful that he was not the only superstitious one. "Who is Anuraja's general?"

He looked at Vidhya as he asked, but it was Sayeh who answered. "His lieutenant commander's name is Zirha. I haven't met him. I think Anuraja arranged on purpose to keep us separated." She hitched her scarf up her shoulder when it slithered down. "Anuraja didn't seem to rely on generals much. I'll say this one thing for the filthy bastard: he led from the front."

Yavashuri rocked on her cushion as if trying to settle her old bones into place. The Dead Man rolled his eyes at himself even as he thought it: she couldn't be much older than he was.

"I'm not reassured by Zirha's reputation in that case," she said. "Would you say he is a weak leader?"

Ümmühan cleared her throat and looked at Nazia, the old encouraging the young. Nazia looked at her hands but spoke. "I would not say he is a strong one."

"Ysmat's beads," the Dead Man muttered. "Just what we need."

Sayeh snorted. "A strong leader could be worse, or better, depending on his ambition."

Yavashuri said, "It seems like we've all independently come to the same conclusion: that our most immediate problem is the unhelmed army in our midst."

"Most immediate," said Nizhvashiti. "But not most severe. *That* would be—" It groped for words of sufficient enormity, which was not a failing the Dead Man associated with the Godmade.

He said, "The predatory necromancers and whomever they serve?"

Nizhvashiti nodded, expressionless. The Dead Man was not sure if its lack of affect was due to mummification, or due to feeling his offering was inadequate to the gravity of the circumstances and being too polite to say so.

The Dead Man didn't mind, if so. He held that dragons, Wizards, necromancers, and monstrous, mysterious forces capable of cracking the lid on a quiescent volcano should all have been beyond his sphere of responsibility. He was a bodyguard, a mercenary.

It was too bad destiny didn't seem to agree with him.

"We can't even disband the Laeish army," Vidhya said, retaining his focus. "They'd just pillage their way back where they came from, and everybody along the way is now Mrithuri Rajni's subject. We need to organize and use them." He looked at Sayeh. "We need to convince them it's in their best interests to work *with* Mrithuri's army rather than squabbling over the pickings."

Golbahar had folded herself into a tidy bundle of limbs. "Once we get them back to Sarathai-lae, we don't need to keep most of them on the payroll, do we? We can send them back to their farms and hang on to the professionals."

"Dire prophecies," the Dead Man reminded. "Terrible things on the wind; the dead walk. We might need a good-sized army. And there's still Himadra to contend with."

Sayeh straightened. "Yes, I at least have every intention of dealing with him, since he's still holding my son. But our most immediate concern *is* finding a way to pay the Laeish army."

Ümmühan said, "Sayeh Rajni is correct. And we must stop referring to them as Anuraja's army. They are Mrithuri's army now. The goal must be to keep them that way and solidify her position as their leader."

"So pay them," Druja said.

Ümmühan nodded. "And get her in front of them to give some kind of speech."

Surreptitiously, the Dead Man made the sign of the pen. How they might expect to get Mrithuri on her feet and channeling her charisma into a political talk—without access to her snakes and their stimulant venom—he did not know.

Yavashuri shook her head. "Somewhere among Anu . . . among the Laeish's things, the rajni's serpents must be hidden. He used them—"

"It's not safe," the Dead Man said, realizing too late how furious he sounded.

Yavashuri held out her palm. "Don't worry. I'm on your side."

Nazia had settled in a corner of the room. She had not spoken except the once, and did not speak now, but the Dead Man watched as her eyes moved from face to face, alertly observing. He wondered what she thought.

Yavashuri shrugged. "Mrithuri is already so unwell because of her overuse."

The Dead Man said, "Where is the money going to come from?"

"There's not enough in the coffers for long," said Yavashuri. "Perhaps I should not reveal that, but—"

Sayeh waved a hand before her face. "Our fates are linked now."

Guang Bao reached over to preen Sayeh's hair. She made a face of distaste that seemed inconsistent with her affection for the bird and with what the Dead Man knew of the bond between daughters of the Alchemical Emperor's line and their familiars.

Ümmühan apparently noticed too. "Is something wrong, Sayeh Rajni?"

"I'm not ungrateful to the austringers," Sayeh said, stroking Guang Bao with a fingertip. He fluffed in pleasure, showing off the black and white bearded vulture feathers spliced to his own damaged ones. "He flies nearly as well as he ever did."

"But?" Ümmühan prompted.

"But he does smell like rotten bones now." Sayeh pinched her nose theatrically. "Yavashuri, I hear you. There's not enough in the coffers. And we can't exactly pry the diamonds from a throne that blasts those who disrespect it with death."

The Dead Man, who did not yet know Sayeh Rajni well, thought, *Here is an effortless leader.*

The thoughtful silence was broken by a scraping sound. The Dead Man did not again disgrace himself by jumping half off his cushion because someone had scratched on the door.

"Come," Yavashuri said, and then looked apologetically at Sayeh. "My profound apologies, Your Abundance."

"It is not," Sayeh said dryly, "my house."

Hnarisha paused beside the open door. "The rajni is awake," he said.

Sayeh levered herself to her feet with Vidhya's assistance. Nazia handed her her crutch; she leaned against it. "Good. Then we can ask *her* where the money can come from."

SAYEH KNEW HNARISHA DID NOT FIND HER HUMOROUS. HE WOULDN'T OUTright scold royalty, but that wouldn't stop him from basting her with dubious glances.

"I know," she soothed, moving toward him. Her leg ached, but she needed to use it, to build the muscle again. "She needs time to recover. But she needs to be alive and free to have that time, so perhaps a little more discomfort now and a longer life to recover in, hm?"

The glance didn't get any less doubtful, but Hnarisha did step out of the doorway. "Not everybody at once," he said.

Guang Bao, always alert to Sayeh's emotions, half-spread his wings to balance on her shoulder, effectively clearing the area around her.

Sometimes it was acceptable to take advantage of one's rank, Sayeh decided, and flared past Hnarisha while the others were still sorting themselves out. It was a creditable sweep for somebody still limping on a crutch. She crossed the hall and let herself into Mrithuri's chambers without scratching or otherwise announcing her presence first.

She moved through the antechambers and did pause at the door to the bedroom. Tsering-la must have left. Ata Akhimah was directing some member of the palace staff toward a covered chamber pot, which was whisked away.

The curtains of Mrithuri's bed were drawn back. She lay among clean covers. Soiled ones were piled in the corner, freshly stripped.

Curls of hair still plastered the Dowager's unlined forehead. Her complexion was greenish and her eyes sunk among bruises. Her collarbones had edges like cut glass.

Sayeh stumped to the bedside and—crutch for a prop—lowered herself among the bolsters and cushions on the floor. She was getting the hang of this crutch thing.

The smell of a sickroom was fading beneath sandalwood and attar of roses.

Sayeh looked into too-bright eyes and said, "It's good to have you back."

"Oh, the indignities of illness," Mrithuri whispered. "The jokes about privy councilors write themselves, don't they?"

"It's a good thing you're still too sick to spank."

"I'd like to see you try." Mrithuri's faint smile failed. "You took a terrible risk."

Sayeh nodded. "I did. And we're not clear of the field of battle yet, Dowager Empress."

"Please." The sick woman swallowed. "Don't call me that."

Sayeh was aware of Ata Akhimah moving around the room behind her. Of Syama beside the wall, head down but not sleeping. Listening, guarding. The chambermaid returned and carted off the soiled blankets and rugs. The miasma of illness lifted.

"It is who you must be," Sayeh said, as gently as she could manage. She felt real sympathy for this child . . . well, not a child, but so young to be a ruler on her own. She had been through a great deal, and there was doubtless more to come. "There is still an army in your city, and they must be *your* army if we are to survive and remain free."

Mrithuri's expression pinched in displeasure. "You think calling me Empress is going to make a difference to those men?"

"If we do it often enough and loudly enough, it will, to some of them." Sayeh smiled. "People want to believe in things. And one way to make them believe is to treat the thing as fact, whether it is or not. Ümmühan taught me that one."

"Fine." Mrithuri waved her hand, paling visibly from that small effort. "I've been overcome with my grief at being so swiftly widowed. I'll recover fast. What do we do next?"

"Get the Laeish to let your people come back from exile. Tell them that you will be bringing them home very soon. Go take control of Sarathai-lae and its coffers."

"Figure out how to pay them until that happens."

Sayeh nodded. Mrithuri was sharp.

"Has there been any looting yet?"

"Not much," Sayeh said, honestly. "So far, their officers, such as they are, are keeping the men in check. I think that will last until the officers start to wonder."

"So. Half a day." Mrithuri sighed. "What do we do when we get to Sarathai-lae?"

"Anuraja was holding Himadra's brothers as fosterlings, you know."

"Yes, I know." Mrithuri's eyes widened as she realized what Sayeh meant. "Oh. Oh! An exchange of hostages? A bargaining chip for a peace treaty?"

Sayeh smiled. "Can you get out of bed to end a war?"

2

THE GAGE WAS PLEASED TO REALIZE THAT HIMADRA APPARENTLY DID INTEND to treat them as honored guests when it could so easily have been a mere euphemism. "Pleased?" Was that the correct word? "Relieved" might be a better one.

The relief was not for him, nor for his companion. It was for the people of Chandranath. No castle built could hold a Gage who did not choose to honor its existence. He felt confident as well that however superannuated she might seem, the transformed dragon walking beside him was capable of handling herself in a crisis.

Dragons were enormous, powerful, and dangerous to be near. Over time, everything in their vicinity became saturated with their poisonous emanations. And a dragon who had lived to be a few million and six—estimating conservatively—probably knew an additional trick or two.

But the Gage didn't want to disassemble a castle. People lived in them, and a lot of work went into building and maintaining them. People got hurt trying to stop you when you had to pull one down without the consent of the dwellers. He was glad to have that particular option set off to one side for the time being.

Anyway, being honored guests rather than "honored guests," there was no trouble when he and Kyrlmyrandal went for a walk.

"Did you expect to find Ravana here?" he asked.

She swung her staff, not leaning on it. "Not . . . exactly. But I'm encouraged by what we *have* found. The raja is not so under the sway of the sorcerer as he might have been."

"Do you believe him?"

"Humans do not lie very well," the dragon said. "He did not seem to be lying."

"He has a reputation as a tactician. And tacticians are all liars. That's half of what tactics is." The Gage sighed without breathing. He was making arguments with the truth because he did not care for its ramifications. "Then this doesn't bring us any closer to catching up with either sorcerer."

Kyrlmyrandal halted her staff at one apex of its pendulation "Did you say . . . *either?*"

Briefly, the Gage explained about Ravani, and about the Dead Man encountering her in Chandranath, in the retinue of Anuraja.

Kyrlmyrandal walked again. "How many times have you yourself met these two?"

"Met? Twice, I think: Ravana for me both times. In ruined Ansh-Sahal, building an abomination of corpses. And again with you, among the Singing Towers."

"And your partner at least once, as well."

"You said the one in your city was a projection?"

"Sure," said Kyrlmyrandal. "Possibly they all are. I don't think either of these sorcerers are, exactly, the creature we are seeking. Or, in a sense, they all are. Have you seen evidence that he—it—can possess things? Take control of their physical bodies from a distance?"

The Gage thought of the twitching corpses in the horrible tower of bodies in Ansh-Sahal. "Not from too great a distance. But there's nothing in that to prove he couldn't, I suppose. Only that I haven't seen it."

"And you haven't seen them in the same place. Both sorcerers, I mean."

"I have not." The Gage flipped his worn brown hood up to cover the reflections of his skull. "Do you think they're the same person?"

The Heavenly River splashed its light from horizon to horizon, casting complicated shadows. Some broad-winged bird glided across that brilliant sky, leaving the Gage . . . well, not breathless, or at least not any more breathless than was usual.

"I don't think they're a person, precisely. By the way, your bird is back again."

Relief and freedom flooded the Gage, sensations so strong he could imagine he had a body to feel them with. "Vara," he said, casting the memory that was his voice across the space between. Mrithuri might hear him, and through her, the Dead Man, in turn.

It must have worked, because the bearded vulture fell sideways toward the horizon like a child sliding on ice. He dropped so hard and so swiftly that if the Gage had had a heart, it would have flown into his throat. He threw up a fist instead. The vulture dropped heavy onto his brass gauntlet, nails scoring the metal with a horrendous sound. Like iron filings caught in gears, like the end of the world.

Vara mantled, enormous wings spread and flexed, head dropped in threat, crest feathers standing on end to make it seem larger and more ferocious. Larger and more ferocious than the largest and most ferocious bird the Gage had even met, and the Gage had met a few.

Its feathers seemed cleaner, less bedraggled. It must have found water and bathed since the night before.

Wandering so long, and so far from its home range, perhaps it had not yet located ochre clay to groom through its feathers, with which to dye itself in shades of umber and vermilion. So it was stark white, weathered-bone white, streaked with black as if by sharp strokes of a charcoal stick.

It glared at Kyrlmyrandal and increased its resemblance to a furry snake by emitting a resonant hiss. It hadn't responded so boldly to her before. The Gage wondered what had changed—but he was no daughter of empire, to understand the ways of animals.

"Be kind, little brother," the old dragon said. "Not all of us are as strong of wing as you."

Whether it was the reasonableness of her tone, or something else entirely, Vara rolled its head suspiciously from side to side and slowly drew its neck back. It flipped its wings and settled, though warily, on the Gage's fist, rocking from foot to foot.

"Everybody's a critic," Kyrlmyrandal said, and moved forward again, clearing her way with her staff.

The bearded vulture seemed calmer with the dragon looking away from it. The Gage followed.

"Kyrlmyrandal, may I ask a question that might seem rude?"

"It wouldn't stop me," she replied with humor.

That seemed like permission. "You are blind—"

"—but I have no trouble discerning the expression of your little friend?"

"I was going to use smaller words, but yes."

"There are other ways of sensing certain things. Things that are alive have a presence in the world. Less so, small objects on the ground." Her staff swung out on a lazy arc, intersecting the Gage's ankle. He rang like a bell and hopped aside.

"You be my guide," she told him. "You do not use eyes to see, do you?"

He thought about that. "The memory of eyes, maybe."

"And the memory of a mind to think, and love, and hope?"

"Are we hoping again, then?" He hadn't meant his tone to sound as bitter as it did.

"All other things being equal—" She shrugged. "Hope can be simulated by choosing to move in a direction."

"Any direction?"

"Whatever direction gets us to this sorcerer, or to whatever beast he is minion to. The beast is of greater import than the minion."

That was an item of information the Gage had not considered before. *There are beasts that feed on war.* The phrase haunted him.

"Kyrlmyrandal?"

She grunted.

What *were* those beasts, and where did they dwell?

He asked her.

She did not answer immediately, leaving him time to wonder if he had overstepped. Until she sucked her toothless gums and said, "When I was young and thought myself clever, I might have answered in a riddle."

The Gage thought of the Eyeless One. If he had been able to smirk, perhaps he would have. "Do you have an answer that doesn't require solving?"

As he said it, he wondered if such a thing existed.

"Unfortunately, no." She swung the staff once more, and this time she struck nothing. "Like my people, they come from somewhere else. Unlike my people, they do not seem to be . . . embodied. Perhaps they are similar to the gods of your folk; perhaps they arise from the same sources. I don't know everything about the Between Places."

"How do you fight something that has no body?"

"Metaphorically? Metaphysically?" She shook her head. "They may be the sort of thing that one summons into one's story by naming them."

"As you say I summoned you."

"One *can* believe things into existing."

"I'd rather be able to disbelieve things *out* of existing," the Gage said. "I could name you a few."

The dragon laughed. "As for where they live, well, at the boundaries of things. Out beyond the Sea of Storms. Out beyond the edge of the sky. In the interstices where the heavens are blank and unchanging."

"In the places no one claims."

"In the places between those places. They are held in those places by a variety of workings. But as it happens, all walls require renewal. All gods require prayer. Everyone must hold up the sky, in their turn, if they wish to have a sky to shelter under."

"I thought," the Gage grumbled, "that you were going to refrain from speaking in riddles."

"Was that a riddle?"

They laughed together.

The Gage asked, "If they live in the places that nobody claims, does that mean they wish to invade the places that are claimed?"

The dragon said, "I do not know. Maybe they come into our world on the ill will and selfishness of those who serve no good but their own gain. Maybe they are just trying to get free again from the worlds that have been stitched up around them. Your Alchemical Emperor stitched up a lot of things."

"Not mine." Then the Gage asked, "Why do they name you the Mother of Exiles?"

"That question, I answered for you when you found me. My people fell here, fell far, in a great cataclysm. We brought destruction and shattering with us, and thus we owe this world a debt." The staff swung faster for a few steps. "For we *do* serve more than our own profit."

"All of you?" the Gage asked.

Kyrlmyrandal's weathered face smiled. "There's always a few moldy fruits in the barrel. So here I am, risen up off my deathbed to pay that debt. Or what of it I can."

"Every bit helps, I suppose." The Gage emulated another sigh. "So what do we do now? Where do we go to find him? This minion? Or the beast?"

The dragon's stick swung hard. It struck a stone, and the stone went skittering away. She cocked her head to listen to it roll.

"Fly past the edge of the world and track him to his lair," she snarled. "An exercise that would once have been trivial."

She hurled her staff down. Vara bated in protest, the Gage ducking its flailing wings for the bird's safety rather than his own. Kyrlmyrandal flung her arms wide, fingers stretching, as if they were the tattered wings that could no more lift her into the sky than could these bony human limbs.

She held that pose for a moment. Then her arms came down. She sighed. "Would you hand me my stick, please? I apologize for the melodrama. It's just very frustrating sometimes, being so damned old."

HIMADRA WATCHED FROM HIS BEDROOM WINDOW, PRINTED COTTON CURTAINS blowing around him in the wind of the heights, a spyglass in his hand. It was dry and bright, which it should not have been: the rainy season should not yet have been over. Because of the clear sky, his attention had been drawn by the flashing wings of a bearded vulture stooping from on high. Now it was kept by what seemed to be an argument.

Not a violent one, and it wasn't easy to read posture or the old woman's facial expression from this distance. But a disagreement of some sort. One that culminated in the old woman—old Wizard, he still suspected—waving her staff around and finally hurling it away, actions that gave every evidence of upsetting the big raptor.

A raptor. Indeed. More specifically, one of Mrithuri's raptors. One of the birds that could serve, so Himadra supposed, as her eyes and ears.

As a means by which, perhaps . . . she could be communicated with.

He would not call these two spies. They had done nothing to deceive him. But it was a good reminder that anything he told them could find its way south.

Not far away, pages and sentries and Himadra's valet busied themselves with their assorted tasks. There was little privacy in an old keep like this, which was a good thing and a bad thing both. It was simple enough for Himadra to send a boy pelting along the long flagstone corridors, careering down the uneven flagstone stairs, and out across the shale-scattered clay of the hilltop to which Himadra's castle clung.

He watched the boy's sandaled feet slap little puffs of dust from the hard earth. Watched him stagger to a halt before the Gage with a force that made

Himadra's ankles ache in sympathy. Himadra held his chin high and kept his eye to the spyglass.

The boy had stopped outside the apparent range of the Gage's grasp but not far enough away to keep from sending the overwrought vulture into another bate. Himadra briefly closed his eyes. He had, he supposed, told the page to hurry.

The Gage got the vulture calmed, and both Gage and Wizard seemed to be listening to the boy. Himadra watched until all three of them—four, if you counted the bird—turned back toward the castle. Then he waved his valet over and made arrangements to be carried downstairs.

He was waiting in the hall when his page led the guests back in. The boy walked with self-conscious dignity now that he knew he was being observed. He had already regained his wind.

Himadra kept his sigh of envy silent through an extraordinary act of will. It was not so much that youth was wasted on the young, or that sound limbs were wasted on the able-bodied. It was how little perspective they were given to appreciate what gifts those things were, so long as they lasted. And here this child was, surrounded by the halt, the old, the entirely mechanized . . . and completely unselfconscious of what he had and of how swiftly it could be lost to him.

Let the innocent keep their innocence for a little while, Himadra told himself, full of pity. *There will be plenty of wars and plagues and famines in life to strip it away.*

"Welcome back," he said to Kyrlmyrandal and the Gage. "Please sit. I know you do not eat, Gage. But will you keep me company at table? And will you dine with me, Wizard Kyrlmyrandal—"

"Pardon," she interrupted, in such a polite tone he could take no offense. "Your Competence. I am no Wizard."

He looked her over again: the staff, the bearing. "I should not have assumed. I would still like it if you would break bread with me."

The Gage made a creaking sound. It might have been meant to emulate a throat-clearing. He said, "I do not wish to incur a debt, Your Competence. As you know, I have promised to serve Mrithuri."

He gestured to the bird on his other enormous paw.

"I have a feeling," said Himadra, "that we would be well advised to join forces."

"Do you think so?"

Himadra had not realized that the metal man was capable of sounding so completely dubious. "I'm not asking you to betray my cousin."

The Gage tilted his massive head. "It would seem to me that joining forces with her enemy would be the basic pattern of betrayal."

"Yes, well." Himadra waved that away as an inconsequentiality. "Setting aside an inconvenient enmity is trivial, provided all involved agree. I've no strong desire to waste my men's lives on invasions, if I can get the trade I need to feed and clothe my people. Some along the borders will always raid, of course."

He shrugged. *What can you do?* Some on the border *would* always raid. What else were borders for?

"And that's all you want in return?" the Gage said.

"Sit," Himadra said. "No debt is incurred. It hurts my neck to crane up at you. And as you intimated when we spoke yesternight, we have a larger problem and a common enemy."

He was acutely aware of the eyes of the great vulture and who might be listening behind them. She would, of course, suspect treachery.

The old woman choosing a low chair, the metal man selecting a patch of floor, they obeyed him. A relief. He gestured for food to be brought. While they waited, he said, "I assume my esteemed cousin can see us, anyway, through the eyes of her familiar."

The Gage, relying on some coaxing, transferred the bearded vulture to his shoulder. "It seems likely," he agreed. "Assuming she looks in on us."

"She's under siege."

Kyrlmyrandal's face reflected in the smooth orb of the Gage's head as she turned toward him. The Gage sat as motionless as a statue. His deep voice resonated in the room. "That seems likely as well."

"I have no desire to see her fall to Anuraja."

Laden plates came, and tea, and wine. Servants moved around the table with the efficient bustle that annoyed Anuraja, who preferred them so effaced as to be invisible. Himadra had bought his people boots after his cousin raja's first visit.

Neither the Gage nor Kyrlmyrandal seemed in the least troubled by the noise. Himadra tucked into his luncheon. After recent short rations on the march, he was in every mood to enjoy food when it was laid before him.

Kyrlmyrandal did the same, handling the food awkwardly with gnarled fingers. Himadra was not certain if it was her cataracts that made her clumsy, her arthritis, unfamiliarity with the local customs, or some combination. He did not draw attention to it by asking.

The Gage poured himself minted tea and folded his metal hands around the cup: his own odd manner of imbibing. He said, "You'd abandon your ally so easily? Then why should anyone else trust you?"

"Ally." Himadra let it roll off his tongue like a dirty word and selected a morsel of spiced mountain sheep.

"We must have ethics," Kyrlmyrandal said. "If we have no ethics, everyone smaller is food. And that places unacceptable strictures on discourse."

Himadra tilted his head. "What if there were something better than ethics?"

"Better?"

"What if there were rules? Not merely customs, or conventions we abide by when they're convenient, or when we can make the argument that they support our position. But actual binding laws. That applied to the Anurajas of the world as surely as to the servants." He gestured to the woman who had just laid a clean napkin beside his plate. "What if?"

"You're talking about a constitution," Kyrlmyrandal said.

The Gage wondered if she knew that Himadra was staring at her. "A constitution?"

"A written document that spells out the rights and responsibilities of government and the subjects of that government. That provides procedures for transfer of power, and protections for the people who live under that power."

"How is it enforceable?" Himadra seemed genuinely curious.

"A constitution is one of those things that exists because you believe in it," Kyrlmyrandal said. "Like gods. And the divine right of kings."

"No one in power is going to like that," the Gage said. "They won't assist it."

Himadra said, "So, what if we arranged things so that the power wound up distributed more widely?"

"Smaller kingdoms?" the Gage asked. "That only means more and smaller wars."

"Something other than kingdoms," Himadra said. "Or even empires. Binding treaties; government by argument and consent. Less worry about heirs and conquest. More concern for the well-being of everyone." He waved a hand, tired beyond belief. "There's some of that in how Mrithuri sits in judgment on trial cases, when they are argued before her. What if there were . . . something more? Written laws, like they have in Song. Something to prevent, say, one ruler from controlling another by taking his heirs hostage. Just hypothetically speaking." He looked at Kyrlmyrandal. "A *constitution*."

Kyrlmyrandal leaned forward, a morsel neglected between her fingers. "It was to prevent that sort of thinking that your notorious ancestor exiled or immured all the practitioners of your Science of Building."

"Notorious?" Himadra said, unable to resist baiting her. "Illustrious, certainly?"

"Depends on who you ask." She popped the food into her mouth and gummed it with a small pleased noise. "It's a different angle on things, certainly. A different perspective of the thought. What you propose would require accommodating such perspectives. Some of which are not . . . flexible."

"You think I don't have to accommodate them now?"

The old woman chuckled. "Are you not the lord of Chandranath?"

"Chandranath," Himadra said, "is not without its neighbors. Nor is it without its minor lords, with their own holdings and liegemen, their own power and agendas. And their own thoughts. So many thoughts. So very many *convictions*." He bit down on a piece of chicken in a sauce of cashews and black pepper. "Convictions they are wedded to."

"And you are not wedded to your convictions?"

He snorted. "Do I look like a man who can afford a lot of pride?"

It was a lie, somewhat. He had his pride, but he did not let it keep him from negotiating. Or from seizing a necessary advantage. It was a hard world, and that was how you kept yourself and your people alive.

Kyrlmyrandal shook her head gently. "We identify with our thoughts, but we are not our thoughts, and they do not need to define us."

The Gage, who had been sitting with such stillness that Himadra had wondered if he were still listening, slapped his metal chest with his hand to make it ring. The vulture on his shoulder awoke with a protest, the draft from its startled wingbeats scattering salt out of the saltcellars. "I'm not sure I am anything *but* my thoughts."

"Do you believe everything that comes into your head? Are you constrained to act on it? Or can you think one thing and consider it, then decide to do something else?"

"If I could not think a thing and still choose not to act on it, there would be fewer cities standing."

"Mm," Kyrlmyrandal said. "And who is it that makes those decisions?"

"Oh," said the Gage.

On a napkin, Kyrlmyrandal wiped her hands. "What I am asking is, how many people can set that aside and choose to learn as you have learned? Can you, Lord Himadra?"

Himadra leaned back amid his cushions, letting the fabric of the chair take his weight. "Maybe," he said. "Can Anuraja?"

Kyrlmyrandal raised her hands before her chest as if they were blossoming. "You know him. I do not."

It was an odd conversation, the Gage thought. An odd conversation, and Himadra was an odd man. Not at all what he had expected. Not the bloodthirsty warlord and raider of reputation but rather a sharp-witted commander of a disadvantaged nation, playing chaturanga to the best of his ability with the limited arsenal of pieces he had inherited.

He was looking at the Gage now with his lips pursed, finger-combing the oiled ringlets of his hair.

"Has she heard me?" Himadra asked.

Careful not to add to the upset of the already-ruffled vulture, the Gage gestured at it delicately. "I cannot tell you if she is listening."

Himadra sighed and reached for his tea.

The Gage added, "*I* am inclined to listen to you."

"Good—" Himadra looked up sharply at a rap on the doorframe. One of his men stood there, and Himadra waved the fellow in. A note changed hands; Himadra read; it must have been brief.

Then he looked up and laid the note on the table. "News from Sarath. Anuraja is dead."

"My lord—" the man began, before the Gage could collect his thoughts enough to react.

"This is my lieutenant Farkhad," Himadra interrupted. "Farkhad, the Gage. And Kyrlmyrandal, who is not a Wizard."

"That is news indeed," Kyrlmyrandal said. "Are there details?"

The Gage allowed his voice to come out slowly. "Is there news of Sarathai-tia and its rajni?" *And the Dead Man,* he thought, but did not say.

As an afterthought, he wondered a little about Chaeri. A subject about which he still did not know entirely how he felt.

"My lord—"

"Go ahead," Himadra instructed. "Let's have it all out and deal openly for droughted once."

Farkhad looked dubious but followed instructions. "Sarathai-tia fell, without too much bloodshed. Mrithuri Rajni agreed to send her troops into exile to save their lives, and Anuraja occupied the city. He married the young rajni—"

"Poor girl," Himadra said, mouth twisting.

"—Indeed. And tried to claim the throne."

Himadra reared back in his chair. The Gage himself might have twitched in surprise, if he had not been a Gage and impassive by nature, and if Kyrlmyrandal had not laid a gentle, restraining hand upon his knee under the table.

"I take it, then," Himadra said cheerfully, "that the curse on the throne actually worked as advertised?"

"That's the rumor," Farkhad said. "Although I have also heard that he had dosed himself with Eremite snakebite before climbing the steps, and you know it has an effect on the heart."

"He was not a well man," Himadra agreed. "How is the young rajni?"

"Collapsed from exhaustion, they say." Farkhad cleared his throat and eyed the Gage and the dragon cautiously. "My sources suggest that Sayeh Rajni has managed to convince Anuraja's army to hold off plundering the conquered city, and to wait for their new Empress to recover from"—he cleared his throat again—"the shock of losing her new husband so precipitously."

"What a woman." Himadra sighed.

Farkhad laughed, then looked guilty for laughing in front of the enemy.

Kyrlmyrandal spoke: softly, with authority. "It sounds as if your royal

cousins have the situation precariously in hand in Sarathai-tia. So what will you do, Himadra Raja?"

"We must march to Sarathai-lae," Himadra said, with the promptness of somebody who has considered this scenario, and already made plans.

"March there and do what, my lord?" Farkhad asked.

"Get this too-big refugee army we've inherited from my cousin Sayeh on its feet and moving toward a purpose," Himadra said. "Get my brothers freed. And make sure nobody else steps into Anuraja's damned oversize boots. The last thing we need is a youthful and vigorous warlord controlling the best port in Sahal-Sarat."

"A warlord perhaps backed by a sorcerer?" Kyrlmyrandal asked.

Himadra whuffed like an amused horse. "I have been paying attention to what you said." He sat back and folded his hands on his stomach. "So what are you going to do about the sorcerer, o not-a-Wizard?"

"Technically," she said, "he—or they—are not a sorcerer, either, if they are drawing their power from a beast."

"Are these allies?" Farkhad asked, with an eye toward his lord.

The Gage made a decision, since it seemed Kyrlmyrandal was not about to voice one. He took it upon himself to answer for both of them. "We are willing to function as allies."

Himadra spread amusement all over them like butter. "Less of a risk for you, who has the ability to take . . . dramatic . . . action should you feel betrayed. But I gather from what Kyrlmyrandal has said that she thinks there are bigger problems at stake than who rules in what shard of our former empire."

"You're right," she said. "You *have* been paying attention."

"Thank you. So, what are they, if they are not sorcerers? A beast, you hinted at our first meeting—"

"Something more like the minion of a beast," she corrected.

"You told me," the Gage put in, speaking meticulously, "that Ravana hated me because I was what I had chosen to make myself. If you call him a minion, does that mean that he has no such choice?"

"He certainly arrives and vanishes as pleases him," Farkhad said disgustedly.

No politician, that one. The Gage was glad he could not smile. He might grow to like Himadra's second-in-command.

Kyrlmyrandal located bread and sauce with deft fingertips. She tore off a piece of the one and twirled it in the other. "I do not think he has much freedom to act on his own. Or to choose who he appears as. I think that his autonomy and even his physical manifestation are constrained."

She put the food in her mouth and chewed.

"So he's not human?"

The Gage felt a little smug that Himadra felt the need to ask the same question that the Gage himself had, not so very long before.

"He—or it—is wearing a human form," Kyrlmyrandal offered.

So are you, the Gage did not say aloud. "Is he also something made? Manufactured, I mean?"

"I cannot be certain." Kyrlmyrandal seemed oblivious to how completely she held the attention of the Gage, Himadra, and Farkhad. "Any more than I can be certain of the exact nature of the beast in question. Or where those human shapes came from, or if there is one minion animating all of them or several. But I can tell you that the beast is a creature of cracks and interstices, and its goal is to feed itself on human conflict, suffering, and division. That, to that end, it thrives on shattering the bindings that your Alchemical Emperor laid upon it in his reign."

"The throne," the Gage said, suddenly.

Himadra stared at him. "What?"

"When we met your sorcerer—"

"Not mine. 'We' whom?"

"We—me. Myself. And a ghost of a dead cleric. It's complicated. But we met him, in the ruins of Ansh-Sahal. And he was building a pile of bodies that looked like the Peacock Throne."

"Sympathetic magic?" asked Himadra.

"Robbing it of power?" Kyrlmyrandal suggested. "Breaking its symbolic hold over your land?"

Himadra sighed. "Sounds like a mess."

Kyrlmyrandal said, "It is."

"I'm just going to spell this out," the Gage said. "To be certain I'm following it."

The others all looked at him.

He said, "Ignoring for the moment all the wars of conquest and succession, and Anuraja's desire to reunite the Lotus Empire under his own control—"

Himadra choked back a laugh.

"—and concentrating only on the supernatural threat here. There's a monster somewhere beyond the edge of the world that wants us all to fight so it can eat our misery. It was held back by the old Empire's binding magic, but that is broken now, and the more we fight each other, the stronger it gets."

"Yes," said Kyrlmyrandal. "Well, theoretically."

They might all have been staring at one another in varying combinations of disbelief, bewilderment, and despair, the Gage thought. Except Kyrlmyrandal was blind, and the Gage, being eyeless, could not stare.

"Presuming for the moment that you are correct . . ."

Kyrlmyrandal waited politely while the raja groped for words.

"How do we stop it?" Himadra finished, after a little while.

She finished her tea before she spoke. "Make peace with your neighbors. Reunite the Kingdoms. Put your angry godlings back to sleep. Drive out the parasites in the wastelands. Find some way to refresh the bindings and chase the hungry beast back over the edge of the world where it belongs—which means you are going to need some Wizards. Some practitioners of the Science of Building. I'm not saying it's going to be a small task, mind you. I am old enough that I don't come out of my home for minor inconveniences anymore."

"You have a way of folding startling revelations into matter-of-fact summaries of peril that is modestly disconcerting," Himadra said. "Would you mind terribly explaining a bit more about the angry godlings?"

Kyrlmyrandal found her staff under the table and leveraged it to shove herself to her feet. "I am tired," she said. "The Gage will explain. He witnessed what I speak of firsthand."

HIMADRA WATCHED THE OLD WOMAN LEAVE, HIS HEAD MILDLY SPINNING—and not from the tea. When she had tapped her way out into the hall, he turned to Farkhad. "Will you get my chair? I cannot stand the smell of cold food much longer."

The Gage waited patiently while Farkhad sent for a valet and helped Himadra into his rolling chair. The Gage followed with a slow, rocking gait as Himadra's valet brought the chair and its occupant along the hall toward the library.

"I thought we'd look in on the young prince," Himadra said. "We've installed him in the nursery."

"How long since it was used for children?" For an automaton, the Gage was entirely too perceptive.

"Since Anuraja decided to . . . foster . . . my brothers."

In Himadra's father's day, the library had been on an upper floor. Being carried up and down the flights multiple times a day struck Himadra as risky and uncomfortable, so he had had the books moved instead. The available space had been close to the old nursery, which would have been awkward from a standpoint of noisy interruptions—except Himadra had never anticipated seeing royal children in this castle again.

More fool he.

The hall was long, and as they progressed, he asked the Gage, "By the way—who the hell is she, if she's not a Wizard? Is she also some kind of supernatural creature?"

The Gage creaked slightly as he shifted. "You're asking me? A random metal man?"

"Set a thief to catch a thief," Himadra answered. "Yes, I suppose I am."

"She's a dragon," the Gage said.

"Dragons are imaginary."

The Gage shrugged, a massive mechanical undertaking. "So are just kings."

They reached the nursery. The valet opened the door without knocking on the frame. Within, Iri the nursemaid and Prince Drupada both looked up and stared.

"Himadra!" the little boy squeaked, and would have run to Himadra and probably tackled him out of his chair—with disastrous consequences—if Iri had not intercepted him. She grabbed him around the waist and picked him up, swinging him into her hip as she rose.

"No!" he bellowed.

"Your Competence," she said to Himadra. Her eyes went to the Gage, and her face went still with fear.

"Don't worry," Himadra said. "This is the Gage, and he is a guest here. Not a monster. He will not harm the child or you. Gage, this is Iri, and Sayeh Rajni's son Prince Drupada."

Himadra stared at the Gage, a look intended to convey the expected behavior. The Gage bowed low with a hissing of lubricated metal. "Charmed," he said.

"Metal man!" shouted Drupada. "Want metal man!"

"Oh, no, my prince," the nursemaid said. Wrangling the squirming child, she shot Himadra an apologetic look.

They'd come a long way since she was threatening to leap off of cliff faces to avoid him. The thought pleased Himadra for whole moments before the toddler began to scream.

"By the Mother, shut the door!" Iri pleaded.

Himadra waved to his valet, and the valet obliged her.

"Some people," Himadra said placidly, "do not respond gently to the setting of boundaries. Come along to the library and tell me about these problematic godlings."

"Only one I know of," the Gage began. "And she is a volcano—"

3

THE FIRST STEP WAS TAKING THE FIRST STEP.

Mrithuri thought, *It is only walking.* It was only walking a little bit and allowing Yavashuri and Golbahar to see to her dressing and the arranging of her toilet. To painting her face and hands and the part of her hair, to dusting her feet with gold.

That was not so difficult. She was Rajni of Sarathai-tia. She was the Dowager Empress of Sarath, ridiculous as that title felt when she weighed it experimentally in her mind.

She wasn't healing a shattered leg, as Sayeh Rajni was. She could manage to walk a step or two.

She was ready to begin when she realized that the first step was not the first step, so to speak. As was so often the case with deceptively complex problems, there were steps that needed to be taken to prepare for that putative first step.

Such as . . . getting out of bed.

Mrithuri closed her eyes. Unfairly, it made the throbbing in her head worse rather than better. Her body ached as if with a fever. The room spun. *Too hard. Guess I'll just have to let the world end.*

But she had not, in fact, died from orphaning, or betrayal, or exhaustion, or withdrawal, or from the sheer existential horror of being forced to marry her evil cousin.

She had survived each of those things.

Her reward for survival, intolerably, was that she had to get out of bed.

When she opened her eyes again, the room was mercifully dimmer. Golbahar, having drawn the drapes, was returning.

"Bless you," Mrithuri said.

"Take it in stages, Your Abundance." Golbahar crouched beside the bed. "Yavashuri is fetching warm water. Would you consent to use my hands to help you sit?"

Not for the first time, Mrithuri wondered where Golbahar might have learned what she knew. But was it such a mystery? Many women cared for elderly relatives, even from a tender age.

Golbahar held her hands steady, elbows braced on her knees, and allowed Mrithuri to pull against them rather than grabbing Mrithuri's wrists and hauling her about. At last, Mrithuri was sitting upright on her own bony haunches, panting with the effort required.

"Surely the Mother sent you in my time of need." Mrithuri did not mean only the present moment.

The edges of Golbahar's eyes crinkled above her veil. "Perhaps She and the Scholar-God struck some sort of pact to answer both our prayers. As for myself, I'd take a siege and a war in your court, my rajni, over a gilded captivity as chattel to any lord of Song."

Mrithuri laughed, and by the time Yavashuri returned with the washing cloths and the chased silver basin of water, she was upright in a sling-seated chair. Her women cleaned her and helped her into underthings and a blouse. They painted and gilded and jeweled her, and they dressed her body and her hair. Ears and paws twitching through a dream, Syama snored lustily beside the door.

Yavashuri brought Mrithuri her golden mask shaped like the muzzle of a tiger. Mrithuri weighed the mask in her hands, thinking of how the padded leather straps chafed her ears and how the buckles pulled at the fine hairs on her nape. Its purpose, other than making her look ferocious and implacable, was to contain the filtering gauze that kept the gold dust swirling around the Hall of the Empty Throne from also clogging her nostrils and being drawn into her lungs.

The thing was bent from gold wire, and it looked airy and fragile and featherlight.

It weighed half a pound. And there was another pound and a half of jewelry—necklaces, arm-rings, hairpins, earrings, anklets—behind it.

The door slid open, framing Ata Akhimah. The Wizard was clad in a white blouse and black trousers, her feet wrapped in high-laced sandals. Her left arm was still in a sling. She stepped around the sleeping bear-dog and said, "The court is ready for you, Your Abundance."

Mrithuri lowered her eyes to the mask once more. The artisanship was astounding. Somebody had spent months, years of their life building this beautiful, awkward, uncomfortable trap. Someone had toiled for the gold, risking—perhaps losing—their life underground. Someone had devoted a lifetime's skill to the artistry of making it.

That gave her a pang. Nevertheless, she extended her arm to Ata Akhimah, dangling the mask by its straps. Weak as she was, the weight made her arm tremble.

"Pull out the rubies," she said, when her Wizard relieved her of it. "Pull out the rubies. Melt the rest down."

"You Abundance—"

"There's a dozen of the damned things," Mrithuri said. "Melt them all down. And sweep up all that gold dust in the throne room and melt it down, too. There's a pile of jewels in my coffers; sell them all, made up with the settings or without, however they are most valuable. Levy a tax; not a high one, and not on the poor."

"The poor will pay it anyway, in rents and prices," Yavashuri said. "Let's sell the jewels first and then levy the tax; we might as well get the merchants and nobles when they're in the mood to buy."

Mrithuri nodded; she knew that. But the money had to come from somewhere. "Taken together—will that pay to get the army . . . my army . . . back to Sarathai-lae?"

Wizard and ladies-in-waiting looked at one another.

"It's a start," Yavashuri said.

Ata Akhimah said, "I'll find the die molds. We can start coining immediately."

"Wait," said Golbahar. She looked at Mrithuri, turned her painted face to the side with gentle fingertips and studied her profile. "Have new dies cast. And let them read *Mrithuri the First, Empress Dowager* around the rim."

Mrithuri closed her eyes and nodded. She opened them again. "The court will have to wait. Send me Sayeh Rajni. And then leave us. I must speak to her as rajni to rajni. As priestess to priestess."

Golbahar said, "I will have refreshments sent in—"

"No," Mrithuri said. "I want nothing to hide behind."

They gave each other skeptical looks under lowered lashes, but they obeyed.

The other women, the women in the walls—those women would hear. There were no secrets from the women in the walls. But those women were nuns who served the Mother River and her Good Daughter, as Mrithuri served the Mother River and her Good Daughter. And in the name of the Mother— she who was called Bountiful, she who was called Giver of Loaves—they would keep Mrithuri's secrets.

Alone for a few moments except for the bhaluukutta now awake and alert by her side, Mrithuri composed her thoughts and hands. She felt curiously vulnerable without her mask and fingerstalls and the weight of all her jewels. She had hated them, and now she missed them. Was that always the way with trappings of authority? With armor, even were it metaphorical?

You could hate something and need it all the same.

Sayeh's approach was heralded by the thump of her crutch. Mrithuri did not wait for her scratch or her tap on the doorframe before she called out, "Come!"

The older woman entered. Mrithuri waved her to a stool tall enough to allow her to sit and rise on her own without struggling, despite her game leg. Sayeh settled herself and leaned her crutch against the wall.

Their eyes met. Sayeh arranged her expression to invite confidences, and Mrithuri almost laughed out loud as she recognized the art of it. She had learned the same techniques as a girl.

It worked. Or at least, it did not make the confidences any more difficult to share. Despite an almost-crippling sense of embarrassment, Mrithuri was determined to keep her courage up, and to plunge right into it.

"This is impudent," Mrithuri said, struggling not to squirm. "But could you get a child on me?"

Sayeh stared at her. "Sister. I see the prudence in your suggestion. It would serve the Mother best if you could get an heir of your own body—and I am . . . flattered—"

"Fear not." Mrithuri temporized hastily. Why had she not arranged for tea? Something to do with their hands? She was such a fool. "I wouldn't expect . . . I mean, I know I am not . . . Dammit, don't Rasan Wizards like your Tsering-la have skills for handling that sort of thing?"

Sayeh, to Mrithuri's advanced chagrin, dissolved into laughter.

Mrithuri put her face into her hands. No mask or fingerstalls to impede that process.

Sayeh stood. She limped over to Mrithuri without her crutch, though Mrithuri—looking up—could see that it pained her. Clutching the tall post of Mrithuri's chair for balance, she bent down and kissed Mrithuri on the mouth.

Mrithuri gasped through her nose, so as not to break the contact. Syama rumbled a small protest but did not intervene.

"O honored empress," Sayeh intoned, "it is not that." Her breath whispered on Mrithuri's flaming skin. "But I had to sacrifice something to prove to the Mother that I was sincere in my desire for a son, and worthy of her consideration. And my Wizard, as you just noted, is from Rasa. Where they perform such operations as a matter of course. It was a decade and more before the Mother accepted my sacrifice, and for a long time I thought it had been in vain. But I got my son. And alas, you see . . . I am not capable."

Mrithuri swallowed. "That must have been terrible."

Sayeh stepped back. She turned away, limping to her chair. "Well, it was not such a sacrifice for me as it might have been for others."

Mrithuri, watching her, firmed her jaw. "We will get your son back, my sister."

Sayeh reseated herself. She smiled the sort of brave smile that did not reach one's eyes. Mrithuri felt it like a nail on the harp of her soul. "Thank you for saying so."

The smile dissolved into a troubled frown. "Drupada, my lamb, is not the only child I need to find. He had a nurse, Jagati, who died to protect him when the earth shook and the walls fell in. She . . ." Sayeh pinched the bridge of her nose for a moment. When she lowered her hand again, her expression had smoothed and her voice had steadied. "She covered him with her body."

"I am—"

Sayeh stopped Mrithuri's rush to commiserate with a raised hand. "She had children. I do not know what became of them. I do not know if they lived when my city fell."

"You want to find them."

Sayeh nodded. "I want to find all my people. Any such as have survived. You should know . . . Ravani promised me that she would bring them to a place where I could find them, if I helped convince you to marry Anuraja."

"Well, you did." Mrithuri offered it with a smile, meaning the words to seem less harsh than they sounded. "It seems the sorcerer owes a debt to you."

Sayeh rolled her eyes. "I may have a hard time collecting."

"You may. But that debt probably gives you some metaphysical claim over her, wouldn't you think?"

"I'm no Wizard—"

"Neither am I. But we do know several. Let's ask." Mrithuri sighed. "I'm just about to make one of them extremely grumpy with me, anyway. And you're right about the need for an heir of my body, of course. I keep thinking that perhaps if I had one, and Anuraja had one, and Himadra . . . that perhaps the sorcerers would not have been so capable at disrupting the rains and calling up monsters and volcanos."

"I have an heir," said Sayeh. "And it didn't help Ansh-Sahal."

MRITHURI SWALLOWED IRRITATION AND LOOKED HER WIZARD IN THE EYE. "My mind is made up, Ata."

"You should not do this, Rajni." Ata Akhimah shifted her left arm in its sling, as if she had meant to gesture and been restrained from it. Her mouth pinched; the broken hand must still be painful. "You are not well enough. Do you wish to give yourself a relapse?"

"Do you wish to be blindsided by another army, then? Do you wish to be devoid of intelligence on the disposition of the Gage and his mission?"

Mrithuri carefully did not look at the Dead Man. It was his partner who was somewhere in the wilds, trying to find the magic that could give her the heir that would cement her claim on Sarath and—perhaps—re-seal the mystic link of rajni and land that had become so distorted. And yet he too would try to forbid her seeking out the Gage, if he could.

As if he could hear the direction of her thoughts, he cleared his throat. She glared at him.

He surprised her. "Our messengers have reached your army, Rajni. Pranaj and his men have camped without the wall. He will await your instructions on whether to enter."

That placed him in a tremendously vulnerable position, exposed to Anuraja's—no, not Anuraja's any longer—larger forces.

"I need to see Pranaj," Mrithuri said. "Him, and then immediately after a meeting with him *and* with the Laeish commander. Lieutenant commander. Has anybody even found out yet what the man's name is?"

"Zirha, Your Abundance."

"Send for him, and some of his staff. The ones Sayeh has an acquaintanceship with. I'll talk with them after I do this little chore."

"Yes, Rajni," the Dead Man said. "May I have your permission to have tea and a luncheon sent in? Pranaj will no doubt be hungry, and you usually like refreshment after you reach out to your familiars."

Mrithuri rolled her eyes. His crinkled at the corners as he smiled behind his veil. "Go on," she said. "Get out of here. Ata Akhimah, if you will stay?"

"I would not consent to leave you," the Wizard said. "Not when you are determined to take this risk. May I send for Hnarisha?"

"Fine." Mrithuri sighed, as the Dead Man eased himself out the door. "And get me some sweet tea, also."

She was surprised by how quickly the tea came, with Hnarisha himself carrying it. That had not been long enough to brew it and bring it from the kitchens. Someone must have made it in advance, set it in a teapot enchanted to keep the tea fresh and hot, and then been standing around waiting for the call...

Her people were colluding against her. Or colluding in her favor. But colluding nonetheless. And there was nothing any ruler could do to prevent that.

She drank the tea and ate the biscuits. She had expected it to be a chore, the sort of thing one did because one had to. Tea had of late been cloying, and the traditional nibbles served with it had been so much sand and grit in her mouth. This tea tasted fresh and sweet, however, and the milk did not turn her stomach. The biscuits had a flavor of herbs and honey. She ate them all.

She paused with half of the last cracker still held in her fingers, her stomach rumbling with renewed appetite. "What did you put in these?"

Hnarisha smirked. "It's not what's in the crackers, Rajni. It's what's not poisoning you."

She wrinkled her nose and considered throwing the cracker at him. Instead, she finished it.

Feeling considerably stronger, Mrithuri reached toward the awareness of the bearded vulture she had sent with the Gage. She stretched to reach the great bird, so far away. So distant, and not linked to her by a fresh taste of her blood. She felt herself weaker without the assistance of the venom, the bridge of her attention more frail. But there—it tickled the edge of her senses, elusive as a remembered scent . . .

Her fingertips stretched into the reaching feathers, grasping and being lifted by the wind. Her eyes saw far and in the most tremendous detail. Stitches on clothing; cowlicks in the pattern of hair. Lichen on stone. The flash of a leaf as a mouse brushed past it.

All from the height of mountains where she soared.

What she saw right now was the wooden palisade and hilltop fastness of Chandranath, and the starlight glittering off the brazen dome of the Gage's head. She saw a tall, lean, dark-complected figure walking beside him, hair pale as the water of the Mother River. The old woman leaned on a staff. With the vulture's vision, Mrithuri could see that her knuckles were knotty with age, the skin on her hands slack between the bones.

They were walking across the barren hilltop beside the keep, toward the open postern. It was far, so far. The wind brought her a scent of carrion, too fresh to be of interest to the lammergeyer. Mrithuri could feel herself falling out of the bird's head.

Too soon, too soon. She needed its memories. She needed to stay with it, to recall. To see what it had already seen. Who was this old woman? Why had the Gage come to Chandranath? What possessed him to wander so far from where he should be, and why was he not coming back to her? Why was he not bringing her what she needed?

Anger unspooled within her, a sharp heat in her chest, a discomfort rising the length of her throat. A kind of pressure that wanted to push out furious words, curses and imprecations. She tried to flow with it, to ride it as if it were the Mother River. She tried to soothe her racing heart—

She tumbled out of the sky, out of the consciousness of the great vulture. She fell off the back of its wings, out of the grasp of its mind, and snapped with bruising force back into her own hungry, shivery shell with its scrawny arms and thin ribcage.

She was cold without the warmth of feathers. She was always cold.

She must have been shivering for real, because when the room stopped spinning enough for her to open her eyes, Hnarisha was draping a cashmere shawl over her arms and shoulders. Mrithuri drew it to her, plucking at the fringe with fingers that did not quite want to pinch and grip the way they ought to. He gave her tea—still hot—and steadied her while she drank.

He should not have been touching her without expressly requesting her permission. But since his hand was the only thing that kept her cup from rattling against her teeth and spilling its contents down her front, she felt not affront but gratitude.

Ata Akhimah, by the door, did not move from her position. Her expression did not change. She most certainly did not say *I told you so.*

She waited until Mrithuri had gotten some tea inside her and stopped feeling cold at the bone. Then, quietly, she asked, "What did you see?"

Mrithuri glanced around the room to confirm that there was no one present except Hnarisha and the Wizard. Reassured, she shared her discoveries.

"There are a lot of things that might have taken the Gage to Chandranath," Hnarisha said, after a few moments.

Ata Akhimah rubbed the bridge of her nose where her reading glasses had left a dent. "It's not exactly along the way!"

"He'd better not have betrayed us," Mrithuri said. It was not a threat. She spoke in exhaustion, as one who had been betrayed recently a few times too often. For their sake, he had better not. "Get me Nizhvashiti, will you? And also get me the Dead Man. I hope he can explain."

She was still keeping the court waiting.

Well, they would wait.

Mrithuri had consumed most of a plate of chickpea-flour wraps and the rest of the pot of tea before Ata Akhimah returned with the Godmade and the Dead Man. The Wizard closed the door behind them.

"Come sit." Mrithuri gestured with her teacup to the cushions spread about near her chair. She did not have the energy—emotional or physical—to look up at them.

Mother, when had she become such an old woman that she needed to sit in a *chair?*

You've been ill, she reminded herself. *It won't be too long before you get stronger.*

She could almost hear Hnarisha lecturing her that the harder she pushed herself, the longer the healing would take. He didn't even have to look at her sidelong for her to imagine him reminding her that she, as rajni, had a duty to her people to care for herself.

She turned to the Dead Man. Contemplated him and decided to see if she could shock him. Trust between lovers was one thing . . . but she had trusted Chaeri, too. Perhaps her standards of who was trustworthy were not to be relied upon.

Mrithuri snapped, "What in all six thousand Rasan hells is your partner doing in Himadra's house?"

The Dead Man rocked forward from the waist. He did not rise; it was a movement born of shock, Mrithuri judged.

He said, "He's *where?*"

"I reached the familiar I sent with him. Both are well, or seem to be. Another person has joined them. An old woman. And they are all in Chandranath."

"He hasn't had *time* to get to Chandranath."

"Not unless he went there straightaway," said Ata Akhimah.

"No," creaked Nizhvashiti. The Godmade's voice sounded as if it worked by means of a stiff old bellows that could not move much air. "He went to Ansh-Sahal and through it. Of that I am certain. I was there, and I told you what we found there—the tower of bodies, the fallen temple. He could perhaps have reached Chandranath by now if he turned west immediately after we parted—"

Mrithuri sighed. "No, my familiar followed him as far as that poisoned desert. Nearly to the Singing Towers. So I suppose he must have gone there. I'm just—"

"We are all overwrought," said Hnarisha.

"So how on God's earth *did* he get to Chandranath?" the Dead Man asked. In a tone of wondering aloud, not as if he expected someone to tell him.

Mrithuri said, "Nizhvashiti, can you go and find out?"

The Godmade frowned and shook its head, a constrained and incremental gesture. "I wish the projection were something I could manage to control. But it . . . happens as it will. I am a vessel, Your Abundance. An ansha, not an architect."

Mrithuri said, "All the things we leave to the will of the gods. The gods could be a little clearer." She looked at the Dead Man. At Serhan, her Serhan. And saw him regarding her, clear-eyed from within the folds of his veil. "What do we do?"

"The vulture's memories . . . ?"

"I could not hold on long enough to reach them." The admission tasted bitter. "I can try again—"

"When you are more rested," Hnarisha interrupted.

"No one in this palace respects a rajni!"

"'An empress,' I think you mean," said Ata Akhimah.

Against her will, Mrithuri laughed. It wasn't much of a laugh, but it was something. "All right," she said. "What do we do?"

"What we were *going* to do," said Ata Akhimah. "Speak with the commanders. Sell jewels, mint coins. Levy taxes. Pay the troops."

Mrithuri finished for her. "March on Sarathai-lae."

"That is so."

She closed her eyes. "I will try again to reach my familiar. Uh, uh—not immediately. I will rest first."

"Your Abundance—" Ata Akhimah protested.

"I need to know," Mrithuri said. "I need to know what the Gage knows, and I need to know it before I brave the damned Dharasaaba. It's the only chance I have of getting them to back us. Let the court know they are dismissed, and we will reconvene this morning. Tell them . . . Oh, I don't care what you tell them. Tell them I am still prostrated by grief, if you deem it politic. Or that an important message has come to me from afar, and my duties as the priestess of the Mother demand I address it."

The room was silent for a moment. Her nobles would not be pleased at the delay. But if she was an empress, she had better act like it if she expected her nobles to respect her.

Nizhvashiti spoke.

"The empress is correct," it said.

4

She's getting better, the Dead Man told himself, as he went in search of Pranaj. *She will recover.*

And she would move on with her life, as was only proper. She was a queen after all—an empress now—and he was a mercenary.

It had all seemed much simpler when death or bondage was inevitable. When there is no future to speak of, there's little point in planning for it. Little point in worrying about it.

Not for the first time, he was glad of his veil. Because, disciplined as he was, old soldier though he be—he was not old enough or disciplined enough to keep his emotions from twisting his expression uncomfortably. And he would not have cared to reveal his inner workings so plainly to anyone who might glance his way.

It was easier to believe in fate and destiny than to accept responsibility for one's own actions and choices. It was so much more pleasant to leave responsibility in the hands of God. To read the book of one's life as the words She had written. As if one's destiny were fiat, passed down without consultation, and one's duty were only to endure it.

It was not very adult, however, to blame God for the consequences of one's own choices. Certainly, much was outside one's control—from the circumstances into which birth or history rendered one, to the decisions others made that affected the course of one's life, to the wild vagaries of fate that had nothing to do with the will of any man. But sometimes one's own acts brought one to a place, and in that place one must for good or ill then stand.

The confluence of the two, like the confluence of rivers—that might be destiny.

Musing, the Dead Man barely noticed the clicks of his own bootheels as he strode along the corridors. The echoes broke strangely through the filigree panels that lined the corridors. Those panels gave into the parallel but separate palace inhabited by cloistered nuns, and the sounds that came back seemed layered over one another, as if they had bounced back from farther away than should have been possible. The cloister seemed empty: he did not glimpse any white robes or hear any plainsong.

It was just as well. He found himself cherishing the rare moment of solitude and quiet. Of uninterrupted thought. Which would continue until he found Pranaj.

Mrithuri's general—summoned from without the walls—was in the war room, frowning over sand tables now stripped of their model armies and with their model terrain raked level. Tall windows composed one long wall of the room. Along the opposite wall were ranged shallow shelves, each tier a few fingerbreadths deep, and a few more fingerbreadths tall.

The shelves were full of tiny models of men, equipment, animals. Pranaj, turning to face the Dead Man as he entered, held a miniature elephant in his hand.

Ivory. O irony.

Pranaj's shoulders relaxed when he saw whom the door framed. With a sigh he set the elephant down. Not in the empty space reserved for shelving her, but on the smooth brown sand.

The room seemed empty and echoing with just the two of them inside.

Pranaj met the Dead Man's eyes. "How is she?"

"Better," the Dead Man said. "Weak."

Pranaj nodded. "She is tougher than most, to have survived."

Those were true words, and not only in relation to the addiction, and the invasion, and the venom of the Eremite snakes. "Did you think she wouldn't?"

The Dead Man phrased it as a friendly question, not a challenge. Pranaj had proved a thoughtful ally.

"I thought"—Pranaj lowered his voice—"that it was unlikely Anuraja would survive the wedding day. And that it was unlikely his men would take kindly to his new wife assassinating him. Now—"

He shrugged.

"Now," said the Dead Man, "we have an advantage. Anuraja, it seems, preferred to keep the majority of his army taking orders directly from him. Or at least conveying those orders through a very few lieutenants and messengers, but he did not give them much latitude to make decisions. There isn't much chain of command. He didn't delegate much authority."

"That's a damn poor means of maintaining discipline . . . not that I judge." The purse of Pranaj's lips said he judged indeed.

"You're not wrong. But it also means that now that Anuraja and Ravani are both gone, there's not much authority in the army to give them cohesion and direction."

"They'll start pillaging, then."

The Dead Man folded his arms. "Not if we can give them that cohesion."

Pranaj frowned. He rubbed his nose with a knuckle. "It will take someone with some charisma to accomplish that."

"We might have a few of those."

Pranaj was not ready to commit to the plan. But the Dead Man could see that he was thinking. These people went around unveiled with all their emotions written on their faces. And it was still half-impossible to figure out which way they were going to jump.

Pranaj grunted, finally, decision still seemingly unmade. "Can we go and see her now?"

THE WALK BACK TO THE ROYAL CHAMBERS WAS SILENT AND MIGHT HAVE remained uneventful. Except that in passing one of the side corridors, both men heard voices.

No one was visible down the hall, but of course there were alcoves and doorways throughout the palace. It was a sprawling, spiraling building with enough wings and connecting doors to seem a maze even without considering the strange, liminal spaces of the cloisters.

They exchanged a glance with one another. It was clear to both their ears: a woman and a man, speaking too low for their words to be made out. Ten nights before, and neither the Dead Man nor Pranaj would have thought much of it. Just a flirtation and nothing to concern serious men.

Ten nights before, despite suspicions, the rajni's handmaiden had not yet been revealed as a spy.

The Dead Man gripped the hilt of his sword. Pranaj, who was technically there under flag of truce, was not carrying one. But he nodded, and led the Dead Man down the corridor, one hand extended to rip aside a curtain or shove back a door.

Nothing so dramatic was required. As they came closer, echoes fell away, and the voices were rendered recognizable. Golbahar, the woman. And the man . . . Ritu the acrobat's son. Amruth, that was his name.

They were standing perhaps a half arm's length apart but leaning toward each other with congenial flirtation. They did not jump apart when Pranaj and the Dead Man rounded the corner, but they did jump with surprise.

The Dead Man laughed. He had not noticed that he was sneaking. Apparently, he could do so even with bootheels on stone.

Golbahar stared at them and then sighed so hard, she blew her veil away from her face. "By God's sand-shaker, you men! Did you think to find assassins in every corner?"

Amruth dissolved into nervous giggles. He was light-complected, and the Dead Man watched that complexion flush scarlet like the pale sky before sunrise.

"I am sorry, my lady," the Dead Man said, as gallantly as he could manage, while behind him Pranaj retreated into a very uncomfortable-sounding coughing fit. "But I do, rather."

The glare held out for a moment before she, too, succumbed to a giggle. "I suppose that's fair." She glanced over at her young man and winked at him encouragingly. "Run along. Everything will be fine."

"Sorry," he mumbled, and edged past the Dead Man. He strode down the hall, failing to look unhasty, trailing his dignity like tattered skirts. Golbahar watched him go, and the Dead Man watched Golbahar. Pranaj had stopped coughing.

"A bit of a naif for you, isn't he?" the Dead Man asked, casually.

Golbahar said, "He'll season, and he is smart enough and humble enough to listen and learn. Besides, in the absence of conquering armies, I do have to come up with something to tell my father about why I'm no longer suited for the dynastic liaison in Song he had in mind for me. A hasty marriage under threat of war seems plausible."

"The war is over," said Pranaj. "Or at the very least, it's between acts."

Golbahar flipped one hand prettily in the air. "Details."

She fished in her sleeve and brought out a folded but unsealed letter, which she offered to the Dead Man. "Here, you should be able to read this. Does it pass the censors?"

It was addressed to the Lady Golbahar's father, the Lord Omer. It was written in the Uthman language; the script of his mother tongue gave the Dead Man a pang under his heart. Between the flowery salutations and protestations of filial devotion and love (all formulaic) lay only a brief paragraph.

The meat of it, written in Golbahar's own trained hand, read: *It is my regret to inform you, dearest parents, that I have been taken in a siege in Sarathai-tia, and that as a result I am not suited for the marriage you had in mind for me. A kind man here has consented to marry me, and I am assured of a place as a handmaiden to the Rajni. Her Abundance looks kindly on me, and my fallen state will not impede my well-being.*

The Dead Man refolded the letter. "Your chain of causality is a little questionable. But there aren't any . . . outright lies. Is your state truly so fallen as that?"

"I am confident that it will be by the time they get the letter," Golbahar said, with a twinkle.

He offered it back to her. She shook her head. "If you could have it sealed and sent in the official mails—"

"Of course," he said. Mrithuri's seal—not her personal one, of course, but the government chop—would lend the contents authority.

"I'm glad you're staying," the Dead Man said. "But you should change that word to 'Empress' and give it back to me. It never hurts to begin establishing a fact before you need it widely known."

Golbahar took the letter back. She looked at him over the bridge of her veil. The corners of her eyes pinched a little. "Let us enjoy each other's company as long as it lasts, uncle."

The affectionate honorific brought tears to his eyes. Suddenly, shockingly, like a blow to the bridge of his nose. It was . . . so *normal*. The sort of thing any young woman might say to an older friend.

He was abruptly so homesick that the hallway reeled around him.

"Dead Man?" she said, concern washing away her amusement. "Are you all right?"

He put a hand on the wall, trying to appear casual. Needing the support. "No one has ever called me that before."

A SIEGE WAS NOBODY'S IDEA OF A PARTY. BUT AT LEAST IT HAD KEPT MRITHURI'S nobles out of her hair. The siege being over, so was the respite.

She sat on her chair of estate in the Hall of the Empty Throne, the gigantic jeweled plinth that supported the Peacock Throne rising behind her, and looked out at the assembled nobles of her court. The Dharasaaba was barely in session, roll still being taken and the assembly being called to order by its various officials and traditions, and Mrithuri was tired already.

She had scandalized them by showing up bare-visaged—unless you counted the full face of makeup that Yavashuri and Golbahar had applied— and naked of jewels. She wore only a simple blouse and drape. Though the cloth and cut were fine, both were devoid of bullion embroidery, stitched-on jewels, costly ornament. She had *shocked* royal standards of dress, and there was whispering behind hands aplenty.

She needed to convince her people to support her anyway.

Nothing in life was ever likely to be simple. Least of all convincing a bunch of wealthy old men whose money she needed to keep her treasury solvent, and whose political support she needed to keep her reign secure, that she was still rajni—no, that she was Empress Dowager now—and that she was still fit to rule. Every single one of them thought he was more capable of the job than she was.

She remembered the lesson she'd learned from dealing with that asshole, Mi Ren, the Song prince who had thankfully taken himself elsewhere. Every single one of them thought he was more capable of the job than she was. But every single one of them would rather piss blood than see one of his peers in her chair.

If she could keep them aware of that without ever seeming to know it herself, she stood a chance of maintaining her office. And saving the world.

No sweat.

During the half-season when Anuraja's army had been camped at her gates, the Dharasaaba's approval had been less critical. The problem had been plain for everybody to see, and her own soldiers had been motivated to stay loyal. Desperate times had emboldened her to take action without seeking permission, and she had not worried overmuch about the consequences.

Now, though. Now the bill was due. Now she had to discern how to keep them paying when the hounds of war were no longer baying at their doors but rather leading them a chase across far fields. They would not want to send anyone to march to Sarathai-lae.

They would not want to back down easily.

Watching them sort themselves into factions and caucuses, she wondered if it were a good idea, meeting them there in front of the throne that had so recently been the death of her brand-new "husband." That death and the suspicion that the throne had rejected him as unworthy and punished his attempt to claim it were the psychological barrier that kept her safe and gave her power now.

The marriage that had by minutes preceded it was the thing that gave her the title of Dowager Empress of Sarath, and some claim on power over the Laeish men.

If she could keep it.

The logic of the two points would seem to contradict each other. But Mrithuri had learned from a young age that most people did not care too much for logic in their politics, preferring justifications.

So she would give them justifications. And a side of patriotic fervor.

She sat, hands folded in her lap, with her advisors arrayed behind her. Ata Akhimah, Lady Golbahar, and Yavashuri. Sayeh Rajni now sat beside her, on a chair a little lower than her own. And on a cushion beside Sayeh's feet sat the poetess Ümmühan.

Quite a crowded dais, really.

It pleased Mrithuri in her heart that every single one of those people was a woman. Perhaps if less of her young life had been devoted to hearing, again and again, that her girlhood made her unworthy to lead ... perhaps if fewer people like those comprising the assembled Dharasaaba had bemoaned her own womanhood and thus her presumed lack of ability to rule despite the mischance that had rendered her as her grandfather's only heir ... perhaps she would have felt less fierce about the women who stood and sat beside her.

But fierce she was, and she would not have traded the pleasure of that emotion for the measure of anyone's approval.

Men were fine. There was plenty of good in them, and she was fond of several. *But in this moment of my need, give me sisters.*

It was a moment fast approaching. The Dharasaaba were sorting themselves out before her eyes. In a moment, they would be waiting for her, and she would seem to be hesitating.

That could not be allowed to happen.

Mrithuri felt slow without the racing pulse of snakebite through her veins and mind. She felt sluggish, as if she must pay much closer attention to proceedings than she was accustomed.

But she also felt clear-headed and coolly rational in a manner she had not experienced since ... well, since when, she could not remember.

The time to act was now.

She inclined her head very slightly. A subtle gesture. But one that would not be missed by Hnarisha.

He was wearing an open-fronted robe of fine white wool over his tunic and trousers, echoing the color of mourning she wore. The placket and the hems of the wide sleeves were stiffened with bands of the gold brocade Mrithuri spurned. When he stepped forward and threw his arms wide, the robe billowed and flared around him like a cobra's hood.

Ümmühan struck a rill on the thumb-harp concealed in her lap. Mrithuri was certain that only she had noticed Sayeh flinch at the sound.

It amused her that Hnarisha's garments were far more regal than her own.

He boomed from the diaphragm, in ringing tones, "If you have a case to make before the empress, stand forth now!"

A stir passed through the vast chamber, followed by a gratifying plenitude of hasty footsteps. Golbahar rested a hand on the back of the chair of estate so her fingertips brushed Mrithuri's shoulder. Nobody else would see it, but Mrithuri felt the clever lady's approbation as a glow.

She had been afraid that she could not do this without the venom. She was still afraid. But being afraid did not mean she would not try.

The first lord to step toward the dais—not too close, as its foot was guarded by the Dead Man, Syama, and a few handpicked soldiers—was a fellow from the fertile hills to the east called Lord Rushabha. He cleared his throat, gestured around him on a sweeping arc like an actor, and spoke in a voice that, in a woman, would have been called shrewish. "Where has the glory of your court gone, Your Abundance?"

"Gone to feed an army," Mrithuri said dryly. "Gone to end a siege."

"But are not the treasures of the realm held in trust for her children?"

Mrithuri smiled. Without the mask on, everyone could see it. It did not sit on her face like a *nice* smile.

"The realm is held in trust for her children," she responded. "And the children of the Mother hold in trust the realm. I will make my court my own now and not my grandfather's, splendid though the court I inherited from my grandfather was."

"But surely," said another lord, "you must don finery to do honor to your court—"

"I am a widow." She flatly interrupted. "Should I dress for a festival?"

It was a stunning hypocrisy, and probably everyone in the room knew it. If she mourned Anuraja, then mourning was a light heart and a sense of joy.

But they were hypocrites as well, and they would not care to have that pointed out before the entire court. And she could carry it off, the appearance of mourning.

Mrithuri spread her hands, knowing that every eye would be drawn to their nakedness, and how the fingerstalls did not glitter over her nails. Her stomach lurched.

"I must be a martial empress now," she said. "That is why I have summoned you here this day, my Dharasaaba. We have learned the meaning of many oracles, and we have discovered that there are worse dangers on the horizon than armies."

This was the tricky part, of course. Many had heard Ravani's words to Sayeh. Only Mrithuri, on her second attempt to contact it, had experienced what the Gage's escorting bearded vulture remembered.

This was her chance to explain the real danger before them, to break it to her lords what Nizhvashiti had encountered in the wastelands. This was her chance to make them all believe in the destruction of Ansh-Sahal.

Sayeh would not be thrilled by Himadra's apparent willingness to switch sides. Mrithuri could not blame her.

Three separate and distinct prophecies of doom. And some bonus doom, unprophesied. A sufficiency of doom for everyone, and what had any among them done to deserve such bounty?

Mrithuri had paused too long, and chatter had started to rise from the cliques of nobles. She raised her hand. Ümmühan struck another rill.

The nobles went half-quiet. Quiet enough, at least, for her voice to carry over them, given the acoustic advantages built into the architecture.

"The old protections on our lands set by my ancestors have failed," Mrithuri said, putting her conviction and her diaphragm behind it. "A great threat is coming for us. A monster out of legend. We have seen its heralds, my lords of the Dharasaaba. We have seen its portents. My royal cousin Sayeh's city has already fallen; she is here to testify to the unnatural evil that overtook it."

Maybe the part about the unnatural evil was an exaggeration, and maybe it wasn't. But a little drama never hurt a stirring oration. And Mrithuri wasn't willing to take that risk.

Mother, she needed an heir.

Mrithuri took a breath. She looked down over her people, who were still not paying quite as much attention as she could have desired. She tried to remember that—cantankerous, obstructionist, and narcissistic as they could be—they were her people.

These lords each protected and ruled over some little fief within the realm, beholden to the Kingdom of Sarathai-tia. Some of them were better and more just rulers than others. Some were petty despots. Yavashuri could have told her all the details about every one—and often did.

What Yavashuri could not do was bring them to heel. Divided, they were the source of the kingdom's wealth and strength, and Mrithuri could rule them. Together, they could oppose Mrithuri and bring her reign to an end. Then they would be faced with the problem of legitimacy and a possibly bloody contest over who would replace her as figurehead. And the Alchemical Emperor's curse that was said to protect his legitimate descendants, as his descendants bound the realm together.

That curse was no doubt fresh in many minds, with the death of Anuraja upon the Peacock Throne.

Better from their point of view to try to control her. Mrithuri had realized that foreign suitors could be kept on a string and played off against one another. She realized now that tactic could be extended to dealing with her own nobles.

So as she spoke, she watched their expressions. She watched who stood with whom. She watched who avoided whom as well.

She reminded them of the portent of the red lotus—had it only been at the beginning of the rainy season that should not yet have ended? It seemed a decade ago. She told them that the Godmade had traveled in spirit as far as Ansh-Sahal and had met there the brother sorcerer to the one whose advice had set Anuraja on the path to war with Sarathai-tia, and sent him also up the steps of the Peacock Throne to his death. She told them of the Eyeless One's prophecy . . . and she told them of the unknown being (possibly the very voice of the Mother herself) that had spoken through Nizhvashiti to offer advice.

She did not know for certain that it was a goddess that had used the Godmade as its conduit. But wasn't being used as a conduit by deities what an ansha was for?

"It's not just my royal husband's army and my royal husband's kingdom that must concern us," she said, concealing her distaste for referring to Anuraja in such terms.

He's dead and I'm alive. I don't need to hate or fear him anymore. I don't even need to think about him anymore except as the source of all these inconveniences. I won. Or, at the very least, he lost, and that's nearly the same thing.

"It is how to unite ourselves and our peoples in order to be ready for the storm that is rising. A storm that we have no choice to face, for it has chosen us. Sayeh Rajni and I are of one mind on this."

Mrithuri looked over at Sayeh to offer the older woman the chance to speak. Sayeh caught the glance and stood without a crutch, using the arms of her chair for leverage. The only sign she gave of pain was a certain tightness at the corners of her eyes and along her jaw. Mrithuri thought she and Ümmühan would be the only ones to see it.

Sayeh said, "This is true. I have personally encountered both of these sorcerers, Ravana and Ravani"—a flinch ran around the room at the names. The sound of them produced an unsavory pang of discomfort in Mrithuri herself—"and I have seen the sway the one who calls herself Ravani holds over people. While I was a *guest* of Anuraja's army, I felt her wickedness, and here among you are your own Wizard, and the Wizard from my kingdom, and the Godmade. These can tell you the grotesque details of how she animates corpses to do battle for her, and how she poisoned the waters in these very cisterns beneath our feet to force you to surrender to their siege.

"The other sorcerer, the one I met in Ansh-Sahal before it was destroyed . . ." Her voice broke, but she held the hall spellbound, and Mrithuri watched as she gathered herself again. ". . . the one who seems to be her brother. He was there, when my city died. From what the Godmade has learned, he forged that destruction. He awakened a sleeping aspect of the one we do not speak of, a dark goddess who made the earth shake and the sea boil with poison."

Again, Mrithuri was not certain the volcano goddess was really an aspect of the Bad Daughter. But they were selling a narrative. Clarity mattered more than nuance now.

"He assisted Himadra of Chandranath to steal my son and heir. And having met them both, I am not certain that either of these sorcerers, Ravani and Ravana—I am not certain that either of them is exactly human."

"They're not," Mrithuri said. "And we have word from a messenger that we sent north that a powerful Wizard there claims these terrible powers only serve as heralds or handmaids to another, vaster power. A power the Alchemical Emperor bound away from our lands, that wants to claim them again now that we are divided and the protections he forged are weakening."

That too was a simplification of what she had learned from the memories of her familiar accompanying the Gage. But in politics as in love, it did not pay to make things too complicated.

I'm not a Wizard, she heard the voice of the very old woman say. But people would understand what a Wizard was.

"That's a superstition!" one of the lords heckled from the back.

Mrithuri sighed. "The Mother Wyrm was a superstition too, until she came to batter down our gates."

A murmur ran through the crowd. She wished she knew if it meant she had lost points or won them.

Sayeh still stood. She raised her voice to carry. Her tone lost none of its sweetness. "He is building a throne of corpses in the palace that was my home. And who will sit on that throne, I ask you?"

The room fell silent. Sayeh's words rang from the dragonglass panes far overhead.

Mrithuri stirred in her chair, directing attention back to herself. "I will tell you who will sit in that throne," she said. "That person is our enemy."

"If that is the case, you must marry again," a man shouted. Lord Partha, she thought—one of the wealthier subjects. Someone whose goodwill, sadly, she needed. "We need a raja to lead us to war!"

"We need an emperor," Mrithuri said. Words that fell like individual coins to ring.

In the silence that followed, she turned and looked up at the enormous glittering bulk of the throne that dwarfed her. Dwarfed her, and Sayeh, and all their counselors, and all the little men standing even farther below. She said nothing. She knew that every one of them could imagine the body of the last man who had dared to sit there tumbling—rolling—ignominiously down the steps again. Either they had been in the room—brave enough to face the conqueror and his officers—or they had heard about it in exquisite and possibly somewhat invented detail from those who either had been there—or were pretending so.

Mrithuri herself had been dizzy with fear and serpent-sickness and exhaustion. She barely remembered her wedding and almost instant widowhood. The mind has its little kindnesses.

She turned back to the crowd. "We have not always had an emperor, you know. It is not a role that has existed since the Moon fell."

They watched her.

She smiled her most inviting smile. "Which one of you would like to be the next to marry me?"

The only sound that answered her was like the shushing of water over rocks: a hundred or so bare or sandaled or silk-slippered feet, shuffling as their owners rocked uneasily over the green- and blue-tiled stones. She was rather proud of her phrasing and how it implied that a lot of men would fail in rapid sequence if they tried.

She gave them plenty of time to step forward, and plenty of time to feel ashamed. And, she hoped, not enough time to start feeling outrage and anger.

"Right," Mrithuri whispered behind her hand to Hnarisha. "Send in Anuraja's fucking lieutenants, would you?"

IN THE CORRIDOR BEYOND THE DOORS TO THE HALL OF THE EMPTY THRONE, the Dead Man stood with his back against a wall and cleaned his fingernails with a sharp little poignard. Beside him was a smaller door, this one leading to an anteroom in which waited what passed for the leaders of Anuraja's army. The Dead Man did not know if it was by happenstance, architecture, or sorcery, but they—and he—could clearly hear the proceedings of the Dharasaaba from there.

They'd gotten lucky. The old monster's own conviction that the sun rose and set in his arse had played out to their advantage, as there wasn't an established hierarchy or a body of institutional knowledge to take his place once he was gone. The Dead Man, product of an organization that was *nothing but* established hierarchy supporting a body of institutional knowledge, found himself moderately dazzled by the lack of foresight.

Being dazzled by a lack of foresight was a frequent state for him. Perhaps he should nurture a deeper cynicism.

As he was chuckling to himself, the door into the antechamber opened and a worried face peered out. It was one of the heathen soldiers. One, the Dead Man thought, that Sayeh Rajni had selected as part of the delegation. He searched his memory for the name, a procedure that seemed to grow more strenuous with every passing year. Vaneer, he thought, and felt an unreasonable flare of triumph for such a small victory.

It was really time to retire and buy some land and grow persimmons, or dates, or something.

"Begging your pardon," Vaneer said to the Dead Man, "but we've been listening to the rajnis speak—"

So had the Dead Man, with half an ear, since he already knew what was to be said. He nodded.

The soldier cleared his throat. "You know these people. And you seem like a sensible sort, for a heathen."

In the interests of harmony, the Dead Man withheld his comments on religious orthodoxy.

The other man said, "If we're going to war, and the Dowager has no heir and Sayeh Rajni has misplaced hers, and Lord Anuraja died heirless, and the cripple up in Chandranath can't get his dick hard to get one . . . and if we need an emperor on the Peacock Throne to hold off demons and sorcerers . . . hadn't one of that lot better get a brat pretty quick? If all that's holding this monster in his closet is the blood of the old emperor and the spells that he put on it?"

Half a dozen answers occurred to the Dead Man. Temporizations, and sly responses. In the end, though, he just said, "I believe they are working on it. And the Lord of Chandranath does have brothers."

He was spared a continuation of the conversation when the door to the Hall swung wide, Hnarisha's fine-featured face peering out. "They're ready for you."

SAYEH RESEATED HERSELF AND WATCHED AS SERVANTS EFFICIENTLY REDECO-rated the echoing Hall to facilitate a smaller, more intimate meeting. A long board was set upon trestles, as for a banquet, and cushions brought in. The majority of the lords of the Dharasaaba were ushered out—or lured out, more precisely, with the promise of refreshments. Though how pleasant those could be in a city still recovering from siege, she did not know and did not care to guess.

Those that remained behind were (from Sayeh's understanding) the wealthiest, those responsible for governing the largest portion of the population. And thusly the most powerful, and the ones most involved in the manning, payment, and disposition of the army. The Alchemical Emperor had not permitted his vassals to levy troops of their own. Part of his technique for maintaining his hegemony had been that *he* provided the armies that defended their land, while conscripting soldiers from his lords' demesnes to defend other lords' cities and provide the bulk of the army.

After the Empire shattered, that had changed. In Sayeh's land and in Chandranath, where there were few people and not much desirable land to defend, the local lords had their little warbands, and the raja or rajni commanded a small army whose main purpose was keeping the roads open and at least nominally free of brigands. Since some of those brigands were indistinguishable from the warbands of the local lords, the situation could become politically complicated. Here in Sarathai-tia, the nucleus of the old empire, the rajni did levy soldiers. In Sarathai-lae, Anuraja had maintained an army as large as all of his neighbors combined.

No doubt some of these Tian lords maintained "personal guards" whose number pushed the limit of law and custom. But the garrisons on their land were still nominally Mrithuri's to command.

Those that had not run away or been wiped out by the Laeish army on its march to the capital. Those whose commanders would choose to follow her orders, not that Sayeh was bitter about the insubordination of her own war leaders.

Well, the captains who had disobeyed her orders to evacuate Ansh-Sahal were all dead now, she thought, and the soldiers who had listened had lived. It was a catastrophic tragedy that they had taken so many of her civilian subjects with them by demanding those folk return to their homes in the face of earthquake and upheaval. She had only been spared herself because when the cataclysm happened, she, Nazia, Ümmühan, Tsering, and Vidhya had been with a small warband of their own, pursuing Himadra and his men through the hills, trying to reclaim her kidnapped son.

She could not bring her slain people back. All she could do was find and protect the ones that remained, and try to find and reclaim her son.

It chafed to be there in Sarathai-tia when Drupada was being held in Chandranath, and when the relatives of Himadra's that she might take hostage and exchange for Drupada were probably in Sarathai-lae.

But all human endeavors involved a certain amount of bustling and thrashing and self-organization before any real work could be done. Sayeh comforted herself that these were necessary arguments. The overture to progress, as it were.

Speaking of which, the bustling and thrashing and self-organization at the foot of the dais seemed to be reaching their inevitable conclusion. The remaining lords had been joined by assorted soldiers, and all were milling around. Sayeh looked over at Mrithuri, who was inscrutable in her own thoughts. Serene, as royal women were taught to be serene, so no lines of character might mark their faces with the evidence of age or—Mother forbid—deep thinking.

Sayeh controlled her fury. That, too, was the habit of a lifetime, trained since she was small. She was glad, suddenly, that she had borne a son and not a daughter. She wondered if, as it became plain that she—Sayeh—was a girl, her own mother had felt the pangs of teaching her to be small, to be soft, to be constrained. If she had felt an undefinable frustration at what she was expected to raise her daughter to be—or if the frustration had all been sparked by Sayeh when Sayeh spoke too loudly, strode too briskly, waved her arms.

For the first time, Sayeh—looking at Mrithuri—realized that her mother's frustration might have derived from feeling trapped in her own sex and being unable to bear watching anyone else stretch the boundaries of it. When she was younger, Sayeh knew she might have been angered by the revelation. But what she felt in her middle age was a tremendous gentleness toward other women and a desire to push wide the bars of their cages.

Mrithuri might have felt the pressure of her gaze, or might also have noticed that the table seemed to be ready. The Dowager—it amused Sayeh smugly every time she thought it—turned to return her regard.

"What do you think, Sayeh?"

Sayeh smiled grimly. "Let's dazzle them, shall we?"

Mrithuri stood, and Sayeh stood with her, the poetess Ümmühan following stiffly a moment later. Mrithuri waited three breaths to allow her women to organize themselves, then swept down the steps, trailed first by Sayeh and then by the others. The Dowager allowed herself to be seated at the head of the table. Once she and Sayeh were in their places, the lords swiftly followed. Mrithuri's advisors arranged themselves in a semicircle behind her while the soldiers and guardsmen found cushions.

Among the lords, Sayeh recognized those who had spoken out during the Dharasaaba: Lord Rushabha, who was some manner of a gentleman farmer, and wealthy Lord Partha. They sat among three others. Among the soldiers was Zirha, the nearest thing to a commander that Anuraja had supported, along with her own former guards Varjeet and Sanjay. Sayeh's guard captain Vidhya was there, and Mrithuri's paramour who was a Dead Man, and Mrithuri's general Pranaj.

It had the look of a creditable council of war.

Tea was served, and once a cup sat before each person, Mrithuri cleared her throat. "We gather," she said formally, "to speak of war."

"That's very nice, Your Abundance," Lord Partha said. "But how do you propose to pay for it?"

Zirha lifted his chin. "Dowager, can you not pay my men?"

Mrithuri made a tinkling sound that some might have mistaken for a laugh, though Sayeh could not imagine how the men in the room would not know it was artificial. Those men seemed, however, enchanted.

She thought again of what her mother had taught her.

Mrithuri turned to Ata Akhimah. "The proofs, if you please."

Akhimah produced a small folder from inside her waistcoat and laid it on the table. She opened it, revealing flawless mirror-bright gold, copper, and silver links and rings sewn onto the chamois. The flat side of each was stamped with a portrait and the legend *Mrithuri I, Dowager Empress of Sarath, 1st Year of Her Reign.* Mrithuri thought the profile was a little over-flattering, but the engraver had done very nice, crisp work, and the details could be seen even on the small gold links.

Bulls, peacocks, dolphins, and even one massive elephant that probably held all the gold from a single mask.

Zirha sighed with slightly too much relief. Sayeh reached out under cover of the table and patted his arm. It was never too soon to start getting on the man's good side.

"You will be paid, Commander." Mrithuri waved Lord Partha aside as if dismissing a child who was being ridiculous. "Have no fear on that account. And what we propose is to bring you home to Sarathai-lae, to your families and children, before all. I must see to the well-being of my people there."

She spoke as low and soothingly as Sayeh herself could have managed, and it had the desired effect. On Commander Zirha at least. Lord Partha seemed less impressed. Or perhaps less credulous.

Zirha would take some shoring up. Anuraja had obviously not chosen the man for his military skills or his strength of character but for his malleability. He was not at all what they needed.

Unfortunately, he was what they had, and she did not think he would take kindly to being set beneath Pranaj or Vidhya. She looked at his soft hands, his jeweled collar, the arrogant bearing—and saw a rich lord's son who had bought a commission, whom Anuraja found useful probably in large part because he had not had a lot of ideas of his own. Sayeh, to her sorrow, knew the type of old.

He had probably never expected to find himself actually in command of anything. Not with Anuraja around.

People had a remarkable ability to ignore contingencies when it suited them. Partha cleared his throat. "*Will* you be assessing taxes?"

He was a bull-fighting dog and not likely to be diverted from the question.

Mrithuri, though, smiled sweetly and said, "Not much more so than the usual, for now. Our treasury will stretch to cover our new vassals. Tian taxes will go to pay Tian soldiers and feed Tian refugees."

Zirha looked smug, and Partha looked disgruntled. Down the table Sayeh saw her own captain eyeing the lord over the rim of his teacup. Vidhya said nothing, but Sayeh had known him long enough to read his expression and know that he had identified Partha as a threat. Sayeh wished she did not so thoroughly agree. There was nothing wrong with being guided by a prudent attention to one's pocketbook. But to let miserliness get in the way of self-protection was a character flaw.

Golbahar murmured into Mrithuri's ear behind her hand.

Mrithuri nodded, smiling sweetly. "And of course, now that Sarath is united as a kingdom once more, our resources are much greater than we have been used to."

Aha. The stiffening of Partha's expression told him that Golbahar had scored a direct hit. His self-regard was of course at stake, as well as his influence. Sarathai-lae was a richer kingdom than Sarathai-tia, with fertile farmland and a port to the Arid Sea. Partha's wealth would not buy him the influence that it once had, when Mrithuri established herself as Dowager in truth.

Mrithuri turned her attention to another Lord down the table. "Lord Taymun," she said, "what are the needs of the border garrisons with Chandranath?"

Taymun was an older man, his hair a thin band around a sun-spotted scalp. From his clothing and from Mrithuri's question, Sayeh deduced that he came from the northwestern region of Sarathai-tia. "They will need to be rebuilt," he said, without temporizing. "Not all of them, but two or three have been completely destroyed and pillaged. Himadra raids when he can and blames it on bandits."

Sayeh was not prepared for the tongue of rage that licked through her at her enemy's name. She spoke through her teeth. "It's truth, if you accept that he is a bandit."

Appreciative chuckles defused her fury enough that she regained her composure. Its return left her feeling let down, drained, as if some animating force had gone out of her. Perhaps she ought to get angry more often and be more loathe to let it go.

Mrithuri stood abruptly. Around the table, others scrambled to their feet. Golbahar and Yavashuri unobtrusively helped Sayeh and Ümmühan stand. Sayeh squeezed Golbahar's hand in silent thanks and caught the wink in reply.

"Our royal progress to Sarathai-lae will begin in two nights," Mrithuri said. "Thank you all for your time."

MRITHURI'S STELLAR WAS NOT CURRENTLY THE QUIET PLACE OF RETIREMENT she usually maintained. It was full of Wizards, waiting-women, and warriors of various inclinations, not to mention her ally and fellow rajni—who was fast becoming a friend. She'd never quite had a friend of her own rank (or close to it, now that she was—laughably—the Dowager Empress of Sarath), and she found it refreshing.

She looked around the room. Besides Sayeh, various cushions supported Nazia, Ata Akhimah, Tsering-la, Lady Golbahar, the Dead Man, Ümmühan, Pranaj, Hnarisha, and Vidhya. With the exception of Yavashuri and Nizhvashiti, she thought, this was her true council all assembled. These were the people beside whom she would go to war.

Some of them she had known only briefly. It didn't matter. They all knew what the stakes were now, and they all believed. Everyone else would have to be swept along beside them.

She looked first at Sayeh. "It's going to be up to you to keep Zirha in line, I'm afraid. I cannot promote Pranaj over him—"

Pranaj shrugged, averting any suggestion that he might feel insult with a turn of his hand. "My self-esteem is not at stake, as long as you do not expect me to take orders from him."

She met his eyes. She had worried that he would not be ready to step into a role as general when he was forced into it. But he had blossomed after the death of her prior commander. "Whatever happens, know that my trust lies in you."

Tsering-la said, "This Zirha may be a little dazed yet from the sorcerer's hold over him."

"Hmm." Ata Akhimah frowned in agreement.

Sayeh tried not to sigh, but it got past her anyway. "I didn't sign up to raise a general, but I suppose I will do it. Somebody has to give that man a little self-confidence to soften the arrogance with."

"If he ever had any, it's obvious Anuraja and Ravani kicked it out of him." The Dead Man leaned against the wall beside the door, so motionless it would be easy to forget him—scarlet coat and all. "But we should not complain."

"I'm complaining now," said Mrithuri, "because now I need to use him. And it would be nice if that didn't involve having to get out and push!"

A light scratch on the door announced Yavashuri. She peered around the edge as she slid it aside. "Well, this is convenient. Hello, everyone."

She crossed the room, stepping over cushions and legs, walking as if carrying a weight. One by one, she removed some half dozen soft chamois bags from a pouch over her shoulder and laid them on the low table beside Mrithuri's tea.

Milky, spiced tea with sugar. Too much sugar for Mrithuri to stomach comfortably at this stage in her recovery, but Ata Akhimah had insisted she take some more sustenance. So she sipped it slowly, leaning back against her bolster while her insides churned.

At least there was, again, Wizardry on the pot and the cup that kept the stuff inside fresh and warm.

"Well done," she said to her oldest confidante.

"It won't be enough for long," Yavashuri said, with a gesture toward the bags.

"It will be enough for now, added to the treasury. And there's nothing to stop us from melting down the silverware." Mrithuri wrapped her hands around the cup for a moment longer. The warmth eased the aches in her bones. "Then we come up with the next thing. I like the dies, Ata Akhimah."

Reluctantly, she set the tea aside and measured each of the bags with her hands, in turn. Two were smaller than the others, so light it seemed there was little inside—but they rustled and clicked when she moved them. The rest were shockingly heavy and clanked in a manner that reminded her of the Gage. For a moment she worried about the metal man, what he was doing in Himadra's court, and the result of his desperate mission east. She did not know what had happened to him in the Singing City. Her bird had not been able to follow there.

Yavashuri pursed her lips and glanced at the Lady Golbahar. Golbahar shrugged with one shoulder.

Yavashuri said, "There's a royal treasure in Sarathai-lae that belongs to you."

"Technically," Mrithuri said. She didn't mention that her brief marriage to Anuraja was a fiction—that it had never been consummated (thank the Mother whose servant she was) and that in any case she had already been married to her foreign bodyguard in a pagan ceremony. She assumed that Yavashuri knew about that, because Hnarisha knew, and those two did not have many secrets from one another. "Do you think his people will give it to me without a fight?"

"It depends on how you approach them," Golbahar said. "Showing up with the air of a royal progress taking possession of one home among many won't hurt your chances."

Yavashuri tipped her head. "He died without heirs."

Golbahar coughed gently against the back of her hand. "And we do have the bulk of his army . . . if we can keep it."

Mrithuri hefted a clinking bag in both hands. She opened it and began to build a tiny fortress with the small bars of buttery gold within. It seemed like very little for how heavy it had weighed in her hands.

"We'll need more gold. And we'll need to strike this all into currency."

"I'll oversee it," said Ata Akhimah.

"Dowager Empress Mrithuri I, first year of her reign," Yavashuri said. "They'll be collector's items someday."

Mrithuri rolled her eyes and pushed the gold toward Ata Akhimah. "This is not easily negotiable. Have you found out if we can sell the jewels? We can't exactly just dole them out to the paymasters. They don't divide very well."

Golbahar asked, "Who in the city has money to buy them? That Partha? I think we'd rather not be beholden to him, though." She blew her veil away from her lips. "My father has the money. But my father is not here."

"I'll check with a few more of the Dharasaaba." Yavashuri sounded tired. "First, I will have some artisans on the Street of Glitter consulted quietly to see what they can move or what they might purchase outright. And at the worst, there will be gold in Sarathai-lae."

"We hope," said the Dead Man, with a roll of his eyes that spoke of long experience with the vagaries of paymasters.

Nazia seemed about to say something but was interrupted by another gentle noise against the doorframe—a scratch as if of an animal's claws. "Come," Mrithuri said.

Drifting in its black robes, Nizhvashiti entered. The hood was thrown back. The bald head seemed shinier, as if shellacked. A scent of herbs and varnish drifted with it.

But what Mrithuri most noticed was the swags of jewelry draped over its wrists and forearms, swaying slightly with its movement. Gold chains dripped from its fingers; gold anklets encircled its wrists.

"Money," it said in its voice like leaves rustling. Its gold eye and its glass eye did not blink. "This should help with the liquidity problem."

Mrithuri blinked, half-blinded by the sparkle. "It should," she agreed. "My goodness. What can we offer you in return, Godmade?"

"Drink your tea, Your Abundance," Nizhvashiti said. "The Good Daughter knows her duty to the Mother, after all."

"Well, that's one thing settled," said Yavashuri. "Next, we should decide who is going on this expedition."

"It's a royal progress," Mrithuri said. "We all are."

As everyone was leaving, she caught Sayeh alone, restraining the older woman with a hand on the sleeve. "If I have to make a deal with Himadra, I will make it. I did not want it to be a surprise, and I wanted you to hear it from me."

Sayeh blinked her stare away and glanced at the ground. "Your familiar? The one who is with your emissary?"

Mrithuri nodded. "We're going to need him."

Sayeh's lower lip pushed upward, stubborn. Quivering. She reined herself in with a deep breath. "I suppose I must promise, if I do not wish to be left out of negotiations."

"I'm sorry," Mrithuri said. "I'll make any deal contingent upon his returning your son."

Sayeh let a held breath out slowly. "I'd like to eat his heart."

Mrithuri held her hand out. "Maybe the beast will do it for you."

Sayeh made a scoffing noise in her throat but took the hand. "All right. I promise."

5

"You are *not* taking this baby on another forced march through a wilderness full of . . . of bandits and hungry animals!"

Himadra, in his chair within the nursery door, crossed his arms in mimicry of Drupada's nursemaid Iri. He tilted his head sideways. "You'd rather I left him here unprotected?"

"I—" She stomped her foot in wild frustration, then looked down at it as if her passion had surprised her.

Himadra laughed. So few people would tell him what they really thought.

"Oh, you infuriating little man. You're mocking me."

Navin, who had been standing beside Himadra as guard and chair-pusher, put his hand on the hilt of his sword. Himadra reached out and touched his sergeant's arm. The man lowered his hand but his tension did not ease.

"I'm infuriating and you're insubordinate," he said. "How on earth did you manage to survive in Sayeh's service? Does she just put up with contumacy and sedition?"

Iri uncrossed her arms. He hadn't used a perilous tone. She was, he assumed, deciding whether his words constituted a threat anyway.

A cowed advisor gave terrible advice. Himadra couldn't prevent his people from mocking his stature and incapacity when he was out of earshot. You could cut out tongues until you ran out of heads, and the outcome would be your victims plotting your downfall in sign language.

Respect was a currency that could not be extorted, only earned.

After thinking it through, Iri must have decided his question was sincere. "I was only a nurse at all because of the emergency. The woman who cared most for him was killed in the earthquake. I was a stable hand." A rueful smile. "They kept me away from the court. But I did care for Prince Drupada's pony, and that was how I had met him."

That explained her skill on horseback, anyway.

Her scowl was likely to etch permanent lines in her face. But it was honest and Himadra found he liked it better than any obsequious dissembling.

"And still you're willing to yell at a raja for him." Himadra shook his head in gentle amusement. "We're leaving tomorrow night. You might as well pack."

✳   ✳   ✳

THE GAGE WAS STANDING ALONE BESIDE THE BATTLEMENTS WHEN KYRLMY-randal came and found him. She seemed tired, leaning heavily on her staff as if climbing the steps had worn on her. She sighed deeply.

"Are the years very heavy?"

Laughter shaded her voice. "They're lighter than the centuries. But perhaps I could ask you the same thing."

"You will have to spot me a decade or ten before I am fit to make any comparisons involving centuries."

"And yet here you are alone, staring off into the sun, getting in the way of the guardsmen on patrol. So if it isn't centuries, what is troubling you?"

"I think you know, Kyrlmyrandal. It was you who told me that I did not want to pass through the same door you used to come here."

"If you wanted to be human, you would be human," she said. "If you had wanted to die, you would not be here. It doesn't require particularly effective detective work to deduce that."

"Human frailty makes me uncomfortable," the Gage admitted.

"It's not just humans that are frail," said the dragon. "Look at me: dragging a leg: flightless and blind and all out of teeth."

"I don't believe you will ever be out of teeth, no matter the contents of your jaw."

As if awarding him the point, she grinned. "I'm sure even that shape you wear has its fragilities."

"Your frailness is of a different order than human frailness. It does not remind me so much of my history. Of powerlessness." He paused. "And before you ask, yes, of course I feel powerless now. In the face of volcanoes and volcano goddesses, of sorcerers and animated corpses—both friendly and unfriendly—and of whatever is looming at the edge of the earth." His carapace rattled when he shrugged.

"It sounds as if it were a relief to you to become a Gage."

"It helps me survive making friends with dragons." He inclined his head toward her. "Is it safe for you to stay here? Will you leave your poison on these stones?"

"There's less of me to poison stones in this shape." She thumped her staff. "And I'm not going to ask to hold the baby."

He snorted, a choked laugh in his own turn. "The pen you gave me?"

"When you find its owner, tell them not to suck on the cap and to keep it in a golden box rather than a pocket. Or lead will do, if they're indigent."

"Lead or gold or a bronze drawer in a clockwork golem's chest," said the pen from its place inside him, "it's all the same to me, as long as they can write. And so long as there's a little velvet cushion to nap on between epics. And a good supply of ink. And—"

"I'll pass your demands along when the time comes," said the Gage. "And what about the Carbuncle?"

"Getting children comes with risks. Children gotten by magic as much as the other kind." The creases of her face rearranged themselves from restrained mirth to sorrow. "My own children came with enough risks, and that's certain. From egg to ancient Wyrm—every one of them broke my heart. Some broke my heart by betraying me, and some broke my heart by standing with me until the bitter end."

"There was a war between them?" he guessed.

"It's just as well," she said tiredly. "Your little world can only support so many dragons. Too many of us and it would all be burned as barren as those mountains there."

He wasn't quite sure how to answer that, and while he was thinking about it, she coughed against the back of her hand and said, "Does your queen know the Carbuncle will get her daughters but no sons?"

"No," the Gage rumbled. "I am fairly certain that she doesn't. Why is that?"

"It's in the father's seed, with you folks, whether the child is female or male. No father, no male children."

"Huh," he said. Then, "Dragons do it differently?"

"Males are young," she said. "If we live long enough, we mature into females."

"If you live long enough? What threatens a dragon?"

She was silent long enough for him to begin to feel stupid, the answer being obvious.

A god. Another dragon. Or a beast.

"Hey," said Heartsblood, oblivious as a toddler to the weight that had settled over both Gage and dragon. "Take me out of the drawer. I want to see the mountains!"

The Gage was not surprised when Himadra summoned him and Kyrlmyrandal to lunch. *We might be the most interesting thing in this edge of the world.* He was surprised when the food was served—to Himadra and to Kyrlmyrandal—and before even tearing into his bread, Himadra said, "Will you come with me to my next destination?"

Kyrlmyrandal gently patted things on the table, locating her plate and bread and tea. She found her napkin and spread it over her lap. She said, "I suppose that depends on why you are going there and what you intend to accomplish once you get there."

"I want my brothers back," he said. "I imagine you might be going to Sarathai-tia—"

The Gage said, "My task does take me there."

"Sarathai-lae is a reasonable place to stop along the way." Himadra popped a morsel into his mouth and chewed with closed eyes.

"Don't you think Sayeh might object to you keeping her son? Or did you plan to return him to her when you got there?"

"That's open to negotiation," Himadra said. "A lot of things change with Anuraja gone. You could try to find Ravana—"

"First and foremost," the Gage repeated, "I have that errand in Sarathai-tia."

"What makes the errand so urgent, anyway?"

"Duty," the Gage said dryly. "And we *do* have a dueling pair of prophecies. Well, I suppose, two prophecies and a portent."

"That seems like a lot."

"Doesn't it just? Who really needs more than two oracles?"

Kyrlmyrandal snorted like a horse. "Who really needs more than one?"

"Tell me about them," Himadra said.

"That is probably providing too much leverage to the enemy."

He shook his head. "You came here. And we've been over my feelings and intentions."

"We came here looking for your sorcerer," Kyrlmyrandal reminded. "And not out of goodwill."

Himadra's smile seemed to spill across his face, slow as water ebbing over the top of a glass. "Have I not taken you in as guests regardless? Have I not listened to your litany of dangers? Have we not admitted that we're allies in this? Especially"—he slurped tea as if it were too hot to drink politely—"with Anuraja dead. Don't we all want the same things? Do we not all share the same enemy? So what's one—or two, or three—little prophecies between friends, that you cannot share that information with me?"

A silence followed. Heartsblood rolled curiously inside the Gage's chest, tickling until he had to fight the urge to clap a hand to the drawer.

Himadra broke the quiet to say, persuasively, "Tell me about these prophecies. And why you think they might be more than balderdash and con artistry."

The Gage could not help but like this little man with his oversized charisma. A charisma that made him an effective leader. And a formidable opponent.

"I want to know too!" Heartsblood said.

Himadra reared back on his cushion. "What on earth?"

"You heard it?" the Gage said.

"A voice but not a voice," Himadra said. "Sorcery—"

"Just a magic pen in my pocket," the Gage said. "It has opinions."

"It shall write the history of what it is you do and fail to do, one day," it replied. "What I witness shall be recorded forever.

"So be nice to me."

"Can I see it?" Himadra asked.

"Dragon-poison," said the Gage. "I'll show you later, away from the food. As for the prophecies—" The Gage gestured to Kyrlmyrandal. Kyrlmyrandal shook her head.

"They're your prophecies," she said. "I respect your judgment."

If the Gage had eyes, he would have rolled them. "Very well. The first was a message that the Eyeless One, the Wizard-Prince of Messaline, sent with my partner and me in response to Mrithuri's request for assistance."

"Wizard-Prince," Himadra said. "That's a relative of mine, isn't it? One of the old Emperor's exiles?"

"Jharni," the Gage said. "That was why Mrithuri applied to her for assistance. She hoped it might come out of felicity."

"So what did she say?"

"Well, she sent my partner and me. And a scrap of paper with the following words: '*A child can come to a maiden; a bride can travel afar. In a stone in a skull lies great wisdom; healing grows strong from a scar. A king ascends from a princess; a harvest arises from war.*'"

Himadra mouthed the doggerel, then washed it down with tea. "Delightfully cryptic. A stone in a skull, ay?"

The Gage decided to reserve, for the time being, the information that the Eyeless One had also sent a chime that shattered illusions, which the Godmade Nizhvashiti had pushed into the socket of its own plucked-out eye.

"WHAT'S THE NEXT ONE?" HIMADRA ASKED.

"That one came through the Godmade that we met in the mountains. It came with us to Sarathai-tia and delivered a prophecy that seemed to come from some other being, using its body as a conduit."

"Hmm," said Himadra. "And whom does this Godmade serve?"

"The Good Daughter," the Gage said, and noticed that Himadra shuddered and looked down at his hands. That was not a goddess anyone seemed to find reassuring. "I do not know if she was the source of the message, though."

"What was the message?"

The Gage was blessed with a better memory than most creatures of squishy, unreliable flesh and blood. He intoned, "Seek the Carbuncle. Seek the Mother of Exiles, blind and in her singing catacomb. Time is short, and more is at stake than kingdoms. Something stirs. Something vast and cruel stirs, to the east, beneath the sea. Your destiny lies with the Origin of Storms."

Himadra thought about it, then said, "Well, I don't see what any of that has to do with me."

"The destruction of Ansh-Sahal might be the thing that stirred to the east, beneath the sea."

"Hmm." The warlord didn't sound convinced. "As much north as east, from Sarathai-tia."

"Some of it's coming plain," the Gage said. "The harvest arising from war—well, Ravana seems to have a use for all those dead people. Unpleasant though it be. And we keep being told about beasts that feed on war." He tilted his head toward Kyrlmyrandal, unsure of what she wished revealed.

"I have been named the Mother of Exiles," she said. "And I have the artifact called the Carbuncle."

"What's it good for?"

She smiled. "Nothing, for you."

He laughed. "A touch. All right, then. So, you came here to trap my sorcerer. My sorcerer is gone. What will you do now?"

"You may find you do not like it," Kyrlmyrandal said.

Himadra peered from under bushy eyebrows. The sclera of his eyes, the Gage noticed, were tinged blue. "I am in a position to judge very few people. I have done many things that were the soul of expedience rather than honor." He shrugged. "I soothe myself that the outcomes I produced were better overall than the ones I would have gotten through a more mealy-mouthed approach."

"Pragmatism," the Gage said. "Better for you, or for others?"

Himadra set down his tea cup and picked up a sweetmeat. "Perhaps not better for my sleep at night. But perhaps more conducive to the long-term continued existence of myself. And of others."

"The more uncomfortable I am with myself," the Gage said casually, "the more prone I am to judging others. The more I like who I am, how I look, what I am doing—the kinder and more generous I can be."

"This is not unique to you." Kyrlmyrandal raised both hands and brushed white hair behind the coppery line of her neck. "The more content people are in their own choices, the less they feel the need to control the choices that are not theirs. The happier they are, the less those who choose a different path and also find happiness threaten them. If you're miserable and pretending not to be, there's nothing in the world more upsetting than somebody who does what pleases them, especially if what pleases them is different from the choices you have made."

"Hmm," said the Gage. "So, Lord Himadra. How severely do you judge others?"

Himadra waved the question away as an irrelevancy. "What if your choices are forced?" he asked. "What if the world has done, perhaps, a little too much choosing on your own behalf?"

"Oh," the Gage said, "that's definitely a recipe for fury. And, in the long run, for drastic action."

"Drastic," Kyrlmyrandal agreed. "And quite probably ill-considered."

"Like stealing your rival's heir?" Himadra asked, with—all things considered—surprising good humor.

Kyrlmyrandal turned her teacup in her hand, tracing the decoration with a fingertip. "I wasn't going to say it."

The raja shrugged. "You have distracted me very neatly, but I put it to you again. What will you do once you've completed your task in Sarathai-tia?"

"We told you about the volcano goddess," the Gage said. "I suppose perhaps I will go back to Ansh-Sahal. To the pile of bodies. And seek Ravana there."

"That's not a good journey for an old woman," Himadra said. "The acid in the air would melt her skin and bones."

"I am made of sterner stuff than I look to be," said Kyrlmyrandal. "But you have a counterproposal?"

Himadra made a face.

The Gage said, "You have Sayeh's son. You have her army. And you will need to feed them all somehow."

"Don't remind me."

"You'll march on Sarathai-lae," the Gage said confidently. "You'll try to take it before Mrithuri can. Then let *her* figure out how to feed *her* army."

Himadra laughed—a joyous and unconsidered belling. "By the Mother, you're not bad!" Then he shook his head. "I'm going to go and get my brothers. And try to strike a deal with Mrithuri Rajni where neither of us lose face or position. Then maybe I can work a trade with Sayeh to get her alliance in return for access to her son. She's going to need a place to live, isn't she? The two of us will be stronger together than apart. Especially"—he gestured—"if a beast is on the move. By the way, what was the third portent?"

"It was the first one," the Gage said. "It happened before I came to Sarathai-tia. And I do not entirely understand the symbolism."

Himadra watched him patiently.

"Something about a red lotus," he said, "and the Ritual of Rains Return?"

The effect on Himadra was instantaneous and shocking. Color drained from his complexion, leaving his sun-ruddied olive face looking ashy and strange. His teacup slopped, though it had not been near full to the brim. He set it down in a small puddle.

"There are worse portents," he said. "But not many."

"Her Wizard found a means to spin it," the Gage said. "But no-one seemed comfortable with the outcome."

"Rains Return is a survival from the old days," Himadra said. "From when we were an empire. And its portent is not just for Sarathai-tia. It's for all the Lotus Kingdoms. It reveals the . . . intention? No, that's not the right word. It reveals what cannot be avoided for the year to come."

"And red is for blood?"

"Royal blood," Himadra said. "Shed violently. It may not mean deaths, at least. But it doesn't preclude them."

The Gage thought dryly that common people never seemed to get portents from the gods that their lives were beginning or ending. It was a pity that even deities who might be expected to bear witness to the end of a cicada's life with as much gravity as they did a human's . . . still only seemed to pull out the signs and symbolism for princes of the land.

He was tired of princes.

6

"Come with me," Nizhvashiti said, and so Mrithuri left the frenzy of packing and preparations for travel behind and followed. Even an Empress Dowager listens, if she is wise, when a Godmade beckons.

Syama padded along with them, a massive, languid presence, muscle rippling under her gold-and-black striped hide.

They moved through the golden corridors as if in a dream, the yellow marble of the outer walls translucent with the brilliance of the Heavenly River behind it, shafts of light streaming through the latticed windows to tattoo patterns on the flagstone floors. A warm haze seemed to wrap Mrithuri, and the Godmade was a slash of black ink.

Perhaps she should have been surprised when Nizhvashiti led her to the rooms of the ambassador from Anuraja whom Chaeri had murdered. It seemed like a thousand years had passed since that bloody day, the excuse for war. It had been months only.

They paused outside the doors. Nizhvashiti produced a key. Mrithuri listened to the tumblers fall over with mechanical clarity and thought, *How was it that I let Chaeri mislead me for so long?*

But she knew. She had loved the other woman. They had grown up together like sisters. And she had relied on Chaeri to tend her familiars . . .

She sighed. Including the Eremite serpents whose venom had made her mind race and nearly destroyed her body.

She would need, she thought, to get Syama more exercise. Well, it would be good for both of them. Even if the court would be scandalized to see a rajni sweat.

And perhaps moving her body would distract her mind from her anger at herself. Because she had not allowed Chaeri to mislead her. No: she had willfully participated in her own deception.

If she thought about it for too long, she would gag on self-loathing. She couldn't afford to waste energy on despising herself. She had a job to do.

Nizhvashiti glanced to her with sightless orbs. "May I open the door, Your Abundance?"

"Yes," Mrithuri said, and watched as the door to the ambassador's chambers glided aside. Nizhvashiti stood back to let the rajni enter. Syama slipped past them soft as a shadow, belying the hundredweights of her, and strolled in first.

Mrithuri paused beside the door, watching Syama sniff her way around the room. She never got tired of how the bear-dog moved, how weight and languorous grace combined to make her seem lazy and slack when she was anything but.

Nizhvashiti stepped over the threshold and stopped beside Mrithuri. Mrithuri scratched her own shoulder, an unqueenly gesture of nervousness. The Godmade would not judge her for human frailty, surely. She asked, "Did anyone ever figure out what happened to Mahadijia's papers? They were found burned when we opened his rooms, but Chaeri would not have had time to do it after she killed him, would she?"

"The timeline is complicated." Nizhvashiti closed the door.

They were alone together, and Mrithuri wondered if Nizhvashiti had brought her there for frank speaking—or to collect what was owed. Mrithuri had made a promise to the nuns cloistered within the palace walls. She had given up her reliance on the Eremite venom in return for the Mother's assistance in surviving occupation by Anuraja's army. Nizhvashiti also served the Mother—or, at least, her surrogate, the Good Daughter, her most terrible and ruthless form.

Mrithuri's throat tightened. How had she not realized until just now that Anuraja had died upon the Peacock Throne after she had made that bargain? Had she murdered him?

The hand that she had pulled away from her shoulder—when had her collarbones begun staring so sharply through her skin?—crept back up to touch the serpent torc coiled at the base of her neck. It housed a flexible stiletto, a razor-sharp little blade with the snake's head as the hilt.

She had been ready to use that on Anuraja. Why did the possibility that divine intervention had struck him down at her behest seem so much more unsavory than a simple slitting of the big artery in his thigh?

Maybe she would have felt differently with blood all over her hands. Maybe her remorse was misplaced.

"But human," Nizhvashiti said quietly, the whispery voice like leaves rustling against dry leaves.

Mrithuri jumped. Syama turned, a low growl of concern at the back of her throat. Hastily, Mrithuri gave the bhaluukutta the sign to stand down. It would be awkward if she ripped the mummified arm off an undead lich-saint.

"You read my mind," Mrithuri accused.

The Godmade's laugh was as brittle as its lips. "You were thinking very loudly."

Mrithuri nodded. "I suppose that's true. Tell me what you mean, about the timeline being complicated?"

Nizhvashiti drifted into the center of the room, not seeming to walk so much as glide. It waved a skeletal hand at rich appointments, heavy rugs, low tables. A bed still made with coverlets and bolsters. The heavy wooden box standing open, the inside scorched; the ashes in the fireplace.

"Two sets of documents were burned," the Godmade said. "The ones in the fireplace, before we managed to find the room and remove the curse of misdirection from it. And the ones that were in the box."

"Chaeri triggered the trap on those," Mrithuri said. "Intentionally?"

Nizhvashiti's nod was singular and mechanical. "It seems likely."

"But we agree that she could not have burned the other papers. So who did?"

Nizhvashiti crossed to the fireplace. It folded itself—Mrithuri would not say that it *crouched* when the movement was so odd and angular—and seemed to stare with mismatched, pupilless orbs into the ashes.

"Mahadijia must have burned his papers himself," it said, after enough contemplation that Mrithuri began to fidget. "He knew he was in danger. He knew he had been slated to die, to provide the pretext for war. He tried to approach you, and when that failed, he burned some papers and wrote the letter to you. And sealed some others away in the trap box."

"Logical," Mrithuri said, despite herself. "But Chaeri killed him before he reached me, and she stole the letter."

"And later gave you the letter. So . . ." More rustling, as the Godmade straightened and swiveled. Its robes wound around it like streamers around a festival pole. Black streamers, for a grim festival.

Mrithuri said, "Whatever was in that box must have been even more incriminating than the letter. All right, next question, and this one is probably for Ata Akhimah. Who cast the concealment spell on these rooms? Was it requested by Mahadijia?"

"Perhaps an even better question for the Gage," Nizhvashiti mused. "He knows much of Wizards."

"Well, he is not here." It came out more snappish than she had intended. "I wish we'd managed this investigation better to begin with."

"We were busy," Nizhvashiti said, amused.

"And I was . . . avoiding the issue." There was that self-disgust again. It would help nothing, though. What was done was done, and the path toward correcting the damage was to move forward, not stare back.

She had not wanted more evidence against Chaeri. And because she was rajni, no one had been able to gainsay her in her avoidance of the truth. Some of her people had tried, she recalled, and she had rebuffed them.

She wanted to bury her face in her hands.

"We all make mistakes, Your Abundance."

Mrithuri rocked back on her heels and shook her head to shake loose her self-doubt. Self-doubt, it happened, was sticky.

Nevertheless, she said, "What was so important in Mahadijia's document box that Chaeri cast further suspicion on herself in order to destroy it before we could see it?"

"I don't know," Nizhvashiti said. "I would guess it must have included communications that incriminated Chaeri."

Mrithuri didn't wish to believe it. But she also knew that Chaeri had been in Anuraja's service for—well, who knew for how long? "Details of payment, something like that. Isn't knowing the truth supposed to make you feel better?"

The Godmade touched her arm, which was lèse-majesté but also a small kindness. It whispered, "There are guards in the hall, and I can send for Ata Akhimah, who might perhaps have answers to your earlier question about who concealed this place with a spell."

When Ata Akhimah arrived, she was accompanied by Tsering-la. Mrithuri, though she had not requested his presence, found herself grateful for it. Though he often denigrated the extent of his powers, he seemed to Mrithuri to be both knowledgeable and quick, which were qualities she valued more than sheer giftedness or the ability to throw primal energies about like so many feather pillows.

Having knocked at the doorframe, they were admitted, and Nizhvashiti closed the door behind them once more.

Politenesses having been conducted, Mrithuri asked, "Who could have hidden this room?"

It bothered her that a place in her own palace had been concealed from her and all her people. It bothered her even more that she had not had the . . . spirit, she supposed . . . to pursue the matter before. There was so much work to be done and so little time to do it in. She had let herself and her people down.

Tsering-la looked at Ata Akhimah. "Not my department, I'm afraid."

Ata Akhimah rubbed her cropped curls. "A Song Wizard, or an Aezin one. Once upon a time, before the purges, any practitioner of the Building Science could have done it better than either of those."

"We could use a few now," Mrithuri said. "Well, I suppose there are the nuns." She scratched her shoulder again, her nails giving no relief to the itch of dry skin. She didn't want to bargain with the nuns again unless she absolutely had to.

"It could have been an object," Tsering-la said. "A talisman."

"Anuraja's pet sorcerer does traffic in those," the Godmade whispered.

"And in illusions," the Rasan Wizard agreed.

Ata Akhimah was looking thoughtful. "A talisman. Like the fire trap." A few silent steps bore her across the heavy carpets. She did not touch the scorched box but bent sideways to peer into it. "It was Nizhvashiti's chime that broke the illusion on this room. If the burning had been an illusion, it would have lifted that as well, based on what we know about the chime."

"The Eyeless One's chime," Nizhvashiti put in, touching its glass eye with a long finger. Delicately, so no peal rang forth. "But it seems she knew we would be dealing with a sorcerer who trafficked in illusions."

"Mm," said Ata Akhimah. "You know, I think it must have been a talisman? Something he brought with him, and with its magic now dispersed, good luck to any of us in figuring out which object it had been."

"Could you have cast that spell?" Mrithuri asked, feeling disloyal and cynical both. She wasn't *really* suspicious of Ata Akhimah. But she watched the Wizard's expression closely, nonetheless.

"I would have done it with geomancy," Ata Akhimah said. "With architecture. Hard to accomplish without rebuilding the entire wing of the palace. You could get some effect of don't-notice-me by arranging . . . objects, decorations in the corridor. A plant on a plinth here, a mirror hung there to swing the observer's attention away. Effective until somebody dusts and sets the knickknacks down differently, so that requires constant maintenance in a way that just . . . building it into the structure does not."

Tsering-la cleared his throat.

"Yes?" said Mrithuri.

"Also—I might be wrong, this really isn't my field or theory—but I don't think *that* would qualify as an illusion. It's a different class of magic altogether, and if the talisman the Eyeless One sent works on illusions in particular—"

"Oh, is that a talisman too?" Mrithuri had always been more concerned with the practical applications of Wizardry—what it could do and what it could not do—than in the theory behind it. She was surprised to find herself interested.

"Yes," Ata Akhimah said. "An object with a particular magic effect built in. Practically the definition of a talisman. Dispelling any illusion at a sound is a subtle and powerful one. Usually the Messaline Wizards just talk to animals or make animate machines."

"Like the Gage?" Mrithuri asked.

"Exactly."

Mrithuri wondered that dispelling illusions would be considered a more "subtle and powerful" effect than building a metal man who could tear down castles with his bare hands, but then, who understood Wizards? "And geomancy is not an illusion."

"It's a manipulation of energy," Ata Akhimah said. "A manipulation of attention, not a . . . phantasm. Does that make sense?"

In an itchy sort of way, it did. Mrithuri stopped scratching her shoulder and scratched the side of her forehead instead. "So what do we do about it now?"

Tsering-la looked at the others. Nizhvashiti nodded.

He said, "Nothing, at this point. But we should make sure we watch out for things that aren't real in the future."

SAYEH WALKED BESIDE THE DEAD MAN, GLAD OF HIS VEILED AND TACITURN company. She was going to sweet-talk Zirha, and he was coming along as her bodyguard.

The Dead Man had no formal rank, which was why he, and not her own guard captain, was with her. He was a mercenary who served the Dowager, and Sayeh herself was a rajni who served the Dowager, and so it was logical that he would come with her on the Dowager's errand. His presence made it seem more that she acted on the behalf of the empire and less as if this were some errand of her own.

All the delicate machinations of politics and appearances, in other words.

But she was also grateful because he was a solid and comforting presence, for all his veiled mysteriousness, the exoticism of his origins.

They crossed a tree-rimmed square, the pavement underfoot littered with unseasonably dead leaves and blossoms. It had rained, but only a little, and then it had stopped again. They were weeks behind. Sayeh worried about famine, with all the fruit trees losing their crop for lack of rain. Would the rice grow? Would the grass, to feed livestock?

She worried about so many things.

She spoke from the corner of her mouth as they approached the barracks and the officers' quarters where Anuraja's lieutenant commander had claimed offices. "Why is it always my job to talk people into doing their own jobs?"

The Dead Man chuckled so softly, it was almost muffled in the fabric of his veil. "Because you're good at it."

They paused outside, beneath an awning that did little to keep off the early heat of the day. The courtyard was quiet and dim under the rise of the Cauled Sun; many in the palace would already be sleeping. Sayeh herself looked forward to a bath and a meal and to her own soft mattress after this.

Because of the dimness inside, they could not see through the gauze-shielded window. Because of the quiet, they could hear quite clearly what was said.

"What do you expect them to do?" A man's voice. "They're here, they have no orders, their commander is dead—"

"I'm their commander," a more familiar voice—Zirha—answered. Perhaps he meant to snap it out, but the words were tinged with a whine.

Sayeh cringed.

"Just in time," the Dead Man muttered.

Sayeh nodded. "Shall we crash this party?"

As an answer, the Dead Man stepped forward, pushing open the thin wooden door. Inside, one man stood before another, who was seated on cushions behind a table spread with scrolls and unbound stacks of paper. The seated man was Zirha. Sayeh did not recognize the other one.

"Hello, officers," she said, aware of the Dead Man taking two steps to remain just behind and to the right of her, as if he were an extension of her body. Even Vidhya would have been impressed by the skill, she thought. "I've come on behalf of the Dowager, to see to the payment of your men. Is there a disciplinary issue?"

Her voice was all sweet reason. Zirha popped to his feet, rocking his inkwell in hasty clumsiness. The other man turned more slowly, with sly insolence.

He reminded Sayeh of her own insubordinate generals. She detested him immediately.

"Who are you?" she snapped while he was still making up his mind if he was going to answer her previous question.

The change of topic startled an answer out of him. "Sekira," he said.

She nodded and dismissed him, turning her attention back to Zirha. "Commander." She leaned toward him—not ostentatiously; just enough to give the illusion of intimacy. "Is there a problem?" '

Zirha cleared his throat. "A small matter of some looting. It's being addressed."

"By 'addressed,' I hope you mean the culprits will be disciplined."

"Your Abundance," Sekira said in soothing, condescending tones. "You sound upset—"

"Upset?" she interrupted. "I am merely disappointed. The *Dowager* will be angry," she said. "I'm afraid there must be real consequences for these men. Severe enough to discourage the next lot."

"You want me to execute them?" His voice rose in protest.

"A flogging should suffice." She waved her hand airily. "And dock their pay by the value of whatever they looted, of course."

Sekira's jaw clenched. Sayeh saw with pleasure how unhappy he was, and wondered if perhaps—just possibly—he had encouraged some of his favored soldiers to exercise a little more privilege than was, strictly speaking, their right.

"If they raped or maimed or murdered anyone," Sayeh continued blankly, "well, then, of course, they must be executed."

Sekira glared at Zirha. Zirha swallowed.

"After a fair trial," Sayeh allowed, remembering that Mrithuri would insist on one.

"Your Abundance," Zirha argued, uncertain of his footing but propelled by his subordinate's displeasure, "these are not even your people—"

"They are," Sayeh said. "And they are your people, too, as you must understand. Emperor Anuraja saw to that. He reunited us. He has made us one people again, as we were meant by the Alchemical Emperor to be." She smiled at him. "The Dowager will, of course, support your leadership in every way."

The Laeish gaped at her, neither sure who should answer. Sayeh took advantage of their moment of discomfiture to secure her advantage. She nodded to the Dead Man with a half-turn of her head.

He stepped forward and crouched to lay a heavy chamois bag on the table by Zirha's feet. It rang softly. Sayeh reached into her sleeve and drew out a folded paper.

"It's handy that you have ink ready," she observed in her most pleasant voice.

"What's that?" asked Sekira.

"A receipt," she said. "For the coin we've just delivered. Payroll for the soldiers."

Silence.

If her tone got any sweeter, it was going to choke her in honey. "We'll wait," she said. "While you count it."

SAYEH AND THE DEAD MAN WALKED AWAY FROM ZIRHA'S TENT LIGHTER BY fifteen hundred gold bulls in links, rings, and smaller coin—and heavier with the certain knowledge of insubordination.

It could have been worse. Sayeh had the receipt in her pocket, and she had assessed the threats. She was not sure if it would be better to recommend that Mrithuri place Pranaj and Zirha on an equal footing in the command structure, she thought, and count on Pranaj to outmaneuver Zirha . . . or if Zirha would after all be relieved to be placed under a capable commander like Pranaj.

The latter would give them more protection against Zirha being manipulated by his underlings. She wondered if Sekira was the only rotten one.

Her own former guards would know. She would ask Nazia to speak with them.

Her train of thought was interrupted by the Dead Man clearing his throat before speaking with obvious disdain. "He's a weakling."

"We're lucky that Anuraja picked him out for it," she answered. "A strong man might decide that *he* wanted to be emperor."

"That other one. He wants Zirha's job. And he was *seething*," the Dead Man said, admiringly.

"Good," Sayeh answered. "Let him seethe."

"He won't give up, that one. He very well *might* see himself as emperor."

"No, he won't give up," Sayeh agreed. "But we can execute officers as well as enlisted men."

The Dead Man's eyes flicked sideways.

"That's not an immediate request," she added.

"Nevertheless," the Dead Man said. "I might just keep an eye out for reasons."

Reasons, Sayeh thought. *Excuses. Are they so different?*

7

THE DEAD MAN WOULD HAVE THOUGHT THAT ONE OF THE FEW REAL, MATE-
rial benefits of a marginal, vagabond existence as a mercenary was that he
would never again be responsible for complicated logistical decisions.

He would have been wrong.

Oh, well. It wasn't the first time.

"Look," he said to Mrithuri, when he'd finally managed to get her attention away from the latest lord of the Dharasaaba who had needed urgently
to confer, "we just can't feed them all, all the way to Sarathai-lae. After the
siege and given the crop failures . . . we'd be hard-pressed to feed just the
Tian army on the march. With Anuraja's troops added to your own—"

"Half rations?" she suggested.

He did the math. He shook his head. "They'll just forage along the way—

"That's a euphemism for pillaging our people."

The Dead Man thought, *They're not entirely my people*, but was wise enough
not to say it. He knew, whatever Mrithuri believed, that his time there would
end. That he would have to move on, much as he longed for a different outcome.

He'd made mistakes. He'd allowed himself to develop attachments. He
longed for a home, and for those date palms. Or persimmons. Eventually, he
and Mrithuri both would pay a price for that.

Enjoy it while it lasts. What he said, though, was the completion of the thought
he'd already begun. "—and we'll still run out of food along the way."

It had been a closed court, and Mrithuri was seated on cushions on the
dais steps, a nod to appearing more approachable to her lords. A calculated
concession to make them feel valued and heard. She looked tired, despite
the tea on a tray by her left hand, but her spine had not sagged nor her head
nodded until the last noble had been excused from the room.

Now she lolled back on her elbows and sighed. "What if we feed them
standard rations until we get to Laeish lands, and let them forage there?"

"It won't endear you to your new subjects."

She sighed. "We can pay for food." She raised one hand. "I know. Can
the farmers and fishers eat silver? Won't food prices be higher with an army
on the move and with crops failing? War is stupid, but I am not the one who
brought the army here, Serhan."

He bowed low over his arm, feeling the cut. "Your Abundance."

"Oh, by the Mother." She stood, pushing herself up with one hand but less frail already, he was pleased to see. Syama rose from the shadows beside the dais and padded toward her. "Fine. Make it happen. Get somebody responsible to talk to the quartermasters and see how much we can feed them if we buy a reasonable amount of food along the way. Let the officers know that we'll not tolerate pillaging. See to it that we do as little damage as we can. I'm going to visit my elephant."

THE DEAD MAN WAS RETURNING ALONG THE CORRIDOR TOWARD THE WAR room when he encountered Hnarisha and Nazia coming the other way. "Have you seen either of the rajnis?" Hnarisha asked. "Or rather, the rajni or the Dowager Empress?"

The Dead Man smiled behind his veil. "That latter is on her way to visit her elephant. She has sent me"—he rustled the stack of papers—"to make sure the army packs its lunch. Hnarisha, if you could arrange with the quartermasters to buy as much food as possible, and move the army to half rations, or whatever they suggest? More is better, obviously, but you know what the treasury can bear better than I do."

Hnarisha's brow creased, but he nodded.

The Dead Man said, "I do not know where Sayeh Rajni is; I have not seen her since we went to pay the occupiers. She is looking for you, though, Nazia. She wants you to ask Sanjay and his friends something. Er, deniably."

Hnarisha snorted. "Nazia here has just come back from a walk—"

"I wanted to see the damage to the river gate from the outside," she said. "And I wanted to swim."

The Dead Man contemplated mentioning the inadvisability of young women wandering around inside cities occupied by armies, and outside cities surrounded by armies, but decided Nazia could probably handle herself in an army camp. Her worried expression suggested that there was something more concerning her than the lowness of the river.

"What?"

Hnarisha gestured to Nazia.

Nazia took a breath. "That big worm thing is still in the river."

"Well." The Dead Man let go a heavy breath that caught in his veil. "That does sound like a problem for the rajni. Let's go find her."

THE RIVER GATES PROVED A PROBLEM. THEY HAD BEEN SEALED BY TSERING-la's magic to prevent that selfsame Mother Wyrm from battering them down under Ravani's direction. They could not be unsealed again, as he had awoken the sleeping spirits of the trees from which they had been hewn, and now those trees were alive again, thick with bark, grown together, rooted in the rich soil of the river and stretching green branches toward the sky.

They were unaffected by the drought, Sayeh saw, whether from the proximity of the Mother River or from the potency of their reawakening. Tsering-la had told her that he had not brought them back to life, precisely: that would have been beyond his power. They had, through the magic of the Alchemical Emperor, never quite been allowed to die.

Even the emperor had not had the power to *raise* the dead.

In any case, she stood and looked up at them, Tsering-la and Nazia on one side of her, the Dead Man and Hnarisha on the other.

They could have walked around, but that would have entailed retracing Nazia's steps—all down through the city, and outside around the walls through an army encampment. Unsubtle, and until they had assessed the situation, Mrithuri thought and Sayeh concurred that it was best to keep it quiet. A monster in the river would not help anyone to forget the anxiety of siege and war.

Especially when most of the fighting men would be leaving soon.

"We could lower a ladder," the Dead Man suggested.

Sayeh tapped her weak leg. "I could do it if I had to. But I don't want to have to. And people would notice. Oh, curse Ravani anyway."

Thinking of the sorceress made her anxious; her thoughts wanted to shy away. She had to force herself to name the problem plainly.

Tsering-la said, "I wish I understood better how she's managed to leave so much influence behind her."

Nazia looked at him. "What do you mean, master?" The honorific fell from her tongue unselfconsciously, with genuine respect. Sayeh was glad. It bolstered Sayeh's confidence in her judgment that the relationship between the rebellious girl and Sayeh's intellectual Wizard was working out. It was a confidence that had taken a few critical blows in the previous months, and though a rajni could never admit it, Sayeh felt she needed a little shoring up just now.

"Indeed," she encouraged, wanting to acknowledge Nazia's useful question without making the girl self-conscious with direct praise. "Please, Wizard. Elaborate."

Tsering-la gave her a sidelong glance but answered, "The rains haven't come. The Mother Wyrm is still sitting in the river—as if waiting for another command. The implications should be evident."

The Dead Man said, "Maybe it has no reason to want to be elsewhere?"

"Maybe." Tsering-la didn't sound convinced. "Animals usually return to their home territory if something is not keeping them away."

The Dead Man winced behind his veil. Sayeh brushed her hand against his coat sleeve. She too felt the bite of exile.

"More talismans?" Nazia asked.

"Maybe." The Wizard shook his head. "When the world is saved, I'm going to research a monograph on the varieties and uses of sorcery. It's time somebody made a serious, systematic study of . . . I'm sorry. Let me start over. What if we just dressed up like peasants and carried buckets down to the river for water, then wandered into the Water Garden when nobody was looking?"

Sayeh thought about it. "Good plan. One modification."

"What's that?"

"Let's send a page to alert the guards not to spear us when we sneak around the fence."

"You were ever," Tsering-la said, "the practical one."

THEY DISGUISED THEMSELVES AS PEASANTS—OR AT LEAST PUT ON ROUGHSPUN— and went barefoot through the streets, carrying buckets and limiting their conversation because Nazia told them there was no hope of them managing to sound like anything except nobility. The Dead Man put on his most worn garb and carried his weapons. Everyone in the city knew there was an Asitaneh mercenary in the Dowager's employ. It wouldn't seem too strange that he was guarding a troupe of servants with buckets along the way.

Tsering-la's feet, used to Rasan boots, were tender. He struggled not to mince over the paving stones, and Sayeh bit her lip not to giggle at him. She wasn't unkind; she wasn't, really. But he looked like an awkward waterbird on land, waddling as he did with the yoke over his shoulders.

The guards at the city gate knew to expect them, and they were not troubled as they made their long way around the city walls. The earth was softer underfoot, and by then Sayeh was footsore enough herself that she was glad she hadn't teased her Wizard. She limped along without a crutch, too, using only a staff for support as if she were an old woman. Her wasted leg trembled with the strain of walking such a distance, even though she only carried one light hide bucket.

They were admitted to the gardens and made their way down to the edge of the water.

The Mother River was low between her banks. This was not Sayeh's land, but she could see where the leaves and stems of the lotus lay draped in the mud, when water should have floated them from the roots. A flight of broad steps led down to the river edge, several of them caked in dry silt that showed they were usually submerged.

Sayeh put her bucket down on a flagged patio with a sigh of relief. "So where did you see the monster?"

Nazia set her load beside Sayeh's. She walked down to the water's edge. "It's difficult to make out from this angle—"

Sayeh followed her as the others unburdened themselves. Nazia crouched. Sayeh reluctantly crouched with her, digging her staff into the mud for support and letting her bad leg stick out awkwardly. So much for the grace of the Bloom of Ansh-Sahal.

"Get your head down close to the water, Rajni," Nazia instructed.

"You can't see anything through it." It was as white and opaque as cream. "Getting closer won't help that."

"No," Nazia said. "Turn your head to the side."

Sayeh wasn't quite sure what it was that she yelped, but her head jerked up and words came out of her mouth. She remembered the silky ripples of something giant moving beneath the water. What she saw now was more like a same-colored bulge in the water, white on white, as if it were thick as honey and somebody had poured one more viscous thread on top.

The thing moved slowly, with oily sinuousness, coated in the river silt and matching it in color. Sayeh thought of parasitic worms coiling in feces.

"That," she said, "is horrible."

"Can you do anything about it?" Nazia asked.

Grimly, Sayeh dug her staff into the mud so it would stand up on its own. She would be balanced enough in her extended crouch, until she tried to rise. She rolled her sleeves above the elbow. "Give me your knife."

Nazia tugged a water-diver's hook knife from under her tunic and unwrapped the short blade. Sayeh accepted it hilt-first. It was honed on the tip and inside the hook.

She set the point against the back of her wrist. Pricking the fingers was a apprentice mistake: they hurt more and one was constantly using them to pick up things.

A drop of crimson slid into the water, went pink as the silty flow diluted it, swirled and vanished. Another and another followed.

Sayeh handed the knife back to Nazia. Propping herself against the staff, she leaned forward and lowered her hand into the water.

This was rightfully Mrithuri's domain, and Sayeh's gut recoiled from contact with the vast slimy worm-thing that inhabited it. But she was a true daughter of the Alchemical Emperor, as the refrain went, and—distasteful or no—what was needed there should be within her powers.

She reached with her mind into the water.

The first thing she felt through her submerged hand was a shiver of vibration. Rising and falling, a thread of keening sounds. Surely, that wasn't the Mother Wyrm? Singing to itself? Herself?

A side-swimming dolphin broke the surface of the river not far from where Sayeh and Nazia crouched, and Sayeh laughed out loud in pleasure. She felt the touch of its awareness, the caress of water along its flanks, the way it felt objects under the opaque water as pressure and a sensation of shape rather than by seeing them.

She felt warmth, and welcoming curiosity, and a bright engaged mind that surprised her with its grasp of abstractions. Even Guang Bao was not so clever as this.

It showed her the size of the Mother Wyrm, and she gasped out loud.

"Rajni?" Nazia stared at her with concern.

"It's bigger than I expected." Sayeh tried to sound calm. "Let me see if I can ask it to go home."

She reached out again, aware of how exposed they all were. She and Nazia were one tail-sweep away from destruction. Tsering-la was behind her with his magic ready to protect them. But she knew also that it could only protect them for so long, and the Dead Man's sword and pistols probably not at all.

There. She found the mind of the monster, and it was not the ponderous, fishy mind she had anticipated. It was agile and bright, aware and intelligent. Without language, as far as she could tell, but not without thought. She might say it even had an intellect.

The Wyrm was unhappy. The water here was too fresh, not salty. Too shallow, so the heat of the day baked its back. It was a creature of the brackish tidal delta, and being this far inland made its skin sting and peel. It *wanted* to leave, but it could not seem to make up its mind.

Why not go home? Sayeh asked it. A gentle suggestion, a sort of push.

She felt it start to turn, saw the surface of the river ripple. The great head with its groping barbels swung around—and then came back, as if dragged unwillingly. Pain, like a hook pulling through flesh. Pain, like a hook in the mind.

"Rajni," Nazia said, urgently.

Sayeh opened her eyes before she realized she had clenched them. She gasped, reaching for the propped staff. "I'm fine," she lied. "Sorcery. There's a sting in it."

Tsering-la and the Dead Man had started toward her, down the bank. She waved them back. "This might get messy. Don't intervene unless I ask . . . or I'm in immediate danger of being eaten."

She heard Tsering-la's sigh even from this distance, but he didn't say anything. She imagined him and the Dead Man rolling their eyes at one another behind her. Insubordination, that was what it was.

She went back to the hook. The *idea* of a hook, and here was she, Sayeh, without the idea of a pliers.

We do what we can.

She took hold of the thought that held the Wyrm pinned and explored it. A fixed idea, a compulsion. A hook, indeed.

"I think it's stuck," she said.

She imagined it, long and smooth, sharp as a needle. Embedded in the mind. She tried to imagine it without a barb—straight, easy to withdraw— but the barbs were there. The barbs were part of the construction.

If you can't pull a thing out, you have to push it through. She'd gotten a fishhook in her thumb once, as a girl. It had not been a pleasant experience.

Be as still as you can, she told the huge creature. Could such an ancient, enormous, incomprehensible mind understand her? She imagined a cricket sending waves of reassurance to a rajni. *I'm trying to help you.*

She wrapped imaginary hands around the shaft of the imaginary gaff and shoved with all her might against it. *Sharp!* As if she grabbed blade edges. The pain felt physical, the struggle as if her own muscles strove. She strained, heard herself gasp. A pain in her chest, burning with exertion.

Slipping. She was losing her grip—

She looked down at her smarting hands. Blood welled across her palms, from her fingers. Nazia had caught her wrist and stared at her with worry. "Rajni—"

So much for my care for my fingertips. "Almost there," Sayeh said. She gritted her teeth, which prevented any other words.

Blood. Her blood in the water. Her connection to the Mother; her connection to the Mother Wyrm.

Close your eyes. Visualize.

She imagined the hook sliding easily from flesh. Imagined pushing it through, pulling it loose without resistance.

The reality was not so smooth. Pain shot up her arms, curled her fingers. Blood slicked her real palms—one held over the water, one pressed to the wood of her staff. Blood slicked her imaginary palms, too. She wrenched at the barb; she pushed and she twisted.

Water splashed her face, or perhaps it was cold blood. She threw her whole weight against the hook.

With a horrible pop, it came free.

Sayeh opened her eyes. A saffron-yellow wall of light floated in the air before her and Nazia. Milky rivulets ran down it. Nazia had not moved but was panting, hands pressed against her belly, looking pale and shaken. A slow ripple spread down the river, a curve sliding before her like a standing wave.

It took a long time for something as long as the Mother Wyrm to turn and glide away.

Sayeh glanced over her shoulder. Tsering-la's hands were raised, Wizardry limning them, but he too was panting. He too was greenish, his face beaded with sweat.

"It thrashed," he said. "I thought it was going to fall on you."

The staff helped her balance again as she pushed to rise. Her hand was slick and painful on the wood; her arm cramped with supporting her.

She looked at Nazia. "Help me up. Daughter, my leg is stiff."

Nazia took her bloody hand without flinching and hauled her to her feet. Sayeh winced but bore it in silence.

Tsering-la handed her a clean cloth bandage from somewhere on his person. "Wrap up your hands. Those will need stitches."

Sayeh did as he bid her, feeling dizzy. All her fingers seemed to work still. That was something.

"You could have just left it there," the Dead Man said while she was still looking down, concentrating on the folds of linen. "It was a threat, sure, but not an immediate one with the sorcerer gone."

"It was in pain," Sayeh said. She looked up at him and met his eyes over the indigo veil.

She could not read his expression. But after a long moment he nodded, and though he didn't speak, the expression around his eyes said, *I understand.*

MRITHURI STOOD AT THE PARAPET ATOP THE HIGHEST SPIRE OF SARATHAI-TIA and trained her gaze to the east. She looked past the plain; past the low hills rising beyond; past the patchwork of fields and into the hazy distance.

She was rewarded with nothing but eyestrain. No clouds dimmed the stars of the Heavenly River, so bright overhead. No cool breeze blew damp against her cheek.

But she was alone for the first time in a long time, and for the first time in a long time, she felt a sort of peace. Or perhaps a sort of resignation.

She recognized the sound of footsteps behind her and was not startled when Ata Akhimah spoke. "Are we intruding, Your Abundance?"

She glanced over her shoulder. "We" was the Wizard and Nizhvashiti. "No. I'm just worrying that we're headed in the wrong direction."

"Seek the Origin of Storms," said the Godmade.

"The Sea of Storms." Mrithuri pointed with a painted nail. "Some incomprehensible distance that way."

"I've been there," Nizhvashiti said. "To the Banner Isles. And back again."

Ata Akhimah had been scratching under her splint with the other hand. The fingers protruding from her sling were still bruised and swollen, but Mrithuri noticed she could bend them a little now. Maybe Hnarisha had been helping to heal her.

Mrithuri needed to make sure *he* rested as well.

Now the Wizard looked up and tilted her head curiously. "How did you travel?"

"It was a long walk," Nizhvashiti answered.

Mrithuri turned away again. Her hands rested on the parapet. This high up, the walls were not embedded with shards of dragonglass. "Would going back there explain what in a Rasan hell is going on with the weather?"

"Not in a timely fashion," the Godmade said.

Ata Akhimah stepped up to the parapet beside Mrithuri and said, "I wonder."

Mrithuri turned to her. The Wizard was frowning into the distance, crow tracks framing her squint. "Well?"

Ata Akhimah shook her head. "What about those dragon-gates Tsering-la used to come here in a hurry? And . . . I admit, I have wondered about the nuns in their cloister. That's a Between Place if ever I've seen one. It's possible it might connect through other Between Places, and who knows where it comes out if it does?"

Mrithuri scratched the healing bites under her collarbone. "I'm not sure I want to ask the nuns for any more favors."

"I would," said Nizhvashiti. It had drifted up on her other hand and hung there silently, somber robes ruffling softly in the wind.

Mrithuri stared down at the Godmade's bony hands, the skin glossy over knots of knuckles. At the colorless flesh of the nailbeds. *A decision,* she realized. *That's what they're waiting for from me.*

"Talk to Tsering-la," she told them. "If he can't help you, go ahead and bargain with the nuns."

"And then?" Ata Akhimah asked.

"Go east," Mrithuri told them. "Both of you. Better two than one. And I will bring the court to Sarathai-lae." She shook her head.

"You should not send both of us away, Your Abundance," Ata Akhimah said. "You might need a Wizard—"

"I *need,*" she said, with infinite patience, "to stop a famine from killing half my subjects. What happens if one of you is hurt upon the journey? You're from different traditions. You have different knowledge. I also need to come up with somebody to leave regent."

"Yavashuri," Ata Akhimah said promptly, though she was still frowning.

"I need her," Mrithuri protested. Panic tore into her. She struggled to keep her voice regal. Calm. She didn't think she entirely succeeded. "I need her with me."

The Wizard shook her head. "Who do you trust more, Your Abundance? And which of your subjects is more capable of dealing with insubordinate lordlings?"

"Oh, Mother." Mrithuri sighed. "I wish—"

But she couldn't say *I wish it were not up to me.*

What she meant, she realized, was something closer to *I wish I were not so alone.*

But there was no answer for that, either.

8

WHEN THEY LEFT CHANDRANATH, THEY WOUND UP BRINGING MORE ARMY than Himadra would have preferred and—he was afraid—less than they might wind up needing. The problem with armies was the problem with anything: if you had one, you wanted to use it. Otherwise, what was the point in keeping it lying around? Eating one out of house and home, making a mess, tracking in mud.

Himadra sat in his padded saddle and tried not to laugh at the hyperbole of his own interior monologue. He was supposed to be sternly reviewing the troops from astride his fancy-bred foreign mare, not making amused faces at them. Besides, his lieutenants and sergeants kept excellent discipline, and if he had to explain to Farkhad and Navin what he was finding so funny, they would rightfully take it as a slight to their organizational skills.

There was an additional danger in bringing so large an army into Sarathai lands: it was likely to look like an invasion. And the locals would not take kindly to the foraging of an army on the move. He hoped this was ameliorated by bringing so many of the soldiers from Ansh-Sahal, who were (technically) not his men at all but Drupada's.

Watching them pass, banners bright in the unseasonable starlight, he raised a hand in blessing. His mare Velvet's ears flicked back. The gesture felt awkward, but the troops didn't seem to sense the awkwardness. A cheer rolled along their ranks and banners dipped in salute, then swooped high again, a wave that began at the head of the column and raced to the end.

Himadra sighed. "That's a lot of people to keep alive."

"That's my job, lord," Navin said cheerily. "You just concentrate on not getting them killed."

A metallic boom drew Himadra's attention, and he saw that the Gage had come up behind them and was, to all appearances, laughing. The horses sidled but not overmuch: they had heard him coming over the clay hillside even if the humans hadn't.

The Gage said, "I can try to let Sarathai-tia know we are on our way—"

"They probably know already," Himadra said. "Given the efficiency of their spy network."

"—and," the Gage continued, very politely, "I can let them know we are not marching to war. At least, there's a chance I can do that."

"Hmh," Himadra said. "The young rajni's familiar?"

The Gage chuckled like a faintly chiming bell. "Indeed."

"Better than being met at the border with troops," Himadra said. "Please do what you can."

ON THE FIRST MORNING OF THE MARCH, WHEN THE ARMY WAS SETTLING around campfires, the Gage found Kyrlmyrandal standing on a hillside near the vanguard. He came up beside where she leaned on her staff, and said, "Hello, dragon."

"Hello, Gage." She sounded peaceful, dreamy. Not at all like an old woman who had marched all day with an army, and not like a fearsome dragon on a quest to prevent the destruction of nearly everything, either.

"I was wondering," he said. "Do you know what the beast is? I mean, more than generally."

"A specific beast?" She smiled, her skin wrinkling softly. She put a hand out as if to measure the distance to him, resting her fingertips on his pauldron. "I met a couple of them, when I was younger. But I cannot guarantee that what we face now is either of those. They don't exactly live *in* the world, these things. I am guessing the one trying to break through now is one the Alchemical Emperor sewed up in the land he built."

The Gage watched the sky all around them grow darker as the Caul rose to cover the brightness of the Heavenly River. He missed, he thought, a proper sunrise, the spill of colors in the east, or west, or wherever the fiery orb or orbs were coming from.

"Where do they live, if not in the world?"

"In the Broken Places." She made a frustrated noise. "It's hard to explain—"

"Try me."

"—it's also embarrassing."

He waited. Waiting, he found, was often the best way to get people to talk to him. "Personally?"

"It's my fault," the dragon said. "As much as anyone's. But it's also not immediately relevant to our problem. I was wondering; do you think we could still try to set a trap for Ravana?"

And that, the Gage thought, was the sound of a topic being changed. "How would you do that? And what purpose would it serve?"

"The first is a sticking point," Kyrlmyrandal agreed. "I'll think on it. The second . . . Well, if we could ask the sorcerer questions without him zooming away, it could answer the question you just asked me—about which Beast it is that troubles us, and what its nature is. And that could help us to defeat it."

The Gage wished briefly that he had eyes so he could roll them. "Well, he came when I was in Ansh-Sahal, a place he had destroyed."

"Not too far from the confused volcano goddess."

The Gage nodded. "And he came to me in your city."

She hummed a musing sound in the back of her throat.

"Another destroyed city," the Gage commented.

"Possibly not a coincidence," Kyrlmyrandal admitted. "Though a long-destroyed city will have little in the way of suffering upon which the beast could dine."

"And a freshly destroyed one will?"

"The emanations . . . linger. For a while."

"Emanations," the Gage said. "Torment of the dying."

The old dragon's mouth arranged itself in a curve that was not a smile. "Maybe what we need is someplace where a lot of people are dying."

The Gage unwillingly thought of the walking cities. Of the workers within, debt-indentured, poisoned by the flesh-rotting dust of the dragon-glass. People of Messaline, sold away to earn a wage that would kill them in the end. It was not so different from all the other sorts of peonage he'd witnessed, from children maimed so they could beg more effectively to galley slaves to chimney sweeps burned and starved. The world was hard, but he didn't have to like it.

He thought of the metallic, olivine-studded knuckle of dragonbone he carried locked inside his body, where its toxic emanations couldn't harm someone if he stood too near. He was full of dragon-poison, between that and the pen.

He wondered, not for the first time, who or what it was that had told the walking city called the Many-Legged Truth to look for him, there in the wastes.

He wasn't, he decided, ready to say anything about that yet. Perhaps they could be used to lure the sorcerer. Or the beast. But was it his place to decide to risk all those lives?

Kyrlmyrandal wasn't the only one who could change the subject.

"I've been wondering" said the Gage, "if *ky* is 'the being' and *myrandal* is that complicated verb, what does *rl* mean?"

"I'm afraid it's just a linking particle," the dragon said blandly.

"Do dragons lie?"

"Perhaps." Kyrlmyrandal arched a white brow over a white eye. "Perhaps we sometimes speak in slanted truths. That fits, I believe, our reputation."

"These Broken Places. Is that what we traveled through?"

"They are the cracks that bind other things together," she said, in the tone of one who was agreeing.

"The dragon-gates."

"Among other uses, yes." She nodded her head in the general direction of the army. "These people used to make a science of manipulating them."

"Ah," the Gage said, thinking that for a change he sounded less informed than he felt.

Kyrlmyrandal's expression probably was a smile this time. "They were not as good at it as dragons were."

9

ATA AKHIMAH WATCHED WHILE ATTENDANTS PAINTED THE HIDE OF MRITHURI'S elephant with lime wash to protect her against the sun. Hathi seemed to enjoy the attention, scratching her back against the long-handled, broomlike brush and leaving streaks that would have to be layered over again.

It should have been a peaceful scene, but both of Akhimah's hands ached: the left one, where it had been injured by a tracing spell gone wrong. The right one, where she was clenching it in the fabric of her trousers.

She hated being the person whose job it was to wait. And wait, and wait, and wait. And, it seemed, to wait some more.

She knew she had not been standing there as long as it seemed. An elephant was large, but with a big brush it could only take so long to paint one. Her emotions were those of anyone used to doing rather than waiting for others to do.

So she managed to restrain her sigh when she saw Tsering-la hurrying toward her, the black petals of his coat aflap about his thighs. Her relief turned to something else when he came close enough for her to make out his expression.

It was . . . well, not grim. But not satisfied, either, and careful neutrality didn't fill Akhimah with confidence.

He held up his left hand, brandishing rolled sheaves of parchment and reed mats covered with writing in at least three systems. Akhimah recognized the Sarathai alphabet and the Song syllabary but caught a glimpse of something else as well. Possibly several somethings.

"Bad news?" she asked, when he came within earshot.

He made an equivocating motion. "Do you want the full explanation or the abstract?"

"Oh, all the details. Obviously."

"Better come out of the wind, then."

He led her up toward the walls, to one of the temporary pavilions constructed there. Silk hangings gusted as they approached, ivory and cream and pale gold. Some workers were in the process of lacing them down; Tsering-la nodded to the men and women and pulled an oxbow bench away from a low table for Ata Akhimah. Circling to the side, he extracted another for himself. "Keep a hand on these."

Wind ruffled the edges of his documents. Akhimah did as he instructed, corralling the portions closest to her, helping Tsering-la spread them out with her one good hand. The injured one ached; she eased it in the sling and otherwise tried to ignore it.

The maps spread out before her soon distracted her from the discomfort. Their outlines were superficially familiar: landmasses and seas she'd seen represented all her life. But superimposed over them were other symbols she did not know.

"Are these the dragon-gates? Pairs of symbols . . . linked to each other?" She saw a cluster of symbols at a place in the mountains beyond the Steles of the Sky and the White Sea. She touched one of those and looked around the map for its twin. There, by the highest mountain in the Steles of the Sky. "So you would enter one and exit the other?"

"Of course," he said.

The paper rustled under her fingertips. "How did you *bring* all of these?"

He smirked. "Secret of my order."

"No—"

He laughed.

She rolled her eyes. "—really. Do you carry them with you everywhere? Sticking out of the back of your coat like a fishing pole?"

"Well, it *is* a secret of my order." He laughed. "They can be made small and then large again. But the magic only works on books and papers."

Akhimah felt a surge of warmth across her cheeks that, after a moment, she identified as cupidity. "Can you . . . teach me this spell? Or technique?"

He sighed. "Alas. It's a tool, and I do not know how to make them." He held up a hand, though the paper curled up when he lifted it. "And before you ask, no, I can't loan it to you to experiment with until you figure out how to copy it. You'll have to go to the Red-and-White Citadel and ask *them* nicely."

"I just might," she said. "I'm sure I have something to trade that *they* might find interesting. All right, I will leave you alone on the subject of maps that are small and then big again."

"Is that the one you used to get here?" She pointed a little west and south of Ansh-Sahal.

He leaned over for a better look. "You're getting the hang of it."

"What I see is . . . not a lot of symbols near the Sea of Storms. Does that mean there are no dragon-gates there?"

"It means that if they are there, the Citadel has not mapped them and does not know where the other ends are."

She grunted, annoyed, and tapped the map. "I guess we could try to get here, into Song, and . . . keep going east on foot. Or get horses."

"Do you speak the language?"

"You neither?" Another exasperated noise escaped her. *Stop that,* she thought, hearing her mother's voice. *You sound like a little hyena.*

He said, "We could hire an interpreter. Or maybe the Godmade . . ."

"Let's go find Nizhvashiti. And see if it has managed to talk to the nuns."

THEY FOUND NIZHVASHITI IN THE RAJNI'S STELLAR. IT HAD MANAGED TO TALK to the nuns. And the nuns had been helpful, without—as it happened—actually *helping* in the slightest.

According to the nuns (according to Nizhvashiti), there was no route through their warrens to the far east. Or anywhere outside of Sarath-Sahal. There had been a way to Ansh-Sahal, but that way had closed when Ansh-Sahal had fallen—not that that would do anybody a lot of good now. According to the nuns, there was a dragon-gate in Sarathai-lae that would take one as far as the shore of the Sea of Storms. One that did not appear on Tsering-la's maps until he drew the symbols in lightly with a sketching lead borrowed from Akhimah.

"I guess we're headed south to go east," Akhimah said with some resignation. That sort of maneuver was not unfamiliar to a Wizard. "We'll stay with the royal progress as far as Sarathai-lae."

"Well," Tsering answered. "That will save on postage."

MRITHURI STARTLED AWAKE FROM AN ANXIOUS, FORMLESS DREAM. HER SCALP had been peeling backward, thick and weirdly chambered like the skin of a pumelo, taking the hair in fistfuls with it. Her heart squeezed painfully. She had, she realized, fallen asleep on a pile of bolsters beneath the window of her stellar.

For a moment, Mrithuri thought she had awakened to a night terror of the sort where a presence seemed to loom over the bed. But by the time she had control of all her limbs again, she realized it was just that Nizhvashiti stood over her, blank orbs looking down under the worn black hood. Mrithuri stifled an unregal scream.

The trailing edge of Nizhvashiti's robe flicked against her ankles. She bolted upright, falling back against the bolsters when the abrupt motion left her dizzy. Somehow, she avoided cracking her head on the window ledge.

"Ugh," Mrithuri said, coherently. She straightened an arm to press herself up to sitting again. "I'm sorry. I must have dozed off."

"Rest, Your Abundance," the Godmade whispered. "You have been very ill. You do not have to keep making things harder for yourself just to prove you can keep going no matter how much weight is piled on you."

"You're a fine one to talk." Her gesture took in the Godmade's desiccated form.

"Would you like to spend twelve years drinking poison and die to become a more effective vessel for your God?"

Mrithuri, lips pursed, shook her head.

"Then the situations are not equivalent." The Godmade's voice was papery. Its lips did not move when it spoke. Or when it sighed as punctuation. "Child, you were placed in an impossible situation, impossibly young. You did well, but you did it by bullying yourself until you broke. And having broken yourself, you need time to heal. Make things as easy on your body and your heart as you can: the world will demand plenty of both. You don't need to add to the toll."

Mrithuri knuckled her eyes. Bright flashes danced against her eyelids. The dizziness receded. A seam of tension bound her neck with neat, tight stitches. Eyes still closed, she pinched the bridge of her nose and said, "I suppose I'm needed."

"Not immediately," Nizhvashiti answered. "I came to tell you that I've bargained with the nuns, and their records indicate that the best way for Ata Akhimah and me to reach the Sea of Storms is to accompany you south and seek a dragon-gate in the vicinity of Sarathai-lae."

"I am embarrassingly relieved to hear it," Mrithuri admitted. She squinted up at the tall figure, like a pole set upright. "Is that all?"

Nizhvashiti did not shake its head so much as rock its whole, hovering body stiffly side to side. "Your serpents are reclaimed."

The Godmade flipped aside the edge of its cloak, showing the inlaid, pierced wooden box under its arm. Within, something slid, heavily.

It was as if Mrithuri had touched a window latch in an electrical storm. All the hair on her arms and nape horripilated. "Are they safe?"

"They are alive," Nizhvashiti answered. "I do not know when they last were fed."

Mrithuri imagined their warm, leathery skins. The patterns on their scaled backs like calligraphy one couldn't quite decipher. Her fingers curled into the stiff bolsters. "Help me up."

Nizhvashiti extended a hand. Mrithuri, having asked for it, forced herself to take it. It felt varnished and hard. She worried for fragile bones and mummified flesh, but the Godmade lifted her to her feet as if she were, herself, no more than a feather-stuffed cushion. It did not even squeeze her rings into her flesh.

"Do you wish them given to you?" the Godmade asked.

Mrithuri squeezed her own rings into her flesh, hiding her fists in the folds of her drape.

She did. Of course she did.

She had made a promise, in return for aid. Would she, now that the aid had been rendered, break that promise?

Was that the kind of rajni she would be?

She didn't even know what means the nuns might have of *enforcing* a payment, if she tried to renege.

She turned away, stumbling over the cushions. Trying to make the mistake look intentional. She stared blindly out the window. "Take them to the nuns."

"Your Abundance—"

"They are promised to the nuns." She swallowed hard, throat aching with affection for her pets. Bones aching with desire for their venom. She hoped it did not sound as if she were sobbing. "*Take* them!"

WHEN NIZHVASHITI HAD DRIFTED SILENTLY AWAY, MRITHURI WENT INTO HER bedchamber. She slid the door closed and latched it. She stripped her fingers bare of the few rings she had kept back from the coiners.

Then she began to punch herself, over and over, on the breasts and thighs where the flesh was soft and any marks would be covered by her clothes.

I could burn myself, she thought. *What would look like an accident?*

She needed the pain. She needed to own the pain. She needed the pain to be hers.

To be her.

She needed it not to be something that came from the outside, something she could not manage. Something that could overwhelm her. She needed to master it, to control it. To control herself.

She wanted to yell after Nizhvashiti. Beg it to come back.

But she couldn't. She had promised; she had made the sacrifice. Now she needed to live with the consequences.

And find a way to ease the gnawing ache inside her. The one she did *not* control.

When she was sore and tired enough, she felt calm again. And a little ashamed of how she had treated herself. She would be more careful, she decided. She would try to be more fair to herself, as Nizhvashiti had suggested.

If she was lucky, the temptation would never be so great again.

WHEN THE DEAD MAN THOUGHT OF PEOPLE WHO WERE GOOD AT GETTING AN expedition from one place to another, he automatically thought of Druja, the caravan master who doubled as Yavashuri's spy. And fortunately, Druja was right there, immediately available, still in Sarathai-tia where he had been stuck during the siege, along with the various members of his caravan.

The Dead Man found Druja in the presence of his brother, Prasana. They had rescued Prasana on the way out of Chandranath only a few months previous, half-dead from torture. Now he was recovered enough to move around, and he and Druja stood on the parapet overlooking the broad swell of the Mother River, looking southwest.

The Dead Man came up behind them, careful to make a few quiet sounds as he approached. The reason Prasana had been captured and tortured by Himadra's men was due to his work on behalf of Mrithuri.

Prasana was also a spy. And possibly an assassin. Yavashuri had quite the network of agents throughout the Lotus Kingdoms.

The Dead Man's attempts not to be too sneaky were effective. Both Druja and Prasana turned toward him, frowning, but relaxed as they identified the interloper.

"Glad to see you feeling better," the Dead Man said. His breath puffed his veil away briefly. "I was looking for both of you."

Eloquently, Druja gestured to the stone benches nearby. The Dead Man remembered other times he had visited there. He smiled to himself. He dusted a bench with his sleeve and was seated. "Vidhya and Pranaj need help," he began.

10

THE FIRST THING SAYEH NOTICED AS SHE WOKE WAS THE PAIN IN HER HANDS. The second thing was someone scratching quietly at her chamber door. What time was it? The curtains were drawn. She had not, she thought, slept so hard since before the earthquake had demolished Ansh-Sahal.

As long as her eyes were closed, she tried her luck at burrowing back under the covers. But the scratching came again. Her interlude of peace was over. She knuckled sleep from her eye-corners, stitches tugging across her palms.

When she sat up, she noticed that Nazia was gone from her trundle bed at the foot of Sayeh's queenly one. Guang Bao was gone from his perch too. The light around the edges of the drapes seemed bright, as if the Heavenly River still shone. Perhaps she had not slept so long?

No, she thought, as she swung her feet into her slippers. Her body, so stiff and so sore, told her she had slept the afternight through, and the day, and into the next night again. She rose in a cloud of silks—unfashionable vintage garments that had belonged to Mrithuri's mother—by using the bedframe in lieu of her crutch. Her hands complained, despite the bandages. She left the crutch lying against the foot of the bed and limped toward the door.

The leg would never get stronger if she didn't use it.

"Come," she called, when she was a few strides shy of the entrance.

The door slid open, revealing Nazia—and Vidhya, who averted his eyes from her negligee. She watched the color climb up his fair olive cheek and felt a little satisfaction that she could still make a man blush. Nazia held a bundle of cloth on her hands. Vidhya was carrying a tea tray.

"Your Abundance," Nazia said. "We let you sleep as long as we could. I've packed your things."

Her borrowed, bartered, and otherwise accumulated things. "I don't understand," Sayeh said, though excitement was beginning to cut through the fog in her brain.

"Your traveling clothes," Nazia said, shaking them out. She held up a tunic and trousers in rich teal, embroidered with gold and pearls and mirrors, for Sayeh's approval. "We're finally leaving."

Sayeh reached for the tea. Something crackled on her skin.

She looked down at it and said, "Can you fetch me a basin to wash my-self? There's still blood all over my arms, and it itches."

SAYEH HAD NOT EXPECTED TO JOIN MRITHURI ON HER ELEPHANT. BUT HERE she was, sitting cross-legged on a carpet, the heat of the animal's body ris-ing comfortably. An awning shaded them from the Cauled Sun. Nazia and Lady Golbahar sat behind them, fanning each other as much as they fanned the rajnis. Behind them Ümmühan the poetess, curled around her cushion, snored like a kitten.

And all around them . . . the army. Armies, rather, combined under the rule of Mrithuri I, Dowager Empress of Sahal-Sarat.

Sarath-Sahal, Sayeh corrected herself silently. *You're in the southlands now. Any-way, she's only got a claim on Sarath so far, so don't get ahead of yourself.*

Yet.

Mrithuri might not be ambitious. But Sayeh was realizing that she, Sayeh, could be ambitious for both of them. And to realize also that ambi-tion on that level might be what it took to keep her people from becoming just chattel to a lord like Himadra.

Hathi had been painted in festival colors over her coat of whitewash. The bright stripes of a tiger extended down her skull and across her ears, a visual joke that accidentally left Sayeh with a pang of longing for her son. Drupada had made up a story about a tiger and an elephant, and thinking about it now left Sayeh with almost more pain than she could conceal.

Fortunately, Mrithuri seemed distracted with her own problems and hadn't been much moved to make conversation. So Sayeh was released from the obligation to entertain the young dowager. She watched the glittering spears weave forward and tried to ignore the pain in her bad leg enough to relax on her cushion. Hathi swayed more like a ship than an animal, her broad back like a carpet-covered deck.

Guang Bao relaxed on a swing perch well off to the side, where any poop would miss the elephant, carpet, and inhabitants. Mrithuri's bear-dog trotted alongside, ranging left and right to investigate smells or rustles in the grass and shrubs along the roadside. A selection of retainers surrounded them, in-cluding Wizards and guard captains and Nizhvashiti, stiffly erect in a chariot drawn by two black horses. All in all, it was a more than satisfactory royal progress, and the unseasonable drought had left the roads in surprisingly good condition. Because their route paralleled the Mother River, if she had been in the full might of her flood, they would have had to navigate the breadth of it on barges and then swing wide up into the hills: much rougher going.

As it was, Anuraja's treachery and the corruption wrought by the sorcerers served Sayeh and her allies for a change. They were making excellent time.

Excellent time on such a long journey was still too much time in which to think. Sayeh eased her throbbing hands on her lap and contemplated empires. Not for herself, no.

But for other people.

She was contemplating them deeply enough that she almost jumped off the elephant when Mrithuri burst out, "You treacherous beast!"

Hesitantly, without wanting to seem as if she were concerned, Sayeh glanced over. She was relieved to see that Mrithuri had reached forward, placed one hand flat on Hathi's hairy, painted skin, and appeared to be remonstrating with the elephant.

She wasn't quite yelling. Her tone was low, but stern, as she continued. "You could have warned me!"

"Could have warned you about what?" Sayeh asked, when Mrithuri seemed to have lost her place in the sentence.

Mrithuri looked up. "Oh. Sorry. One of this girl's jobs"—she reached forward to scratch the elephant's head, looking so precariously balanced that Sayeh wanted to grab the back of her blouse to steady her—"is to warn me of chaos and upheaval and dread creatures from outside reality coming to eat us all. They say elephants can smell the future, you know."

"I did not know that," Sayeh said. "But we haven't any elephants in Ansh-Sahal. Not enough for them to eat."

Mrithuri looked back over her shoulder. "Pity. Anyway, as I was just now explaining what I said, I also realized that I was wrong about it. Sorry, girl." One more scratch and she leaned back into the cover of the awning.

"So she did warn you about the . . ." Sayeh cast about for the term. ". . . the beast that feeds on war?"

"We perform a divination ceremony at the beginning of the year, when the rains return. And I was just thinking about that. I had been assuming that the dire portents were about Anuraja and invasion . . ." she sighed. "Things can always be worse."

Sayeh made a noise the uninformed might have mistaken for a laugh. "I had a dire portent too." She looked over her shoulder at Nazia. Nazia, of course, was listening intently and without any pretense otherwise.

The girl winked.

Sayeh rolled her regal eyes at her. She spoke to Mrithuri. "But now you think it was this she was hinting at?"

Mrithuri rolled her neck, stretching it until it cracked. Sayeh watched with a little envy for the flexibility of youth. She didn't feel any envy, however, for the distracted picking at the scars on her arm that Mrithuri's right hand was doing, seemingly of its own volition.

"It could all be balderdash," Mrithuri admitted. "Who knows if portents mean anything, or if we bend our experience to meet the expectations?"

"Or the portent to meet our agenda," Sayeh said dryly, not looking at Nazia this time.

"Oh, that, definitely." Mrithuri seemed to settle into herself, staring out over the heads of the army that moved like a glittering flood across the river plain. A gyre of black birds followed. At first, her heart sank as she remembered the bewitched birds of the sorcerer Ravini. After a moment, she saw the way they held their wings and realized that these were only common vultures, following the army with a learned eye toward taking advantage of sky-burials. There would be men who died along the way—of typhoid, cholera, and other rigors of army life. Someone had to dispose of the bodies, and the vultures were experienced.

"Have you checked in on your emissaries?" Sayeh tried to make it sound casual, as if the question of what Himadra was doing had only now occurred to her.

"I've been avoiding it." Mrithuri's forthrightness could sometimes set Sayeh aback. It was an attractive quality nonetheless. "I'll do it now."

She closed her eyes. Her body settled back against its bolster, and Sayeh once more had to stop herself from reaching out and steadying the empress. Mrithuri didn't slide off the elephant. Didn't even threaten to: just swayed in time with Hathi's movement. Breathed slowly, each breath a little deeper than the last.

Sayeh smelled the dust, the warm animal scent of the elephant, and the sharp tang of paint pigment. She heard the marching feet, the rattle of soldier's kit. She looked down at her folded hands and noticed the calluses she'd grown from her crutches, and the way the threads of her stitches drew the swollen flesh together. She smoothed her untidy mind, as best she could, and waited.

Mrithuri seemed to struggle. Her brow furrowed. Her fingers tightened. A little while passed before she opened her eyes again. The look she gave Sayeh was the frown of somebody deciding whether to share bad news.

"Out with it," said Sayeh.

"They're coming to Sarathai-lae."

"They?"

Mrithuri's voice was slow, reluctant. "The Gage. His friend the dragon. Himadra."

"Oh," said Sayeh, her pulse accelerating uncomfortably.

"He's bringing your son," Mrithuri said. "And your army."

It was all going entirely too smoothly, and the Dead Man did not trust it.

The army—or armies—made good time, by the standards of armies. The men so recently at war with one another bickered, threw punches, and

once in a while drew blades both across and within their various factions—
but the stabbings, when they happened, were minor. Under circumstances
such as this, a lack of violent, needless deaths could be considered a luxury.

For the first three nights of travel, nothing of any significance went
wrong. For the first two days of rest, the Dead Man slept as soundly as
he ever did. His peace came at the cost of Druja's calm and well-being,
as the little caravan master was run ragged keeping up with the needs of and
conflicts between a few tens of thousands of animals and men. But that, the
Dead Man thought, was why you hired a caravan master.

So that someone else could handle the worrying.

General Pranaj, Captain Vidhya, and—the Dead Man presumed—
Lieutenant Commander Zirha were all being harassed off their feet as well.
But the Dead Man was finding himself with a rare, strange moment of peace.

Nobody needed him for anything, for a little while. His attendance upon
Mrithuri as anything other than her personal guard was curtailed by a lack
of privacy. And she spent most of her night aloft on Hathi, surrounded by
Wizards, a Godmade, and familiars who were far more effective protection
than he could be.

His luck wouldn't hold. And on the third day, when he was awakened by
the clash of blades and multiple voices shouting, he knew that it had broken.

The Dead Man plunged out of the low tent he slept in, still securing the
tail of his veil with one hand and shoving his sword into his sash with the
other. In instants, he had located the direction of the ruckus, through the simple expedient of identifying Pranaj's back as the general swept a path through
men on his way to intervene. The Dead Man hastily followed.

"Make way!" a voice bellowed—someone just in front of Pranaj. Two
other Tian soldiers knocked men who did not dodge quickly enough aside
with heavy sticks. The Dead Man wished he had Mrithuri's elephant. The
only thing better for crowd control would be one of those indrik-zver they
used for draft beasts in Kyiv. Or maybe the dragon—the *ice-drake*, he corrected himself—that had tried to eat their caravan coming over the Steles
of the Sky.

Well, the elephant wasn't there. And it was useless longing for her. Not
only did you go to war with the resources you had: logistics and supply
chains being what they were, you went to war with the resources you had
right there.

The ring of weapons became audible over the shouts of men as the Dead
Man pressed forward. He felt in the pockets of his hastily donned coat for
his guns. There they were, though his powder horn and lead balls were still
in his pack next to his bedroll.

He shoved the guns through his sash as well, just before he came up on

Pranaj's back. He announced himself, so he wouldn't get killed accidentally. Pranaj sidestepped and let him in.

"Glad you're here," the general said, without looking over.

"What's going on?" the Dead Man asked.

"Insurrection," said the general. If he had been about to say more, he ran out of time, because they came upon the place where the fight was happening.

The Dead Man drew a gun. The one Ata Akhimah had made for him, he realized, recognizing its less-familiar weight in his hand. He cocked it, keeping the barrel low beside his leg. If he had to make a snap shot from there, he could do it as fast as thinking.

Ahead was a whirl of horses, flashing blades, dust, running men. The Dead Man heard screams and hoofbeats and the slam of metal on metal and on other things. He could not see over the crowd, and he needed to see.

There were no elephants. But there were horses, which would provide an improved vantage point.

He turned to the nearest mounted soldier in Mrithuri's colors, a smooth-chinned youth on a bay. He didn't grab the man's stirrup, feeling that under the circumstances he was likely to lose a hand to reflex if he tried. He shouted up, over the clash of weapons and the cries of men: "Loan me your horse!"

The soldier scowled down, and the Dead Man could see the moment of resignation when he identified who was making the request. An internal wrestling match was visible across his features.

Mouth twisted, he swung down and handed the Dead Man the reins. "Her name is Rose," he said. "If you get her hurt, I know who you are and I won't forget it."

The Dead Man instantly liked and pitied the kid. "I'll do my best," he said gruffly.

The mare was a nag, but she was elevation—and the Dead Man supposed that even nags had friends.

There's someone for everyone. Being old, he accepted it when the young soldier offered him a leg up, though he was sure the kid did it to save the mare's back more than the Dead Man's dignity. At least he made it astride without embarrassing himself, despite the threatening pop of his hip when he slung his leg over.

He settled into the saddle. The mare sidestepped, feeling a strange rider up, and the Dead Man let her calm herself. He wasn't the best rider he'd ever met, but he could stay on under most circumstances and not cut his mount's ears off in a swordfight. He hoped he wouldn't need more than that.

The horse left her rider with as much reluctance as he'd shown to hand her over. The Dead Man put his leg on, sending her through the crowd. She didn't like that, either, shaking her head and grunting, but she did it.

Now he could see. And what he saw made him wish he hadn't forgotten his bullets and powder horn.

Ahead, a group of cavalry advanced in a disciplined wedge formation. They were all, based on the colors, soldiers who had been Anuraja's men before they became Mrithuri's men. And the one in the middle, on the big dapple gray, was indubitably that fellow Sekira.

They were pushing through the crowd, aiming toward Zirha's command tent and the administrative hub that surrounded it. The rajni and the empress were housed elsewhere, away from the rank and file of the army, which was at least one less thing to worry about.

"Well," said a voice beside the Dead Man. "We all knew that was coming."

He looked over to see Pranaj settling into the saddle of another borrowed horse.

The Dead Man lifted his pistol. "I could just pick him off."

Pranaj raised a hand. "Zirha's got to do it."

"Zirha's useless."

Pranaj huffed. "Then it's our job to make him less useless. At least until Mrithuri can win the men over. Then she can replace him with whomever she likes."

The Dead Man sighed. "Well, this is shit."

General Pranaj, reining his horse forward, chortled. "This is the army!"

Pranaj had assembled a company of foot soldiers who pressed forward in good order, moving on a diagonal to cut Sekira off. Horse soldiers, including the Dead Man on Rose, followed behind. The seething crowd between the two groups parted to make way, but only slowly. The Dead Man imagined dragging caked feet through clay mud, or the nightmare heaviness of limb that attended trying to run toward or away from something in a bad dream.

Where had all these men come from? Was it just the ones who had been sleeping nearby, awakened and attracted by the shouts?

Well, at least they were slowing Sekira down as much as the Dead Man and Pranaj.

"Turn and face me!" Pranaj bellowed. "Sekira! Attend!"

If you got to be a general because you were able to make your orders heard across a noisy battlefield, Pranaj qualified. His voice rang in the Dead Man's head.

Sekira heard them and turned. Just his head at first, and the Dead Man had the sickening sense that Sekira was going to ignore them and ride down on Zirha's tent, where Zirha was apparently still inside.

They were so close now that the Dead Man could see the lines of Sekira's sneer etched beside his nose. It made him want to curl his own lip in disgust and fury. He held the reins in his left hand. His right palm sweated on the butt of his gun.

He wasn't sure yet if he was going to follow Pranaj's orders.

They kept closing the distance, surging forward now as men on the ground scrambled aside. Sekira must have decided that it was too much risk to turn his back on them, because almost within spitting distance of the command tent, he swung his horse around, letting men dodge its hindquarters as best they could. He leveled his sword at Pranaj.

"This doesn't concern you."

Pranaj kept moving forward, his own weapon sheathed, his bearing proud and negligent. He had guts. Whether he had any sense was a different matter.

"Oh," he said, "but our empress has made me an equal commander with Zirha over this *entire* army. So I'm afraid it *does* concern me."

Setting all the commanders at one another's throats is one way to make sure they don't unite against you, the Dead Man thought. Anuraja must have regularly promoted soldiers over the bodies of their comrades.

It was not a functional way to run an organization if you cared about long-term results and efficiency. But if you cared about maintaining power and making sure nothing happened unless you personally commanded it, on the other hand . . . that was a different story. Let the dogs fight, and throw a bone to the winner.

Off to his right, the Dead Man saw the flap of the command tent drawn aside, Zirha stooping slightly as he emerged. He looked about at the mounted and unmounted soldiers on his doorstep. He blinked mildly at each group and raised a hand to bring the placket of his coat across and button it.

"You're unfit!" Sekira snarled, pointing at the lieutenant commander. "I am in command of this army. Not you!"

Not bad technique, the Dead Man thought. Present it as a fait accompli; make the other guy scramble to keep up. There was something to be said for taking control of the narrative. Even if you did it with a series of bold-faced lies.

A blatant lie could be effective if the people hearing it wanted to believe it enough. The Dead Man had been a soldier long enough to know that soldiers would believe anything negative about a commander they despised, while believing that one they respected walked on water. It was a sort of strangeness in the thought, a superstition brought on as all superstitions are: by powerlessness in the face of compassionless, inexorable forces.

He wasn't even under Zirha's command, and he despised him. Anuraja had probably picked him out to de despised, so that Anuraja could seem golden in comparison.

Zirha drew himself up. "Get off your horse," he commanded.

Sekira laughed at him. "I don't take orders from anybody's lieutenant.

And none of us"—his gesture took in the men surrounding him—"take orders from a scheming snip of a girl."

Even the title "General" might have helped Zirha a little. But Anuraja had made sure he didn't have that title. And from Sekira's smirk, he was banking on his rival's lack.

Zirha surprised the Dead Man. He looked over, caught sight of the red coat on horseback, and calmly ordered, "It is treason to speak of the Empress Dowager in that manner. Shoot that man."

The Dead Man's experience had turned him into the kind of person who thought through contingencies and considered potential outcomes as a background function of existing. He didn't always have a plan, but he always had a series of branching decision paths under consideration. He was very rarely blindsided by events. The last time he'd been completely gobsmacked was when the dragon—the *ice-drake*—attacked them out of nowhere somewhere in a pass above Chandranath.

He was so surprised by Zirha's order that he almost fumbled his gun.

He didn't think of disobeying. Any show of reluctance on his part would further undermine Zirha's fragile authority, and he needed Zirha to keep Anuraja's army in line and more or less under Pranaj's orders. Not that *that* was going particularly well at the moment.

The Dead Man did not lower his veil, as there were so many other people around that he had no intention of murdering. He leveled his wheel lock, and he fired.

Then he was suddenly too busy with a spinning, panicking horse who apparently had no prior experience with gunfire near her ears to see how the shot resolved itself. He heard cursing, chaos. The renewed clatter of weapons. His own cursing added to the mix. Two or three impacts tried to shake him out of the saddle as the horse banged herself against other horses and bowled over foot soldiers. He hauled Rose's head around until she whirled herself dizzy in the space she had cleared. She staggered to a halt, no longer fighting to bolt. The soldiers nearby would have to look out for their own toes.

When the Dead Man had the mare straightened out again, he looked up to find himself at the center of a silent eye in a whirlpool of utter chaos. He sought out Sekira. The insubordinate leader was on the ground, standing. But he still held the reins and was being dragged in a circle by the horse that the Dead Man guessed had thrown him. It still seemed rather put out by the proceedings.

Sekira didn't seem injured. Apparently, the Dead Man's shot had missed, which was not surprising, given the mare's gyrations and the distance involved. Disappointing, however. And Sekira's frantic horse wasn't making it any easier for anyone to handle the others.

The Dead Man reined his borrowed bay in another mincing circle. She sidestepped. He stayed in the saddle and didn't drop his empty pistol despite the too-long stirrups, so he felt moderately pleased with himself. When he got the mare steady again, snorting and shaking her head, he was close to Zirha. So was Pranaj, who had the lieutenant commander by the elbow and was shaking him. "These are your men, Lieutenant Commander. You need to discipline them!"

"I just tried! Oh, bother. Give me that!" Zirha reached out a hand to one of Pranaj's aides and snatched a cone-shaped object out of his hand. It was a speech amplifier, used for yelling orders across a battlefield. The Dead Man had seen them used before.

This one must be magically enhanced, because he'd never heard one make as much of a racket before. Zirha's voice felt like it nearly split his head. He couldn't even make out the words yelled through it. The noise was unbelievable.

The mare was so stunned by the explosion of sound that she froze in place. The Dead Man shook off his own bewilderment enough to stick his gun in a pocket, get the reins organized, and draw his sword. Sekira was still struggling to get his own horse under control, his footwork nimble enough that the Dead Man felt he would not care to engage the fellow in swordplay unless he had the opportunity of cheating.

His own had been as swift, once. But he was no longer a young man, and Sekira . . . was.

With a heartfelt sigh for the indignities of getting old, the Dead Man kicked the mare forward. She was only too happy to plunge away from all the terrible noises; it was steering and stopping that seemed likely to be the problem.

One stride, two, and the Dead Man became aware of somebody coming up on the ground behind Sekira, turning sidestep by sidestep to follow as Sekira wrestled his horse. It was a figure—a man, apparently—wrapped in a ragged cloak, masked beneath a cowl. He slipped a hand into his opposite sleeve. The Dead Man knew it was Prasana only because he recognized the dagger the figure produced. Straight-bladed, razor-edged. Useless in frontal combat, because a blade that fine would snap at contact with the enemy's weapon. It wouldn't even slow down a good swing with a moon-curved blade like the Dead Man's.

But that's not what it was for. This knife was for surgical bloodletting and stealth.

Prasana reached down with the blade, toward Sekira's leg and the big arteries from which a man could bleed to death in instants, if a wound went unstanched. He turned the blade . . .

The Dead Man's horse nearly ran him over.

Sekira's dapple ran into the bay's shoulder, slamming her sideways. The

Dead Man went forward over her neck, staying in the saddle only because he grabbed at the mane with his left hand. Prasana avoided being trampled through some combination of luck, magic, and skill—and then somehow Sekira was back in the saddle.

"Dismount," the Dead Man yelled. "Or it won't go easy on you." With a mental apology to the bay's owner, he drew back his sword and kicked her forward again, completely losing a stirrup in the process.

Sekira didn't exactly have control of his mount, but booting a panicked horse into a run was working with the tide. His horse was willing, and it ran—crashing through the weakest spot in the ranks of men, leaving at least one hopping around, swearing at a stomped foot, and another sprawling.

The Dead Man watched him go. There was no way his borrowed nag could match the speed of that blue-blooded courser. He gave up the chase and pulled his lathered horse into another tight loop, looked around as the sound of Sekira's escape died away. A few dozen mounted men kicked their horses in pursuit of the fleeing man and his horse. The Dead Man had no idea if they were followers, Mrithuri's loyalists, or a mix.

The other men who had backed Sekira were already fading into the crowd. The Dead Man marked a few for later. He wondered if any of them would be foolish enough not to desert immediately.

"Shit," Prasana said through his mask, staring after the escaping insurrectionist. He looked down at the blade in his hand. There was no blood on it. He grunted and slipped it back into a sheath inside his clothing, where it became invisible.

General Pranaj looked over at Prasana, obviously having no idea who he was, other than an ally. "Yes," he agreed. "That's going to be a problem later."

THERE WERE A SEEMINGLY LIMITLESS NUMBER OF WAYS FOR PEOPLE TO INJURE themselves or fall ill while traveling, and Ata Akhimah was starting to think she might learn them all by the time the armies reached Sarathai-lae. There were burns and blisters, sprains and turned ankles, heat exhaustion and plain old malingering—all of which Akhimah was now unfortunately well acquainted with. There were people kicked by horses and butted by goats. Some were poisoned by scorpion stings or snakes or by unfamiliar plants that bore a passing resemblance to safe forage herbs of the coast—or simply poisoned by drink. There were childbirths and broken limbs and feet run over by cartwheels. There were parasitic infections and a small plague of dysentery and a minor cough that traveled around the camps for twenty nights or so before it ran out of victims. During that time, it seemed everyone caught it—even Ata Akhimah herself. So did Tsering-la, and between them they probably passed it on to dozens of people they treated.

There was nothing to be done about it. One couldn't refuse to set a broken bone because your nose was running. Not when there were so few hands to do the work and so much work that needed doing.

One poor fellow had the flesh of his arm laid open when a lever he was using to pry a wagon out of a rut snapped and impaled him. Another had slashed his own hand to the bone sharpening his knife.

Ata Akhimah was not even a healer, though she thought by the time they reached the mouth of the Mother River, she might have served an apprenticeship. Her Wizardry was of a different school, and for the first part of the journey, she herself was still one-handed. She served as Tsering-la's assistant, or sometimes Hnarisha's.

Mostly, the people they treated were Mrithuri's. Well, all the people were Mrithuri's. But in this case, she meant the ones who had come originally from Sarathai-tia and not the ones that she and Tsering-la had once ridden out on an elephant to do battle with.

The soldiers who had been Anuraja's men were suspicious of Wizards. Based on what Ata Akhimah had seen of Ravani, she did not blame them.

The situation confirmed Akhimah's feelings on two things. One, she preferred her patients dead before she cut into them. There was so much less screaming. And two, she hated travel passionately.

Things did not improve much from Akhimah's perspective as time passed and rations grew sparser. With Hnarisha's help, her hand healed enough to come out of the sling, though it pained her whenever she used it.

The stitches needed to be pulled out of Sayeh Rajni's palms, leaving angry red centipede tracks, long before Akhimah was ready to give up on splints and wraps. Sayeh met Akhimah in the medical tent. Tsering-la said he was too busy, and anyway, Akhimah was competent to handle something so simple on her own.

"One of the worst things about getting older," Sayeh remarked as Akhimah bent over her palm. Akhimah squinted through her reading glasses, plucking the ends of snipped threads with the tweezers held awkwardly in her off hand.

She was getting better at using it.

"Pardon?" she muttered, distracted, paying more attention to the stitches than to the conversation. Inattention was as much a mistake with royalty as with Wizards.

"Healing more slowly," Sayeh said. "Worst part of getting older."

Akhimah looked at her over the top of her reading glasses, judged the angle of Sayeh's smile, and decided to risk a joke. "Well, maybe not the *absolute worst.*"

Akhimah snipped the last loop of transparent gut with a pair of flint-bladed spring scissors she had modeled on the pattern of the obsidian ones in Tsering-la's surgical bag. Rasan Wizards had the best medical kit, and they seemed to make most of it out of chunks of volcano.

Tsering-la said the sharpness of the blades and the spirits in the stone prevented infection and speeded healing. The Wizards of Akhimah's own birth-folk had a beer that was said to do something similar, though having been trained in Messaline, Akhimah did not have the secret of its brewing.

Whatever the explanation—sharpness, healing spirits, or something else entirely—Akhimah thought the glass blade worked. Having no obsidian, and being of a scientific mindset, she was trying the technique with knapped flint. Results were not conclusive, but nobody she had worked on had died of blood poisoning so far.

As she tweezered the curl of gut from Sayeh's flesh, her mouth did not even tighten. As if having stitches pulled were such a small scrap of pain as to be entirely beneath the rajni's notice. Considering what Sayeh had been through, Akhimah could only assume that was the truth.

She leaned back and discarded the thread into a tray.

Sayeh said, "What do you think of Zirha now?"

Akhimah's first impulse was to roll her eyes. That was her second impulse, too, but one did not survive an apprenticeship in the Uncourt of Jharni the Eyeless One, Wizard-Prince of Messaline, without learning a tiny bit of self control.

"Our people—sorry, the Tian people—respect him a little bit more now. The Laeish folk—" She shrugged.

Having picked up a cloth, she began dipping her medical tools in boiling water kept hot over a spirit lamp and wiping them dry. Tsering-la insisted that this was part of the process for keeping the spirits appeased, or fed, or something. Whatever the logic behind rituals, Akhimah respected the order and substance of their steps. Wizards usually ordained such things for reasons.

As her master had said, just assume that every step is written down a particular way because somebody lost a limb doing it differently.

She folded the tools away in a boiled lint cloth to protect the brittle edges from chipping.

"I haven't heard a lot of positive things," Sayeh agreed levelly.

"How do you know that?"

"I listen," Sayeh said.

"Nobody talks in front of royalty."

"No," Sayeh said. "But they talk in front of animals."

What sort of animals, Akhimah wondered, trying not to think of Ravani's flocks of black, corrupted birds. "People would tend to notice a phoenix fluttering overhead."

Sayeh laughed and rubbed at a spot of blood on her palm. "I've been branching out. I thought about all the empress's familiars, and the dolphins in the river, and the . . . the Mother Wyrm."

It became evident that the silence was stretching on. Akhimah made a noise of encouragement.

"Marching is boring," Sayeh said.

Outside the medical tent, the noise of feet and animals and voices rose and fell. "It is," said Akhimah.

"And . . . and I realized that I had been holding myself back."

The tools were wrapped and tied so they would not even click together. Akhimah slipped them into her pocket. She leaned over to blow out the lamp. She was going to have to find something else to do with her hands now. She kept her expression soft, listening.

Sayeh cleared her throat. "I think I had been afraid of being judged. Of seeming pretentious. Of trying too hard to seem like something I wasn't."

Sayeh flushed and glanced down as if realizing she had made herself too vulnerable. Was that fear of pretension at the core of every human's self-image?

Akhimah took her time in selecting her words, as if she were selecting the tools for a delicate repair. "I think . . . I never appreciated how much expectations must have shaped your life and Mrithuri's."

"Not just our *lives*." Sayeh put a hand on the edge of the table and levered herself up without a wince. "Our power, or what power we can wield as royal women, as . . ."

Her dirty, well-dressed hair brushed the tent ceiling. Her expression stayed smooth. If it had matched her tone, her brow would have scowled and her lips would have twisted in scorn.

". . . as proxies . . . it's all based on seeming like good wives, good mothers, dutiful daughters. Conscientious widows."

Akhimah snorted her agreement. "Women can do anything, as long as we appear plausibly as the cat's-paw of some man."

Without warning, the ambient noise of an army camp beyond the canvas escalated. Cries and the clash of metal startled Akhimah to her feet. Sayeh, already standing, had the advantage despite her game leg and beat Akhimah to the tent flap. She charged outside unarmed and unguarded into an unknown situation—and all Akhimah could think was that it wouldn't matter if Sayeh came to harm or just risked it; Vidhya was going to kill Akhimah either way.

One could not just grab royalty by the sleeve and drag them away from a poor decision. So, cursing her sense of responsibility, Akhimah nerved herself and plunged after Sayeh. She emerged blinking in the dazzling starlight and almost ran into Sayeh's back. The rajni had drawn up short and braced herself, staring at a scene of chaos bordering on mayhem.

Akhimah sidestepped to avoid bowling her over. *Well, why not?* she thought, and continued the motion to put herself between Sayeh and the fight.

For a fight there was.

Not for the first time, Akhimah wished she were educated in a more martial school of Wizardry. Tsering-la's ability to throw around walls of force would have come in handy right now. The price, however, was more than Akhimah was willing to pay for convenience.

Perhaps two or three dozen men were engaged in combat around the approach to the medical tent, which was cleared so the injured could queue outside. All of the combatants wore the gaudy orange and blue of Sarathai-lae, but based on the way they were hammering away on one another, they were currently experiencing a violent difference of opinion.

Akhimah wondered how they knew what side each one of them was on and who they were supposed to hit and whether some of them might not be hacking away at allies in error. Wasn't that the entire point of putting soldiers in livery? So they could tell at whom to swing a weapon?

Well, she did have one tactic that might serve to get the attention of everybody assembled, though it wasn't a weapon of fine distinctions, and it was also personally costly. And since she couldn't decipher which side any of the various combatants were on, it was probably best to avoid incinerating anyone. There were always political repercussions if you responded to a riot by turning everybody into crackling.

A man went down amid the skirmish. Another took a blow to the shoulder that spun him around. The fight surged toward the two women. They could run, but Sayeh couldn't yet run well.

A man who seemed somewhat familiar stepped between Akhimah and Sayeh and the fight. He brandished a sword, and since his back was to the women, Akhimah assumed he was defending them.

Whatever she intended to do, Akhimah needed to do it quickly.

"Stay well behind me," she said over her shoulder, and hoped Sayeh heard her through the noise.

Akhimah's old master had reprimanded her many times for using gestures as an aid to focus. Akhimah found them viscerally satisfying and the advice irritating. But now, as her hand failed to flex against the splint, she was belatedly grateful.

She imagined, instead, lifting her hands up and jerking them down decisively. A crackling pillar of sparkling electricity leaped up from a bare, unoccupied patch of earth just in front of the soldier defending them.

He startled sideways, leaped back, and fell. He hadn't even managed to get his skinned hands off the cracked rough earth—it was dry, everything was dry, Akhimah was going to start a brushfire if she was not careful—when Akhimah strode past him, Sayeh at her heels. Sayeh paused to help the soldier up. Akhimah did not stop moving forward until her conjured pillar of lightning hissed and sparked behind her shoulder, curling the hairs on her nape.

The fighting had stopped and everyone was staring at her.

Akhimah looked at the soldiers and the soldiers looked back, all wide-eyed except the one who lay on his face. Blood pooled around him on earth too dry to soak it in. The one who had been knocked to his knees was struggling to stand, blood running from his shoulder and his scalp.

All the people in the world who stopped to think things through never accomplished a thing. Akhimah lunged forward. Soldiers scattered out of her way like farmyard chickens, though she was bare-armed and wearing only shirt, boots, and trousers. She snatched the wounded soldier by the seam at his uninjured shoulder and hauled him to his feet with her unsplinted hand.

The rest of the soldiers had drawn back into a loose semicircle surrounding three sides of the tableau made by Akhimah, the wounded soldier, her pillar of energy—and behind them, Sayeh and Sayeh's soldier friend. Akhimah felt the emotional pressure of that ring of men, as if they shoved against a door she held closed. Their differences were temporarily forgotten. If one of them moved against her, they would all fall inward like a breaking wave.

And then either they would overwhelm her, or she would have to set all of them on fire to stop them. All of them, and possibly herself also.

Still clinging to the unwilling man, Akhimah took a half a step forward. "Well?" she called, as if she were in fact yelling at a flock of chickens. "Go on, get out of here! Get!"

She stretched her attention into the column of energy, willing her legs not to wobble with the effort. The world wobbled instead, but her knees didn't buckle. She made the thing flare and hiss and spit stinging sparks like a swaying cobra.

The ring of men broke . . . and fell back like a wave draining into the sea. They scattered. Akhimah could not see in what direction most of them ran. They vanished among tents and gawking onlookers.

The injured man leaned away from her like a scared dog leaning against its collar. "Let me go."

Akhimah let her Wizardry go instead. The pillar collapsed into the ground like a sigh. Akhimah staggered but stayed on her feet. Her grip on the prisoner's sleeve saved her.

He cringed. "Please let me go."

"Oh, shut up and come inside," she responded. "You're bleeding."

AKHIMAH WOULD HAVE LED THEM ALL RIGHT BACK INSIDE THE MEDICAL TENT, but Sayeh's pet soldier—Sanjay was his name, a thing Akhimah remembered instants after being reminded of it—insisted that they were not safe.

He was probably right, she admitted grumpily, but she wanted to sit down as soon as possible. She made him go inside to retrieve her coat and her grip. She would have done that herself, but she wasn't about to relinquish her grasp on her patient-prisoner for an instant.

By the time Sanjay ducked back outside, the Dead Man had arrived with Vidhya and a squad of Tian soldiers. Akhimah's captive stopped trying to get away. The new arrivals probably would have taken turns upbraiding Sanjay for leaving Sayeh alone outside the tent if Sayeh hadn't stepped in to lie and tell them she had ordered him to retrieve Akhimah's Wizard tools. Neither the Dead Man nor Captain Vidhya liked that much, but there also wasn't much they could say about it.

Akhimah was grateful. She suspected that Sanjay was more so. Nobody really wanted the Dead Man angry with them.

The Dead Man and Vidhya accompanied Sayeh, Akhimah, and their respective Laeish soldiers back to the royal encampment. The balance of the guard remained behind, in place around the medical tent.

Akhimah considered asking them to pause so she could slap a quick dressing on the man she'd rescued, but he was bleeding less heavily than he had been, and the encampment was only a short walk away. It would be faster and safer to hustle him along and let Tsering-la and Hnarisha deal with it. Along the way, he continued pleading with them to let him go until Akhimah lost her patience and snapped, "We're only going to save your arm and possibly your life."

"I don't want your witchcraft!"

"Tough," she said. "You're getting it."

11

AKHIMAH WASN'T SURE IF ANYONE ELSE SAW HOW SAYEH'S MASK NEVER SLIPPED until they were safe inside the Empress Dowager's encampment, but Akhimah did. Sayeh kept her appearance of calm and dignity, aloof and impenetrable, until the guards drew aside to let them enter. Even then, her spine only relaxed a little, and—Akhimah noticed—she began to limp more visibly.

It must have cost Sayeh something to stride out with such confidence. Akhimah did not think she would ever admit it.

Vidhya had charge of the patient, who stumbled along as sullenly as if he were being taken to his execution. Akhimah asked a passing soldier where Tsering was, then sent a page to warn him that they were coming to him with an injured man. The Laeish soldier hadn't fainted, at least. She would have hated to carry him.

Sayeh said, "Can you take this from here?"

It took a moment before Akhimah realized that Sayeh was talking to her and not Vidhya. "Er, yes."

"Good." Sayeh stepped back and lowered her voice, shifting to the Sahali dialect, which Akhimah could understand well enough, though not speak fluently. "I'm going to go fill my royal cousin in on events. If further intelligence emerges . . ."

"I'll let you know at once."

Neither one of them looked at the Laeish soldier. He seemed too wrapped up in his pain and what Akhimah could only assume was increasing dizziness to worry much about women muttering in a Northern dialect.

The remaining party continued toward Tsering-la's quarters. Around them, the soldiers were beginning to break tents down and harness animals for travel. Akhimah wasn't too worried; it took a while to get an army on the march, and Mrithuri traveled back from the vanguard in case of ambush.

Tsering-la came hurrying out to meet them. His expression of concern smoothed slightly when he realized the patient was still more or less ambulatory. The frown returned when the soldier spotted the black six-petaled Wizard's coat and began waving around the hand he'd been using to apply pressure on his wound. The blood didn't spurt, which was a good sign, based on Akhimah's burgeoning medical knowledge. But it definitely spattered a fair distance.

"Get that witch away from me!" the soldier cried.

Tsering-la rolled his eyes. He looked at Vidhya. "Well, *I* can't make him sit still to be stitched up."

"I can," the Dead Man answered. "Get a chair."

The page, who was still standing by, ducked inside Tsering-la's quarters and came back out again with a backless ox-yoke chair. As he put it down, Tsering-la leaned over and muttered something in his ear. He vanished within the tent.

The light was getting dimmer. Ata Akhimah looked up; clouds scudded across the Heavenly River. It seemed laughable to think there might be rain.

The Dead Man took one step toward the soldier, who had clutched at his wound again and whose pallor was beginning to look distinctly greenish.

"Sit down," he said.

The soldier sat without even checking where the chair was, but Vidhya managed to guide him into it despite knees that seemed to buckle as much as bend.

"It's worth my life," the soldier said. "If they think I'm taking favors from—" He paled a little more as the Dead Man squinted at him. He swallowed and tried again. "Gener . . . I mean, Sekira's got folk in the troops. Informers."

"Mmm," said the Dead Man, noncommittally.

Sayeh's soldier friend—Sanjay—stepped forward. Akhimah moved aside. "What's your name, friend?"

"Who are you?" the soldier asked.

"Sanjay," Sanjay said.

"Azee," the soldier replied.

"I can make sure it's put about that you resisted until you fell unconscious, Azee." Sanjay crouched to get on eye level with the wounded man. "But only if you help me."

Azee looked around. Akhimah made her face implacable. She crossed her arms, then wondered if it was too much. Well, too late to uncross them.

Sanjay's voice was increasingly reasonable. "What are you so worried about, Azee?"

"You can't keep me safe from . . . from *her*."

Vidhya looked like he was about to speak, but despite the difference in ranks, he stilled himself when Sanjay put out a hand, low and casually. "Her? Not the Empress Dowager, I trust?"

"The Tigress," Azee said.

"Ah," said Sanjay. "You've heard that she's working with Sekira?"

"Everybody knows it." Azee first looked as if he wanted to clap his hands over his mouth. Then he looked stubborn and said nothing more.

"What caused the fight, Azee?"

He shook his head, his expression changing to puzzlement. "I don't . . . remember?"

"Turn out your pockets." Urgency filled the Dead Man's tone.

Azee glared at him, leaning away.

"Turn them out," said Akhimah, "or we'll do it for you." She looked at Sanjay. "The man who died. You need to burn the body. Strip him; go through his belongings. Wear gloves. But first burn the body."

Sanjay nodded grimly. "I'll get it done." He stepped outside the tent.

Azee seemed to have been bullied into cooperation. He turned out his pockets, struggling to reach the one on the wounded side. A few links of money, a fire striker, a smooth green river stone. A handful of nuts in the shell. A small gold ring with an empty setting.

Akhimah pointed to the ring. "Did this have a stone in it?"

"I got it at dice," said Azee. "It didn't then. Ow!" He looked at Tsering-la with betrayal. Tsering-la kept right on cleaning the wound on his scalp.

The Dead Man leaned close to Akhimah's ear and murmured, "Do you think half a ring is enough to do the job?" in the language of Messaline. His accent was Uthman but light.

"If I were Ravani, I would have left plenty of my talismans scattered about," she answered.

"Remind me never to take a gift from a Wizard."

Pointedly, she looked at his gun.

He didn't laugh, but a little puff of air blew his veil out. "How can we find them?"

It was an excellent question. She was still thinking about it when the page came back with a steaming kettle. Tsering-la directed him to hang it on a rack outside the tent door, and Akhimah realized she should go assist with the surgery. "I'll see what I can come up with," she said, and began taking her coat off again. There was space on the rack for it as well.

"We're going to need a travois for this fellow once we're done." Tsering-la snipped his thread into manageable lengths in preparation. "Or a wagon. Ata—oh, there you are. Can you get started cutting the tunic away? Vidhya, I will need you to send over a couple of men to help if we need them. Strong ones. With strong stomachs."

As Akhimah stepped forward, it began to rain. Not hard, not with the steady beat of the monsoon. But a weird scattering of enormous drops, followed by intermittent sprays of modest-sized hail crystals that smarted when they struck flesh. As if the sky couldn't hold it anymore but was still trying.

"Damn it," said Tsering-la, holding an arm over his ducked head. "To at least four hundred of the hells."

"I'll get a tarp pitched," the Dead Man said.

THEY TRAVELED ON, FOLLOWING THE RIVER PLAIN SOUTH, TOWARD SARATHAI-lae. The wounded soldier lapsed into a fever and did, as expected, need to be drawn along on a travois. It was nobody's favorite way to travel—Sayeh remembered her own time in a horse litter without affection—but with Tsering-la tending him, he rallied. He kept the arm. How much use of it he'd get back was a matter of time, luck, and effort.

As Sayeh, to her discomfort, knew.

She was grateful for the flatness of the terrain. The rain grew heavier for three days, so she dared to hope the weather had broken. Her crutches stuck in the mud, so they mostly resided in a baggage cart, heaved along by cattle that struggled as the wheels grew caked. Soldiers had to slog alongside, knocking clods loose with long sticks in an endlessly repetitive process.

Sayeh walked too when she could, building the muscles in her weak leg. She rode—horses, or Hathi, or in carts or beside Nizhvashiti in its chariot—when she could not walk.

Every mode of travel hurt. But every mode of travel hurt differently, so at least varying them helped a little.

She went to sleep each day in pain, on a hard pallet she was lucky to have under the circumstances. She awoke each night in different pain, having traded the discomfort of overuse for the discomfort of stiffness while she rested.

At least her hands were healing and all the tendons worked. And at least she had the landscape to distract her. She'd never come this far south before, and the way the sharp-edged mountains on the horizon gave way to terraced hills and eventually rolling lowlands fascinated her. Bluffs rose beside the river, so it traveled through a broad steep-sided valley. The land was so rich, so eager to be cultivated. There was so much food, and that abundance supported so many people.

People who lined up several deep along the roadside to watch the army pass. People who sometimes cheered the Dowager Empress on her gaudily painted elephant, who sometimes watched with clasped hands or folded arms and frowning faces.

Everyone was hungry. Everyone was thin. General Pranaj had appointed Druja quartermaster and ordered him to pay for anything foraged along the way. This did not make him popular with the supply masters.

That was acceptable. It was Sayeh's job to make herself popular with those who had been Anuraja's people, and with Ümmühan's help, she kept at it. She built her own little network, amused to discover that Sanjay was becoming her spymaster, and she kept in touch with Ata Akhimah over the question of who among the troops might be under sorcerous influence.

Sayeh deduced that the supply masters were accustomed to a more *liberal* style of "foraging" under Anuraja, and would as soon have kept the extra coin for themselves. Especially since the Dowager had not promised them another payday until they reached Sarathai-lae. But Mrithuri was not eager to alienate her new people so soon after becoming—very tenuously—their Empress. If there had been a virile adult male heir available, Sayeh honestly didn't think anything she and Ümmühan could have done would have carried any weight with the army or the people. But in the absence of anyone more likely than Himadra and his brothers, who were still children, Mrithuri looked like a chance at continuity. Rank-and-file soldiers, unlike their leaders, often preferred to avoid a fight. Theirs were the lives on the line if it came to war.

No one ransomed an infantryman.

Sayeh and Ümmühan moved among the soldiers with their honor guard—and their honor guard was all Laeish. They hadn't *convinced* the army. With Sekira doing whatever Sekira was doing in the shadows, and with Zirha the ineffectual person that he was, they were unlikely to win over the rank and file.

But these soldiers had been mustered for a long time, as such things went, while Anuraja pursued his plans of conquest. Now that they were headed home, with the promise of being paid out and returned to their own beds, keeping them equivocating was enough.

They didn't want to start a fight. They just wanted to go home.

And that was Mrithuri's advantage over Sekira.

As long as Mrithuri's faction held the army and didn't give the population unbearable grievances, they could keep the people on their side. And if they managed to win the people over, they could keep the army for good.

It was all a matter of balancing the pans on the scales.

SOMETIMES, SAYEH WATCHED THE PROSPEROUS VILLAGES ROLL BY FROM HATHI'S back, the towns with their tradesmen well fed and richly clothed—and she felt angry. She was careful to keep the rage from her face: noble women were serene and did not express emotions that might distort their features in unpleasing ways or—worse—cause wrinkles.

But a smooth brow meant that what she did not display, she felt even more strongly.

Why should these folk have so much more than her folk? These folk had never hoarded water, or dived for it at risk of their lives as had Nazia, and Nazia's mother. They had never scraped a living from a difficult hillside and prayed that it would be enough to keep all of their children and old folk alive through the dry season.

I would like to be Empress, Sayeh thought, from her place on Hathi's carpeted back. *If I were Empress, I could fix things so that wealth was shared more evenly.*

She forgot herself enough to press her lips together. Looking at the back of Mrithuri's head, she wondered. If they made it through this precarious situation, if they managed to fight this monster stalking them from some metaphysical realm . . . would Mrithuri be moved to share the wealth of the southern nations with the hardscrabble north? Could trade routes bring some of this prosperity to Ansh-Sahal, if there ever was again to *be* an Ansh-Sahal?

And if Mrithuri did not think of it on her own, could she be, perhaps, convinced?

Sayeh sighed under her breath and closed her eyes, reaching out to songbirds in the shrubs along the roadside once again. They were as much her agents as Sanjay.

MRITHURI COULD NOT STOP WATCHING THE HORIZON. SHE WASN'T SURE WHAT she expected to find cresting it, but the foreboding was real. As was the sense of presence that made it seem that the gaze of an enemy fell upon her.

She knew she seemed distracted and distant to those closest to her, the friends and family who shared Hathi's back or stayed close in the protected center of the column. Perhaps Ümmühan's and Hnarisha's skills at politicking would be enough to make those farther away see Mrithuri as remote, queenly, and stern. She missed Yavashuri desperately. Even having been convinced that her maid of honor's abilities made her best suited as regent, Mrithuri could not help but feel those skills—those networks of informants—were what might have brought them all some peace and confidence on the road.

Intellectually, she knew that networks of informants would, in reality, provide a lot of contradictory and unsettling reports, making her even more uneasy. But logic didn't always help with feelings.

She did have Druja and his brother, and Ümmühan, and Sayeh's connection to the friends she had cultivated among the enemy that now belonged to Mrithuri. It would have to be enough, because she knew that things would be even more precarious once they arrived in Sarathai-lae.

A whole palace of intrigues lay before her. But she didn't think that apprehension was causing her sense of eyes boring into the back of her neck.

She wished she could have talked to the Dead Man about it in private. *Really* talked with him: bared her heart and her fears. He was an excellent listener, and his manner of puncturing her self-pretension and cycles of worry with a sardonic comment would have made her laugh and then relax a little. But there was no privacy on the march, and there was especially no privacy in front of the army that had belonged to her supposed husband. And when her claim was based on that supposed marriage, she could afford no rumors.

How was it, she thought, that the more temporal power she seemed to accrue, the less she got to just do what she wanted? When she had been a girl studying to be a priestess, the most frustrating part of her day had been the necessity of wearing slippers and reciting the old prayers letter-perfect.

Time passed, the days much like one another apart from the incident with Sekira and the other one with Sekira's retainers. With much support from Mrithuri's people, Zirha seemed to be coming out of his paralysis. She wondered how much of it had been induced by fear of Anuraja's retribution if he made any decision without first consulting the warlord. Mrithuri came to enjoy dinners with him every few mornings. She tried to bring each of her senior staff into her presence on a regular basis.

There were small problems to be solved, but none of the matters of discipline were large enough that she needed to involve herself directly. So, mostly, she made herself available as a sounding board—and to her surprise, Zirha seemed to blossom when given some freedom and a certain amount of authority.

Mrithuri knew that the storybook retainers surrounding her did nothing to lessen her glamor. Nizhvashiti in its black robes, moving awkwardly— woodenly puppet-like when it moved at all—had come to seem common-place to her, a sort of friend.

But it was a Godmade and a revenant, and it would seem not at all com-monplace to the regular folk, to the soldiers who followed Mrithuri more or less wittingly. To have such a being at her beck could only make her seem a tiny bit legendary herself, especially when considered in combination with the other characters in her retinue: the exiled rajni of destroyed Ansh-Sahal; a dashing and somewhat dissipated swordsman; two foreign Wizards; and the rest of the crew.

Mrithuri regretted not bringing tumblers, but Ritu and her family had remained behind in Sarathai-tia to support Yavashuri, much to Lady Gol-bahar's regret. Still, Mrithuri thought with some satisfaction, her entourage was more than fancy enough to exceed whatever boost in magnificence An-uraja had enjoyed as a reflection from his flamboyant sorcerer.

Never more so than when Nizhvashiti came floating up beside Hathi's head, hovering alongside Mrithuri to keep her company as Mrithuri rode. Usually the Godmade was silent, a stroke of black ink against the elephant's papery, whitewashed ear. But sometimes Mrithuri spoke to it, as priest to priest or as sister to sibling, and listened as it replied in whispers.

One night, with the dawn creeping closer, with Ümmühan behind her somehow contriving to write on a lap desk despite the moving platform of the elephant's back, with Golbahar asleep across the rug, unselfconscious as a cat, Mrithuri said to the Godmade, "Godmade. You might know the answer to this. How did we come to have a Cauled Sun, when in other lands they sleep by night and wake by day?"

"I am a Servant of the Good Daughter. Not that other one."

That intrigued Mrithuri, with its suggestion Nizhvashiti *did* know. "And I am a servant of the Mother, but the story is not in my lore."

She did not mention that her acquaintance with that lore was, perhaps, a little truncated by the early death of her *own* mother.

Nizhvashiti made a sound like ripping paper. It might have been a sigh. "The Mother had two daughters," it said. "Half the sky belonged to each: one for the night, and one for the day. But the daytime daughter was jealous of the other, and jealous of us"—its gesture took in soldiers, farmers, and everyone else—"and so she made her own sigil so hot, it scorched the land unbearably, and she wrestled with the Good Daughter and ripped that daughter's sigil from the sky and threw it down far to the west, where it utterly destroyed those exotic and distant lands."

"The sun and moon?" Mrithuri asked.

Nizhvashiti nodded. "In so doing, she made the night too dark to see in. And the day too hot to bear. She would have driven all the people in her Mother's lands away or to death."

"But—"

"But the Good Daughter intervened. She found her blackened and blasted sigil and raised it up again into the heavens, using it to shield the land from the burning sun. She raised a mirror into the night to reflect her Mother's visage in the sky, that we might have light to see by. She did this all with great sacrifice to herself and asking nothing."

Mrithuri hummed. "And the Ba—" Nizhvashiti's already-stiff posture seemed to stiffen further. It was a warning. "And the Other One? Do you think she is the beast?"

"No," Nizhvashiti said. "But I think she might be its mother."

MRITHURI KNEW THEY MUST BE GETTING CLOSE AT LAST WHEN THE PEOPLE lined up along their route to watch the army pass started calling out to loved ones on the march. She gave instructions that men were not to be disciplined if they broke ranks to hug families, lovers, friends, or children. Progress slowed; there were a few desertions. Not too many. Not with money owed.

She did see care packages being handed from wives, mothers and fathers, and what she presumed were sweethearts and siblings of both genders. Everyone was thin with the short rations. Except for her. She was putting flesh on, which made her wonder how badly she had starved herself before.

It was two marches later, halfway through the night under the gaudy banner of that same Heavenly River, that she first caught sight of Sarathai-lae. It glittered; it shone. Its banners snapped blue and vermilion against the glowing sky.

A sound began to rise around her. Ethereal, layered, thin and strange.

It was thousands of soldiers singing softly, some song she did not know. She was as far from the land of her birth as she had ever been. And they . . . they were home.

12

THE GAGE COULD HAVE COVERED THE DISTANCE TO SARATHAI-LAE MUCH faster on his own, but he had to admit that it was nice to have company. Mostly, he walked beside Kyrlmyrandal while the gullied mountains gave way to verdant plains. Himadra and some of his command staff were interesting, but the political entanglements felt tiresome. And there was always the risk Heartsblood might say something impolitic.

The soldiers often went hungry. The supplies the army had brought from Chandranath were tightly rationed. Once they were beyond its borders, Himadra severely limited foraging—or pillaging, if one preferred accuracy. Himadra's men—accustomed to raiding these very borderlands on a somewhat regular basis—grumbled.

The soldiers from Ansh-Sahal kept to themselves. They were, the Gage thought, watchful and quiet. He couldn't quite tell if they were cowed or if they simply observed and waited. Or if they were quite reasonably suffering from grief, despair, and terrible loss.

Their nation had been shrugged off the shore of the Bitter Sea by one lift of a volcano's shoulder. Shrugged off—mothers, grandfathers, children, lovers, childhood homes, beloved vistas, picnic trees, and all.

It would traumatize any human. The Gage remembered enough to know.

Though the company was nice, the slow pace occasionally frustrated even the Gage's machine patience. He didn't like to admit it, but he was looking forward to rejoining the Dead Man when they reached Sarathai-lae. He missed his partner. He wondered, when all this nonsense was done, where the road would take them.

Back to Messaline? Or farther out in the world?

Don't get so attached to humans, he reminded himself. *They never last for long.*

He was not insensible to the irony of having that thought while walking beside Kyrlmyrandal, to whom he must seem a similarly ephemeral creature. Nobody, to his knowledge, had tested the limits of how long a Gage could endure. But gears must wear out, brass must eventually corrode . . . and he had experienced, himself, how his joints could be gritted and fouled until they froze, if a fine-enough dust infiltrated them. He might end his days as a living statue, motionless but self-aware.

It was the inorganic equivalent of the creeping stiffness of mummification that seemed to affect Nizhvashiti. Perhaps when they were both frozen in place and unable to stop existing, the Gage would manage to convince somebody to prop them up side by side—for the company.

Blessed Kaalha! For an ageless automaton built for vengeance, he'd gotten maudlin. And dependent on having people around.

Kyrlmyrandal was pleasant company, anyway. She seldom spoke much, but when she did, what she had to say was usually trenchant, amusing, or informative. The Gage learned more about the natural philosophy of rock formations in a week's march than he had in decades spent around Wizards.

And the pen was witty too, if a little too truculent for some company.

Himadra usually rode on his gray mare on the Gage's other side. The Gage thought it was half curiosity and half keeping an eye on them. Though right now, the raja seemed deep in conversation with the boy prince. Drupada was on the other side, riding a pony led by his nurse, who herself rode another mare. Himadra and his adopted heir weren't exactly having a conversation of consequence. What *did* you discuss with three-year-olds, anyway? As near as the Gage could make out, this particular conversation involved Drupada explaining in great detail how the elephants came and built the road every morning, and then came at night again and chopped it up and carried the sections away with their tusks, only to lay them down again in front of "his"—that is to say, Drupada's—army.

Himadra wondered if that didn't take a lot of elephants, and Drupada, with a sly tone, explained that they were magic elephants that moved very fast and could fly.

"And why would they move the road around like that?" Himadra asked.

"The elephants like me," Drupada answered in all seriousness. "So they move the road so that my army has someplace to walk on. Mama told me a leader has to take care of his people."

A spike of forgotten tenderness sliced into the Gage's hollow breast. It made him want to pick Himadra up and shake him—a process that would likely be fatal for Himadra, so the Gage remained calm, reminded himself that humans were indeed very fragile, and waited until the prince's nursemaid eventually drew him away.

It was easy for the Gage to forget, sometimes, that he and the Dead Man had more in common than not, in terms of the losses that had set each of them on the road they still walked. And somewhere, the Gage knew, Drupada's mother was suffering.

Himadra watched them go, proprietary. After a few moments, the Gage asked, "Why did you bring that boy? It's not just because you like his company. And he'd be leverage over Sayeh as surely in your holdfast of Chandranath."

Himadra gave him a sideways look, as sly as Drupada's. The momentary resemblance startled the Gage, until he remembered that man and boy were, after all, cousins. "I do like his company."

The Gage made a sound like a creaking hinge: his closest approximation of a disbelieving hum.

Himadra sighed. "I *like* children, you know. He reminds me of my brothers. And there's no safety in a city when mountains shrug and seas boil. When sorcerers are on the roam. I can keep an eye on him if he's with me."

"Does that mean you won't sacrifice him, if you have to?"

"Define 'sacrifice,'" Himadra retorted. "Define 'have to.'" He shook his head—the gentle, limited motion with which all his gestures were made.

"And you have learned that Mrithuri's forces will reach Sarathai-lae before yours do. With Sayeh Rajni, perhaps, accompanying them."

"There's one with no reason to like me." Himadra pointed out over the army with his chin. "You know how many of these are her people. Drupada's people. Having him along might keep the Ansh-Sahali soldiers willing . . . if it doesn't come to a fight."

"Do you want it to come to a fight?"

Himadra turned, scrutinizing the Gage as if he studied his own reflection in the Gage's polished, egg-shaped mirror of a head. "Under the circumstances, aiming for a fight would be a poor tactical choice on my part."

It was true. Himadra's agents must ride like the wind. If their information were trustworthy, by the time Himadra and the Gage reached Sarathai-lae, Mrithuri would be in possession of it. And a larger army, one that would have had time to rest and recover somewhat from their own long march, to boot.

Even the soldiers late of Anuraja's army would be unlikely to abandon a woman for a cripple, given the choice of leaders. If there were a sound adult male of the bloodline anywhere in the Lotus Kingdoms, he might have been in with a chance.

The Gage was not fool enough to think that Himadra's stature and brittle bones rendered him any less able to rule than did Mrithuri's sex. But the Gage was not most men, and to most men it mattered.

"Drupada reminds you of your brothers."

"They were both much younger than me." Himadra's mare sidled. He gentled her straight again. "I was not the only son of my bloodline born under this curse. I was just the only one to survive past infancy."

"Do you think your brothers will remember you?"

Himadra's words were soft. "It seems unlikely."

"They must be teenagers now."

"Rayesh is twelve," he said. "And Vivaan is two and a half years older, so he would be fifteen."

"And you haven't seen them since Anuraja took them into custody. As hostages."

"The polite euphemism," Himadra said, "is to say that he 'fostered them.'"

The Gage waited, to see if anything else would follow. Sometimes he thought he richly understood the strategy behind Kyrlmyrandal's silences. They invited others to fill them. Sometimes he thought that she just didn't see much point in talking most of the time.

Himadra also apparently saw no point in talking currently, but Heartsblood seemed to have no compunctions about breaking the silence. It spoke from the seclusion of its drawer: "Euphemisms are like metaphors. They can clarify as well as elide." It paused. "But not in this case, apparently."

The Gage felt responsible enough to correct the awkwardness. "How long since you saw them?"

Himadra appeared to count inside his head. "Nine years, more or less."

"And you think you can trade Drupada for them?"

"It's an option. I like having options." Himadra's mouth quirked inside his beard. "I enjoy a novelty."

HIMADRA HAD A TENDENCY TO RANGE UP AND DOWN THE LENGTH OF THE column as they progressed, and so the Gage and Kyrlmyrandal ranged with him. He really must be keeping an eye on them. And perhaps he was trying to demonstrate to the Gage—and through him, to Mrithuri—that he had nothing to hide.

Perhaps he had accurately identified the Gage and the dragon as the most dangerous creatures likely to be found on this side of the Steles of the Sky, and looked upon them as protection.

The Gage was never sure later if it was coincidence or enemy contrivance that they were all near the head of the column when a plume of dust, moving fast, became visible on the horizon. It rose like a narrow column of smoke into the heat of the brilliant night. Two horses, the Gage thought. Three at the most.

Rapidly advancing.

On this particular occasion, Himadra was accompanied at his right hand by his lieutenant, Farkhad, mounted on a white-splashed roan that, after weeks of hard traveling and failed rains, was much the color of the road. Farkhad lowered a spyglass from his face and exchanged a significant look with his raja. Himadra pinched the bridge of his nose.

"What is it?" asked the Gage.

He didn't expect Kyrlmyrandal to answer, "The beast's pet."

"Our alleged ally," Himadra agreed. "That fucking sorcerer."

✳   ✳   ✳

THE GAGE WAS BRACED FOR ANNOYANCE. HE WAS BRACED FOR RIDDLES. HE was braced for mockery. He was frustrated that they had not managed to work out a plan for a trap, after all.

He was not braced for Ravana to rein his unhappy, lathered bay horse up before them with a companion on his left hand, her chestnut less unhappy but no less lathered, blowing with the heat of the run.

It was Chaeri, her blouse and pantaloons as dust-coated as her face above the kerchief through which she breathed, her ringlets tied back in a scarf. Some were coming loose, straggling and greasy. Her sandaled feet looked chafed at the instep where the stirrups rubbed. One arm was bound across her chest with a filthy bandage. Dried blood crusted her tunic. Her eyes were wild.

Pity pressed out from inside the Gage's chest. His metal ribs were un-yielding. The emotion caused pain. *Steel yourself,* he admonished, the joke bad enough to break his own emotional spiral.

Ravana tugged his kerchief down. He looked, amused, from Chaeri to the Gage. His gaze skipped over Kyrlmyrandal as if he were a cat ignoring an inconvenient fact. The Gage rarely minded that his own face was expressionless, a perfect mirrored oval. Now he was glad.

The bay mare tossed her head, spattering the Gage's tattered rough-spun robe with froth. They stood with an army behind them; the Gage had a dragon at his hand. They had quite recently been plotting to find and per-haps capture this creature. But under Ravana's gaze, the Gage felt small.

The air filled with the reek of corpses. The Gage was glad he lacked the equipment to gag.

"Why don't you go and talk to your little friend, metal man? She wants a word. I have private business with my lord," Ravana said, his undershot jaw more than usually pugnacious. It was not the greeting the Gage would have expected. Based on Himadra's expression, it was not the greeting the raja had expected, either.

Kyrlmyrandal, though, laid a hand on the Gage's sleeve. "Go ahead," she said. "It will be fine."

I won't let anything happen to you, Heartsblood said. For the Gage's inner ear only, apparently, as no one else responded.

The Gage had a brief mental image of the little sliver of wood and metal and lacquer prancing about with a rapier and was glad he had no expression to keep straight.

"I will wait here," the Gage said, speaking not to Ravana but to Himadra, and to Farkhad. "Don't go too far off, Your Competence."

Farkhad winked at the Gage across Velvet's shoulder. Kyrlmyrandal, word-less, detached herself from his sleeve and followed as Himadra and the other two reined their horses aside.

Leaving Chaeri staring at the Gage, and the Gage . . . Well, one with no eyes could not be said to *stare*.

"You've fallen in with bad company," the Gage said, in a metallic murmur.

"'Fallen' is the right word," Chaeri agreed.

"How did that happen?"

So formal, when they had been . . . well, friends. When Chaeri had been, so he supposed, romancing him.

Chaeri whisked a frightened glance at Ravana. She whispered, "Save me."

"How did you come to be here?" the Gage asked. "Why aren't you with Mrithuri?"

Chaeri pulled her kerchief down from the bridge of her nose. "I could tell you I had been kidnapped."

"I suppose you could tell me that," the Gage agreed. He had an unsettling premonition that he knew the true answer, however. And Chaeri could not know how little he knew.

He folded his arms and tried to look implacable.

"Mrithuri's people drove me out. They were jealous. Anuraja . . . captured me, then sold me to him. To her. To . . . well, I suppose, to both of them." She touched the sling binding her arm up. "Your partner shot me. I can't use this arm. Ravana tells me I will not be able to use it again. I don't think he really cares."

The manipulation was transparent. The information that the Dead Man had shot her told the Gage what he needed to know. The Dead Man did not generally go around shooting people who had not done something to deserve it.

Somehow, the Gage did not think it was a matter of jealousy that Chaeri had left Sarathai-tia in a hurry. As for being captured . . . that seemed like embroidery.

Her horse was too relieved at being allowed to rest to take advantage of her distraction. It stood very still, breathing heavily. And, well, Chaeri had always had a way with animals.

The Gage said, "You're Mrithuri's half sister, aren't you?"

The way she gaped was as good as an admission. "How—"

"You're as gifted as all the royal women, in your own way." The Gage tipped his dome in the direction of Himadra. "The men, too, though I suppose they think it's some sort of effeminacy to admit it. But look at how Himadra rides that mare, when you'd think she'd break his fingers the first time she objected to his hands on the rein."

Chaeri's jaw worked silently.

The Gage thought back to what he had seen before he left Sarathai-tia. He said, "And then there's how much nonsense Mrithuri put up with from you. Some of that is because you made her dependent on you emotionally, for the serpents. But some of it was guilt, wasn't it?"

"Mrithuri didn't know."

"Not admitting something, to yourself or others, is not the same thing as not knowing, Chaeri. You're not the first royal bastard kept around the court on a sinecure that I've met."

Her sideways glances after Ravana, who was now speaking in low tones with Himadra, were either artful or revealed real fear. The lower part of her face was clean and soft, skin fair against the road dirt that banded her forehead and eyes. She softened her voice further and ignored the inconvenience of what the Gage had said. "You could protect me from him. From them."

"It's possible," the Gage admitted. "I wouldn't lay odds."

"I love you." Her voice swelled with emotion; her eyes welled with tears.

"You have a funny way of showing it," said the Gage.

His callousness took her completely by surprise, he saw. She had been preparing one reaction. Now she was caught out into an honest response. And it was fury.

He was not surprised when she cast the emotions she was feeling back at him.

Arranging her face in an attitude of condescension, she said, "How you must hate me."

"Hate you?" It struck him in a peculiar way. Maybe he was becoming numb to her. He tipped his head and thought, then shook it slightly. "In all honesty, I had not considered you overmuch."

Her expression stiffened because she would not allow it to crumple. The Gage felt a little bad for her. He knew she must have betrayed Mrithuri and placed the Dead Man's life in danger. Despite everything she had done . . . the Gage thought she had done it, in part, because she had never managed to feel herself important. And perhaps that was a lack within her . . . and perhaps it was that nobody else in her life had very much helped.

"You cared for me!"

He said, "You tried very hard to make me care for you. And it is easy to confuse enjoying the appearance of being wanted with wanting something yourself. But I am older than you think, Chaeri. Oh, and by the way . . . was it you that poisoned her parents?"

Her hand covered her mouth. "That was my father, too. I could not even mourn in public."

"True," the Gage said. "But their deaths made you handmaid to a queen in waiting and gave you far more influence over her than you would have had with your father and his wife alive. I wonder, was it you that suggested that she use the serpents to make herself sharper, more focused of will? To live up to her grandfather's expectations?"

It hit home. She rocked back and forth, so upset that even her tired horse reacted.

The Gage struck again while she was still gathering herself. "I'm sure Ravana and his master would love it if you joined us, pretending contrition, begging redemption. Ready to betray us again."

"If I had been a boy," she said, "it would not matter that I am a bastard. If I had been a boy, I would be raja. I'm older than her! I could have married her off to anybody! I deserved . . . I deserved something better than being her servant."

And of course, she was not wrong. The Gage knew it, from when he had been a woman. Women, everywhere, were held to higher standards than men. Women were never accorded as much respect as men. Women worked toward incremental change and gain, because they were systematically kept from the positions where they could order a sweeping reform with a gesture of their pen. Even a woman in power, like Sayeh, like Mrithuri . . . her lords would bear less from her than they would if she were a man.

But what the Gage said, turning away, was "And how would you sending her off to that fate have been more fair than you being accorded a servant's place? It was you, back in Sarathai-tia, that reminded me that women always get the worst of it."

CHAERI DID NOT GIVE CHASE WHEN HE WALKED AWAY, BUT HE SAW HER DIG IN a pocket before her arm went back. Something small and glittering *chink*ed off his armor, bouncing away into the dust.

She'd thrown a link at him, a small piece of change. He hoped it gave her satisfaction.

He could not hear what the others spoke of while he approached. Given the acuity of his senses, he could only assume that Ravana was using sorcery to mute the conversation. Closing the distance was like wading through molten glass. The flow wanted to divert him to left or to right. Keeping himself from being swept aside became a little more difficult with each step.

It was as if the Gage pushed himself forward through a vast silence, and the silence itself was a moral and spiritual weight.

He almost fell forward and measured his brass length on the ground when Kyrlmyrandal's voice broke through like a gunshot, easing the pressure and the muffling silence at once. Even though she spoke in measured tones. "I hope you are very unhappy for a very long time, Ravana. I hope you see how you have failed, but that even in self-knowledge you are incapable of repairing your errors, because you will not take responsibility for your crimes. And I hope you don't even learn anything from it. That is the curse I curse you with!"

Ravana smirked. But the Gage had noticed the flinch that preceded it, and the way his horse fussed and sidled. He raised a hand, though, and with the raising of that hand, everything stilled. All the little noises that had come rushing back with Kyrlmyrandal's curse were muted and silenced once more. That weight—that great, muffling weight—fell over the Gage again like the mass of a featherbed. He had not breathed since his lungs were replaced with cogs and clockworks, but he felt airless.

Himadra and Farkhad sat their horses as if frozen. Kyrlmyrandal struck forward with her walking stick, but the arc of the staff was weirdly slow. The Gage took one more step forward.

Ravana looked down his nose at Himadra and said, "Well, don't say I never offered you a chance."

He yanked his horse around and kicked her flank, sending her plunging back toward where Chaeri still waited, looking more stricken than the Gage thought their conversation warranted. Her horse half-reared when Ravana's bolted. As Ravana swept past, her mount fell into his wake as if dragged.

Soldiers turned, watching the galloping horses, and as they raced into the distance, the sound of their hoofbeats rolled back like the echo of thunder, louder than it had been when they first passed close.

The Gage spoke to Himadra. "What was he saying before Kyrlmyrandal laid her curse on him?"

Himadra blinked like someone coming back from far away. "I don't actually know. As if . . . what he said didn't actually mean anything? Or it contradicted itself? It sounded convincing for a minute, though."

It bothered Himadra for nights afterward, that sense that whatever Ravana had been saying to him was important, and importantly disturbing, but that he couldn't quite remember its freight. It reminded him of the foolish, shamefaced anger one sometimes experienced after a strenuous argument, of not being able to remember how one had been moved from measured and reasonable disagreement to being forced to defend a sequence of increasingly more ridiculous propositions.

An unsettled sensation woke him often, along with the usual pain. His dreams were anxious and amorphous. He could never quite remember the content of any of them, either, even immediately after they awakened him.

He'd eventually nerved himself one morning to send for Kyrlmyrandal to come to his tent. She'd arrived with a tapping of her cane, and Navin, the trusted guard at the door, had held the flap aside and guided her to duck her head to enter. When she was settled, Himadra gave her tea and assisted her in finding the cup.

She seemed to have no trouble locating and navigating around living things. It was only when interacting with the inanimate ones that her sightlessness became manifest.

It seemed rude to ask, though, so he kept his questions to himself.

He had considered his approach before he summoned her. He had a sense that she was probably somebody who appreciated directness. So, once she was settled, he cut right to the point.

"Why can't I remember what the sorcerer said before you sent him away?"

She had been holding the teacup under her nose with both hands, inhaling the steam. Now she sipped, quietly, and breathed in over the tea to further enjoy the aroma. She gave the air of one thinking over her answer, and he did not hurry her.

She set the cup down. "It wasn't so much what he said as how he said it."

"I don't understand." This was why you invited someone over for tea. Tea was a useful thing to fiddle with.

She steepled knobby fingers that reminded him of the bones in a bat's wing. The long nails curved over the tips like claws. To his relief, she refrained from rattling them against each other while she pondered. "You had proved resistant to his more subtle influences," she said at last. "More so than Anuraja, I imagine. You're used to filtering out the distractions of your pain?"

He couldn't take offense, when he had watched her own limping stride. He nodded.

"So he resorted to more blatant attempts at control. Puppetry, if you will. Do you carry any talismans that he provided you?"

"I did," Himadra said. "Or rather, he gave me one some time ago. I never quite trusted it. It's in a coffer, back in Chandranath."

"Hah!" The bark of laughter was as abruptly ended as begun. "They should call you Himadra the Wise."

He sipped tea. "When there are so many more colorful epithets available?"

THEY CAME OUT OF THE HIGHLANDS AT LAST, AND IT BECAME EASIER TO BUY food and keep the men at least partially satisfied—for a while, and then the gleanings again became slim. They were too deep in enemy territory now to raid without inciting a response, and Himadra did not want a war.

He tightened his belt. So did all of them. Occasionally, Himadra wondered who he might have been if he had been born into as rich a land as this one. His whole life might have been different. He might have been a scholar. He might have been anything.

He might, he supposed, have been dead.

When he rode beside Iri, he found her looking around herself with an expression that led him to imagine she experienced similar emotions. Ansh-Sahal was an even poorer kingdom than Chandranath.

They had argued, he recalled, about whether he should be foraging—

pillaging—to feed his own men and the men of Ansh-Sahal he had taken in. What did she think of this and why he made those same men go hungry now?

Maybe she did understand the nuances. She was a listener and a thinker, the sort of person who was content to keep to the background and let herself go unremarked. And she'd demonstrated more than once that while her own moral compass was inviolable, and that she would argue it ferociously, she was capable of understanding the expedient decisions others made.

Understanding, though she could not be made to condone them.

You're starting to like her, Himadra thought in amusement. *Don't be tempted to make her an advisor, Boneless, or you'll be stuck listening to her lecture you about your ethical failings until the end of the world.*

Literally, perhaps.

One thing he did like about the roads they traveled now—other than the roads themselves, which were well surfaced and broad—was the way the people along them came out to view his passing army. In less-safe lands, there would have been no enjoying the impromptu parade. All would have hidden away, in bolt-holes in the hills kept as well stocked with food and clean water as the economics of daily need would allow. They would have taken their children along with any livestock and valuables they could move, and fled.

"They don't look as unhappy to see us as I would have expected," Iri murmured.

Without turning to catch her eye, Himadra replied, "We're not the tax collectors."

She struggled to hold back laughter until her cheeks puffed out and she snorted.

Himadra found himself scanning the crowd, nodding and waving as regally as his decidedly nonregal self could manage. Some waved back; some murmured excitedly. Some drew away. He counted children, and discovered that there were many, and that most did not look malnourished or diseased. The children were the most likely to return his gestures. One little boy in particular—six or seven years old—caught his eye. The child was straining enthusiastically against a shirt collar held by a more cautious parent, waving his arms and jumping up and down.

Himadra met the kinetic child's gaze and made a sign of blessing over him.

"There is another one ahead of you!" the boy shouted, before his mother clapped her hand across his mouth and vanished him away into the crowd as quickly as a cat scruffing an endangered kitten.

Himadra watched them melt back into the crowd and felt a pang.

He mocked himself silently for feeling disappointed. The trust only went as far as was wise. Catching the notice of the great was not safe—and if the child didn't know it, the parent did.

"Another what?" Iri asked, pulling him back from contemplation.

Himadra looked at her sideways this time. "Another army."

13

THE PROBLEM OF UNCOVERING RAVANI'S—OR RAVANA'S—INFLUENCE WITHIN the Laeish army was complex, and Ata Akhimah needed to decide where to begin. The task seemed so vast, the parameters so undefined, that the mere act of selecting the thread from which to unravel the whole tapestry of information left her daunted.

She had to shed this frozen feeling. She would choose a thread—any thread at all—and start unpicking.

She didn't have contacts in the Laeish army. Other than Sayeh's acquaintance Sanjay, Akhimah didn't know people she could ask. This lack argued that she should prefer a mechanical approach over an interpersonal one. Which meant somehow—on the road, separated from her tools and forge and workshop, without knowing exactly what she was looking for—she needed to build some kind of . . . evil-talisman detector. Better yet, she would ideally build a talisman of her own. A small, portable, inexpensive, easily duplicated one that could be employed not just by Wizards and magic-users but by all sorts of people. From Mrithuri herself down to the most scantily trained enlisted man.

After that, the Laeish army needed to be prepared to do its work against the infiltrators. To see them as a threat not just to an Empress Dowager to whom they had as yet no reason to feel loyalty, but also as a threat to their own integrity as individuals and their fealty to the institution to which they belonged.

That, Akhimah realized, was a morale problem. Morale problems, thank the red saints, were not Akhimah's department.

Morale problems belonged to Ümmühan, and since Ümmühan *did* have contacts with the Laeish army from the time during which she and Nazia and Sayeh had been held captive by them, Akhimah was more than happy to let the poetess handle it.

Akhimah, meanwhile, sacrificed her own sleep—and Tsering-la's—to work on the magical and mechanical problem.

They had an example of Ravani's work: the padparadscha ring that had been used to disguise an assassin as Ümmühan . . . and later to reanimate his mutilated corpse. And all its various severed fragments. They had their training and their theoretical knowledge of how sorcery must operate. And they had their native wits. They had the damaged ring that had affected Azee.

It was little enough to go forward on.

First, they had to find a means to detect the one and a half example talismans they did have. The man killed in the brawl had had no such object on him. Either he'd just waded in to fight because everybody else was, he'd had his pockets picked, or he'd been defending against the possessed soldiers.

And nobody seemed able to identify who had been in the fight, or on what side. Akhimah did not know if that was due to soldiers protecting one another or Ravani's ability to muddle memories.

Until they had more to work with, the talismans were still the most likely thread for Akhimah and Tsering-la to unpick. After what seemed like dozens of experiments, they discovered that if they stroked a needle against the ring repeatedly, then floated the needle on a bit of cork, it would swivel to point at the talisman, just as a needle stroked against a magnet would swivel to point to the north. Both Akhimah and Tsering-la were careful never to touch either the padparadscha ring or the energized needle with their bare flesh. Akhimah also had no intention of finding out what might happen if either of them were to prick themselves, so they wore thin leather gloves for the experimenting.

They tried several times and discovered that the needle trick worked reliably to detect the complete talisman. It would not detect the stoneless ring Azee had surrendered to them—but it shivered a bit if you got the ring close enough.

The next problem was that a bit of cork floating in a basin of water failed the requirement of being easily portable. Akhimah had to find a glassblower among the troops, convince one of the army's many blacksmiths to loan them his portable forge (getting the Empress's say-so helped there, at least), and then stitch padded leather harnesses to contain and cushion the resultant globes full of water with needles floating in them.

The globes had to be neither too small to be easily read nor so large they were extremely fragile. The bits of cork tended to stick to the edges, and the stoppers had a tendency to come out and spill water and enchanted and potentially cursed needles everywhere. The first problem was solved with a drop of soft soap in the water. The second was solved with wax.

Most annoyingly, though their talisman-detecting talismans showed promise, either there were no more of Ravani's poisoned gifts in the camp, or the detectors' ranges were too short . . or the detectors simply could not detect evil talismans other than the one they had been energized from.

Akhimah had an uneasy feeling that the last of those possibilities was the one most likely to be true. Maybe if they got another one close enough, it would cause a little shiver, like Azee's ring. But once they had a talisman in their hand, they wouldn't need the detector to find it.

* * *

"WELL," SAID TSERING-LA, AS THEY WANDERED DUSTY AND THIRSTY AND even more unslept than usual back toward the Empress's encampment in the dark of midafternoon, "if we got our hands on another example of Ravani's spellcraft, an intact one, maybe we could use it to tune the needles to a broader spectrum of sorcery."

Akhimah wiped gritty sweat from her forehead. "That's not the worst idea I've ever heard. But . . ."

"I know. We won't make it any easier for Mrithuri to win their loyalty if we have Tian soldiers start tossing Laeish billets, looking for contraband. Assuming we even knew what the contraband would look like."

"Probably studded with coral-colored sapphires," Akhimah said with poor grace. "Too cursed even to sell to pay soldiers."

Tsering-la pursed his lips and tipped his head from side to side. "Too cursed to sell *ethically.*"

THE FOLLOWING MORNING, AKHIMAH WAS SO TIRED, SHE FELL ONTO HER PALlet as soon as the tent was pitched. Rocks, lumps in the bedroll, her empty and grumbling stomach: none of it mattered.

It seemed that she had barely closed her eyes when she was blinking them open again—gritty, unfocused, and aching. Somebody was hissing at her from the low doorway.

She pushed herself up on her elbows and said, "If you haven't brought coffee, I am going to turn you into a frog."

"Don't tell me your lot have been holding out on us with transformation magic," Tsering-la said, ducking to enter.

She bared her teeth at him, but he squatted and held out a tray upon which perched a tiny steaming stoneware cup. "How on earth—"

"You're not the first Aezin I've met in this lifetime," he said, with a grin.

She buried her face in the coffee, which was sweet and bitter and almost as gritty as the corners of her eyes. While she was blowing and taking tiny sips that still scorched her tongue, he put the tray aside and rested his patched elbows on the patched knees of his trousers. Hard travel had faded everyone's magnificence.

"What if it *is* sapphires?" he asked.

Akhimah moved the coffee away from her lips. It had been so long since she had tasted any that she could feel it sizzling through her veins already. "We don't have a lot of orange sapphires just lying around—"

"No," said Tsering-la. "But we could just . . . detect all kinds of sapphires."

She sipped coffee. It had cooled enough now that she could let it sit on her tongue before she swallowed. "Hmm. You'd wind up with so many false positives. There are a lot of ways for that to end badly."

"Sure. Story of every Wizard's life, I imagine."

The bottom of the cup was thick with grounds. Akhimah swallowed it anyway, leaving a trail of sediment behind. She studied it, winced, and held it out to Tsering-la. "Do you know how to divine with these?"

He shook his head. "Good news?" he said, mock-hopefully.

"Well, it augurs success in our endeavors. Which I suppose means that there are evil talismans to be found, if we can but find them."

"Great," he said. "Now, who do we know in this army camp who might have some sapphires?"

Nizhvashiti had sapphires, in a predictable turn of events. Some time after the Wizards spoke to Hnarisha and asked him to check around, the Godmade sought them out. Withdrawing a hand from its pocket, it produced a fine gold chain linked at either end to a looped pin. On the bar of the pin were threaded a few dozen or so drilled translucent stones, organized by color into a muted rainbow.

Nizhvashiti uncurled fingers that seemed stiff as twigs and laid the chain gently in Akhimah's palm. "Will this serve?"

It served.

They did, as predicted, uncover some contraband.

The Wizards considered themselves clever for first trying the prototype sapphire detector within the confines of the royal encampment. If they were going to offend already-touchy troops by tossing their bedrolls, they wanted to make sure the technology worked, first.

The first time the detector flickered, Akhimah suffered a surge of unpleasant, intrusive memories of Chaeri's unmasking and escape—because it pointed directly to the low tent being used by the Lady Golbahar. Akhimah winced from an imagined twinge in her nearly healed hand and shared a nervous glance with Tsering-la.

He said, "I'll just see if Vidhya is free."

He returned in a little time with the guard captain in tow. Together, they approached the tent, and Vidhya and Tsering-la kept watch while Akhimah—elected because she was the woman—went through Golbahar's underthings as tidily as possible.

She had just opened a coffer to uncover a bag that clicked promisingly—thereby making her heart sink—when she heard Vidhya say, "Lady, my apologies, but please wait where you are."

"I beg your— Oh, you're looking for sorcery, aren't you? Go ahead; never mind."

Akhimah turned around to see the lady with her arms crossed, her darkened eyebrows arched in amusement. Akhimah held up the bag, which was silk and several layers thick.

"A portion of my wedding goods." Lady Golbahar cast her eyes down, lashes fluttering. "My dowry."

Akhimah rather thought that, behind her veil, Golbahar was smirking. The Wizard picked the bag open with her fingernails—not all of the twinges in her hand were imaginary—and peered through the earrings and nose rings and finger rings and arm rings and necklaces within. A pair of dark blue earrings and a matching necklace caught her eye, so she plucked them out.

"Try it now," she told Tsering-la.

The needle in its glass bubble swerved toward the blue stones and did not react at all to what remained in the bag.

"Looks like it works," Akhimah said. "Thank you for being our test subject." She handed jewelry and bag back to Golbahar.

"Charmed," Golbahar said, holding the earrings up to the light.

The next time the needle twitched, they were near the great royal tent Mrithuri had inherited from her late and unlamented husband, and which she was now sharing with Sayeh Rajni. At first, Akhimah thought the detector must be responding to whatever jewelry Mrithuri might have kept back, or perhaps to the royal stores of currency. But as they grew closer to the billowy orange-and-blue monstrosity and the needle began to depress the bit of cork into the water because it was pointing downward so strongly, the Wizards realized that it was indicating the bottom edge of the tent.

Akhimah considered herself enough of an authority in the court that she didn't see a need to send a runner to fetch the Empress. So she hunkered down again and this time drew a knife, and began to unpick the stitching along the tent's hem. There was something inside, a series of small smooth weights to keep it from flapping in the wind.

"Common river rocks," Akhimah said, as Tsering squatted down to see what she spilled into her hand. "Look, white quartz weathered smooth. Granite. All water-worn."

Tsering pointed with his chin. "That one might be a river rock, but these others aren't. Or if they are, they're very *uncommon* ones."

One by one, Akhimah held them up and away. On the sixth stone, the needle flickered.

"Huh," she said. "So he was smuggling jewels with the ballast."

"Not a bad place to hide some emergency money," Tsering-la said later in Akhimah's tent, as Akhimah used beakers of oil and her scales to confirm which stones were jewels and which were the more common sort of smooth rock. The diamonds were easy: they had a distinctive crystal structure. But what bit of quartz was tumbled, unpolished amethyst or citrine, and what was merely a rather hard stone?

"Sure," Akhimah said. "Until you have to take to your heels without pulling your trousers on first, and leave all your kit behind."

Tsering-la snorted. "You know that's one possibility that probably never distressed His Competence."

It was the Dead Man, unsurprisingly, who provided the idea of combining their search for evil talismans with a barracks inspection. Well, Akhimah supposed it couldn't be a barracks inspection when there was no barracks to inspect, just rows of bedrolls interspersed with the tents of those whose rank rated them. But she had no idea what to call it, otherwise. Perhaps just an *inspection* inspection.

That meant they had to use the Laeish noncoms to carry out the bulk of the work, but that was as much an advantage as not. The Tians wouldn't be blamed for the inconvenience, and the Laeish—even the officers—didn't need to know what the inspections were for. Just that a member of the Tian army would be joining each of them in order to observe and learn.

The noncoms might not like that, but casting them in the role of teachers would soften the blow. The Tian soldiers had orders not to interfere unless they had reason to think something was hidden and not being discovered.

They also were not told exactly what they were looking for. Just that if they found anything that made their detectors twitch, they were to slide it into a silk bag (provided) without touching it with their bare hands, and without allowing anyone else to touch it, either. And then they were to detain whoever the object seemed to belong to, and summon one of the empress's personal guard immediately.

Akhimah could catch up on her sleep, finally, because the whole affair would be carried out most smoothly if she and Tsering-la were nowhere in evidence. The more Wizards hanging about, the more suspicious everything would seem. Somebody would come and get her if it was deemed important. Her standards had fallen so far that a little rest seemed like an incredible luxury.

She was sound asleep when the attack came.

She might have died in that sleep. She would have died in that sleep, if she had not been a Wizard who, through her origins and training, knew a little of the Aezin and the old Sahali arts of geomancy. She had built wards and warnings into the design of her living space—such living space as it was—and she had built workings to discourage vermin.

The anti-pest spell was effective. Akhimah spent the rare hours when she did get to sleep pleasantly free of biting insects.

It was the destruction of that spell that warned her.

She came abruptly awake in the darkness, aware of the oppressive heat of day seeping through the tent walls. Something else was with her. Something had pushed through her spell with an agency no such creature should have been able to muster on its own. She thought the force of the spell breaking had overturned a candlestick and one of her carefully placed sandals, disarraying the order of the objects that sustained the enchantment.

Rats and scorpions were not well-known for their strength of will. Whatever this was, it had shoved through the aversion, brushed aside the discomfort. And now it was in the tent with her, slipping through the dark. She could not sense its location, only deduce its presence. She must assume that it was seeking her. That it had been sent. And that it meant her ill.

She could call out for help. There were guards all over the camp, and Tsering-la's tent was right beside her own. But anyone who entered would be a target as well.

The tent was as hot as a womb, and darker. She wished she had Tsering-la's ability to summon baubles of witchlight with a thought. If she moved, would it attack?

She strained her ears and heard nothing. She thought of the corrupted birds that had assailed Sarathai-tia at Ravani's behest. Did something like that wait above her, ready to pluck out her eyes?

Well, if Ravani was sending monstrous emissaries to hunt her in her sleep, it was a sign they were looking in the right direction.

Akhimah sat bolt upright among the tangles of her sweat-creased linen coverlet before she remembered that she was frozen with apprehension. Tsering! If some eldritch assassin had been sent for her, there was probably one in his tent as well. And he wouldn't feel it creeping in.

He'd hear her yell, however.

She took a breath. In the pitch blackness a heavy body slithered. *Snakes!* Or a snake, at least. *One for me and one for Tsering-la . . .*

Her pallet on the ground didn't give her the option of scrambling up and away as a bed would. Her breath held, that scream on edge at the back of her throat, she felt something rustling along the border of the reed mat, something dragging a scaled belly over each rush so they twitched under her thigh. If she strained her vision, she could convince herself of a long shape moving against the pale margin.

She heard it, though. She definitely heard it. The individual tick of each reed stem against the belly scales, soft as wind in grass but much more definite. And she had a knife beside her pillow.

If she could reach the knife without being bitten. She did not think she would care to be bitten by any creature corrupted by Ravani. And she assumed that if Ravani were corrupting serpents, she would have saved a step and chosen a poisonous one.

The heavy curve of a body brushed her leg, startling that teetering scream out of her.

A huge flare of yellow light burned through the tent walls. Before she lost it in the dazzle, Akhimah's dark-adapted eye saw the outline of a snake longer than she was tall as its head swung toward the sudden incandescence. Screaming didn't stop her from acting. Navigating by memory, she snatched for the knife.

She cut herself as she whipped her hand around, letting momentum throw the sheath aside. She couldn't see the snake. She slashed blindly at where it had been, using the long side of the knife. She hit dirt and rushes, yanked her hand back, and heard the thump as the snake lunged for the motion but missed her arm.

Now she knew where it was. There were some advantages to the damn thing being the size of a caravan.

She slashed again, bruising her knuckles on the earth through the ground cloth. *Don't break your hand again.*

Cold blood spilled over her fingers and splashed her thigh. Sightlessly, she slashed again. Something that felt like a leather belt with sand weights inside slapped her hand, knocking the knife flying. She scrambled away, scuttling like a crab. The tent wall caught her.

She went to knuckle her eyes, but the stickiness on her left hand stopped her. She blinked, and blinked again. The yellow light was still burning, less fiercely now. It was the color of Tsering-la's magic.

Akhimah could see the snake, half-beheaded, coiling and thrashing in a pool of blood that spurted with every contraction of its heart. She grabbed at a robe to cover her nakedness and fumbled the knife up again. It had fallen by the door.

Poor snake. It's not your fault you got enspelled.

Barefoot, belt fluttering, she stumbled into what should have been the darkness of day and found herself plunged into a confusion of lanterns and running men. She danced about for a moment, avoiding their boots, realizing that it was brighter without than within, and that the beacon of light was coming from inside Tsering-la's tent.

Someone caught her elbow, steadying her. Akhimah managed not to reflexively knife them. It was Hnarisha, who opened his mouth to speak but never got the words out.

Something sizzled. The acrid smell that followed told Akhimah it wasn't meat, which was . . . sort of a relief, she supposed. The robe flapped around her ankles as she sprinted toward Tsering's tent.

None of the soldiers seemed ready to go charging in. Akhimah's stride broke as she saw they had drawn back into a ring, holding swords, holding lanterns. Except the one who had his hands raised, and nothing in them.

Only amateurs need to wave their hands around. The memory of Jharni the Eyeless One's voice echoed in Akhimah's inner ear.

"Hnarisha," she said, but he had seen it too and was already racing forward.

"Grab him!" he yelled to the soldiers. Akhimah would have to trust them to handle it. She resumed her interrupted lunge toward Tsering's tent and whipped the door hanging aside.

Tsering-la stood there, clad in his shirt-sleeves and a pair of carpet slippers, surrounded by a wall of brilliant yellow light that outlined him like an enlarged carapace.

He looked up at Akhimah, frozen in the doorway, and blinked.

His brow furrowed. "You have blood all over you."

"Somebody tried to kill me. You too, I presume?"

"They bit you?" The flare of light died, collapsing back into his skin as he took two quick steps toward her.

"They?" she said. "You got more than one?"

He stopped, outreached hand dropping back to his side. "What attacked you?"

"A snake," she answered. "You got . . . several snakes?"

She felt a little offended in her dignity or her professional pride or whatever. Did Ravani take her less seriously because she was a woman?

He threw back his head and laughed until tears started in the corners of his eyes, and he had to grab the door pole for support. Akhimah knew it was the hysteria of death averted. She couldn't help but start to chuckle too.

"Mosquitoes," he said. "Fucking plague vectors."

Somebody yelped behind them. Akhimah remembered the scuffle and whirled to see if Hnarisha and the soldiers needed help. She had the sense to rotate away from the door, so Tsering-la was beside her in an instant.

They were not needed. Unfortunately. Hnarisha and the other men were staggering backward as the soldier who had been making the gestures sparked, fizzed, and began to burn. Flame so hot it was nearly invisible raced over his skin, setting his clothes alight, leaving charcoal in its wake.

"Shit," Akhimah said. "So much for asking questions."

Tsering echoed her earlier thoughts. "Well, now we know we're looking in the right direction, since we're attracting attention."

"If that's attention, I'd hate to experience focus." Akhimah fumbled for her belt and finally tied the front of her robe. "I guess he must be keeping an eye on us. Still, *shit*," she said again.

She waved to the crumbled pile of char on the ground.

"Yeah," said Tsering.

Hnarisha, panting, straightened up. He lifted one hand, displaying a wad of silk. An embroidered handkerchief. With something wrapped in the folds that glimmered in the lanternlight, orange-pink.

"No." Tsering-la broke into a grin.

"It was around his neck on a cord," said Hnarisha. "Don't worry; I haven't touched it."

"I could kiss you," Akhimah crowed.

"Please don't," said Hnarisha, but he was grinning. "Are you both unhurt?"

Tsering-la was inspecting his arms anxiously. "I don't think they got me. There was a swarm." He sighed and looked up. "I guess I'll find out if I show any welts by evening."

Akhimah held out her hand. "I cut myself with my own knife. Bloody amateur."

Hnarisha bent over her. Tsering-la dimmed his light again. That was good, because a horrible headache had begun tightening behind Akhimah's eyes. It eased, one throb at a time, along with the sting in her hand as Hnarisha touched her lightly.

He said, "Mosquitoes, huh? If he can do that, why doesn't he just send disease pests to sicken the whole army?"

"Because he wants a fight," Tsering said. "And he doesn't much care who wins it just as long as the whole thing is sufficiently nasty."

"Because a *lot* of mosquitoes would be a huge investment in energy," Ata Akhimah added.

Nizhvashiti drifted toward them, its robes seeming an extension of the darkness that trailed after it. "I believe Tsering-la is correct," it said. "The more we fight, the more we are divided—the stronger the beast becomes."

Akhimah almost bit her knuckle before she remembered it was covered in snake blood. "It can't break through, can it?"

Nizhvashiti's head inclined. A nod. "If we make it strong enough, it can."

THEY HADN'T BEEN GOING TO WAKE MRITHURI TO TELL HER, BUT THE RUCKUS had handled the waking for them. She sent a sleepy-eyed Golbahar to fetch them just as Akhimah was starting to wonder if she would be able to sneak away, set her wards up again, and go back to bed. If she had wanted to be short of rest, food, and baths, she would have chosen a less-comfortable career than court astronomer.

Oh, well. There was always something. At least Golbahar brought along a footman with water to wash in and gave her time to pull on a pair of trousers while he took the cobra carcass away. Tsering-la would want to dissect it as soon as possible. Seeing it in the light, Akhimah was relieved she hadn't known what kind of snake she was dealing with.

Around that time, Nizhvashiti vanished. It had a disconcerting habit of going silently missing when you took your gaze away.

By the time they reached Mrithuri's tent, the Empress Dowager was sitting up on a cushion, drinking tea, apparently having given up on any plans she might have had to go back to sleep. Which meant that nobody else was getting any more either. And Akhimah still had to clean up the snake blood.

Akhimah sighed and accepted the tea when Golbahar offered it around.

Sayeh and Ümmühan were present also, along with the girl Nazia and Mrithuri's and Sayeh's particular personal guards. It was always amusing to watch the Dead Man lift his veil and slip a cup beneath it. Especially when he burned his tongue.

Observing the tea incident out of the corner of her eye, Akhimah realized that the vertical pillar behind him, which she had taken for part of the structure of the pavilion, was actually the Godmade swathed in its tattered black robes.

"I'm sorry if the yelling woke you, Your Abundance," Akhimah said, when tea had been passed to everyone. She thought it wasn't the first time the leaves had been brewed. Would the troops think less or more of their leader to know she shared their shortages?

Something to discuss with Ümmühan.

"Actually"—Mrithuri's tone was astringent enough to tan leather—"it was the enormous conflagration."

Tsering-la shifted uncomfortably. It seemed like a bad time to point out that he had caused no fire, only light, so Akhimah did not bother.

Mrithuri continued, "Did you catch him?"

"Er," said Hnarisha.

The Empress Dowager raised her eyebrows.

"He spontaneously combusted," Hnarisha said. He held out the wad of silk. "We got a talisman, however."

"Barren Mother," Mrithuri swore. Akhimah was a foreigner, and not any more devoted to the local gods than she had to be for the sake of appearances, but she saw a couple of the others look aside or smirk, embarrassed by the blasphemy. "I want to string the body up on a pole as a warning to anybody else who might sell themselves to that sorcerer. They should know how she will honor their service."

The Dead Man rocked forward slightly, as if seeing merit.

Hnarisha said, "It burned to ash."

Ümmühan held her hand up. "Just as well. Stringing up bodies might be unproductive."

Nazia stage-whispered, "But satisfying."

Ümmühan made a pirouetting gesture with her hands. Akhimah did not know what it symbolized, but these Northerners had entire languages of gestures, even more elaborate than the stories the Lotus Kingdoms told through ritualized dance.

Hnarisha sighed. "Very satisfying. But with the likely effect of turning morale further against us."

"Yes," said Sayeh. Her voice was a husky murmur, but the authority in it still silenced the room. "But in the absence of a body, I think Ümmühan can probably spin enough of a morality play out of the agent's immolation to help our cause. If the empress agrees, she could even suggest that anyone who has accepted a gift from Ravani might be pardoned and protected if they surrender it to us."

Mrithuri's lips tightened, then relaxed reluctantly. She set aside her tea. "Fine."

"That has the advantage of getting us more talismans," Akhimah said.

"Which we can use to find even more of them," added Tsering-la. "I mean, we hope. Some of them, anyway."

"Now we can test the detectors on this one," Hnarisha said.

"We will be in Sarathai-lae before we can find all of them," the Godmade said in its rustling voice, making Akhimah jump embarrassingly.

Mrithuri picked up her tea again. "Is that a prophecy?"

"No," said the Godmade. "But I have a good idea of the size of your army. And I looked at a map."

14

Dusty, thirsty, road-weary, and not a little triumphant, the Dowager Empress and her people came into Sarathai-lae. Sayeh chose to ride the elephant a little behind Mrithuri, as befitted her rank. She had made herself as magnificent as possible under the circumstances—weighed down with mirror-embroidered silk and bells, a gilt headdress woven into hair that needed washing even more now that it had been dressed in scented oils to hide the way the road dust dulled it.

Mrithuri was slim and straight in shining white, and the only jewels upon her body were the Queenly Tiger in her navel and the wedding bangles on her wrists. She looked older than her years, and out of flesh, and Sayeh worried for her.

No one farther away could have seen that she was drawn, however, so cunningly had Golbahar made up her cheeks and lips to provide the illusion of health and color. Her eyes were pools of kohl whose direction could be read from as far away as anyone could have seen her face at all.

Sayeh had hoped to see the time away from the serpents bringing renewal to Mrithuri. But whatever health she had gained at first from giving up her drug, she had lost again to the rigors of travel.

Still, her people cheered her. They lined the streets and waved pennants and threw dyed rice in blessing. They leaned from balconies and dropped the petals of marigolds. Sayeh was sure she was not the only one who watched the Dead Man and Mrithuri's guardian bear-dog both fret, and circle, and stare first one way then another as they struggled to train their senses in all directions at once.

It was a gamble. To let the people see Mrithuri, to let them close enough to her to feel as if they had personally been recognized by their Empress—it built a bond. It made them feel like *her* people.

It also gave them the opportunity to strike against her. If anyone would risk the wrath of the Mother by raising a hand to Her priestess, or the wrath of the land by raising a hand to its Empress. Or if they were under the influence of Ravani and her damned cursed baubles. There were probably plenty in the city who were.

The Wizards' sweeps of the army had turned up several more talismans—two of which had been in the possession of soldiers who swore they did not know the rings were among their belongings—and Ümmühan had encouraged three more to turn their rings in with promises of lenience.

Her effectiveness was probably not hurt, Sayeh suspected, by word of the incinerated soldier having gotten around.

But there were no doubt more secret assassins concealed in the ranks, biding their time. Waiting for what, Sayeh did not know.

She tried to pull her thoughts back. She could not afford to think about it now. It would be an embarrassment to her rank and to the Empress Dowager if she started rocking with panic, thinking about all the ways this progress could go wrong.

Besides, the Dead Man and Syama were worrying enough for everyone. Sayeh should strive to be more like Hathi, who paraded along with her trunk lifted, waving her ears with pleasure at everyone applauding her.

You only come into a city for the first time once, Sayeh thought, and decided that if the professionals were there to worry about their safety, she would focus on noticing other things.

The first of those was that Sarathai-lae was not built of the same grim granite as Ansh-Sahal, or the wood and adobe and brown stone of muddy Chandranath. Nor even of the golden translucent marble of Sarathai-tia.

No, it was a city of shining white and blue—marble and lapis lazuli and blue tiles from far Asitaneh, brought by ship down the Arid Sea. That was not all that came by ship, either: Sayeh saw rich clothing in a dozen styles and faces of a dozen complexions. She saw turbans dyed blue or brown or orange, and headwraps in bright prints, and a man sweating in a fur-lined cap that he must have brought with him, stubbornly, a relic of whatever cold climate had spawned him.

She saw a man with more tattoos than Mrithuri, shockingly blue against skin that was shockingly pale. His straight, braided hair had been dark once, though it was graying fast. She saw a woman darker than Ata Akhimah, her skin reflecting blue highlights from the Heavenly River overhead. She saw houses five or six stories tall, their upper floors ringed with metal balconies and hung with flower gardens.

Sarathai-tia might be the once-capital of the fallen empire, but there was no mistaking that Sarathai-lae's place as the rich hub of trade.

The jealousy of the Daughters for each other made perfect sense to Sayeh. How could the Mother give so much to some of her children and so little to the others?

As if reading her mind, Nazia leaned forward and whispered near her ear. "What are you thinking, Rajni?"

"That I would like to trade cities with these people," Sayeh admitted.

Nazia chuckled. "I was thinking I'd like to burn it all down."

"Stone doesn't burn well," Golbahar said from behind them, her voice as dry as Nizhvashiti's flesh. "Consider using black powder."

They had not brought the whole army into the city, which was just as well. The boulevards were broad and straight, with long sight lines. As they came within view of the palace grounds, it was evident that the soldiers would have filled up the whole of the route from city walls to castle gates, with plenty left over. Sarathai-lae was wealthy, then, but not vast.

That was, on some level, reassuring.

Some people dealt with the fear of meeting new people by imagining them naked. Sayeh preferred to imagine all the palace inhabitants scrambling to make ready for their new and unknown empress, rushing to and fro, scrubbing floors and bringing in armloads of flowers. She looked at Mrithuri's hands clenched on her trousers and leaned forward herself to whisper, "They need to impress you more than you need to impress them."

Mrithuri gave her a tight little smile. Sayeh wished she could lay a hand on the young woman's shoulder and comfort her. Rajni, empress, dowager, precariously holding on to a position of power she might lose at any time— and half Sayeh's age. It was unfair what the Mother asked of so many of them.

A runner came out of the palace ahead, feet slapping in a street swept so clean that no puffs of dust followed his sandals. The gate—gilded ironwork— stayed open behind him. Mrithuri's vanguard moved to intercept, and the slim young man bent himself low.

He held up a scroll bound in a great number of ceremonial ribbons and dangling an orchard of dull lead and bright wax seals. One of the men took it and brought it to Vidhya, who was the ranking officer present. Pranaj and Zirha had stayed outside the walls with their armies.

Vidhya accepted it with all due ceremony and reined his mincing horse back until Hathi caught up. He held the scroll out, and there were gasps and cheers from the onlookers as Hathi plucked it daintily from his hand with her trunk and passed it up to Mrithuri. While the elephant walked on, Mrithuri passed it to Sayeh. "Read it to me."

Sayeh was not entirely confident in her ability to read the southern dialect of Sarathani with clarity, but—well, when the empress says "Go and die," one does one's best.

She broke the seals, unknotted the ribbons, and by the time they passed under the arch of the gate, she had puzzled the words out as well as she was likely to.

Within lay a courtyard, meant for reception and not defense. Mrithuri's honor guard fanned out, facing a revue of what must have been palace guards and various dignitaries.

"It's from the chancellor," Sayeh said. "He offers greetings and the usual assurances. He says that you will be guided to your private apartments, and once you have refreshed yourself, he will attend at your convenience."

Mrithuri turned and looked over her shoulder. Her lips pursed. "Oh, shall he?" she drawled.

Sayeh smirked. "The power grab begins already."

Mrithuri lifted her chin: an implicit command. Sayeh knew what to do. Leaning down, she handed the scroll back to Vidhya.

"Send me Sergeant Sanjay, would you?" She'd made sure that her favorite members of Mrithuri's army—the ones who had been her guards, when she was Anuraja's prisoner—came into the city. She was now pleased with her foresight.

Sanjay was with them in a moment. Up ahead, functionaries intoned meaningless greetings in loud voices. It was Hnarisha on their side, and some man in a sleeveless, embroidered, open-fronted long coat that looked like a token of office on the other.

Sayeh leaned down, steadying herself with one hand, and spoke in a low voice. "Do you know where the apartments that belonged to Anuraja are?"

He nodded. Sayeh hid her smirk. Anuraja's tendency to command his men directly was useful to them once again. As was his tendency to mistreat them, which had enabled her to make the ones she'd befriended fast allies in so little time.

"Catch me," Sayeh said, and slid down the elephant's shoulder.

Surprised, Sanjay caught her, lowered her more or less gently to her feet, and stepped back.

Sayeh said, "Give Her Abundance a hand down and lead us to the raja's rooms, would you? Send . . . oh, send Nazia, with a couple of loyal soldiers who know the way, to put eyes on the princes and protect them. And get somebody to tell that chancellor that he's wanted immediately. Not later. He can bring the snacks himself, if he requires them."

Sanjay's eyes cut sidewise. "Where were *they* sending her?"

"Lord Chancellor Dehan hasn't specified, but at a guess it'll be some consort's apartment."

"Oh, no," he said. "That won't do at all."

"Don't worry," Sayeh said. "We'll soon have it all handled."

The palace staff protested. The raja's rooms were not ready. It was not fitting. There were no facilities for a noble lady in that place.

Sanjay, delighting Sayeh, nodded politely and walked right past them, leading the rest of Mrithuri's inner circle forward in a knot with Mrithuri at the center. Guang Bao perched on Sayeh's bare fist, so gentle with his talons that she did not need a glove. He had started to molt out the repaired feathers and looked less motley but more threadbare.

Syama paced at Mrithuri's side, nails clicking on the elegant tiles. Her quiet watchfulness and muscled size no doubt helped limit the strenuousness of any protests.

The interior of the palace was cool and shady. Arched colonnades caught the sea breezes, and Sayeh became aware that the scent of the Arid Sea, which she had not yet glimpsed, was very different from that of the Bitter Sea. Fresher, but also more rank, as if a great deal of organic material were composting along its margins.

This palace was not a citadel built for defense but a gigantic airy house, gracious and sprawling. The rajas of Sarathai-lae obviously relied on their ability to pay good soldiers and sailors—and lots of them—in order to stay safe.

It seemed like a long walk to get to the raja's apartments that were the Empress Dowager's apartments now. Sayeh's leg hurt, but not more than usual. She had become strong on the road, and her limp was now more a matter of the bone not having healed straight than one of weakness. The door stood open: there was a guard outside, and a flurry of just-commenced cleaning within.

Sayeh walked past the guard as if she had every right to be there, enjoying his consternation as he reached for her arm, saw the phoenix on her fist, did a double take, and snatched his own hand back again.

"Your Abundance!" he protested.

"Never mind," Mrithuri said, a step behind her. She turned her attention to the flurrying in the room, as servants loaded with armfuls of books and papers and miscellaneous other objects turned toward the newcomers, looking just as shocked.

Sayeh said, "What are you doing? Put those things down!"

They stared like rudely awakened children. One dropped an armload of scrolls, the wooden spool cases clattering.

They looked at one another, obviously at a complete loss. In the doorway, the guard cleared his throat. "Begging your pardon, Your Abundances. The Lord Chancellor ordered the raja's personal belongings put away."

Mrithuri held up her right hand. "My *husband's* belongings will stay right where they are. Out with all of you!"

She didn't have to snap twice. They scurried away like startled mice, leaving behind a scene of disarray.

Sayeh turned in time to catch the guard in the process of withdrawing. "Have someone bring tea," she told him. "And some sweets."

He completed his vanishment with a mumbled acknowledgment. Mrithuri looked at Sayeh as others filed into the room: Golbahar, Ata Akhimah, the

Dead Man, Ümmühan, Hnarisha, Tsering-la, and Nazia. Vidhya glanced around the doorpost and said, "Empress, I will guard this entrance."

"Thank you, Captain," Mrithuri replied. Sayeh contemplated protesting that her own guard captain's first loyalty should be to her, not to Mrithuri. But he had been working with the empress and her people directly for some time while Sayeh had been captive. And Mrithuri, through an accident that Sayeh had in part engineered, now held the higher rank.

She would worry about re-establishing her chain of command in a less critical moment.

For now, she simply crouched—thrilling a little with her ability to do so—and began collecting the scattered papers and books.

"Leave it," Mrithuri said, sinking onto a cushioned bench beside the window with a sigh. She kicked her sandals off.

"Let me make them safe, at least."

Mrithuri smirked. "Let this Chancellor find out how effective his tactics are. Then we can have them tidied, and go through them at our leisure to discover what in the contents needed hiding so badly."

Ata Akhimah said, "Do you think he's likely to get here before the tea? Because I for one would enjoy reading them."

"I think he's likely to make us wait as long as he thinks he can get away with."

"Mm." Sayeh put the books down and sat on a cushion as well. "Sergeant Sanjay, thank you for your assistance. If you would join Captain Vidhya at the door? If Lord Chancellor Dehan shows up before the tea, let him in. If he doesn't, keep him waiting but let us know of his arrival."

"Your Abundance," Sanjay said. He bowed and turned to thread his way past bear-dog and courtiers. He stopped and turned back. "Your Abundances," he said. "I should tell you that now that we are home again, there has been renewed muttering among the soldiers."

"They'll be paid soon," Mrithuri said.

Assuming Dehan hasn't stripped the treasury. Sayeh wondered how many of the scrolls and volumes scattered about the floor might be ledgers. Accountings that could be used to prove how much money the kingdom should have and where it ought to be held.

Sanjay cleared his throat. "It's not that. There are men now saying openly that we ought to join Sekira, that he's raising an army. That a Dowager isn't an Empress. That there ought to be a revolution. Begging your pardon, Your Abundance."

"Who is spreading this sedition?" Sayeh asked.

"I don't know the root of it," Sanjay said apologetically. "Things were quiet after"—he glanced at Ata Akhimah, who had folded her hands together and leaned forward with interest—"the assassination attempt and the result. Maybe people turned away from Ravani then. But now . . ."

He shrugged.

"Something loves fighting," said Tsering-la. "It gets no joy if we avoid a civil war."

"Is he nearby?" Mrithuri asked. "Sekira?"

Sanjay shrugged. "Maybe."

"And Sekira thinks he ought to be a prince, is that it?" The Dead Man's voice came dry through his veil.

"That's one version. Another is that the army should back Himadra or his brothers."

"A child would be a useful pawn," Mrithuri said. "What about—pardon, Sayeh—Prince Drupada?"

Sayeh smiled tiredly. There was no keeping a royal child from being used as a pawn. Not once his father was dead. Not when he had fallen into the hands of the enemy.

"Fewer support him," Sanjay said. "And anyway, he's with Lord Himadra."

"I imagine," said Ümmühan, "that once we wipe out Sekira, or Sekira wipes us out, Himadra will be encouraged to fight the surviving faction."

"Famine is coming," Sayeh said. "That's a good excuse to keep everyone feuding until all pretense of a government collapses."

Sanjay bowed deeply. "Shall I keep my ears open?"

"Yes, Sergeant," Mrithuri said. "And thank you. I will not forget what you have done for us this evening. Ask Vidhya to send someone to locate and guard the treasury, please. You shall remain, yourself, outside the door."

WHEN THE SERGEANT HAD LEFT, MRITHURI TURNED TO HER ASSEMBLED friends and retainers and said, "Well, we have a whole new barrel of politics to play now."

"And a joyous one." Hnarisha sighed.

Mrithuri transmuted the urge to scratch at her travel-dry skin with untidy nails—how unregal—into waving him onward.

"A raja on our tail, three princes young enough that any ambitious servant might think he could raise them to be biddable, and a government that's no doubt full of contrary civil servants to bring to rein."

"One of those princes is my son," said Sayeh.

Hnarisha inclined his head in acknowledgment. "No disrespect intended."

They were interrupted briefly by the arrival of tea. Sanjay smirked as he admitted the servants, then ushered them out again with Golbahar's request to bring further refreshments, as more guests were expected.

"Who knows," Sayeh said. "This Lord Chancellor Dehan might very well have either or both of Himadra's brothers under his thumb. How long have they been here?"

Ata Akhimah, Mrithuri noticed, was quietly piling some of the closer documents on the table in front of her.

"Most of their lives," Hnarisha replied. "Certainly, it seems unlikely that either of them remembers Chandranath or their family of origin."

Tsering-la, leaning against a pillar, folded his arms. "That might mean they don't have much loyalty to him. That might be useful."

The Dead Man commented, "Sometimes it is easier to have loyalty to an idea than to a person. People are complicated and messy. Ideas are sleek and clean."

It had the ring of personal knowledge. Mrithuri cocked her head at him, but she was still working out what she might have said when her speech was pre-empted by the sound of Sanjay outside the door, challenging some newcomer. Another voice answered, though the words did not ring clearly through wood and stone.

"Look like you belong," Mrithuri said.

Her people began arraying themselves about the chamber in attitudes of long possession. When the door opened, the only one that turned to look was the Dead Man, his hand on the butt of his gun.

Sanjay poked his head in and said, "The Lord Chancellor Dehan and assistants to see you, Your Abundance."

Mrithuri glanced over. There was a shape behind the guard. "Give us another quarter-hour."

She wasn't naive enough to think that it would teach him not to play games with her. But she couldn't be seen to rush to wait on anyone whose role was to serve her. She stretched her legs out for a moment. She was stiff with all the riding.

"Hnarisha, will you bring me a cup of tea?"

Ata Akhimah had claimed a low table on one side of the room. She began spreading the rescued papers upon it. Tsering-la sat down across from her and helped her sort things into piles. It was an act of will for Mrithuri not to ask what they were doing, and whether it was theatre or legitimate assessment.

Some of both, probably.

The second tray of tea arrived. Raised voices beyond the door heralded the servants before they entered with their trays held high. The Dead Man, who had been moving toward the commotion, relaxed when the Lord Chancellor did not barge in with the tea. Judging by the voices, Captain Vidhya must have returned, and he and Sergeant Sanjay had prevailed.

Tea and little cakes were passed around. Mrithuri was surprised to discover that she was famished. It had been so long since she felt an appetite for food that she made three cakes disappear in a matter of moments. And then felt slightly nauseated.

She was licking her fingers clean of the sticky honey glaze from the last one when Sanjay opened the door again and allowed three men in, each thinner and more mean-looking than the last.

The one in the center was doubtless the Lord Chancellor, by the height of his headdress and the richness of the cloth from which his severe tunic and trousers had been cut. Raw silk, natural ivory in color, spun so the texture of the nubbins along each woven thread was visible. Mrithuri wondered if he had taken the time to change into something near-white in order to mimic what she was wearing, or if they just both had similar ideas of how to dress to dominate a room full of colorful silks and vivid clothing.

The other two men flanked the Lord Chancellor. They dressed in more garish but less expensive clothing. One of the gold-flecked lapis stones in the Lord Chancellor's headdress would have bought the entire outfit of the man on his right, who was the tallest of the three. The one on the left rejoiced in a mustache that might have been sketched in with a stick of charcoal. He wore a particularly ingenuous expression around the eyes that Mrithuri did not trust for a moment.

Not one of them looked the least bit cowed. Well, that would come in time.

If Mrithuri was going to survive this.

She was not overjoyed to see that there were even more papers loaded into the arms of the secretaries, or aides, or whatever they were. Lord Chancellor Dehan apparently did not tote his own impedimenta.

Hnarisha was the person most nearly of equal rank to Dehan. He stepped forward and introduced himself—and the rest—with such flowery formality and precise etiquette that no one could have avoided taking offense.

But nor could anyone have found the grounds to claim it. Thus, they learned that the tall aide was Kannla; the ingenuous one with the mustache was Marnor. Mrithuri got bored and lost her attention halfway through the recitation of her own ranks, but hearing her given name at the end of it jolted her out of distracted thoughts.

She smiled. None of her people, other than Hnarisha, had risen. "Please," she said, taking the role of host. "Sit, and join us for tea."

The Lord Chancellor's mouth twitched, but when she gestured him toward a place along the side of the long table, he went. With a hand from Golbahar, Mrithuri rose, stepped to the head, and resettled herself, Syama padding alertly at her side. Dehan's aides sorted themselves out to either side of him, and Mrithuri gestured Lady Golbahar to the foot of the table. The Wizards stayed where they had been at the smaller table in the corner, sorting through piles of documents and muttering to one another. Hnarisha moved to Mrithuri's right hand, Sayeh to her left, and the Dead Man stood behind her. Ümmühan took a place across the table from Dehan, pretending obliviousness when he eyed her with distaste.

All these power plays, disguised as the most exquisite politeness. All of these strategies hidden beneath courtly manners. It could make one very tired, if one permitted.

Lady Golbahar served out the tea while the Lord Chancellor and his aides glowered. Dehan and Kannla did not fidget. Marnor twisted the ends of his mustache. His squirming reminded Mrithuri to keep her own hands still upon the table. Sayeh's impassive gaze reminded her to keep her face smooth, too.

When the tea had been shared, Mrithuri looked directly at the Lord Chancellor—no simpering, no indirection—and said, "You brought some documents for my review?"

Once you've grasped the upper hand, never let go.

She thought her unwomanly directness unsettled him, but he kept his expression under control and, sadly, did not immediately crumple.

"Contracts," Dehan said. "Letters from the . . . from your late husband. Documents pertaining to the succession."

Without being told, Ata Akhimah rose from her place amid the other scrolls. She picked her way over Tsering-la and assorted documents before coming to the Lord Chancellor. She held out one hand to the aide most burdened with reference material. He passed his armload over to her, and she made three trips to gather it all.

"These are copies?" she asked, once they had all been relinquished.

"The originals are in the Royal Archive," Dehan confirmed.

Ata Akhimah reclaimed her seat and became busy unrolling scrolls while Tsering-la thumbed through bound books, not having looked up at all.

"Aren't you going to read these?" Dehan demanded of Mrithuri. Supercilious but not quite sneering. Mrithuri wondered if she should have him assassinated. Prasana would no doubt be happy to do the job. But no, that would be obvious. And unethical. And probably result in no progress, just an obscuring of who the adversary was.

"Our Wizards will inform us of the substance of them," Mrithuri said casually. She saw Sayeh's mouth quirk at how she avoided *exactly* claiming Tsering-la's service while nevertheless implying it.

The Lord Chancellor lifted his chin, revealing a bony throat with a prominent larynx.

"They will," Mrithuri continued blithely, "acquaint me with the legal peculiarities involved, once they've had the time to review thoroughly. But perhaps you could give me the—the filet of it now?"

"Certainly," Dehan said. "Kannla is our legal scholar. I'll let him share the details."

Kannla cleared his throat, obviously surprised to be thrust center stage, and a little bit flustered. "Well, Your Abundance—that is to say—there is no precedent for a Dowager reigning, except as regent for a minor child."

"Mmm," Mrithuri said.

Ümmühan leaned forward, her native charisma commanding the attention of everyone gathered. Mrithuri concealed her amusement under regal serenity as the Lord Chancellor tried to dismiss the diminutive old woman—and failed.

The poetess said, "Is there precedent for a Dowager Empress who has a better claim by blood on the seat of Empire than her deceased spouse?"

Kannla sputtered. Mrithuri could tell already that Dehan would never allow himself to be moved to such a transparent display. With that emotional control, he might have been a woman.

He said, "That's a conjecture unsupported by the genealogy."

"I'm a historian," Ümmühan said familiarly. "Perhaps I'll do a little research while I'm here."

"After all," Golbahar added, "the Peacock Throne rejected Lord Anuraja's claim. *Most* unmistakably. Which would suggest that there was someone with a better claim."

"Indeed," Sayeh added. From where she was sitting, Mrithuri could not see the wink that Sayeh sent Golbahar, but she was utterly confident of its existence. "Perhaps there was some flaw in his bloodline. An inaccurate pedigree. There *are* conflicting versions of the line of descent."

Feigning boredom, Mrithuri dismissed it all with a wave of her hand. Whatever she had to do to stave off the giggles. The Lord Chancellor might have an excellent chaturanga face, but from the furrowed dismay of Kannla's expression, none of the Laeish dignitaries had expected a pack of women to run rings around them.

"The bloodlines," the Lord Chancellor said, "clearly indicate that the heir to Sarathai-lae should be Vivaan of Chandranath."

"Mmm," Mrithuri said. "Isn't he also the heir of Chandranath?"

"Perhaps," he said. His gaze flicked significantly toward Sayeh. "In any case, it does not matter if he is. The Kingdoms can be re-united."

"I'm glad you think so," Mrithuri drawled. "I will meet with him, of course. And Rayesh. Actually, I will host the princes for dinner tonight. Arrange it."

"Your Abundance!"

"Oh, don't pretend to be scandalized, Dehan. Just see to the invitations and the menu. Somebody in this palace must know what they like to eat."

He sputtered.

She smiled. "As for the rest of this"—she gestured—"it can all be discussed after our Wizards have reviewed the documents. In the meantime, I'm sure my generals will want to speak with you about the quartering and feeding of my army. If you would be so good, Lord Chancellor, as to arrange that meeting at your earliest convenience? Sergeant Sanjay, who you met on the way in, will be pleased to carry your messages."

The Lord Chancellor regarded her, inscrutable. "Yes, Your Abundance."

"Is there anything else you needed to discuss with me immediately?"

"No, Your Abundance."

Mrithuri steepled her naked fingers and smiled brightly over the tatty nails. She should see about a manicure. "Excellent. Then there won't be anything to prevent you from working with Hnarisha, here, to set up my calendar for the next few days."

"Your Abundance?"

"I need to meet the advisors, and the staff members, and the household, of course. The nobles and officials, the ladies-in-waiting, the gentlemen of the court. I expect a full schedule until I've been introduced to them all, down to the least runner, pot-scrubber, or chambermaid."

He stared.

She fixed that smile as if it were carved upon her. "As I said, please work with my confidential secretary on the arrangements. He understands my needs. Oh, and this is Lady Golbahar, my chief lady of the bedchamber. Please have her introduced to the ladies-in-waiting and the body servants." *Don't let that smile turn into a smirk, Mrithuri, or you'll ruin the whole effect.* "We are weary from the road. Does this palace have a baths?"

"Your Abundance . . . the raja never troubled himself with, with mundane details—"

"I know," Mrithuri interrupted. "But there are going to be some changes around here."

15

Hnarisha shot Mrithuri a bleak look as he escorted Dehan and his aides out the door. Mrithuri managed to keep from bursting into laughter until that door was safely shut and the footsteps had receded down the hall. Then she lay back on the cushions and laughed until she was forced to press her fists to a cramp above her hip bone and gasp to a stop.

When she opened her eyes, she found the Lady Golbahar leaning over her. Golbahar held out a dainty hand—somehow she had managed to keep *her* skin looking dewy—and assisted Mrithuri in rising. She sat up, breathless, and took stock.

"He's skimming off the royal treasury," Golbahar said.

"Of course he is," Mrithuri answered. "Is your bookkeeping good enough to catch him?"

Golbahar smirked.

Mrithuri leaned over on her elbow, looking toward the table where the Wizards were still sorting documents. Ümmühan had gone to assist. Watching them work so intently, Mrithuri felt as useless as a double thumb.

Perhaps she was easier to read than she thought, or perhaps Sayeh was more than usually perceptive. Whatever the cause, Sayeh came to stand at her elbow, crouched down—steadying herself on the table edge—and said, "Come on. Now would be the time to get cleaned up before that dinner. While they were leaving, I found out from Marnor where the baths are."

Baths. A magical word.

And trust Sayeh to have one of the enemy half-seduced already.

"Amazing," Mrithuri said. "Did it have to be the one with the mustache?"

"The one with the mustache doesn't have much self-love," Sayeh said. "The Lord Chancellor Dehan should be kinder to his subordinates if he expects to retain their loyalty."

She winked, a slow drape of kohled lashes across a cheek, and Mrithuri's insides squirmed. She could imagine what such a gesture would do to a downtrodden functionary.

She dusted her hands on each other to disguise her discomfiture and stood to join her royal cousin. "Lady Golbahar, are you coming?"

The Dead Man accompanied them—as did Syama. The bear-dog gave a less convincing impression of nonchalance than the warrior, and *he* kept one hand on the butt of his gun. Sayeh, Mrithuri noticed, still walked with a hitch, and her foot turned out slightly at an unusual angle. But she kept up well and had mostly abandoned both crutches and cane.

The long walk had been good for both of them.

Sayeh had either obtained very good directions or been poring over plans of the palace while Mrithuri kept the Lord Chancellor waiting as she drank tea she had been too distracted to remember the flavor of. Sayeh led them unerringly through a maze of corridors, along which bustling maids and bored guards snapped to attention when they realized who was passing. One dropped a dustpan. Another they caught mid-scratch, and he ducked his head between his shoulders and yanked his hand out from under his tunic, staring straight ahead.

"Well," Sayeh said, "The garden quarters would have been more convenient to the women's baths."

"Nothing about this is convenient," Mrithuri replied under her breath. Sayeh and Golbahar laughed out loud, and Syama bristled at the sudden sound.

They smelled the attar and sandalwood and felt the steam on the air before they came within sight of the baths. They abandoned the Dead Man—much to his chagrin—by the entrance, but Syama would not be left.

Rows of pierced screens—carved of rosewood, sandalwood, and perhaps other less familiar incense-trees—created a corridor through which one wound until privacy was achieved. Beyond the last screen was a young girl stationed by an array of baskets and cubbies. She jumped up as they came in sight, then bowed low over her rope belt when she identified them.

Word must have flown through the palace. "I'll need clean clothes," Mrithuri said. "And so will Sayeh Rajni and Lady Golbahar. Is there someone you could send?"

Big-eyed, the girl nodded. She wiped her hands on her undyed linen wrap. "Please give us a moment to prepare your bath, Dowager—"

"No need for anything special," Mrithuri said. "I am just here to get clean before tea."

Silently, the attendant offered towels and robes and combs and scrapers, and a tray of cleansers, soaps, unguents, and scrubbing sands. Sayeh took it all heaped in her arms, a queen acting as lady-in-waiting to an empress. Golbahar unfastened her veil with a sigh.

"This way," the girl said, and showed them.

The baths were something out of a fairy-story. Pierced and carved stone vaults hovered over a space made soothing with mosaics of lapis lazuli, malachite, and jade. Deep pools ranged like the petals of a flower, some steaming briskly and some apparently clear and cool.

Sayeh found a standing rack for their tray and towels, and together the women stripped out of their sweat-marked travel clothes. They used oiled cloths to clean the makeup from their faces and sluiced themselves off with dippersful of heated water from a cauldron. Sayeh scrubbed Mrithuri's hair, then Golbahar scrubbed Sayeh's and her own. Mrithuri would have offered, but there were other women in the baths, carefully ignoring the newcomers, and she had to perform the dignity due her rank. However much it made her want to roll her eyes.

The water felt incredible. Merely stripping off the stiff clothes had been an inexpressible relief. It was not the first time any of the women's outfits had been worn on their journey, and there was only so much airing and washing one could do in an army on the march. Actually being clean . . .

They rinsed the various pastes and scrubs from themselves, then climbed into the otherwise-unoccupied pool that seemed the hottest. For a moment, Mrithuri thought it would boil the tender skin of her arches. The tiles on the bottom were smooth and warm as she sank down into the water. Heat and buoyancy eased the stiffness in her legs, spine, neck.

You wouldn't think sitting on an elephant and sleeping in a cot would provoke such misery.

"I'm getting old." Mrithuri sighed.

"Yes, Your Abundance," Sayeh answered wryly. "In a year or two, you will be half my age!"

Mrithuri almost splashed water at her but remembered just in time: her Dignity.

Golbahar, whose wickedness was tempered by a natural dignity, let herself slide down and float, arms extended and long neck back, eyes closed. She seemed utterly unselfconscious and at peace, and Mrithuri looked down at her own scar-pecked torso and envied her.

To distract herself, she looked at Sayeh. "That must have been a hard journey for you."

Sayeh let the water lift her arms. "I've had worse."

Mrithuri thought about Sayeh's broken leg and how she had come all the way from Ansh-Sahal in a horse litter. "I suppose you have."

Sayeh swam a lazy backstroke across the pool. Mrithuri leaned her head against the ledge so she would not stare rudely at the scars on Sayeh's lame leg, or at the other marks upon her body. *It's none of your business,* she told herself firmly.

Animal curiosity was no excuse to be rude.

Sayeh turned and came back toward her. She was beautiful in the water, a strong swimmer. Mrithuri wondered if she had learned in the Bitter Sea. She glanced aside. Golbahar was watching also. Golbahar winked, much more saucily than Sayeh's earlier languorous performance, and Mrithuri was glad the heat of the baths meant her mortified flush would not be recognized.

Golbahar was such a blessing. The only friend Mrithuri had ever had of noble rank and close to her own age was Chaeri. They had been bound together since they were girls. As much grief and guilt as Mrithuri still felt about the loss of that friendship, she could see now that it had not been good for either of them.

Sayeh dove and broke the surface gasping. Steam rose from her head. With Sayeh cleansed of cosmetics, Mrithuri could see the fine lines at the edges of her eyes, the silver threads in the black masses of her hair. It did not, she thought, lessen Sayeh's legendary elegance or beauty.

She settled down against the wall beside Mrithuri, on the opposite side from Golbahar. "I want to live out the rest of my life in this water."

"Me too." Golbahar sighed. "But you'll get hungry and have to pee eventually."

"I'll eat fish," Sayeh said. "They'll already be parcooked. I wonder how they get the water so hot."

"Hypocausts," said Mrithuri. "The water flows through pipes over beds of coals and is circulated back into the pools. It cools as it flows out; that's why the hottest pool is the highest up."

"Huh," said Sayeh. "At home we have—we just had hot springs." Her voice caught a little. If her eyes were moist, it was explained by the steam. "The water welled up out of the rocks steaming and stinking. A terrible smell, but it felt good down to your bones. I wonder if the same volcano that destroyed Ansh-Sahal heated it."

There didn't seem to be a way to answer that. Golbahar broke the awkward silence by hoisting herself from the bath and padding naked across the wooden slats to fetch cups of cold water. While she was filling them, Mrithuri, without looking, reached out and rested her fingertips on Sayeh's shoulder.

For a moment, all she felt was stiffness and resistance. She was afraid she had made it worse. But then, with a sigh, Sayeh settled lower into the water and leaned her shoulder into Mrithuri's palm.

ATA AKHIMAH LOOKED UP FROM THE DOCUMENTS SHE HAD BEEN STUDYING. She pulled her spectacles down her nose to ease her aching eyes. Hnarisha sprawled backward on the pillows, a robe thrown across his legs, a scroll held above his face. Tsering-la had dozed off, his temples propped on his fists and his arms propped on his elbows.

"Hey," Akhimah said to the secretary, "look at this."

The scroll she had been studying was stiff and old. Rather than handing it to Hnarisha, she nodded him to her. Grumbling, he got to his feet. She held the document open on the table as he bent over her shoulder to read.

The hand was old-fashioned, the shapes of the words archaic. He mum-

bled under his breath, sounding it out. After a little time, he leaned back on
his haunches and looked at her. She had to crane her neck around to make
eye contact.

"The Peacock Throne can do all that?" he asked. "Raise up storms, call
rain? Pull mountains from the earth?"

"Well, small mountains. A big conical hill, anyway. We did know the
Alchemical Emperor raised the mount that Sarathai-tia sits upon—"

"Hmm," he said. "Once the Dowager is back, you need to show her that."

The unsettled feeling in her stomach was only getting worse. "It makes
me wonder what that pile of corpses in Ansh-Sahal that Nizhvashiti found
is for."

WHERE WERE THE WINGS THAT HAD BORNE HER UP ON AIR AS SECURELY AS IF
she stood upon stone? Where were the eyes that saw the minutest detail, the
flash of a stem of grass ruffled by some scampering creature? Where were
her feet like blades, heavy with talons?

Mrithuri sat at the table where she would soon take tea, and tried yet again
to discover how her far-flung subjects, allies, and enemies were faring. She
reached out to her familiars and found—yes, Hathi, and Syama. But beyond
them, she had only the sense that she had tossed a rope into the darkness and
it had fallen to earth, uncaught. The vultures were too far for her to reach, no
matter how she strained. Her range had been fading slowly while they traveled.

What was happening with Yavashuri? With the Gage? Was everyone in
Sarathai-tia still safe? Not knowing gnawed at her.

If only she had her serpents; if only she had not bargained away their
venom. Then she could reach her pets, see through their eyes, have an idea
what transpired back in Sarathai-tia and on the road with her cousin's rival
army.

A hand brushed her arm, soft and gentle. She opened her eyes to see
Golbahar, bent over and concerned.

It took a moment to shake herself back into her own body. She was
chilled despite the heat of the day. Somehow, Golbahar noticed and draped
a soft goat-hair shawl around her shoulders. "They're here."

Mrithuri glanced toward the door. The Dead Man stood on one side of
it, arms folded, impassive. Syama lay on the other, massive head on mighty
paws, eyebrows twitching. She might have been a strange sort of tiger, tawny
stripes on black instead of the other way around.

Mrithuri smoothed her plain ivory blouse under the vivid colors of the
shawl. "Let them in."

WHEN NAZIA BROUGHT THE BOYS INTO THE ROOM, THEIR HEADS WERE BENT
together and they all seemed to be giggling behind their hands. Their

distraction gave Mrithuri a moment to assess them. A moment she was grateful for, because given that time, she noticed a few things.

Actually, the younger lad isn't laughing. Rayesh smiled, but it was a tight smile, and he hid his mouth behind his hand. His eyes flicked from Nazia to his brother to Mrithuri and back again. The older boy, Vivaan, seemed more carefree, but nobody knew better than Mrithuri how young a royal child learned to calculate each gesture and weigh the impact of each action.

The lads showed no evident symptoms of the affliction that crippled their brother. (Lads! How could they seem like children when they were six or eight years younger than Mrithuri?) They were straight and strong, well-grown. She guessed. Mrithuri suddenly realized she had no idea what children of any age were meant to look like.

It seemed Anuraja had at least been feeding them.

Nazia noticed Mrithuri behind the table. Instantly, the apprentice Wizard's demeanor shifted. She straightened her spine and made a very pretty courtesy, exactly as if she were impressed with royalty. Mrithuri knew better.

"Dowager," Nazia said, "Forgive us. I hope we have not kept you waiting."

Vivaan folded his hands nervously, at last seeming apprehensive. Mrithuri pushed aside the latest stack of papers that Ümmühan and the Wizards had left her. Golbahar whisked them away. Bookworms had been at the sheets in a few places, and their musty smell had been giving Mrithuri a headache and undoing all the relaxation of her bath even before she started trying to reach her distant familiars.

Mrithuri said, "You are right on time."

Nazia began to move toward the door. Vivaan kept his attention forward, but Rayesh was still young enough to be unable to contain the sideways flick of his gaze.

"Nazia, stay," said Mrithuri. Nazia must be roughly the same age as Vivaan. Mrithuri did not think of royal children as usually being sheltered, but she had to admit that the Sahali girl seemed . . . much older.

Judging from the relief on the boys' faces when Nazia turned back from the door, they were already starting to see her as a protector. The hero worship might be useful; the speed with which it was happening made Mrithuri wonder how desperate they were for the guidance of peers.

She had no direct experience of her own but she understood that fosters usually traveled in packs, royalty and nobility together, building the friendships and alliances and connections that would remain with them for the rest of their lives.

She sympathized. She'd been a lonely child herself, without peers in the palace. Her grandfather had not sought out the children of his nobles to be playmates and hostages. Her only near agemate had been Chaeri.

Chaeri.

The name still sent a pang of distress through her. Betrayal and heartbreak, that the woman who had been her closest friend—her only childhood friend—had turned against her. She still didn't want to believe it, even in the face of incontrovertible proof.

Maybe she had been naive. Maybe she had deserved it. Maybe she could have been a better friend herself.

But then again, maybe naiveté was not a sufficient reason to betray someone.

Whether it was or was not, she had been raised to be a rajni, and heartbreak was inadequate cause to shirk those duties. Even when the pain welled up inside her as sharply as if Chaeri's treachery had been yestereve. Mrithuri had her duty before her, and her duty was winning over a couple of teenagers who had no reason to like her at all.

She gestured to Vivaan and Rayesh to be seated. They found cushions, and Nazia sat down as well—away from the royalty, at the bottom of the table on the far side of Lady Golbahar.

"Do you care for tea before dinner?" Mrithuri asked, taking refuge in formal inflections. "And some cakes, perhaps?"

Watching the boys eye each other, she remembered what it had been like to be a young person subjected to the scrutiny of noble adults. A spasm of sympathy pierced her. Weren't boys always enthusiastic about food, especially sweets? Did their hesitance mean that they were used to navigating traps?

Mrithuri caught Golbahar's eye and directed her attention toward the princes. The Asitaneh lady was much the same age as Mrithuri, a couple of years younger. And much more worldly. Mrithuri had never asked, but she got the impression from chance comments that Golbahar had quite the assortment of siblings, half siblings, and allomothers back home. It would explain her facility with politics at such a young age.

Golbahar leaned forward, making her voice girlish and musical—a trick Ümmühan used sometimes, too. "It's delicious tea," she said. "It comes all the way from the mountains. With honey and cream and spices in it. And there will be honey sweets, and some with orange-blossom water."

"That sounds very nice, Your Abundance." The embarrassment of everyone staring at him while he sat in silence seemed to help Vivaan find his voice.

The Dead Man opened the door and reached a hand outside to gesture. A runner poked her head in, and Golbahar mimed sipping tea. The servant whisked away.

Well, they could sit there in silence staring at one another until the tea and food came. Or Mrithuri could take charge of the conversation.

"I wanted to meet you," she said. "And I wanted you to meet me, as well, so you could see and judge for yourselves who I am." She gestured with both hands to her chest and shoulders. "I'm not used to having very much family around. My parents also died when I was young."

Maybe she had overstepped. Rayesh, who had been fidgeting slightly, froze. Vivaan leaned back on his cushion just a little. He was watching her face intently. His fingers steepled.

This young man has had his confidence presumed upon too often.

There was a scrape at the door. The Dead Man opened it and allowed two servants inside with the tea service. They distributed steaming pots, trays of dainties, and tiny plates around the table.

Mrithuri thanked them, then poured the first tea with her own hands. She served the princes, and Nazia served Golbahar. The plates of treats were passed around. Both boys took less food than she thought they ought to.

Before he tasted anything, Rayesh elbowed his elder brother with what he obviously thought was great subtlety. Vivaan flinched and glared sidelong.

Mrithuri bit her lip to keep from laughing. A terrible habit; it would leave marks.

"Are you—Nazia says you are our new foster-mother."

That drew Mrithuri up short. The boys' well-being was her responsibility now. They were her wards, as she was the widow of their previous fosterer.

"I suppose I am. But more importantly, I am your cousin."

Yes, that was definitely where the sore spot lay, and having met Anuraja, she suspected she knew why.

"Drink your tea," she said, and took a bite out of an orange-blossom water, pistachio, and honey pastry. The tea was too sweet with the pastry; she longed for something savory instead. Or tea without honey.

Well, there was time to re-educate the chefs. Maybe. If the Lord Chancellor Dehan didn't succeed in wresting all power away from her.

The boys were apprehensive, but they were boys. After a moment or two, the sweets won out, and they ate and drank less nervously. Their eyes didn't stop flicking toward her every few moments, though.

She waited until they started to slow down before she tried again. "Look. I'm not going to try to sell you some nonsense about family duty or how we all need to pull together because of the blood we share. I'm not going to tell you that you need my protection, or that I'm counting on your felicity. You've been Anuraja's hostages for most of your lives."

They flinched when she said the word *hostages,* but she could also see them becoming more and more curious. They hadn't expected her to be honest with them. They had expected adult lies and prevarications.

Manipulation and mind games.

It was refreshing to feel anger at Anuraja for someone else's sake. It made her feel stronger and more secure in the validity of her emotions. Which almost made her laugh. Why did it feel petty to be angry on her own behalf, about her own mistreatment, when that same rage felt righteous on behalf of another?

"It's fine for you to speak up to me," she said. "I'm the Dowager, but I also know I'm not much older than you." She smiled. "And I've not been to Sarathai-lae before, and you have lived here."

"What do you want from us?" Rayesh asked, when Vivaan sat and stared at his hands.

Mrithuri looked at Nazia and Golbahar. Nazia mouthed *Go ahead, then* with a perfect lack of subtlety.

"We need each other," Mrithuri said, simply. "I'm not going to pretend that what we're up against is easily defeated, or that I can protect you no matter what. I'm not going to pretend that I understand what you've been through, or what living with the old raja was like. But he forced you to come and live here and he forced me to marry him, and that's something we have in common."

Rayesh stared at her with giant eyes, mouth open. Vivaan stared down at his tea and poked the surface with a pastry.

"What is it?" Rayesh asked.

"What we're up against?"

He nodded. Vivaan looked up through his lashes.

At that moment, someone scratched at the door.

Damn it. I think I was getting through to them. Mrithuri looked over as the Dead Man opened the door. He peeked through and then opened it wide so that she could see Hnarisha, hands folded inside his sleeves, brow furrowed.

He had the look of someone who desperately needed to have a conversation that he was not looking forward to.

Mrithuri stood. Around the table, her subjects scrambled to their feet. She bit back the urge to apologize. It would have been politer to fuss about a little before rising so tea didn't slop everywhere.

"Nazia and the Lady Golbahar will explain," she said. "Please excuse me. It seems I am needed. I will try to come back for the main course if I can."

16

The Dead Man fell in behind Mrithuri and her little secretary. Hnarisha led them along the hall with as much haste as decorum permitted. The Dead Man, having grown to manhood in a society where many people went veiled, had no difficulty deducing Hnarisha's state of worry from his movements. Tension rang from him like peals from a bell. The echoes crept into Mrithuri's carriage and breathing. She clutched at the shawl Golbahar had draped around her with a pale-knuckled hand.

The room they came to in a few moments already held Ata Akhimah. The Wizard stood by a window, head bent over some spindled papers. She glanced up as the Dead Man shut the door behind Syama.

He set his back against the wall and the bear-dog settled beside him. Together they watched as Ata Akhimah moved around the perimeter of the room. She picked up some small objects and moved them elsewhere. She hooked a stool out of a corner and turned a vase of flowers askew. As she returned to the window and re-draped the curtains, a hush settled over them. A sensation like the pressure of deep water pricked inside the Dead Man's ears.

"There," said Ata Akhimah. "We're secure."

Words burst from Mrithuri. "What's wrong? Hurry, tell me."

All the difficulty of the last months strained in her voice. Akhimah glanced at Hnarisha.

Hnarisha said, "We have word of another army on the road. A night's travel away, no more."

"What?" Mrithuri asked. "Himadra? Or a third one?"

The Dead Man half-stepped forward. It seemed this conversation might require him to participate as more than bodyguard. "Sekira?"

Syama nudged his hand with her massive skull, as if to offer comfort. The bear-dog was generally a good judge of character. Her trust flattered.

"Most likely," said Ata Akhimah.

The Dead Man realized that he was resting a hand on one pistol. He peeled his fingers delicately off the scrollworked butt.

"There *have* been a lot of desertions," Hnarisha said apologetically. "It's easy for any soldier to walk away when they are billeted outside the walls and they know the land so well."

"How far had Himadra gotten?" Mrithuri asked. "Are we still expecting that he will want to protect his brothers?"

"If we're right that Anuraja was using them to enforce the alliance, that seems likely."

Mrithuri said, "I just met them. They are suspicious of familial goodwill, to say the least. I do not think they have enjoyed being fostered by Anuraja."

"Don't you know how far off the Gage is?" the Dead Man asked. "With your birds?"

He had been trying not to sound too worried. Of course, he realized, he'd failed at that by naming the Gage in particular.

Mrithuri touched the serpent torc, one last piece of jewelry she seemed determined not to abandon. "I have been . . . struggling to reach my familiars. If I had not left the vultures behind, I could send one out and link to it using blood and bone."

"Sayeh Rajni has Guang Bao," said Ata Akhimah.

Mrithuri turned and paced, turned and paced again. Bare feet padded across carpet on blue and silver tile. "Sayeh Rajni would trade anything to regain her son," she said reluctantly. "It's quite understandable. But can we trust her in this thing?"

The Dead Man saw the shadow of Chaeri's betrayal in those words. Tightness bloomed in his throat. Grief for this woman he called wife in his heart, if never again out loud.

It occurred to him that in this room, before these witnesses, he could go to her. He could offer her the shelter of his arms. Hnarisha and Akhimah already knew. And Akhimah had said the room was warded.

The Dead Man stepped forward and reached out to Mrithuri. She whirled on him as if startled or furious. A touch of kohl on her lids made the ring of white around her irises seem all the more wild.

"Let me hold you for a moment," he said.

She stared from Hnarisha to Ata Akhimah and seemed to remember what he had remembered, too. She came to him and leaned her forehead on his shoulder, clasped her hands behind the back of his red coat.

He held her gently until she had calmed herself, and wondered if it were for the last time. When she stepped back, he opened his hands and let her go.

She was young; he was not. Though she had been orphaned, so had he. Perhaps his longer experience had given him a better understanding of how everything was transient: homes, callings, friendships; even life itself.

It seemed unkind to tell her, and he would have been too shy to speak of his feelings before others. He held his tongue.

Mrithuri turned back to the Wizard and the secretary, who were standing around, awkwardly staring into corners in that way people had when confronted with another's vulnerability.

"Not another siege," said the Dowager. "Not in this city."

Hnarisha shook his head. "We couldn't fit the entire army within the walls of this place. Even if we could trust most of them to defend it."

Mrithuri rubbed her eyes as if she were trying to chase a headache away. The Dead Man's temples throbbed in sympathy.

Mrithuri said, "I will speak to Sayeh. I will place the situation before her in honesty and see what she says. I will not be the kind of leader who maneuvers my allies and friends."

Hnarisha grinned. "As long as you're willing to maneuver your enemies, I don't see a problem. Maneuvering friends is why you have a staff."

Mrithuri's smile was more restrained. The Dead Man thought it might be genuine. "Send my royal cousin to me, then. Akhimah, would you watch the door from the outside? I need to speak to my bodyguard in private."

The door closed behind Hnarisha and Ata Akhimah, and the Dead Man's heart beat faster. Mrithuri gestured him to the cushions. He joined her seated in the corner farthest from the door. There was no tea, nothing to occupy their hands or distract them from the conversation.

She said, "You have been avoiding me."

"I have been avoiding the appearance of impropriety," he said. "There is no other reason."

She said, "Hm."

"You should divorce me," he told her.

She laughed. "Balderdash! What nonsense is that?"

"There is too much danger for you, for all the Kingdoms, if we are revealed to have a romantic relationship."

"I have the privacy of my rooms." She smirked ironically. "Anuraja's rooms."

"No royal person has privacy. Especially not in the house of her enemy."

She pinched the bridge of her nose. "Can a queen not have her favorites?"

"Not when she can afford doubts about neither the validity of her marriage nor her widowhood. There can be no scandal, no question of your chasteness."

He hated what he was saying. He hated the truth of it.

"I'm an old widow," she scoffed.

"The Gage is still trying to return to you with the Carbuncle," the Dead Man reminded. "If he has secured it, and if it works, can your reign survive any question of how the child it produces was conceived?"

"We have never been at risk for getting a child!"

"Do you expect the Lord Chancellor to take our word for it?"

She sighed. "He wouldn't, would he?"

The Dead Man shook his head. His veil caught against the collar of his coat.

Mrithuri reached out gently and unhooked it. Then she lifted the edge to reveal part of his face, and kissed him on the mouth. She lowered the veil again. The corners of her eyes sparkled bright. "I should regret what we have done."

He touched her hair. "I do not."

THIS WAS A STRANGE CASTLE, SAYEH THOUGHT, THAT HAD SO FEW DEFENSES. It had no battlements. Its fair white towers were finished with pointed domes, and around the rim of each ran a delicate balcony.

Sayeh stood at the edge of the northmost one, called the Tower of Ijanel. The city spread below her. A distant column of dust rose pale against the star-strewn sky.

Guang Bao reposed on her fist. She bent her head beside his and whispered, "If you see that sorcerer, you must fly away far and fast, before he sees you in return."

Mrithuri had told Sayeh about her feeling that Ravana had gazed right out of the past and seen Mrithuri, though Mrithuri had done no more than look into Guang Bao's memories. For this reason, and for simple safety, Sayeh was not alone on the tower. A door stood open behind her. Just inside it, out of the wind that loosened her braid and snarled the freed strands, waited Tsering-la. He wore a new black coat courtesy of the palace's tailors, one not rubbed to tatters at the skirts and elbows nor bleached to grayness by the sun.

On the balcony itself stood the Godmade. Its garments were as ragged as ever. It waited with twig-arms folded, a thin gold diadem encircling its hairless red-black pate, hems and sleeves aflutter like torn banners.

Sayeh stroked Guang Bao's head with a fingertip and scratched under his crest. He fluffed his feathers and stretched his neck, eyes closed as he luxuriated in the grooming.

For all his size, he felt light on her glove. She lifted him into the updraft without strain. Her leg ached from climbing the ninety-eight steps of Ijanel's Tower but she was not winded. Having walked from Sarathai-tia, and having spent so much time bearing her weight on crutches, she was fitter than she had ever been.

She had a small knife at her belt. She drew it in her right hand, moved it to her left, and scraped the back of her right hand against the blade.

Guang Bao didn't like the taste of blood, preferring mangos. She had no fresh fruit, so she rubbed her hand against the side of his beak. If birds had the ability to make faces, he would have grimaced. As it was, he fanned his wings and leaned away from her in disgust. "Not a treat!" he squawked, offended. "Not good! Nasty!"

She might as well have dosed him with some unpleasant medicine.

Enough of the blood infiltrated for her purposes. His eyes were bright; his wings were strong. He had molted out the majority of the repaired feathers that had tugged so oddly on his skin. She felt his restlessness from the inside as her own body dropped away.

They fell from her fist into the wind.

The sky wheeled above. The city reeled below. The updraft bent their feathertips and fluttered the elaborate frills of their tail.

They rose in a spiral, higher and higher, until they were far out of bow-shot or the range of a rifle ball. From Sayeh's vantage on the tower, Guang Bao was nothing but a slender cross of darkness eclipsing the stars of the Heavenly River a few at a time. Perhaps they would slip across the sky entirely unnoticed by their enemies.

Sayeh almost forgot to keep her own body breathing as she rode within Guang Bao. The concentration demanded by her task made it far too easy to feel her way into his existence and lose herself there.

It wasn't just the flight. It was the focus they needed to locate and identify so many things on the ground. Things that were of little interest to the phoenix, that his eyes were not well adapted to see. But which might be a matter of life and death to the humans within and around Sarathai-lae.

She needed to maintain enough awareness of her own body not merely to breathe but to speak. She needed to relay what they saw to Tsering-la and Nizhvashiti.

There were horses, and riders on those horses. Did one have a tiger-skin saddlecloth? It was hard to tell one rider from another when all you could see were their hats and their shoulders. But Sayeh thought one did.

She winced at the size of this army, at the number of soldiers. How were there so many of them? Where had they all come from?

How had Sekira found so many men in all of Sahal-Sarat?

The eyes of the bird were a wonder. They could make out details from leagues in the air that would have defeated Sayeh from mere yards of distance. Some colors, ordinary to Guang Bao, were entirely beyond Sayeh's perception. But telling strangers apart from one another? That was not something a bird usually needed to do.

There were two armies upon the road. The closer, Sayeh judged, was indeed less than a night's ride away. The farther one—she marked their column of dust in the air—was not too much behind.

Sayeh and Guang Bao looped and gyred farther from the city walls. They could see the white finger of Ijanel's Tower reaching upward. The strain of maintaining contact over the distance made Sayeh's temples pinch. Sweat broke across her brow. Discomfort made it all the more difficult to sustain the connection.

But there, in the midst of the second column, they saw the glitter of a featureless brass head, a robed figure that moved with the heavy stride of a massive machine.

It was Himadra's army, and the Gage of whom she had heard speak was in their midst.

Sayeh did not know this Gage. She had never met him. She was disinclined to trust anyone who walked beside that wicked prince Himadra. But the Gage was the Dead Man's partner, and the Dead Man had earned her trust.

War made strange allies.

Who was that small figure riding alongside the not-much-larger figure that must be Himadra? Who was that child on a pony, a nurse on another horse managing the reins?

Sayeh's half-abandoned body clutched the balcony rail with both hands. Her son, her son was there. And that Chandranathi pig was riding toward a war with him as if it were nothing.

Before they consciously decided to do it, Sayeh and Guang Bao slipped into a dive. If there were a sorcerer with Himadra and he saw them, so be it.

Guang Bao skimmed low over men both marching and mounted. Sayeh was dimly aware of restraining, supporting hands on her body's shoulders. She was much more alive to the gasps and unexpected cheers that went up from the army.

Some of those cheering and waving wore the colors of Ansh-Sahal. Some of them were her own people, the loyal ones who had followed her orders to desert the doomed city, against the commands of her insubordinate generals. They must have come as refugees to Chandranath. And then Himadra had brought them here.

They were technically Drupada's troops and not Sayeh's. She was only her son's regent—if she was even that, with no kingdom left and Himadra claiming to foster him. She wondered if Himadra had brought Drupada along in order to ensure the loyalty of these borrowed men. She could not decide if their presence would be to her advantage or to her detriment.

The cheering gave her hope. It was time to find out.

Guang Bao winged down to the Gage. As they approached, they saw another bird on the Gage's metal fist—an unhooded bearded vulture, its black and white feathers streaked russet and orange with ochre. It bated as Guang Bao swept past, beating its broad wings and flaring nape feathers around a gaping beak.

There would be no landing there! They whisked about the Gage's head, red-gold feathers fluttering. Denied her first choice, Sayeh wanted to land on Drupada's saddlebow, as if she could somehow sweep her son up in phoenix wings and carry him back to her body on the tower.

He was pointing and waving and shrieking joy, and his pony was rather unhappy about the performance. A flurry of wings would endanger him, the pony, *and* Guang Bao. Her instincts would have to wait.

But there was an old woman a few strides away from the Gage, her dark skin seamed with creases, her eyes white as boiled eggs. She held a staff in one hand, and as Guang Bao circled, she lifted it. The wooden end looked comfortable for perching, nicely rounded and knobbly for talons. They alighted, and both felt surprise when the stick barely bobbed despite the length of its lever arm.

There was some strength beyond human in the old woman's wrist. The staff stayed firm as a thick bough while she grounded the butt. Guang Bao balanced easily, his long neck compensating for the motion to keep his head steady. Sayeh turned their eyes upon the wicked prince.

The little man sat his gray mare in an odd, padded saddle. He rode with a strong bit, but at least the mare's mouth wasn't bloody. Sayeh didn't think any better of him for it.

She gritted her own teeth. In an echo, Guang Bao's beak clacked. He hissed like an outraged goose in Himadra's face. The Chandranathi prince startled, making his horse dance back. Sayeh wanted to laugh. Petty vengeance was not beneath her.

The human voices registered on bird ears as so much noise unless Sayeh forced Guang Bao to concentrate very hard. Drupada was shouting something from the other side of Himadra's horse. His nurse seemed to be pulling his pony close, trying to keep him from spooking it.

Himadra's bird-ear-distorted voice said, "That's the rajni's familiar."

"Mommy bird!" Drupada confirmed excitedly. "Mommy bird, mommy bird!"

They could probably peck out Himadra's eyes before anybody could stop them. But then Guang Bao would be shot full of arrows before they could escape. And Drupada would be left here defenseless in the midst of the enemy.

Fuck this. Himadra had Sayeh's son. Himadra was her son's protector, no matter how angry and jealous that imposition made her feel. Therefor, she must help Himadra, though rage twisted inside her, thick and poisonous as Mrithuri's Eremite serpents, at the thought.

Sayeh coaxed her familiar to open his beak. Her first attempt at speech emerged a garbled squawk. Her second one was better.

"Traitors!" Guang Bao croaked in his harsh voice. "Traitors on the road!"

Himadra stared at them. His lips curved behind his beard. "Sayeh Rajni?"

Grudgingly, they nodded.

"Traitors. A rebel army—between us and the city?"

"Yes," they clucked.

The smile showed teeth. "Then we have them in a pincer, don't we?"

✳   ✳   ✳

"IF DEHAN IS GOING TO MOVE," THE DEAD MAN SAID, "HE'S GOING TO HAVE to move fast."

Mrithuri looked up at him stiffly. There was redness at the corners of her eyes, and it was not all from the dust and eyestrain of poring over an endless series of documents. Some of it, the Dead Man knew, was his own doing. "Are we ready for him?"

The Dead Man looked around the table. Mrithuri shared it with the Lady Golbahar, Hnarisha, Ata Akhimah, Tsering-la, and a grimy pile of paper and parchment. They each looked up one by one.

Ata Akhimah extended the bound book she had been studying. "What do you think?"

The Dead Man took it from her hands. He flipped through the pages, feeling the deckle edges with a fingertip, examining the color and the way the ink was faded. He found the page with Mrithuri's name and geneal-ogy, then turned back until he found Anuraja's. The illuminations on the would-be emperor's page looked a little hurried, the gilding a little shoddy.

The edges of the royal blue hide cover were mouse-nibbled. Borer worms had been at the pages at some point. When he bent the pages gently with his thumb and riffled them, the wormholes seemed to dance in spirals, recapit-ulating the path of the worm.

He let the cover slip closed. "I can't tell," he said. "The Scholar-God must have guided your hand, because Mrithuri's lineage looks better than Anuraja's."

"Does She take an interest in the doings of foreign nobles?" Mrithuri asked, amused.

Golbahar set her tea aside. "She takes an interest anywhere there are books."

The Dead Man offered the tome of royal genealogies back to Ata Akhi-mah. "This would put Mrithuri next in line for the throne of Sarathai-lae, in her own right."

"A closer blood claim than Anuraja's, at least insofar as relationship to the most recent emperor." Ata Akhimah agreed. "But she was born after Anuraja and is the Alchemical Emperor's great-granddaughter where he was a grandson."

"I suppose it all depends on your thoughts on primogeniture," said Gol-bahar.

Hnarisha answered, "I think the throne made its opinion clear. This document also demonstrates that you have a closer link to the Alchemical Emperor via his oldest daughter from his first wife, on your mother's side. I didn't know your parents were cousins."

He grinned at her.

She said, "Every royal family is nothing but cousins. I'm related to half the nobility in the known world. Even the princes of Kyiv."

"Civil wars have been waged over less," said the Dead Man. He looked at Mrithuri. "Are you sure about this?"

"I think it's all a travesty," she said. "But I'm not sure what choice we have."

Lady Golbahar came up from the table without using her hands. Her crossed legs unfolded and unwound and she rose to her feet, her body describing a spiral. "Let's get you to the throne room, then. It's time you became more Empress than Dowager."

"Now?" Mrithuri reflexively smoothed her simply dressed hair. "I'm hardly—"

"If you're eloping anyway, there's no point in wasting a lot of time embroidering your veil! Come on, Your Abundance. Somebody send a page to fetch the Godmade. And the poetess. And wake up Sayeh Rajni! She won't want to miss this for the world."

"Lord Chancellor Dehan is not going to like this," Mrithuri said.

Golbahar waved a ledger. "I can handle Dehan."

She caught the Dead Man's gaze over the lines of their veils. The way the kohl crinkled at the corners of her eyes told him she was frowning sternly.

"Yes," he said, touching the hilt of the sword that had been a gift from Mrithuri. "We can handle Dehan."

Hnarisha slipped toward the door. Mrithuri half-turned, finger pointing imperiously. "Where are you going?"

"To fetch the crown, Your Abundance." His smile was impish. "Make sure you practice that commanding look, though. You're going to need it."

"Dehan probably keeps the keys to any crown jewels."

"That's okay," Tsering-la said, crossing to lead Hnarisha out the door. "The first thing a Wizard of Tsarepheth learns is how to pick a lock."

17

MRITHURI'S ENTOURAGE SWEPT HER TOWARD THE THRONE ROOM IN A WHIRL even more precipitous than the one prefiguring her wedding. She had been sick and frail then, terrified, plotting a murder of her would-be husband that would have resulted in her own execution. The Eremite venom had been burning itself from her veins and she had struggled through a haze of confused thoughts and waves of illness.

This was more of a whirl, too, than her first enthronement, after the death of her grandfather. Then she had prepared by fasting and anointing in the waters of the Mother River. The ceremony of keeping vigil had given her a chance to grieve in private for a few hours and to get used to the idea that she would soon be rajni.

Now she paused on her way to the throne room only to bathe her feet in the clear, cool stream of filtered sacred river water that one must step across in order to enter. Her people probably would have hurried her past even that if she hadn't pointed out that first, she needed to purify herself, and second, they couldn't do anything until the Godmade arrived to perform the ceremony. *And* until Hnarisha and Tsering-la got back with the regalia.

The water whisked over smooth jade in its channel. The cold and the swift tickle of the current against her ankles and arches gave Mrithuri something to ground her attention in. The craving for her serpents' venom lodged in her throat. She tried to swallow it, but—a bitter spikiness—it remained.

It didn't matter. The serpents were back in Sarathai-tia. She could not reach them even if she were desperate enough to go and beg the nuns for their return. And everyone knew the nuns never gave back a price once it was paid, just as they never themselves reneged on a bargain.

She walked out of the water and through the arched doorway into the throne room, leaving a trail of wet footprints on the precious flagstones. Syama padded at her heels. Syama had kept *her* princess paws dry by stepping over the water.

As they entered, Mrithuri realized that in her haste to secure Anuraja's rooms and papers, she had not even glanced into the seat of his power.

It was smaller than the Hall of the Empty Throne, and not of course dwarfed by that namesake edifice upon its tower. Who ruled in Sarathai-lae had no strong lords to contend with, no equivalent of the Mrithuri's Dharasaaba.

That was good. It meant one less group of political figures to manage if she were going to make Golbahar and Akhimah's ridiculous plan into an accomplishment. And it was bad, because it meant she had no kingmakers to bargain with or play against one another. A powerful enemy to Lord Chancellor Dehan would have come in handy about then.

Well, Mrithuri would just have to be that person herself.

The hall was not empty of people. So few places in a palace ever were. It wasn't crowded, either. A half-dozen of Mrithuri's new subjects stood around, soft voices echoing off the vaulted stone ceilings. They turned when Mrithuri and her party entered. She nodded to the four men and two women, all richly dressed. They returned much deeper courtesies—a little delayed as they realized who this plainly dressed woman was—but did not approach, as they had not been invited. Mrithuri made a note to ask Golbahar who they were.

So many subjects and courtiers to learn about. Her head was already full of the families and familial relationships of Sarathai-tia. Would she forget it all as she learned the politics of her new acquisition?

Ata Akhimah still clutched her book to her chest. She went to the courtiers and spoke with them. Mrithuri could have tried to eavesdrop, but she didn't really feel like it.

She tipped her head back to examine the interior of the onion-shaped dome. The windows were tall and breezy. Beyond them, to the southwest, Mrithuri could see the long steady march of the waves on the Arid Sea. They hissed on rocks far below.

She had not known they were so close to the ocean.

She walked to the windows, which stretched from a handspan above the floor to far above her head, and she leaned her hands on the stone frame. Smooth and warm, it still held the heat of the Cauled Sun. Syama leaned against her hamstrings. Mrithuri was distantly aware of Ata Akhimah moving around the room, rearranging things to suit her sense of aesthetics or geomancy. Golbahar followed, adjusting the angle of ornaments and drapes to suit Akhimah's instructions. Two of the courtiers had left. Others began filling it.

Witnesses. Of course, there would need to be witnesses.

Mrithuri felt the presence of the Dead Man more strongly. He stood just a little behind her, turned sideways so that his back was not to the room. He and Syama were always guarding her.

"What are you thinking?" he asked in a low voice.

"I've never seen the ocean before."

It wasn't actually what she was thinking. What she was thinking was that she was scared; that she had not asked for any of this; that there seemed to be no avoiding the duty that was dragging her into a more and more inescapable death. Either she would die of these political machinations, or she would die fighting the nameless beast that lurked at the edge of all these maneuverings. Maybe there was no difference. Maybe if Dehan got her, or Sekira did, that would just be the beast's claw in a human-seeming glove.

"It's so big." She waved at the horizon. "Akhimah's homeland is on the other side. I think I . . . never realized before how far she had come."

She glanced at the Dead Man. She had learned how to tell when he was smiling behind his veil, even when he tried to keep it out of his eyes.

"And you, too."

"A long way," he agreed.

A wistful feeling kept her pinned by the window. The breeze on her face smelled brackish and alive. "What's the sea like?"

He folded his arms. "Frightening," he said. "Pitiless. As you say, huge. There are places far from land where the sky is dead and the air grows cold enough to make your breath turn to ice on your veil. There are other places where you sail from one sky to another and the waves and currents are wild and treacherous, as if the sea wrestled itself. I think it has to do with tides, but I am no sailor."

The breeze felt fresh on her face. She wanted to lean out into it, spread wings she didn't have, and fall into flight over the ocean. She wanted to shrug off duty and never come back.

"Are you going to look at your throne, Dowager?"

She supposed she must. Her throne, if she could take it. If she could keep it. Not Anuraja's throne.

It was bigger than her own chair of estate at home. Probably wood underneath, but the frame was covered in beaten gold, so pure the yellow metal seemed nearly orange. Cabochon sapphires big as dove eggs studded the surface, their dark blue laced with milky flaws. The cushions were blue-and-orange silk brocade, and there were plenty of them.

It could be worse. At least he's dead, and I'm not, and I didn't have to kill him. With my own hands, anyway.

"Well, at least it should be comfortable," she said out loud. "We'll need chairs for my advisors. Sayeh Rajni, Ata Akhimah, and Lady Golbahar."

"After the enthronement," Golbahar said, having wandered close enough to overhear. "For that, you should sit up there alone. Splendid isolation. It projects power, do you see?"

Mrithuri did see. All she felt was despair. "You should be empress. You have the knack for it."

"But then I couldn't marry my fiancé," Golbahar said. "I'd have to marry some boring prince or Qersnyk barbarian."

"Mother!" Mrithuri said. "Don't remind me!"

But she had started laughing, and she was still laughing—scandalizing the small crowd that had assembled—when Tsering-la and Hnarisha came in, carrying a glass-topped case and a velvet pillow to which was pinned an utterly ridiculous crown. The thing was lined in orange silk and shaped like a beehive wearing a corona. It was gold—or, she hoped, gilded—and it was studded extensively with rubies, emeralds, sapphires, spinels, pearls . . . all arrayed to represent the path of the Heavenly River.

"Oh, no," Mrithuri said, feeling all the weight of the masks and regalia and hairpieces she had so gladly melted down and coined straining her neck again. "That's a man's crown. I can't wear that! It must weigh as much as a baby!"

"We'll get you a smaller one for everyday," Golbahar promised. "A nice light diadem. But this is the crown of the ruler of Sarathai-lae, and you must wear it at least once."

Golbahar jumped in her slippers as a rustling Nizhvashiti swept up behind her. The Asitaneh woman turned, hand to her veil, then breathed out a nervous giggle.

Nizhvashiti raised a hand, revealing a vial of river water—silty, milk-white—wound in skeletal, dark fingers. Mrithuri glimpsed Sayeh coming in at the same side door through which Mrithuri had entered.

"All right." Mrithuri squared her shoulders. "Let's get this done."

As she walked toward the throne, Ata Akhimah and Nizhvashiti fell in on either side behind her. There was no music; there should have been music. Zithers and horns.

Saffron-colored rice grains and marigold petals snowed upon her. Mrithuri realized that her new subjects must have procured them from somewhere. There would be offering tables set about the palace.

Someone was singing in a high, sweet voice. It was Lady Golbahar. Another voice joined, cracked but true: the poetess Ümmühan. Perhaps she had come in with Sayeh; Mrithuri had not seen her. The vaults and the dome overhead caught their voices and amplified them, filling the hall with textured echoes.

The steps of the dais were worn from many feet, the precious blocks of rose quartz smoothed, scuffed, dished, and uneven. They felt neutral under her bare feet, as if she stepped on the impervious skin of a living thing. The throne was low. She kept her eyes upon it as petals fell all around her. The aroma of incense joined that of the sea. Mrithuri looked down at her hands and saw that she was limned with golden light. All the tiny mirrors embroidered into the throne's awnings caught the light and amplified it, scattering brilliant droplets on the ceiling, the walls, the floor, the sea of faces.

Tsering-la's doing, no doubt.

Effective. She could be made to seem regal even in her plain white trousers and blouse.

The arms of the great chair had lions on them. The back was carved to resemble the head of a trumpeting elephant.

She slipped the shawl from her shoulders, letting it drape through the crook of her elbows gracefully, revealing the sacred beasts tattooed upon her arms. She turned and found herself facing a room that had somehow become filled with people.

It seemed no one wanted to miss this, even if they had to pull themselves from their meal, a nap, or—based upon wet hair and hastily donned clothing—even the bathhouse.

Mrithuri drew one last breath, taking strength from the aromas of myrrh and sandalwood.

Nizhvashiti drifted beside the throne, its height made greater by the handspan its robes trailed between its feet and the floor.

"Be enthroned," the Godmade said. Its whispery voice seemed loud as a rush of cyclone wind through a forest. Mrithuri could imagine the creak and snap of boughs, the whoosh of leaves tearing loose and blown.

It sounds like the ocean, she thought. The incense and the lights were making her dizzy.

Gratefully, she sank onto the cushions. Syama padded up the stair after her, circled around the back, and lay down beside the throne with the heavy sigh of a big dog. Nizhvashiti was a pillar of blackness before all the dazzle of colors and people behind it. Mrithuri focused her eyes on the soothing darkness with gratitude. She looked up, lifting her chin.

"I anoint thee in the name of the Mother and the Good Daughter," Nizhvashiti said, and stroked the part of Mrithuri's hair with a finger. Wetness told her the substance was river water.

"I bless thee with courage and wisdom," Nizhvashiti said. This time, its fingers were scented with sweet almond oil as it repeated the gesture.

"I bless thee with competence and strength," Nizhvashiti said, with fingers stained red with slaked turmeric.

It was, Mrithuri realized, the ritual for enthroning a king, not a rajni. Her heart, which had seemed to sop within her bosom, squeezed painfully and accelerated.

"I bless thee and acknowledge in the name of the Mother and the Good Daughter thy right to rule." Necklaces were lifted from the cushioned box and settled around her shoulders. One snagged on the serpent torc. Nizhvashiti gently untangled it.

"I bless thee and name thee servant of and intermediary to the Mother and the Good Daughter for thy people of Sarath."

Mrithuri extended her wrists and allowed Ata Akhimah and Golbahar to slide bangles on, where they rang against her wedding jewelry. Mrithuri rested her forearms along the carven lions, trying to look languorous, feeling as if she were pinned down with iron manacles.

Oh, here came that crown. Mrithuri hoped Golbahar had thought about hairpins. It would be a terrible omen if the thing got dented from crashing to the floor.

Nizhvashiti lifted the crown as if it weighed nothing, despite the frailness of arms revealed when the black sleeves slid down. The Godmade lowered the crown toward her head, intoning, "I bless thee and elevate thee. Thou art Mrithuri the First, Empress of all Sarath—"

"Stop!" someone shouted from the door. "Stop that at once; it's blasphemy!"

Mrithuri blinked dazzled eyes as Nizhvashiti set the crown on her head, disregarding the order. It weighed, as predicted, as much as a small child. She didn't dare try to rise; she'd be struggling against a hundredweight of gold, and she'd probably wind up breaking her neck falling down the steps of the dais.

"Who is it?" Mrithuri asked.

As Nizhvashiti stepped to the left of the throne and turned to face those assembled, Golbahar whispered in Mrithuri's ear, "The Lord Chancellor. And his pair of puppies."

Nizhvashiti folded its hands within its sleeves. "Are you accusing an ansha of blasphemy?"

Its whispery voice sounded so calm, so reasonable, that one could be forgiven if one missed the threat implied. Dehan was apparently a little smarter than Mrithuri had been giving him credit for, because he drew up sharply and didn't move another step. He wore brilliant red tunic and trousers embroidered in heavy bands around each hem. The leather on his sandals was gilded. His associates—Kannla, the tall one, and Marnor, the innocent-looking one—flanked him on either side.

"You cannot crown this woman Empress simply because she is the Dowager—"

He stepped closer. The otherworldly glow around Mrithuri intensified. She suspected Tsering-la was putting up his walls of light to protect her. His forethought filled her with gratitude.

"You are a woman!" he said. "You can be regent to the rightful heir, and even then, propriety dictates that your orders must be delivered through the Lord Chancellor. I have documents here explaining the bloodline—" He held out a hand to Kannla, who filled it with an ornately wrapped scroll.

"Vivaan is my ward," Mrithuri said. She might not be able to move well or see much, but at least she could talk. "And I think you will find that my claim to the throne by blood is closer than his, on my mother's side. Ata Akhimah, that book, please?"

Akhimah did not relinquish the ragged hide-bound tome. But she did riffle through it until she found the appropriate page, then turned it to face the Lord Chancellor.

He barely glanced at it and sniffed. "An obvious forgery."

"That book was in the raja's papers," Ümmühan said in her quiet, carrying voice. "It has the mark of the palace's own librarians upon it."

Neither statement, Mrithuri noticed admiringly, was a lie.

Dehan was turning a particularly vibrant shade of mahogany. "A nice claim from an unchaste whore who dishonors her husband's memory!"

Spittle flicked from his lips with the force of his words. Mrithuri leaned back to avoid the spray. She let her mouth pinch in disgust. "That is treason, Lord Chancellor."

"Not if it's true! Will you submit to an examination?"

Shocked laughter from the onlookers.

"I will *not*." She snorted. "I've been surrounded by Laeish soldiers and my own women every hour since my husband conquered Sarathai-tia. You have no evidence, and I have plenty of testimony to my chasteness. I should have you executed. But I won't have you executed for *that*."

Golbahar knew when she was summoned. She stepped forward. "Lord Chancellor," she said, "I've been going over the books, and I'd be interested to know where"—she consulted a column of figures, squinting down her nose—"this approximately fifteen thousand gold leopards has vanished to. There was a series of small subtraction errors, repeated over time, that makes the balance in the royal treasury seem lower than it should be—"

Dehan had self-control. Mrithuri had to grant him that. She thought *she* might have taken a step back, confronted with Golbahar's interested condescension. The raised eyebrow said a lot, over the veil.

The crowd of courtiers behind Dehan, who had been murmuring and shifting about, fell into a profound hush.

He said, "We shall have to have an inventory."

"Oh, we have," she said. "We just finished. Fifteen thousand, two hundred and thirteen gold leopards and fifteen silver cranes are definitely missing from the treasury. I believe your colleague Marnor is the bookkeeper?"

Marnor had gone suddenly greenish-gray, a color that did not look well with his sunshine-yellow tunic. His hands were clasped in front of him, skin stretched over the knuckles.

"My Lord Chancellor keeps the books for the main vault." His voice shook. "I keep the pay slips and the accounts of expenses."

"We'll need those," said Golbahar with a reassuring smile. "It will be interesting to see where the Lord Chancellor's debits differ from those you have recorded."

Mrithuri kept the smile of victory off her lips with an effort. Maybe there was something to that veil thing after all.

Dehan's clobbered expression filled her with glee, especially since Mrithuri knew how hard Golbahar had worked to uncover his fraud. The lady had not slept, for ingratiating herself with servants and undersecretaries—and of course, her new special friend Marnor the under-chancellor. Her bookkeeping and interpersonal skills and cleverness had allowed her to find the documentation to catch Dehan, if not red-handed, at least with his pockets full.

Mrithuri said, "Syama can smell when you are lying."

The bear-dog heard her name and looked up. Now Dehan *did* take a step away.

"There is an army at the gate," the Lord Chancellor said. "Surely, now is not the time for civil conflict."

"Mmm." Mrithuri examined her fingernails. "I think you mean to say that there are *two* armies at the gate. Not counting the one that I brought with me. Do you have expectations of assistance from one of them?"

"I—" He had been, she judged, surprised to hear of the second army. And now he was gobsmacked by her allegation that he was working with Sekira.

But the particular kind of gobsmacked that probably meant he was.

She said, "Perhaps we should let them all fight and see which one wins."

As she had foretold, the crown was slipping on her head. Putting a hand up to steady it would be too obvious. All of Anuraja's people were watching her, and even such a tiny breach of decorum could undermine their confidence. It didn't matter that the effect was all out of proportion to its significance.

She was forced to hold her head at an uncomfortable angle to balance the damned thing, though her neck protested the maneuver.

None of this political theatre was really about the truth. It was about who was spinning the most compelling narrative. And a young widow fighting to preserve her kingdom and her autonomy from a treacherous counselor was a strong story, the sort that people would like.

Mrithuri was lucky to have found a counselor like Golbahar. Golbahar was good at this sort of thing.

She stepped forward now, brandishing her sheaf of papers. "Go with the under-chancellor," she said, gesturing to two courtiers who happened to be standing close to the front. More were still packing in from the back, slowly pushing the crowd forward. "Observe while he collects his ledgers."

The three men hurried away. One glanced back over his shoulder as if sorry to miss the rest of the show. Well, his friends could fill him in later.

Mrithuri's neck twinged dangerously. "Dead Man," she said.

He stepped forward. Her feelings as she watched him did not bear examining. They were complicated, and they hurt, and there was nothing she could do about them.

"Place the Lord Chancellor under house arrest until we have time to hold a trial. He is to be confined to his chamber. Set a trusted guard."

"Your Abundance!" cried Dehan. His other advisor—Kannla, the tall one—had edged away from him so subtly that Mrithuri only noticed because a couple of rods had opened between them. The Dead Man's hand was on his sword-hilt. He moved between Dehan and the closest door.

Mrithuri did not see a signal, but the soldier Sanjay and Sayeh's guard captain Vidhya were suddenly there, stepping away from the wall and positioning themselves to intercept the Lord Chancellor's escape. The Lord Chancellor whirled, at bay, throwing his hands up. Long sleeves swung.

He took a running step toward the throne. Crystals of ice seemed to form in Mrithuri's chest; she was too weighted down with ceremonial finery to fight or flee. But Syama was there in front of her, between her and the threat (as Syama always was). And there was Tsering-la's boundary of light.

Dehan recoiled. He dove toward Captain Vidhya and snatched at his belt, where a jeweled dagger hung. Vidhya struck his arm aside with one hand and drew the dagger by its hide-wrapped hilt.

He had no opportunity to use it. The Dead Man's sword whistled through the air. It struck Dehan cleanly across the side of the neck. Dehan's fingers grasped at his throat, then fell slack. Blood spurted from the wound, but he was dead before he hit the floor.

Vidhya jumped back from the spray, not entirely successfully. The Dead Man's curved sword had been yanked from his hands and stood upright, wedged into the Lord Chancellor's vertebrae. Mrithuri had not even seen him lower his veil. She did see him draw it up again before walking forward to prise the sword free. He braced a boot on Dehan's back. When he twisted the blade loose and bones cracked, Mrithuri momentarily forgot to project serenity.

For a moment, no one was looking at her. She put a hand up and smoothed the crown back into balance as nonchalantly as possible. The damage to her neck was done. A muscle along her spine had locked itself into white-hot cramping agony.

The Dead Man examined a nick in the edge of his blade and shook his head theatrically. Then he turned to Mrithuri and bowed low. "Empress," he said. "Your humble servant begs your forgiveness for this unsightliness."

"You acted in my defense," she replied. She turned to Golbahar. "Lady, please see that this regalia is returned to the vault. And send for some armor that might fit me, and some that might fit my elephant."

GOLBAHAR CAUGHT UP WITH MRITHURI, SYAMA, SAYEH, THE DEAD MAN, Hnarisha, and the Wizards before they made it back to the royal chambers. Vidhya walked ahead of them, dagger drawn, still leaving a sticky trail of smudges that Mrithuri paid extra care not to step upon. The lady was breathing heavily, but when she fell into step with the others, Mrithuri saw that it was only from running to catch up—and from the excitement.

"We'll display that book in a crystal case in the receiving room," Golbahar said. She turned her head the other way and lowered her voice to ask Ata Akhimah, "How did you get the wormholes to match on the pages you inserted?"

Silently, Akhimah reached into the pocket of her trousers. When her scarred left hand emerged, she held a twist of wire pinched between her fingers. A thin blade like a flexible razor was corkscrewed around it: a kind of tiny drill bit.

Mrithuri had to assume that her people would not have this conversation if anyone was within earshot. She could not have turned her head to check for spies if offered a wagonload of tea and precious spices. The pain in her neck was bearable only if she kept her eyes focused directly ahead.

She tried not to think about the armor she was about to be buckled into. At least there would be a gorget to support some of the weight of the helmet.

"I need to draw up documents immediately in favor of Vivaan as my heir," Mrithuri said to Hnarisha. "And then we need to get him and his brother out of the city. In case Sekira *does* kill me. Or capture me, even worse."

She touched her snake torc. The warm metal was a comfort.

"I'll see to it," said her secretary.

Mrithuri turned to her cousin. "Sayeh Rajni, I hate to ask—"

"Yes," Sayeh said. "I will send Guang Bao to Himadra with a copy of such documents."

It might mean more war. More for the beast to feed on. The young prince could prove a rallying point, and Sekira had proven his ability as a populist. But making sure Himadra knew should concretize their alliance—if Mrithuri could keep Sayeh from having him assassinated.

In an undertone, Mrithuri asked Golbahar, "Why did you pick those courtiers to retrieve Dehan's papers? It wasn't at random, though you made it look that way."

"I was watching their expressions," Golbahar said. "They kept leaning away from Dehan. And he flinched when I looked at them, so I knew they wouldn't hide evidence on his behalf."

"He did us a favor when he tried to attack you," the Sayeh said. "That was a mistake."

"Geomancy can encourage people to make mistakes." Ata Akhimah's voice was dry, her attention seemingly focused somewhere down the corridor.

Tsering-la glanced over at her, fighting a smile. "Is that strictly ethical?"

She said, "No. But then, neither is forgery."

18

IF SHE NEVER HAD TO SEE ANOTHER FORCE AT ARMS, SAYEH WOULD NOT MOURN. Unfortunately, she had a good vantage point atop Mrithuri's elephant, and from there she could clearly see at least three different armies: that of Sarathai-tia, that of Sarathai-lae, and the rebels.

The one comforting point was that this time, one of the armies was hers. Well, not precisely her *own* army: the soldiers owed Mrithuri service as rajni of Sarathai-tia and as empress of all Sarath. They had been freshly paid in links freshly minted with her image and titles. Sayeh *did* have a personal claim on the soldiers who marched with Himadra. But it would probably cause another civil war to press it, and she would never fight against her son.

It pained her to acknowledge that Himadra was right. Between their forces, they had Sekira in a pincer. Sekira—who now styled himself as General Sekira—and whichever sorcerer was riding beside him.

Nizhvashiti floated alongside the elephant's ear. Both Wizards rode behind Mrithuri and Sayeh. Nazia had been left behind, over her protests. The Lady Golbahar and the poetess Ümmühan were charged with holding the fort. Himadra's brothers were at sea in one of the armada of trading vessels that had fled Sarathai-lae ahead of the advancing armies. They could be called back, if Mrithuri or Sayeh or Himadra survived the coming battle.

And if not, the future of the realms would devolve on the shoulders of a boy of fifteen.

Hathi had been decked in mirrored armor and hung with charms. Silk trappings draped her sides, rippling in the wind, embroidered in every imaginable color.

Sayeh found herself thinking how excited Drupada would be to meet a real elephant. She bit the inside of her cheek.

Mrithuri too was in armor. The style was decades old; the gilt-and-blue enamel pattern on the breastplate was a lion with a sunburst mane. The helm had a blue-and-orange crest of feathers and was hopelessly out of fashion. Sayeh was reasonably sure that it had been intended for some royal boy of Anuraja's generation. Perhaps even the dead would-be emperor himself, when he was a slip of a thing.

If they lost and Vivaan was all that was left to hold back the beast, it would hardly be the first time children went to battle. Mrithuri herself had been barely more than a child when she inherited. She was not doing too badly, all things considered. Sometimes, her fragile bravery caught in Sayeh's throat.

"Sekira will think you're Vivaan in that kit," Sayeh teased, trying to lighten a grim silence.

"Only if Vivaan came from fifty years ago." From her position on Hathi's neck, she stroked the elephant's domed head. "Anyway, it's just as well if he does think I'm a boy. Otherwise, he'll probably want to marry me too." The new empress sounded exhausted.

Sayeh could not blame her. Most women's lives would be better for a little less marrying and a little more choice in who they were to marry. And a little less childbearing, too.

"We can't fall back to the city," Tsering-la said, breaking Sayeh's brief, bitter reverie. "There's no way to defend it."

"We'll just have to rely on Himadra," Sayeh said. Her tone came out savage. There was no inflection that could give voice to the fury that curdled in her stomach. Maybe he would ride right up Sekira's ass and vice versa until they both vanished in a puff of reciprocal proctology.

Sadly, the Mother was never so kind.

A FEW RANKS BACK FROM THE VANGUARD, THE DEAD MAN RODE BESIDE GEN-eral Pranaj. The newly promoted General Zirha and the Laeish men had been placed in the left flank, in the hopes that they would not have to come into direct contact with friends and former shieldmates—and the tempta-tion to switch sides or just remove themselves from conflict.

How many soldiers could Sekira have, in a reasonable expectation? There hadn't been *that* many desertions, and there just weren't that many men of military age left over in and around Sarathai-lae. The sorcerers might have access to mercenaries, but . . .

When they came within sight of Sekira's army, those hopes evaporated. The Dead Man, to his displeasure, had plenty of experience estimating the size of forces, and it looked as if Sekira had three times the men that Pranaj and Zirha together commanded. They were well-formed-up and—as he peered through a spyglass—seemed rested. It was infuriating. Where had they all come from?

Himadra's force was on their tail. But Himadra's force was smaller and had just marched from Chandranath. They would be footsore, weary, and ill fed. And they would need time to come up and harry Sekira.

"It's going to be a rout," Pranaj said under his breath, for the Dead Man's ears alone.

The Dead Man stroked his dark brown gelding, a graceless rawboned animal with a ratty tail and well-angled shoulders that he'd liberated from

Anuraja's stables. He didn't care what the animal looked like. He cared about the power in the slanted hindquarters.

"Give me the banner," he said to a nearby foot soldier. The man passed it up and the Dead Man couched it in the guide that should have been for his lance. He was no lancer. But he could wave a banner around with the best of them.

This one had been freshly and crudely sewn. It showed a blind white dolphin of Sarathai-tia leaping over a golden lion's head, all on a deep blue field. It didn't have to look good for the man holding it, though. It only had to look good across the width of a battlefield.

With his other hand, the Dead Man reached for his gun.

"That's one hell of a dust cloud," Himadra said, looking toward the sea and the pale towers of the city before it. The shape of the cloud and its movements against the sky told him of two armies moving toward one another—one much, much larger than the other. "I guess Sayeh Rajni relayed the message."

The Gage and the old woman Kyrlmyrandal walked alongside his horse. Farkhad rode on his right.

Iri and Prince Drupada had been left back in camp with a small honor guard led by Himadra's best tracker. They would evacuate if things went badly, regroup, and try to make it to Sarathai-tia to connect with any other survivors. There was no point in sending a toddler with no army back to Chandranath. It would just lure enemies down upon the Chandranathi people, who could ill afford it.

Himadra's brothers were in that city ahead. Things could not be allowed to go badly.

One advantage of having fielded such a small force: there were horses enough for everybody, though Chandranath would be relying on buffalo for its plowing and sowing if the rains ever came again. If there were anything to plow for or to sow with.

"Can you keep up with a cavalry charge?" Himadra asked the Gage.

"I can restrain myself," the Gage replied.

Himadra almost called the old woman Ata, and remembered in time that she still claimed not to be a Wizard. "Grandmother, I can offer you a horse."

"Don't worry about me," she said. She tapped her staff on the stony road beside the Gage's enormous brass foot. "I can follow this one. He makes enough noise for an army."

Never tell a person what they are not capable of, Himadra reminded himself. "I'll be behind you, then. I'm going to ride up that bluff for the view, with my flagmen."

There was no point in being down among the chaos of combat where he couldn't see, when he could not swing an axe, where he could not give commands. He had his javelins and his crossbow, but he could not take a blow even on a shield without breaking bones, and he could not direct troops if the troops were overrunning him. The bluff he had in mind overlooked the road and the city and the plain upon which two armies were about to meet. His men would be able to see his flags, and he would be able to see their movements.

His inspirational speeches had been delivered as the Cauled Sun set. There was nothing left now but the fight.

"Go on, then," he said, and patted Farkhad on the elbow. "I'll see you on the other side."

He wondered if his bravado sounded as empty as it felt. He coughed. "And watch for my flags this time, dammit."

Farkhad laughed. "Liar, my lord. You know I always do."

The Gage watched the Lord of Chandranath ride away. Farkhad, too, had turned his head. The lieutenant frowned. Ahead, down the sweep of the road, two dark, amorphous shadows on the brightly starlit earth were moving toward one another. There were banners, and men, and horses, and the Gage's inhuman vision could make out the shape of an elephant like a slightly larger ivory toy amid all the specks that might be tiny soldiers carved from splinters of bone.

He said to Kyrlmyrandal, "This is not your fight. Are you sure about this?"

"Oh," she said. "I think you need me."

The shadows met. Now the sound floated up from the plain, thin and distant, voices raised and metal clashing. The Gage felt hollow in his metal heart.

Farkhad lifted the lance with the banner on it once, twice, thrice. Together, the men of Chandranath and Ansh-Sahal, one cavalry now, reined forward at a walk. The Gage walked with them, steadily, tall enough to top the horses' shoulders.

They parted in front of him. Kyrlmyrandal followed, outrunning the horses, her staff swinging and her robe swishing with each prodigious bound. The Gage surged into the van with a clear path. Strides lengthened, the steady clop of hooves breaking into a rolling thunder. He too lengthened his stride, breaking from a heavy trot to an earth-shattering run as the enemy came within clear sight and the horses began to gallop.

The rear of the enemy was turned to meet them. The gap closed. Arrows fell now, ringing off the Gage's carapace. He threw his arms wide to give what shelter he could to those behind him. His well-oiled joints clicked and glided. The ground struck his feet with hammerblows. Swords, spears deflected from his body as harmlessly as rain. His arm swung like a scythe; men fell like wheat before it.

Wheeeeeeee! cried the magic pen.

He laughed, a tolling bell, and lost himself in the tremendous joy of not having to hold himself back, not having to make himself small.

MRITHURI WATCHED FROM THE HEIGHT OF HATHI'S BACK AS HER VANGUARD plunged forward. The Sarathai troops were stretched thin, their line half as deep as the enemy's. They would have to fight like demons to hold long enough for Himadra's cavalry to arrive. Her forces were less than half the usuper's.

You're one to talk, she thought, remembering a certain forgery. Sarcastically, she reminded herself, *It's different when we do it.*

"We're doing a great job of preventing conflict," Mrithuri said. "It looks like we're doing the beast's work for it. Damn everything!"

Nizhvashiti seemed as insensible as if it had finally died for good. It floated beside Mrithuri and did not speak, and took no action.

Tsering-la grunted. His eyes were raised, his hands folded in his lap as he concentrated on the sphere of protection around them. Akhimah stood on the arch of Hathi's back, her boots stripped off, her stockinged feet spread for balance. She peered through Tsering-la's veil of yellow light, panting with exertion as columns of crackling power erupted from the earth among the enemy again, and again, and again.

Mrithuri fancied she could see the Wizard's skin growing tauter across the bones of her face with every use of power. And yet, the flanks of the Sarathai army had begun to bend back under the onslaught of Sekira's men. Units rushed to reinforce—she saw banners moving, surging through the sea of fighters—but it would not be enough, and they could not leave the center vulnerable.

Where was Himadra? Where was the Gage?

As if it were returning from a great distance, Nizhvashiti whispered, "Of course. I think I see."

"See what?" The energy of hope surged from Mrithuri's breast, sizzled along her limbs.

But the Godmade did not answer. Instead, it began to rise, floating amidst a fluttering of bleached-black robes. It sailed up like a leaf on the wind, passing through the protective globe of light as if it were no more than the rays of the sun.

"How on earth did they do that?" asked Sayeh. "And where are they going?"

Mrithuri had no answer.

✶ ✶ ✶

THERE WERE JUST TOO MANY OF THE ENEMY. THE DEAD MAN LED HIS MEN again and again against them, moving his unit at speed from place to place, wherever the push came, wherever the line grew thin. Men fell around him. The brown horse heaved for breath. He had lost Pranaj somewhere in the battle, but once in a while, the general's voice came to him, shouting orders above the din of combat.

He could feel as much as see the line of the defenders bending back, the flanks starting to collapse. It was a sense born of too many battles. He charged pell-mell the length of the army to shore up the left flank, the brown horse thundering along with a turn of speed he hadn't expected. General Zirha was there, fighting hand to hand like a madman, his sword a blur. He might not be much of a commander or tactician, but the Dead Man had not seen anything to exceed his personal ferocity.

The Dead Man felt it when the movement of the enemy shifted. Some of their momentum was broken. The weight came off the line. There, there was Himadra, somewhere on the other side, distracting the enemy. Some of them were turning, defending their rear.

Some. But so many of them remained. It was not enough.

The Dead Man brought his men around to fill the hole in the line, faced down six or seven times as many of the enemy as what he had to fight them with. Something cold took him in the chest.

He'd felt it before, in Asitaneh. He had been one of very few who had survived the fighting then.

His pistols were empty. He still had his sword. He raised the blade before his eyes for a moment and made his peace with the Scholar-God.

"There's a lot of sweet grass in Paradise," he said to his gelding. With leg and rein he lined the lathered horse up for a charge. It blew heavy breaths, but he felt it lower its head and lift its back beneath him.

A sound struck him like the swell of a wave lifting a wader. Sweet, pure, crystalline. It washed through him and over and left him buoyed, left him clean.

The sound of Nizhvashiti's chime. The one the Eyeless One had sent with him and the Gage from Messaline. The one that destroyed illusion.

Half of the men in the enemy charge shivered and vanished like smoke rings blown into a breeze. Gaps opened in the ranks; gaping holes; plenty of room to lead a charge into.

"Ysmat's sacred arsehole," the Dead Man bellowed. "That fucking sorcerer!" He gathered his wits and his reins. "To me, men of Sarath! TO ME!"

IN THE WAKE OF THE SOUND, A GLOOM LIKE THE SHADOW OF A THUNDERCLOUD fell over the Gage. Kyrlmyrandal's staff dropped to the ground behind him.

Something enormous loomed. For a dizzying moment, he thought the walking cities had come out of the desert and followed him there, to Sarathai-lae.

But no: the thing that loomed over him was a dragon. Bleached white with age, scales marred and dull over wrinkled hide, rent wings streaked crimson and vermilion between the gaps where the stars shone through. It was Kyrlmyrandal, restored to her true form by the peal of Nizhvashiti's illusion-destroying chime.

That was the sound that had washed across the battlefield.

She laughed. The air shook with the might of it. Horses squealed; men shrieked. There was the distant trumpeting of an elephant. The Gage let fall the man he had been grasping. Half the enemy had burned away like a morning mist.

The dragon took a step forward, picking her way, putting talons as wide as a wagon-bed down so carefully. Her head lowered. She cast from side to side, lids dropped over blank white eyes, nostrils flaring. Men scrambled away from the enormous head, climbing over one another. Horses threw their riders. The screaming didn't stop.

"I smell you, little sorcerer," Kyrlmyrandal said, in her voice that shook the hollow places in the Gage's carapace until he rattled like a box full of stones. "Where are you? Here *I* am."

MRITHURI LOOKED UP AT THE DRAGON. A SENSATION CONTRACTED THE TISsues of her mouth, astringent as over-brewed tea, as underripe persimmon. Tsering-la's jaw dropped; the orb of light protecting them dropped also.

"Shit," he said, and struggled to reconstruct it.

Nizhvashiti dropped from above in a swirl of cloth. It placed a desiccated hand upon his arm. "Let it be. The Mother of Exiles is not an enemy."

"Dragon," Sayeh said.

Ata Akhimah nodded. She swallowed. "The Mother of Exiles is a *dragon?*"

19

WHEN THE ENEMY LINE BROKE BEFORE THE DEAD MAN, HE THOUGHT AT FIRST he had died in truth and that the ghost of his hammerheaded gelding was carrying him across a rolling plain to heaven. But then the enormous laughter carried to him, a sound like the booming of a giant. When he looked up, he saw the shape looming over the battlefield. It was so huge, so overwhelming, so incomprehensible in scale that the brown horse didn't spook or shy. He just kept galloping, as if the monstrous pale legs were merely pillars, as if the bulk overhead were the roof of a training arena. Other horses screamed and scattered, but the brown gelding was already running and apparently didn't see any reason not to keep at it.

Two more strides while the Dead Man tried to talk him into settling from a breakneck charge to a more collected canter—or even, perhaps, a walk!—and then the horse did shy, planting his feet and sliding to a halt as if a wall had sprouted before him. The Dead Man pitched up the horse's neck, managing to stab neither himself nor the animal. Nor did he wind up flat on his face in the dirt, which—under the circumstances—he counted a victory.

This time, his stirrups fit.

When he pushed himself up again, he blinked twice before he could make himself believe his eyes. A shine of grimy metal through the dust of the battlefield; a surface no longer mirror-bright but dulled to a satiny finish.

The Dead Man was out of his saddle and hurling himself at the hulking figure in the tattered undyed robes before he realized he was moving. He threw himself at the Gage like a child embracing a returning mother, hugging the metal man as far around the waist as his arms could reach. The pommel of his sword rang off the Gage's back as if he had struck a gong.

The Gage stood with arms spread gently, not returning the embrace but holding very still. The Dead Man squeezed him harder, thumping on his back until he pealed like a slightly muffled bell.

The Dead Man's horse tugging to get away brought him back to the moment. Reflexively, he had held on to the reins. Whatever towered above them was apparently so far outside of the gelding's experience he couldn't be afraid of it. But he could manage to be afraid of walking statues.

The Dead Man stepped back. His cheeks hurt from grinning. The Gage, of course, was expressionless.

The gelding stopped leaning against his bit, but he stayed well behind the Dead Man.

"It's good to see you, too," the Gage said calmly. "I missed you."

"Since you brought an army, you're forgiven for your long absence. Did you find the Carbuncle?"

"Not exactly. But I did bring back a magic pen." The Gage pointed toward the shape looming over them. "And a friend."

"What's that?" asked the Dead Man, looking up.

"That," the Gage said, "is an *actual* dragon. Not an ice-drake. Would you like to meet her?"

The Dead Man swallowed. "Are you sure this is a good idea?"

The Gage boomed a laugh. "What's the worst that could happen?"

"I'm *edible*."

The Gage bent toward him quizzically, then straightened. "Oh, right. That. It'll be fine. She's friendly."

"Easy for you to say, metal man." But when the Gage walked toward the towering creature, the Dead Man followed.

It was a rout. And not the rout of his own side that Himadra had been more than half-expecting.

He'd bitten his own lip in self-exasperation when the illusionary soldiers vanished, gotten a beard hair stuck between his teeth, and still managed to signal a rally and charge to take advantage of the usurper's disarray. A rally and charge that never happened because as Himadra's men responded to the flags, the dragon appeared.

By the time Himadra got Velvet back under control, they were halfway down the back side of the bluff. He eased her to a walk. She shook her head, complaining, while several of Himadra's men on their horses galloped after. She wasn't about to let just any horse beat her in a race.

He got her turned around and headed back up the hill, resisting each step but too well trained to make a fight of it. Her head was high, her neck taut, her ears straining.

He wouldn't have made her do it if his need hadn't been so dire.

A sensible man would let the horse bolt, and take off into the mountains.

Well, very few people had ever called Himadra of Chandranath "sensible."

He talked to Velvet under his breath. "I know, girl. I know it's scary. I know you want to run. Just a step. Another step."

Rocks scattered down the slope as the others caught up to them, and Himadra had everything he could do to keep Velvet pointed in the right direction. By some miracle, not one horse went heels over head bolting down the hillside. If Velvet had fallen, it would have killed him, and the coldness in his palms and at the back of his throat told him his body knew it.

Himadra saw that the flagmen had remained behind. He swelled with appreciation for their courage. Velvet calmed a little at finding herself among the herd again. Now they had a half-dozen horses to wrestle back up the slope.

By the time they regained the vantage, the action was over. What remained of Sekira's army was evaporating like a fog when the wind blows through it. Sekira himself was nowhere to be seen, though Himadra had to admit that the enormous dragon looming over the battlefield was something of a distraction.

"What the hell?" said Navin through his grizzled mustache.

"Dragon," Himadra replied succinctly, with an air of worldly indifference. "There's the white elephant. Let's go see if we can join forces with the Empress."

"You want us to ride down there?"

Himadra surveyed the horses, their lathered necks, their trembling ears. "Maybe you had better lead the horses."

THE GAGE STEPPED AWAY FROM THE DEAD MAN MOSTLY BECAUSE HE WAS tired of the horse fussing. That, and the repetitive thumping on his lumbar region caused a disconcerting vibration inside his carapace. The armies had parted around them—Himadra's men regrouping at a signal, Sekira's in rout. The line of Mrithuri's soldiers was moving in a hasty but orderly fashion away from the dragon. They seemed to be falling back to the bulky shape of Hathi in her glittering armor.

There was something on the battlefield brighter than the Gage. That armor would have outshone him even if he retained his usual sparkle.

Kyrlmyrandal's head lowered over them. The Gage said, "Are you going to come back down here?"

"The seeming is broken," the dragon said. She settled her wings against her gaunt sides as best she could. The tip of the crooked one dragged. "I'm afraid this is what you get."

"Well, that's not going to be easy to hide," said the Dead Man.

"Come on," the Gage replied. "Your usurper is escaping. Let's go and get him."

He sprinted after the fleeing army while the Dead Man, taken by surprise, struggled to remount. His horse was done with this nonsense. The Dead Man managed to thrash into the saddle despite its resistance. He kicked it after the Gage.

It had a surprising turn of speed.

The Gage's feet pounded rutted earth. He ran through scorched patches, altered his stride so as not to splatter the bodies of the fallen. The fields looked as if they had been harrowed without first bringing the crop in. Armies were not the best thing to roll across your farmland.

Men and horses scattered before him as his pace increased. Each stride came a little longer, a little faster than the last. Each foot fell a little harder in the rutted earth, sticking briefly until his momentum pulled it free. The Gage was not designed for sudden starts—or stops. But when barreling across a field without obstacles, he could come on like an avalanche.

The Dead Man on his brown horse followed gamely, the horse hurtling obstacles the Gage simply plowed through: hedges, stone walls, a thatch roof somehow come loose from its moorings and resting upside down like a vacant turtle shell. They were patently a spectacle.

Fleeing soldiers to both sides glanced over their shoulders at the earth-quake rumble of the Gage's charge. They staggered, stumbled to a halt. Turned back to stare, stock-still as the prey observing the predator.

Those ahead, those in the Gage's path, kept running. He overtook them. They scattered like a covey of quail. Those closest fell to their knees or tumbled onto their faces as the earth shuddered away from his stride.

More running steps, and the battlefield—and most of those fleeing the battlefield—fell behind.

There. Just cresting the line of a hill, the Gage saw two horses. The rear-most one's haunches were draped with a tiger skin. He charged up the slope, his own weight and the huge clods of mud booting his feet dragging against his momentum and his redoubled effort. Despite all he could do, he slowed.

But he crested the hill still running, and without breaking stride he headed down the other side.

He didn't know what a sorcerer could do to him. But Wizardry, at least, took some time. So he hoped that if he hit them fast enough, and kept hit-ting, they wouldn't have time to try.

He'd far outstripped the Dead Man and his mount by now. The Gage ran alone, and as he pelted down the far side of the hill his gait became a series of huge bounds. Two horses, yes, and they heard him coming. They stretched out their necks and fled as if some Rasan demon were behind them.

Two horses. But only one rider.

The Gage cursed in a language he had not had occasion to speak in de-cades. He ran faster. He'd followed a decoy. He wouldn't find Sekira unless he caught the sorcerer—it was the female half of the pair—and got the information out of her.

At least this gadfly would be a useful captive in her own right.

The sorcerer had to know he was coming. She could probably hear him, even above the thunder of hooves. She bent low over the withers of her mount, her braid bouncing behind her, her hat lost to the air. She let go of the horse she was leading. It split off to the left. She kicked her own mount, which didn't need it. The bay was already running as hard as it could.

A moment later, the air in front of her began to twist in a manner the

Gage, experienced with magic, did not like. He gathered himself and leaped as hard as he could, hurling himself through the air toward the horse and its rider. It would not go well for the horse when he landed, and he felt bad about that, but there wasn't much he could do about it now.

His outstretched gauntlets brushed the sorcerer's coat hem, gusting behind her. He clutched; the fabric tore like gauze. There was a moment of resistance, a sense of the sorcerer beginning to be dragged back—

And then the horse leaped; the rider clutched the saddle; they vanished slice by slice like the weighted streamers he had seen thrown into sword-dancers' whirling blades.

He struck the ground face-down, arms extended, and churned through it like a badly designed plow, ripping through roots, hurling clods and rocks in every direction.

The Gage lay there, assessing the damage. Grass and dirt were ground into his joints. There was, perhaps, a dent here and there. Cleaning himself would be a tedious process. But he was unbroken and largely unharmed.

The beat of hooves warned him the Dead Man was approaching. When the horse's shadow fell over him, he saw its heaving chest and lathered sides. The Dead Man was wild-eyed above his veil, scarf ends and whatnot escaping.

Something dangled from his right hand. The sorcerer's emerald-green cloth hat.

The Gage dragged his arms out of the dirt, braced his hands beside his shoulders, and pushed himself to his knees. Creaking, joints grinding, he stood.

"You missed," said the Dead Man.

The Gage said, "Fuck you."

ONCE THEY ASCERTAINED THAT THE DRAGON WASN'T ABOUT TO START EATING anybody, Sayeh went to help with the wounded. There were so many of them, men sitting on the ground or lying in uneven rows. She had more empathy for them than she might have before her own misadventure of the shattered leg. In the aftermath, it was hard to look at their wounds without re-experiencing her own pain.

She wished she had a veil like Lady Golbahar's, to hide the unregal manner in which her face wanted to pinch. Distress was not reassuring.

Sayeh was not a skilled healer. But she could hold a dressing in place or flush out a wound, and that made her useful. She could help care for those who were not under threat of immediate and various mortal dangers. Hnarisha and the Wizards and the army doctors were more than occupied with cases that lay beyond her small skills.

The men she helped were awake and aware, for the most part, and to her surprise they did not seem bothered that a rajni condescended to bathe their wounds with her own hands. Once upon a time, Sayeh would have worried about preserving the dignity of her office. Now, illusions of dignity long abandoned, she was just happy to have something useful to do. Something to distract her from waiting for a message to be returned from Himadra regarding her request to meet with him.

And the men were extremely grateful. She heard them whispering when her back was turned. *The rajni came to help us. The rajni is here.*

One of the men she treated was Sergeant Pren, Sanjay's partner as her guard when she had been Anuraja's captive. He was hurt in the calf but, she thought, not too badly. He might walk with a limp like hers when he healed.

She squeezed his hand before she left. He almost wept with gratitude.

Drupada was right there, somewhere near. So close she could almost feel him. If she paused for even a moment, she would think of nothing else except her son. Her beautiful, beautiful Drupada. Her body ached with longing. She wanted to sit down on the ground beside the wounded and wrap her arms around her knees and do nothing until Himadra surrendered him. She wanted to ride into Himadra's camp and demand his immediate return.

But that would gain her nothing and might lose her everything. So she bathed her hands in blood, because the need of the wounded men was immediate and distracting. She finished with one, stood up again on her lame leg, and forced the aching limb to push her on to the next.

So intent was she, limping her way down the lines, that she startled back a step when the soldier she had just smiled vaguely at did a double take and blurted, "Your Abundance!"

His clothes were tattered and grimy with more than the damage of the battle they had all just come through, but he wore the emblem of Ansh-Sahal. And his accent—his accent had the soft vowels of home. She didn't know him. She wouldn't have expected to: a leader couldn't know every subject of their nation unless their nation were very small indeed. But she knew who he was. Or, at least, where he had come from.

She crouched and held out her hand. "Soldier," she said. "Your voice is like music to me. Are you much wounded?"

He showed her the gash in his leg. She soaked the cloth of his trousers loose and used scissors that had once been meant for embroidery to trim it away. Across the front of the thigh, and the muscle was cut though not severed. It would need stitches, but he would not bleed to death before someone with the skill to do so could manage. He told her his name. It was Abbus.

As she wound cloth around his leg, she asked, "How many of your compatriots came south?"

He had leaned back on his elbows, looking resolutely up at the sky. It hurt, what she was doing. And perhaps he also found it embarrassing. "Four hundred and some," he said.

She closed her eyes against the tears that started.

Perhaps he noticed, because he hastened to add, "That's just the soldiers. There's another ten hundred, perhaps, back in Chandranath. Not fighters."

"So few," she whispered. She gave herself a moment to feel it, feel the loss of ten thousand people or more, the majority of the folk of Ansh-Sahal.

"Some others went east, my rajni," Abbus said. "I don't know how many. And maybe some went into the mountains, north."

She thought of telling him not to call her *rajni*. How could she be, when her city was broken, obliterated from the earth. When she herself had only survived by a fluke. Because she had been chasing Himadra.

But perhaps he needed her to be his leader now. And his priest.

She laid a hand on his forehead. The dust of the battlefield gritted between their skins. "The Mother bless you," she said. "That wound will need stitches. Here, you must drink some water."

He drank what she offered. At least there was enough of that for everyone.

"Will we go home, Rajni?" he asked her. His eyes seemed to shine from the bottom of their sockets, like water reflecting light in deep wells.

"We will find another home," she promised him. "Ansh-Sahal is dead."

She hadn't said those words before. Spoken in her own native tongue, they hung in the air between her and Abbus. They had a weight and reality that left her stunned. As if she had pronounced out the life of a loved one.

She squeezed his hand one last time and stood, almost blind with unshed tears. The boy carrying her water buckets and bandages scrambled to follow; she waved him off, stumbling only slightly as she walked away as quickly as possible. She'd come back, she'd come back. She just needed a minute.

It was all so much.

And it wasn't yet over.

SAYEH WAS NOT CERTAIN FOR HOW LONG SHE WALKED, BUT SHE DIDN'T THINK it was more than a quarter-hour. Her leg had ached already, so she couldn't use pain as the meter of her exertion. But when she looked up, she had somehow come a fair distance from the carnage, the smells of smoke and blood, the shouts and the screaming.

The injured horses suffered in silence, as horses will. The injured men made noise.

She found herself on a bank above the milk-white water, standing on an undercut bluff overlooking the sprawl of a delta so broad and slow that it seemed more like a vast lake striated with almond-shaped islands than the outflow of the slow old peripatetic Sarathai. Caution told her not to go too close to the edge, so she stood on tiptoe to see better. The light of the Heavenly River reflected in the surface of the earthly one. The waters here seemed more like skimmed milk, bluish and dilute. The tang in the air had a brackish note.

Tides, she thought. *Tides push the seawater up into the body of the Mother. This is where the Mother Wyrm makes her home.*

As if it heard her, Sayeh saw something massive lift in the distance. Like a white, rolling hill, the long body of the creature she had rescued lifted above the surface and fell again, one smooth glide. She reached out to it, her fingers absently pressing in the numb patches on her palms. Her mind brushed its mind, ancient and slow. She felt quick and ephemeral by comparison, and as shallow as the starlight glinting off the surface of the river.

Her friend the Wyrm had beaten them home, slipping downriver faster than armies could march, swimming with the current, sliding along the silty channel. It was healthy now, strong and contented, no longer in pain. The raw patches on its hide were healing, coated in protective slime.

She felt proprietary toward it, protective. She felt its amusement in return.

This was better than a battlefield. Better than a ruined city. Better than the faith of men she was not certain she could protect. This was a thing that did not need her. That had only ever needed her because one of her kind had dragged it from its home and harmed it. Had stuck it on a hook and made it squirm.

Something dark engulfed her without warning. She drew a breath to shout—for help, in surprise, equal parts of the two—and a strong scent made her head spin. She would have fallen to her knees but someone supported her, tugging her elbows although her hands were bound to her sides somehow. She stumbled, felt herself spun in place. There were hands on her, dragging her along. It was dark, and the smoky, sticky sweetness cloyed at the back of her throat, made it impossible to think. She gasped and the world rocked under her feet.

"Careful there," a man said. "That's a valuable package. Bring the horse over; there you go. Upsy-daisy, my girl."

Somebody planted a hand on her backside and pushed. Something hard dug into her stomach. She tried to complain. Her words came out furry and far away.

"Crap, what is that?" A different man, voice muffled. "It's coming this way!"

Through the cloth, Sayeh heard a swishing like a tremendous wave. Somebody swung into the saddle behind her. Knees dug into her hips and shoulders. Bile rose in her throat. She wasn't going to vomit in this sack, this sack full of . . . poppy smoke?

That was the smell, the tarry sweetness. She recognized it; Tsering-la had given it to her for pain after the violent birth of Drupada. That was why she couldn't think. Her mind was full of poppy.

The rushing sound grew louder. A great splashing followed, a muddy sound like an elephant belly-flopping into a mudbath.

The Mother Wyrm. The Mother Wyrm felt her fear and confusion.

The Mother Wyrm was coming for her.

The horse squealed in terror and whirled underneath her. She would have been thrown off, but somebody had looped ropes attached to the sack they'd stuffed her into over the pommel-tree. So she slid around in the sack, instead, bruised against the saddle and the rider.

"Go!" a man shouted. "Go, go, go!"

The horse didn't need any encouragement. It bolted. She slid into the rider's lap, jouncing painfully on his knees. He cursed; apparently it didn't feel too good to him, either.

Something crashed heavily behind her, a great body striking the earth of the bluff. The horse staggered as the earth shook under its hooves. Then it flattened out, running as if all the devils in a Rasan hell had broken loose and flooded behind it. Sayeh heard chunks of earth falling, great boulders splashing, the wet slide of a mighty body falling back into the river. Men shouted, their voices fading backward.

Her head swam. She struggled to stay awake, to keep her eyes open in the smoke-stinging blackness. She couldn't see. She held her breath but the horse's strides jolted it out of her.

There was too much poppy. She was drowning in musty sweetness.

She slid downward into the dark and hoped the horse would run out of terror before her ribs broke.

ATA AKHIMAH WORKED THROUGH A BLUR OF WOUNDED LIMBS AND DENTED heads. A medic from the Tian army followed her to assist, handing her bandages and restraining wounded men. Her hands did what was needed; her eyes barely lifted to register a face. There were too many of them.

Each pause beside a soldier was time during which another had to suffer. They were losing the light and cool of night. Soon they would be toiling in the heat and darkness of day. Men were dying while they waited for care, and there was no one even available to cart the dead away.

She found herself treating men of all the principalities of Sarath-Sahal, including soldiers abandoned by Sekira when he fled. Mother, where was Sekira?

She'd met, briefly, Mrithuri's metal friend. She'd heard his report of the chase, of Ravani's escape into what she could only assume was a dragon-gate.

So focused was she on her work that she noticed her assistant staring over her shoulder with a horrified expression before she even registered the terrific crashing noise.

She turned, straining over her shoulder, the awkward pose reminding her of how much her neck and upper back hurt. She was in time to catch a glimpse of something pale and enormous sliding back into the water, having left an enormous muddy dent in the river bank.

"What the hell?" said the man whose arm she was stitching. She turned back to him. She still held a needle and thread.

"The Mother Wyrm," she answered, and made the last two knots quickly while he winced and made himself hold steady. Arms were better than hands and fingers any day. Scalps were her least favorite because of the blood and the way they tended to pull back from the wound, but working on them didn't upset the patient as much as stitching fingers.

"I need to investigate," Ata Akhimah told the assistant. "I'll be back as quickly as possible. See who you can bandage; do whatever you can."

"Ata—"

"Monsters," she said, rising to her feet, "are on the list of things that are my job."

SHE WAS SO TIRED, HER RUNNING FEET HIT THE GROUND LIKE BAGS OF SAND, each impact jarring her knees and body. She called it a run, but it would have been fairer to describe it as "stagger." She felt light, frail, dried out—like a husk when the wind has blown all the seeds away. And yet somehow her weight seemed to have tripled.

She reached down into the core of herself, trying to find the strength to call up one more blazing pillar. It was like trying to blow out a candle after exhaling until she was dizzy. There was just nothing left inside her.

She didn't think she could do more than discomfit the Mother Wyrm, if it were being driven to hump its entire incomprehensible length out of the Sarathai and attack the armies as it had attacked the gates of Sarathai-tia. Sayeh Rajni had released it from the command that drove it upriver. Where was she now?

But as Akhimah drew a little closer, she realized that the Wyrm was not climbing the bank. It had stretched itself to a great length, and the curling catfish fronds surrounding its blind face groped outward. One gripped a man by the ankle; he screamed and clutched at the stones.

Akhimah heard hoofbeats: three running horses galloping away. Only two had riders. The third man must be the one on the ground.

He yelped for help. She thought the tendril clutching him didn't have the strength to haul him back toward the Wyrm's mouth . . . but now the Wyrm itself was sliding down the bank, and where it had mass, not much strength was necessary. The frond stretched. The man began to grind backward, hands flailing.

There was something a Wizard of Ata Akhimah's school could do about this. She bent down, touched the tendril, and reached inside it with her mind. There were currents . . . traces inside the meat . . . paths of energy. And if she touched one, tickled it in just the right way—

It was a technique she usually used to ease the pain of sore muscles. But under these circumstances . . .

The tendril released.

Ata Akhimah grabbed the man by his wrists and hauled him, scrambling, away from the Wyrm as it fell back down the bluff and toppled into the river like the greatest imaginable tree. Wet silt splattered around them, splashing Akhimah's black trousers like thrown milk. The man was abominably heavy. He fell, scraped his bloody hands further, and eventually managed to prop himself on his knees, panting.

"Thank you," he said. "Thank you!" He looked up at her face, and his eyes showed a bright ring of white. "Oh, shit."

If he'd managed to keep his composure, she might have thought very little of his misadventure. But the moment of panic gave him away. "Stand up," she said. "I guess you must be one of Sekira's men? We have some questions to ask you."

✴   ✴   ✴

SAYEH WOKE, AND IMMEDIATELY REGRETTED HER EXISTENCE. HER HEAD ached, a hangover worse than any she'd gotten from wine. Her body ached worse than if she'd been thrown by a horse. Thrown by a horse, perhaps, and then run over by it. She lay in the dimness, hurting, feeling the lumps of a thin pallet on the earth under her body. She did not know where she was.

She tried to put her hands up to rub her eyes and discovered that they were not only numb, they were tied behind her. She was lying on her side. Her shoulder hurt from the pressure. Her neck, when she lifted her head, sent spikes of discomfort across her scalp and down her back. Her internal organs felt as if somebody had scooped them out and rearranged them, and she had the experience to make an accurate comparison.

Her eyes were crusted shut. There wasn't much light on the other side of the lids. Blinking them open was a slow, gritty, uncomfortable process. The tears generated by the pain of trying to unstick her lashes from each other helped, eventually.

It seemed to be dim daytime, though her view of the sky was blocked by rocky outcrops. The Cauled Sun was low rather than overhead, out of sight. Its heat either waned or was not yet formidable. Sayeh guessed the latter. She did not think she had been unconscious for hours.

Memory returned bit by bit, and with it the patient simmering of her rage. It was not just that she had been kidnapped and was presumably being held hostage. *Again.* It was that they had stuffed her into a sack like so much baggage.

Not even Anuraja had dared to so degrade her.

Anger was good. She felt the pain less when she was angry. It was easier to plan without the pain distracting her.

First thing: to get her hands free. And the first step to that was to get her hands in front of her.

No point in rolling around like a fool if the hostage-takers were watching her, though. She thought she could hear breathing nearby.

She'd wiggled around enough that anybody looking on would know she was awake. Whoever it was hadn't said anything, though, or called out to warn anyone. So there was no harm in sitting up and trying to ease the cramp between her shoulders.

So she told herself, trying not to think what a kick in bruised ribs would feel like if a guard took exception.

She struggled up and discovered to her surprise that the person whose presence she had sensed was no guard and not even any stranger. Rather, it was Nazia.

The apprentice Wizard lay on the ground about the length of Sayeh's body away, trussed up as Sayeh was trussed. Nazia was frowning at her as if trying to project her thoughts across the space between them.

Sayeh kept her voice low. "You could have said something."

"I didn't want to startle you until I was sure you were awake." Nazia sat up also, more nimbly than Sayeh. The young would never appreciate their youthfulness until it was gone.

Nazia's still-short hair was full of bits of chaff. She blew the fringe out of her eyes.

Sayeh asked, "How did you get here?"

The girl's nose wrinkled. "It turns out some of the palace guards are still friends with Sekira."

"Hm," Sayeh said. "Would you recognize them again?"

"Oh, yes."

They kept their voices low. Sayeh stretched her neck and looked around. In the faint light of day, she could see that they had been placed on some canvas sheets spread among boulders. The ground beneath them was just as unforgiving as she had thought. When she opened her mouth and turned her head from side to side, she could make out voices but not what they were saying. There was no smell of fire or food or brewing tea.

Well, if their captors planned to keep them for any length of time, that did not bode well for comfort.

"How long have you been here?"

Nazia glanced at the sky. "Since just before sunrise. I gathered that they intended to use me as bait to lure you out." The girl's voice softened. "I'm surprised it worked. I didn't think you would come for me."

"It didn't," Sayeh said. "They spotted their opportunity before anyone told me you were gone. Possibly before anybody outside the city knew."

"Oh." Nazia was not one for giving away emotions. But Sayeh had gotten practice at reading them.

"Of course I would have come for you once I knew," Sayeh said. "But I would have brought a Wizard. And probably a couple of swordsmen."

They regarded one another, Sayeh rewarded with the faint brief flash of Nazia's grin. White teeth glimmered in the twilight.

Sayeh winked. "Well, they don't seem to be paying much attention to us for the time being. Let's not give them a chance to re—"

She cut herself off at the sound of footsteps. She half-expected Sekira, but the man who came alone around the rocks was some soldier she had never seen before. One of command rank, by the quality of his clothing and the amount of decoration he wore. She could not read the Laeish rank insignia.

He paused not too far away, hands on hips, gloating visibly. No one else joined him. That could be a miscalculation on his part, if he underestimated Sayeh and Nazia. Or it could be a very bad sign for both of them, if he were about to attempt something that no one wanted remembered.

"Vice-commander Sethu," Nazia said, surprising Sayeh. But of course Nazia had spent plenty of time running wild among the troops on the long trail there. It wasn't surprising that she should know some of them. Or that some of the ones she knew might be among the defectors.

Sethu smiled faintly. "Miss Nazia. I hope your wait hasn't been too uncomfortable?"

A year ago, Sayeh might have found his politeness reassuring. Now she knew how often the polite ones were simply the ones who didn't feel the need to make a performance of being intimidating.

Nazia apparently wasn't fooled either. "Have you come to let us go?"

"Not just yet." He went a few steps closer to Nazia. Sayeh shook her hair back from her face, ready to use whatever wiles middle age had left her to distract him from the girl. He made no overt threat, however; he just stood near her.

He said, "You must ally with me, Your Abundance. You must pretend to throw your allegiance behind Sekira. For a time, until we are ready to depose him. Then you can be my empress, Sayeh Rajni."

His voice made it seem as if what he was proposing were perfectly calm and reasonable.

It was not. He was deluded. Or power-mad. The states were not always distinguishable from one another. Especially, Sayeh was coming to understand, when the sorcerers got involved. "What do you think that will accomplish? None of these men follow me. I have no armies."

He shook his head at her, sadly. "You don't need to worry your pretty self about strategy. It is always a help if the enemy is divided and their morale is frayed."

There are beasts that feed on war, Sayeh thought. The object was not victory. The object was just chaos and disarray. They were all deluded by the whisperings of the sorcerer.

He said, "I would rather have your willing assistance. I can rescue your son from that half-sized cripple. I can free you of your obligation to the false Dowager. Surely, it gripes one such as you to bow down to one such as her."

"Only a little," Sayeh said, trying to lighten the tone. His intensity frightened her. It was not the mood of a rational man.

He did just kidnap you and Nazia. You might be looking for rationality in the wrong place, Sayeh.

He touched Nazia's head gently. Her eyes wide, she kept herself from leaning away. He said, "It would be better for you, Your Abundance, if you worked with me."

She cleared her throat. Behind her back, her hands twisted against the ropes. She accomplished nothing but cutting and burning her wrists, warm blood dripping over her hands. "You cannot intimidate me."

He smiled. "But what will you do to protect the child here?"

Suddenly, his hand knotted in Nazia's hair. He dragged at it hard enough that she yelped.

"Let her alone!" The ropes were merciless.

"Boo-hoo," he said.

He picked Nazia up by the hair and slammed her body against the nearest outcrop of rock. She didn't cry out; the sound she made was air being forced from her lungs by the impact. A kind of breathy squeak, and then a terrible rattle as her diaphragm cramped and she struggled to breathe back in again.

He let go of Nazia's hair and smoothed it down. Dirty as it was, it sprang back up in spikes.

Nazia lay against the stone, eyes open, hands still bound behind her. Gasping.

Sethu smiled at Sayeh. "Let's bargain."

"All right," she said. "All right. You've made your point. You don't have to hit her again."

He wasn't a terribly big man, though not small. But the horrible power with which he had driven Nazia into the stone left Sayeh almost as stunned as the girl. Sayeh disciplined herself, allowed her voice to shake only a little. She had to keep his focus on her and buy Nazia a little time to recover.

If she would recover. If the blow hadn't broken a rib, driven it into a lung.

"Yes, Vice-commander," she said. "Let's bargain. There has to be more in this for me than just life."

"Life for you, life for your pet here. I don't know who you think you're fooling, pretending your little nymph is a budding Wizard."

He sneered. Sayeh wondered if he realized how much he was revealing about his own character. And proclivities.

"You want my willing assistance," Sayeh said. She stretched herself and smiled as seductively as possible, gambling that Sethu would both react to her and be enraged by his reaction. It was a risk; men were known to lash out at people who made them examine their own hypocrisies. "You think you can win my son away from Himadra?"

And use him as further leverage against me.

He smiled patronizingly.

Whatever he was about to say, however, never escaped his mouth. He gasped, yelped, and clutched at his thigh. Then grabbed wildly at Nazia, who—with youthful agility—rolled away over the rock she had been lying against. As Sethu's hands came up, a fountain of blood spurted from his leg, driven from the artery by the hard squeeze of his heart behind it.

Nazia landed on her feet, a pale blade glittering in her hand. Her diver's hook knife, which Sayeh had almost forgotten she still carried. She jumped back from the splashing blood and said, "This is the sort of thing that is only going to keep happening if you *will* underestimate women. You should have had three men at least."

"I—"

He fell over.

Shaking her knife, Nazia came to Sayeh and crouched.

Sethu's hands clutched feebly at the ground. Blood pooled on the dry earth. He moaned; it died away into a whisper.

Sayeh said, "How did you hide the hook knife? And how did you hang on to that all the time we were prisoners?"

Nazia held it up and smirked. "No one takes a servant girl very seriously." Nazia looked at the knife. Her lips twisted. "I was looking for a chance to drag it across Anuraja's filthy throat. But I guess you made that irrelevant, my rajni. Now hold still, please. I do not want to cut you."

Sayeh was distracted by the heat of the sensation of pins and needles savaging her hands. She lay back. Returning blood brought pain so strong, she flopped her hands against her chest, trying to massage the life back into them. Her feet, at least, had not been tied so tightly. When Nazia had cut the bindings, Sayeh curled up, hugging her own knees, gasping.

"Is he dead?" she said, when she could manage to string three words together.

Nazia looked over at Sethu disinterestedly. "If he's not, he's well on his way. Will you miss him?"

Sayeh shook her head. She put one hand on the earth to push herself to her feet and felt a faint shiver like a distant earthquake, followed by another. The third one was strong enough to shake the stones she sat upon. She heard a distant hammerblow, and then another. "Bad Daughter, what *now*?"

The Gage burst over the rim of the rock outcrop at a dead run and seemed about to topple down upon them. Sayeh scrambled aside, dragging Nazia with her.

With a prodigious bound, he leaped clear over them and landed on the other side of the hollow among the stones. Now the earth really jumped with impact, striking Sayeh's palms and soles and nearly pitching her to her knees again.

She and Nazia straightened up, balancing against one another.

The Gage turned. "I came to rescue you." A note of amusement colored the metallic voice. "I see I am just in the nick of time."

It wasn't that funny, and yet neither Sayeh nor Nazia could stop laughing. They both sagged. Sayeh put a bloody hand out to the nearest boulder and leaned against it. It was relief, blowing through her like a strong wind.

"How did you find us?" Sayeh asked, when she could breathe mostly normally.

"Ata Akhimah captured one of the kidnappers," he said. "Or rather, a large Wyrm did, and the Ata relieved it of its dinner." He turned his featureless head ostentatiously from side to side. "Have you seen another one?"

"Just this one," Nazia said, looking as if she wished to spurn the corpse with her foot. She had become civilized enough that she restrained herself.

Sayeh wondered if, just this once, manners weren't a pity. "He wanted to take on Sekira and all the rest of us," she said. "I have a feeling those mind-warping sorcerers are at it again."

The Gage made a sound as if a gust of wind echoed around the inside of a mill. "I suppose it was too much to hope that we might have seen the last of them. Can you walk, ladies? I saw three horses at the bottom of the hill."

21

Sleep had been brief, despite his exhaustion, and now Himadra sat upon a round shield cushioned with leather as the sky brightened with sunset. The camp was just stirring. His soldiers had fallen into their bedrolls like so much timber.

Farkhad, who had come from the main camp, crouched beside him. "Three men were assassinated in the night," he said. "Throats slit in their beds. Nobody saw anything."

Himadra blinked at him. "That's a doozy of an opening. Our men?"

Farkhad nodded. "They were on the southern border before"—he gestured—"all this."

"Same unit?"

Farkhad said, "Anti-espionage."

"Hmm," said Himadra. "What did you think of them?"

"Frankly, they were assholes. These are the same ones who captured and interrogated that Tian spy not too long ago, but he escaped."

"Interrogated," said Himadra. "Hmm. Any other torturers in that unit?"

"I don't know," said Farkhad.

Himadra sighed. "Well," he said, "we know the empress has good agents. Possibly one holds a grudge. If it doesn't get out of hand, we'll just chalk it up to the cost of doing business."

"Right," said Farkhad. "Do you need anything else?"

Himadra gestured to the horizon. "Stay within shouting distance for a little while."

Himadra thought he was probably the first besides the perimeter sentries to notice that they were about to have a visit. As Farkhad withdrew, Himadra might have been more concerned about the two riders, leading a spare horse, who were coming down the slope of the hill across from his encampment if they hadn't been accompanied by the hulking, familiar silhouette of a metal man. And if his camp hadn't been bulwarked by the gigantic form of a relaxing dragon.

Kyrlmyrandal lay sprawled on her stomach like an enormous, long-necked, long-legged monitor lizard. Her forked tail-tip twitched idly, making Himadra think of a tiger that was half-awake and half-dreaming. Her bleached body was as big as a hill.

He had been trying to decide how to ask her, without giving offense, why a dragon got involved in human politics. Or upon any conversational opening, really, because it made him nervous to be sitting in the shadow of a dragon and not acknowledging her presence as a guest. He was relieved to have an obvious change in the environment to comment upon.

"Someone is approaching with the Gage," he said. "Do you know who?"

The dragon lifted her head. She inhaled deeply, her damaged wings rising from the roots with the volume of the breath. "Sayeh Rajni," she said complacently. "And a female retainer. They are both covered in blood."

How the dragon knew Sayeh's scent, Himadra decided to leave consigned to the domain of all his other unanswered wonderings. The answer could never be as interesting as the question.

"Covered in blood?"

The dragon tilted her head at him. Well, he supposed many people were. There *had* just been a battle.

"It is not," she said, "their own blood. Mostly."

The more interesting problem was what he was going to do with Sayeh Rajni, and whether she was likely to kick him from there back to Chandranath like a horsehair-stuffed ball as soon as she caught sight of him.

He had a little bell in his pocket that he hated to ring but carried because there were things, sometimes, that he could not do without assistance. He rang it now, wondering if Farkhad would return or send someone else and keep watch.

It wasn't long before a valet was beside him, disheveled from the bedroll he had obviously just dragged himself out of. Himadra would need to remember to reward this one somehow, because the man had been sleeping alongside a dragon in order to stay close to him.

"Company is coming. Royal company. Have them met pleasantly. Bring them warm water for washing, several basins. A table, please, and tea. Sweets if you can find any."

Ladies who were covered in blood would presumably find comfort and utility in hot water and honey in various combinations.

Himadra thought of something else. "There's distillate of wine in my personal stores. A flask of that, also."

Ladies who were covered in blood would presumably also find comfort and utility in something stronger than honey.

Someone brought the table, a long, low thing with legs that folded out from underneath on hinges. Someone else brought a rug to set it on, and cushions to put beside it, two amenities that Himadra had not thought to mention but was glad to have.

He combed his hair and beard in a pocket mirror—a little vanity and a social advantage never hurt a prince—and allowed himself to be assisted from the shield to a cushion at the head of the table. Tea arrived, and small cups, and plates of sweets. Himadra disciplined himself not to ask for the tea to be poured before the guests arrived.

A little respect. A little formality.

The women who arrived, flanking the Gage, were damp indeed, and dusty. But though their clothes were filthy and spattered with red, their hands and faces were clean, and their hair was combed and—in the case of the older one—braided.

This was Sayeh Rajni, whom he had briefly met before. She was still tall, and fair, and even in her battered state quite lovely. She looked different, though. Harder. More wary.

Well, he supposed some of that was his fault.

The much younger woman who accompanied her was broader, muscular, her hair growing out cowlicked spikes. Himadra had no guess who that was.

But he knew how to find out. "Forgive me if I do not rise," he said. "I am Himadra, raja of Chandranath. Welcome to my table."

Sayeh's full lips pressed white. She swung down from her horse, stood grasping the stirrup for a moment while she straightened painfully, and handed the reins to her equally filthy handmaiden.

Himadra steeled himself not to flinch away from her as she limped heavily up to him. She loomed, bloody fists clenching. Her wrists were ringed in scabs.

She took the kind of breath people take when they're making an effort not to punch something, and in eminently reasonable tones she said, "Where the hell is my son?"

Sayeh's nails bit into her palms, and her efforts to uncurl her fists were not having much effect. She tried very hard to keep her glare on Himadra and not look up at the enormous white bulk of the dragon stretched out behind him.

"Please." Himadra indicated the pile of cushions heaped around Sayeh's dirty sandals. "You look like you could use some tea. And possibly a little alcohol."

"Do you think I would eat rice with you?"

"Your son is safe and is being brought here," Himadra said. "You can use this opportunity to loom over me and glare if you like, but I have not had breakfast yet. So I am going to eat. You and your handmaid are welcome to join me. Gage, would you like some tea?"

"I would like some tea," the Gage agreed. He settled to one side of the table, leaving Sayeh the choice of the foot or Himadra's right hand.

She chose the foot. As soon as she settled onto the cushions—with some difficulty, as legs and rib were both troubling her—she regretted it. Not because she was uncomfortable but because she realized that getting up again was going to be a miserable proposition.

She looked over at Nazia and the horses. One of Himadra's men had taken the reins of the gray gelding—Sayeh was at best an adequate rider, but sitting astride him was definitely superior to being slung over his back—and the other horse the Gage had been leading. He was waiting politely for Nazia to hop down.

"Spoils of war?" Himadra asked, following her gaze.

Sayeh pressed a hand to her tender ribs. "You could call them that. Did you say there was wine?"

"Better," he said. "Spirits of wine."

He pushed the flask toward her.

She uncorked it and sniffed the opening. The fumes knocked her head back, eyes watering. "Better by whose standards?"

"Well. More medicinal. You needn't drink it."

"Actually, I rather think I had." Sayeh poured some into a teacup and swirled it around to try and let the vapors dissipate. As Nazia was settling down, Sayeh knocked the whole cup back. It was a proper northern teacup made of gritty unfinished clay from Chandranath.

She gasped, then poured tea quickly—both to soothe the burning and to hide how homesick she had suddenly become.

"Here," she said, putting the flask in front of Nazia. "Try a little of that for your bruises."

Nazia looked at her sidelong but poured a very little into her cup. Inside Sayeh, the burning was settling down into a comfortable warmth, banked by the honeyed tea.

The dragon lifted a head big as an oxcart and curled around to regard them. "Greetings, Rajni," she said. "And greetings, apprentice. I am Kyrl-myrandal."

Sayeh knew a lot of protocols. She had studied them for forty years. Among them were several ceremonies for meeting a dragon. She hadn't re-freshed herself on those since childhood, when she had been quizzed on them by royal tutors. And she had never expected to use them.

She gave the seated bow she would have offered an equal, and said, "It is a pleasure to make your acquaintance, O dragon."

"It came as a surprise to me as well," Himadra said.

"It's not as if I didn't warn you." The Gage reached across the table and filled his own clay cup with spirits. Sayeh wondered where he was going to pour them, not having a mouth. But he just folded enormous hands around the eggshell cup and sat like a statue.

"Oh, sure, you told me she was a dragon. But I was just humoring you." Himadra tilted his head back to look up at Kyrlmyrandal. "I concede now that I was mistaken."

Sayeh did not want to find him charming. And perhaps the liquor was loosening her tongue. "Do you concede that you were mistaken to steal my son?"

"I should not have done that," he agreed. "My very profound apologies. I cannot be happy that I caused you such grief and fear." He made a face as if something tasted bitter, and he washed it away with tea. "I cannot be unhappy that he and you both survived the destruction of Ansh-Sahal, however, Your Abundance."

He made a gesture toward her leg, which she had propped on cushions rather than in a ladylike fold. "I'm sorry for your pain. I know what that feels like."

Anger flared. How dare he offer her fellow-feeling? How dare he offer her sympathy, or anything?

She reached out and took the flask back, adding a splash to her tea. The lessening of pain was a wonderful thing. Nazia was taking tiny sips and making faces.

Sayeh stretched her arm out and put the spirits down at Himadra's end of the table. It would be easy to get too fuzzy, and she couldn't afford that. Seeking to distract herself until her anger subsided enough that she could act with reason rather than reacting with rage, she picked at rosewater-soaked pastries. Not what she would have expected from the grub line of an army on the march, but she supposed clay ovens were portable.

She placed one into her mouth to soak up some of the alcohol. The burst of sweetness left her more lightheaded. Perhaps she was closer to a state of shock than she had realized.

She pressed the back of a sticky hand to her eyes and waited for the world to stop spinning.

"Forgive me. We just escaped a kidnapping attempt." She let that linger a moment while Himadra studied the backs of his hands. "I'm not at my best. How long will it be before Drupada is here?"

"Minutes," Himadra said. "I thought from your appearance that you might have had an adventure. That's why I had the snacks brought. And sent for your son. And his nursemaid, I presume, will be accompanying him."

Sayeh's throat dried. She'd barely thought of the nursemaid, kidnapped along with her son. She didn't even know the woman's name: she had been a temporary replacement, because Drupada's real nurse had died protecting him during the earthquake.

Sayeh still needed to find Jagati's own children, somewhere in the wide world, and make sure they were taken care of as well. If they were still alive.

She had, she realized, neglected her responsibilities shockingly. She had some excuses—war, kidnap, life-threatening injuries—but she was still the rajni of Ansh-Sahal, and even though Ansh-Sahal was gone, its people needed her. She pinched the bridge of her nose and pulled herself together.

She was not any less angry with Himadra. But she was ready, perhaps, to accept that some of her anger at Himadra was also anger at herself. She didn't have to like him to understand that they did need each other.

And Nazia and the Gage certainly weren't about to carry the conversation. Nor, apparently, was the looming dragon.

Sayeh said, "Do you still propose to make my son your heir?"

"If I get my brothers back, they will of course take precedence." He sipped tea. "Where are my brothers, by the way?"

His elaborate casualness hid real pain. Sayeh watched his face. The lines around his eyes made him seem older than she, though he was in truth some ten years younger. She thought about Drupada and how she would not have another child. How she would do anything to protect him—even give him away if that was what it took.

"I did not expect to have fellow-feeling for you," she said slowly. "But your brothers, they are the only family you have, aren't they?"

He turned his teacup with his fingertips, back and forth, its unglazed base making an anxious scraping sound. "Drupada is the only family that you have, also. So yes, I think we understand one another."

Sayeh made herself speak calmly. "You are wondering how one such as I gives birth to a child."

"It is not known to happen," the Boneless admitted. "But it may not be polite to ask."

Sayeh, watching his eyes flicker, thought perhaps she understood. He had no heirs of his own body, and the rumors that attended any royal household hinted that this was because he was not capable.

The Boneless drank tea. "I had assumed your foreign witch has something to do with it. Him, and perhaps . . . an artifact? A stone?"

He was watching for her to flinch. If he thought he knew some secret, it was more than she did.

"Tsering cut my beloved child from my belly, it is true," Sayeh said. "And stitched me up again, alive. I can show you the scar."

From the arch of his eyebrows, he was curious enough to take her up on it. Perhaps she could parlay that into advantage. She lifted her blouse to show the line, with its centipede tracks of stitches along either side.

"But." Sayeh shook her head. "The Rasan Wizards have great power and great skill, but none over the generation of life. It is what they sacrifice for their magic. And no, I used no arts at all. Except prayer, as would be expected of a daughter of the River. And my own personal sacrifice. I was simply blessed by the goddess. Just blessed. That is all."

"It is not always a good thing to have the Mother's attention," Himadra said.

"No," she agreed. "Not always such a good thing at all." She raised her eyes to the lightening sky. "There are worse things whose attention we might get."

"I think it's safe to say you have it," Kyrlmyrandal said, so slowly it did not seem like an interruption.

"It hasn't been a good war," Sayeh admitted.

Himadra flashed her a grin that amazed her with its charm. She was forgetting to hate him, damn his eyes. "Yes, but did you have a tactician like me before?"

Her answer was interrupted by the whinny of a horse. One of her own recently liberated trio, calling to two others coming down the long slope of the bluff. Himadra had picked his campsite well: there was a good long view of the approaches.

What Sayeh saw made her try to leap to her feet, forgetting her bad leg and her bruises. She fell back hard but didn't look down. She saw a woman on a horse leading a child on a pony. Somehow she scrambled up, through pain that made her dizzy. She reached out to clutch the table edge and found instead the Gage's hand, steadying her, solid as the arm of a chair.

"You didn't lie," she said to Himadra. If she had trusted her body more, she would have run up the hill to Drupada. As it was, she stood and watched him come, already anticipating the solid, wiry warmth in her arms. She ached with the need to hold him. Soon. Soon.

"I do try not to."

"Your brothers are on a ship," Sayeh said. "They are safe. The empress sent them away to keep them safe, but we can easily recall them."

"Mother, thank you," Himadra murmured, and closed his eyes.

Sayeh barely registered him, just as she barely registered Nazia leaving the table—stuffing one last sweet into her mouth as she rose—coming to stand at Sayeh's elbow. Nazia steadied her as the nurse swung down from her saddle—she was a better rider than Sayeh, for sure—and it was only then that Sayeh realized she was trembling.

The whole time the nurse was crossing the space between them, lugging Drupada in her arms, Sayeh was afraid to reach out. Afraid that this was a dream, and the instant she moved it would shatter. That Drupada would vanish, or be replaced by a leering monkey, or—

She didn't even know what she was afraid of. But she stood stock-still until Drupada—how had he grown so much in a few short months?—turned in the nurse's arms and saw her face. Whatever changes the hardships of those months had wrought on her, he recognized her instantly.

"Mommy!"

He reached out with both hands and she grabbed him, clutched him to her chest, buried her face in his hair. He smelled more like dirt and horse than the sweet, clean child she remembered. But it didn't matter. They were both crying. He was there, in her arms, both heavy and real.

"ARE YOU SURE IT'S SUPPOSED TO BE HERE?" SAID ATA AKHIMAH, FEELING bruised and out of sorts on the back of her horse. Beside her, Tsering-la looked dusty and equally out of sorts. His horse at least was fresh. It made its displeasure at standing still in this incomprehensible spot known by shaking its head and stamping. If people were going to insist on standing there on an empty plain miles from the rest of the herd, the very least they could do was get down to some serious grazing.

Five men-at-arms accompanied the Wizards. They spread out in a perimeter, watching outward.

"Yes. And wherever it's supposed to be, it's not." Tsering rattled the map. "Here, you look at it."

"I don't know how to open the doors," she protested. "Or even to see them."

But she took the map and started matching cartography to landmarks. Not that there were many landmarks there—but there was the river, behind them. And there was the curve of the rise just ahead. And there on the map was the symbol for the door they had come looking for.

"We're in the right spot," she confirmed. "So how do I spot the doors?"

"Some are marked with an arch, or a stone set in the ground."

"Like the Dragon Road."

"Yes."

She shaded her eyes with her hands. "But not all of them, I take it?"

He scratched his restive horse under the mane. It stretched out, accepting the contact. "So unfocus your gaze. Look past the horizon, and—I don't know enough about your tradition to know. Do you have a way of calling power?"

"Yes," Akhimah said, feeling for the strength at her core. She was still depleted from the battle, and trying to focus left her lightheaded, but she settled herself in the saddle and did it anyway.

"Imagine a lens of the power before you."

"As if I were looking for the flow of elemental energy in the earth and sky?"

"Yes," he said, "I suppose? Is that what you manipulate?"

"One of the things," she said. "Yes, I have a lens."

"Look through it. Toward the horizon. Unfocus your gaze. You're looking for a . . . a discontinuity. A shimmer. Like a mirage or haze over water. As if there were a prism, sometimes. Or the refraction you get through water. It's subtle and faint."

She looked. There was grass, and the ridgeline, and the sky. There were the men and their horses.

There was nothing that looked like haze or blurring or diffraction.

"Nope," she said.

"That's what I was telling you."

Ata Akhimah felt a surge of childish outrage. "But we came all this way! All this way in the wrong direction! And that damned sorcerer—" She noticed herself avoiding the name, and forced herself, despite the discomfort, to say, "That damned Ravani, *she* used it! The Gage saw her!"

"You don't have to rub it in!"

"*You* don't have to snap."

He sighed. "I know. The map is wrong."

"Could it have . . . I don't know. Drifted off or something?"

"I don't know. They have, in my experience, always been right where we left them. Or right where previous generations left them. I suppose the Alchemical Emperor might have learned how to take one apart. Or move it. Or maybe Ravani knows how. It's all academic, anyway."

"Yes," she said. "We're going to have to find some other way of going east. And it will probably be a lot more work, also."

She squinted through the lens again. The sky was strange. The sky had been strange all season, the flow of energy through the heavenly regions tangled and constrained. She'd stopped looking at it, because it bothered her so much. But now there was movement again—and the movement looked wrong.

"Huh," she said. "That's funny."

"What?" Tsering-la's horse sidled as he leaned forward unconsciously.

"Those lines of power. They've been twisted in knots all season. It's been tying up the rains, holding the monsoon at bay. Nizhvashiti worked a miracle once, the Mother intervened, and there was some rain after that—"

"I remember. Is something changing?"

Akhimah's innards twisted with anxiety as she thought about the power involved. Her own horse sensed the mood and stamped once, tail flicking. "All those knots. Something is pulling them east now."

"What does that mean?"

"I'm only guessing. It looks like how I channel the elemental energy of lighting to create a pillar of energy. But it's not just fire . . . sun-heat, lightning, I mean. It's air and water, too. And it's huge. The whole—" She waved helplessly. "It's everything."

"A monstrous invocation."

It hurt, but she still swallowed. "If I were powerful enough to do something like that, it would be because I was building the mother of all storms."

✳   ✳   ✳

PRASANA WAS WAITING AT THE PALACE GATE WHEN MRITHURI, HER ELEPHANT, and her entourage returned. Three dead men lay at his feet, their throats slit. Prasana looked as scruffy and unassuming as ever, a slight man whose scarred hands hung a little crooked at his sides. He reminded Mrithuri of a plain-looking tomcat standing proudly over a pile of rabbits.

"I took the liberty," he said. "When I heard what happened to Sayeh Rajni and to Nazia."

Mrithuri looked down from Hathi's back. Maybe she should have been horrified, or gratified. Possibly she should have worried that Prasana had gotten the wrong men. This was not justice as she had been raised to believe in justice. This restored nothing.

But it did remove a threat. And mostly, she just felt tired.

"Thank you," she said. "Dispose of them."

Prasana bowed low. Mrithuri glanced down toward her left hand, where the Dead Man rode his dark brown horse, his head about the level of the elephant's eye. He was looking up at her. At the question on her face, he nodded.

She shouldn't need the reassurance, but the knot inside her softened a little. She'd just won a war. Shouldn't she feel better? Why did people go about conquering and building empires if it all just left one empty inside?

Perhaps most emperors enjoyed it more than she did. Or perhaps they just weren't as worn out by all the marching around and having people executed as she seemed to be.

And now she would have to meet with Himadra, her northern cousin who had mostly been a pain in her ass throughout her short reign. She'd never met him, but she'd dealt often enough with his people raiding on her border.

She was tired of men. Tired of them wanting things, and tired of them being disappointing.

She could have laughed to herself. Here she was, sulking like a child because her lover had rejected her. And, she had to admit, not even rejected her. But stepped away at a cost to himself, as well, in order to maintain her legitimacy.

For a moment, she wanted to toss it all, throw whatever kingdoms she had a claim to into the crowd of her cousins and let them all squabble. Take off for the hills with the Dead Man and never be seen again.

Even as she thought it, she knew it was a fantasy. She might delight in imagining freedom, but she could not abandon her responsibilities. And—if she were being honest with herself—she did not *want* to abandon her power. She'd kept her self-determination, and with Sayeh's help, she'd survived Anuraja. They'd *defeated* Anuraja.

She couldn't walk away now. She was just coming into her own.

Boys ran to meet them as they entered the inner courtyard. Mrithuri slid down from Hathi's shoulder, not even waiting for the elephant to drop a leg. She landed lightly and turned to the Dead Man, who was handing his horse over to a stable lad. "I'm going to bathe," she said to the Dead Man, who was still mounted. "Send Sayeh Rajni to meet me when she's back. Afterward, I will convene my council, and having done that, I will meet with Himadra Raja. Also, can you figure out how to fit a dragon in here?"

"Your Magnanimity," he said, and bowed in the saddle. The horse bowed as well, which he obviously had not anticipated. He pitched forward on its neck and saved himself by grabbing the pommel.

When he straightened, he was laughing. "So much for elegant gestures."

"Disgraceful," Mrithuri agreed. "What's his name?"

"I don't know," the Dead Man said. "I suppose I had better catch one of these stableboys and ask. And find out what other tricks he knows, before one of them gets me killed."

THE BATHS WERE JUST AS GOOD AS SHE REMEMBERED. IT WOULD BE WORTH fighting to keep this place just to have access to these huge tubs full of hot water. She was still floating and soaking when someone slipped into the water beside her. She opened her eyes and saw that it was Sayeh.

Bath attendants were nowhere to be seen. "Did you send them away so you could assassinate me?" she asked.

"Assassinating you is the last thing on my mind." Sayeh took up a sponge and began to wash her long arms. "I sent them away so we could have some peace and quiet. And a private conversation, since I assumed that was why you sent for me."

Mrithuri stared at her through the steam. The laugh, when it came, startled her. "You know me too well already."

Sayeh grinned. "What do you want from me?"

"First," Mrithuri said, sinking down in the water, "how is Drupada?"

"Settled," Sayeh answered. "Sleeping. I took him to visit Hathi first, and he was beside himself with joy. He loves elephants."

"I'm surprised you managed to drag yourself away."

"Oh, trust me," Sayeh said, "I didn't want to. Honestly, though, he's in better shape than I am."

Mrithuri began to shampoo her hair. The grit of the battlefield coated her scalp and every strand. "Children can survive nearly anything, because they don't know any better. It's not good for them in the long run, though."

Sayeh was looking at her funny.

Mrithuri said, hurriedly, "I was thinking of Himadra's brothers."

"Mmm," Sayeh answered.

"Can you work with Himadra? The Dead Man reported that he's broken with the sorcerers. He talked to the Gage about it."

"I don't have a city anymore," Sayeh said. "My people are scattered to every direction a lotus petal points at. I don't think I have much choice about who I work with anymore." She sighed. "Actually, he seems like a decent sort for a kidnapper."

"Maybe once the existential threat is dealt with, we can all just go back to raiding each other's borders. That would be nice."

"Is that what you want? When all this is over?"

Mrithuri lifted her hand and wiped droplets of condensed steam from her lashes. "What I want has never had anything to do with it. I might be growing into this rajni thing, however."

"Just in time to become an empress." Sayeh balanced herself to scrub at each of her callused feet in turn with a brush. "Who are you?"

Mrithuri drew herself up, her shoulders chilly as they broke the surface. Beads of bathwater rolled down her skin. She knew what was expected. Grit. Determination. No merely mortal frailty. "Rajni of Sarathai-tia; Empress Dowager of Sarathai-lae. I am the Empress of all Sarath."

Sayeh frowned at her and shook her head. "No, who are you when you're *you*? Not when you're doing what people expect of you. When you're being who you want to be."

Mrithuri stared at her. "I . . . don't know."

"No hobbies?" Sayeh said. "No outside interests? Nothing you do in your spare time?"

"What's spare time?" Mrithuri asked, trying to make light of it. Failing.

"No wonder you started using the snakebite," Sayeh said. That stung. Perhaps because it was true. "Have you thought about playing a musical instrument?"

"I have my familiars," Mrithuri said. "I have . . . I don't know." She felt her face screwing up, her eyes stinging. Her body contracting around a coldness in her core.

"It's all right," Sayeh said. "It really is all right. You are young, and if we beat this thing, you have a long life ahead of you to decide who you want to be."

"And what about you?" Mrithuri asked, when the spasm of pain passed. "Your city is gone—"

"I just said so."

"I do not mean to be cruel. But where will you go? What will you do now?"

Sayeh began to laugh behind her hand. "The deal I made with Ravani," she gasped. "She paid the debt. And there is nothing I can do with her payment. She has made it useless to me."

"Deal?"

"To bring my people to a place where I could gather them again. To reunite me with my son. I promised her I would convince you to marry Anuraja. And I did. And she kept her part of the bargain. And—" She shook her head. "I still have no place to bring them home to."

Mrithuri could not be angry about whatever bargain Sayeh had made. She had made that bargain, and she had turned it into Anuraja's death and Mrithuri's salvation. She had done what she had to do, as a prisoner and an exile.

"You could marry Himadra. Bring your people to Chandranath. The ones that aren't already there."

Sayeh knuckled tears of mirth or grief from her eyes. "Chandranath has to raid your lands to eat. If I brought my people there to stay, it would be a famine. And Chandranath has that caste system." She shook her head. "How are my folk ever likely to fit into it? They'll chafe; there will be violence if they stay too long. Himadra's people might throw a revolution. Mine might be pushed into enclaves and eventually riot."

Sayeh was right, of course, as much as Mrithuri did not wish to admit it. There had to be a way to provide for the folk of Ansh-Sahal, though. If Mrithuri was Empress, then they were hers to protect as surely as the people of Sarathai-tia, and even of Sarathai-lae. She could not be ruler of all Sarath-Sahal if she favored one region over another.

And then she realized the answer, which had been staring her in the face the whole time.

Mrithuri shook her head. "Oh, of course."

"Of course what?"

"Sayeh Rajni." Mrithuri climbed naked from the pool, dripping wet, too conscious of her scars and the thinness of her body. Nevertheless she dropped to one knee, her hands reached out across the pool rim toward Sayeh. "O most beauteous. Star of the north. Your limbs are like the pale limbs of young trees. The shining part of your hair enchanteth me."

". . . Mrithuri? What on earth are you doing?"

"Marry me, Sayeh Rajni," Mrithuri said. "Isn't it rich that I've only just now come to realize that women, raised to be helpmeets to men, are completely capable of being helpmeets to one another instead? Join your kingdom to mine. Marry me."

Sayeh stared into her face, eyes wide, her fair olive skin pink with scrubbing or emotion. The moment stretched. Her lips parted, and Mrithuri thought that her mad, impulsive plan might work.

"I can't marry you!" Sayeh exploded.

Mirhutir sat back on her heels. "Why not?"

"I . . . am not sure I have those feelings for women." She did not sound convinced, though, as she said it.

"If that's true—and I remember you saying that it wasn't my femininity that was the problem, back in Sarathai-tia—if that's true, well, so? It's a dynastic marriage. Take a lover. What about that Sanjay fellow? He likes you. He's clean enough."

"I am a widow!" The steam softened Sayeh's lovely features and made her look young. "And he's far too young for me."

"So am I," Mrithuri said. "On a technicality. But we're royalty. That automatically makes us attractive."

"What about *your* lover?"

Mrithuri pressed her palm to her face. Her skin was damp and wrinkled and smelled of sandalwood and amber. "He dumped me."

"And he's still got kneecaps?" Sayeh demanded. "Why would he do that?"

"Dynastic reasons," Mrithuri said on a convulsive breath. It might have been a sob or a laugh. "Too many fucking Laeish around looking for a reason to delegitimate my ridiculous marriage to their ridiculous raja. Even if he hadn't, it would still be no barrier to marrying you. He's . . ." She sighed. "He's a pragmatic man."

"I can't give you a child."

"We'll think of something. Maybe I can still talk the dragon out of her magic jewel."

Sayeh waved her hand. "Anyway, I can't marry a woman."

"You are third-sex. Legally, you may marry whomever you desire." Mrithuri rose and dusted off her knee. She was getting cold. She eased herself back into the water. "Besides, I have heard that two queens married once in the far northlands. Surely, Ata Akhimah can find us a precedent."

"Wait, what about the horse tribes? They've got that male-shandha chieftain married to another chieftain. That's a precedent."

Mrithuri smiled. "See, you're starting to see the logic in it. There's room in Sarath for a few unhomed Sahalis. A few thousand, even."

Sayeh shook her head. "You're not suggesting—"

"Hell yes, I am."

"You're supposed to send a child to propose to me."

"Fine. Let's go wake up your son."

22

MRITHURI CALLED THEM TOGETHER IN THE INNER COURTYARD TO ACCOMMO-
date the dragon. Though the Gage didn't say anything, he also found it
more comfortable than the palace interior. There were no carpets to shred
underfoot, no delicate ornaments on plinths to totter at a careless footstep.
Human habitations were just not very relaxing for someone like him.

Outside, he could settle on the ground alongside the dragon, in a ring
with the others sitting on chairs, and not tower over anyone. It always dis-
turbed him to be reminded of how small and fragile humans were. How had
he ever borne being like that? So easy to hurt, once upon a time?

Because he hadn't any choice, he supposed. And when he had been given
one, he accepted it.

On his shoulder rested the bearded vulture that Mrithuri has sent with
him, a bird he called Vara. He had sewn a bit of leather into his robe to give
Vara a secure perch, his huge fingers making clumsy stitches with the awl
and needle. The bird was even more fragile than the humans. But despite the
Gage's mass and power, Vara seemed to think he made a fine place to rest.

Kyrlmyrandal, especially in her dragonshape, was more reassuring. She
might be ancient, blind, and earthbound. But she wasn't going anywhere.
Not in a human lifetime. And he might be able to break her, but he would
have to work at it.

The others filed out and took their seats: Mrithuri with Syama; Sayeh
carrying Guang Bao; Himadra wheeled in a chair. The Dead Man, who
looked uncomfortable sitting in a chair and kept fussing with the hang of
his sword. Lady Golbahar, Hnarisha, and Marnor the new Lord Chancellor.
General Pranaj was still busy on the battlefield.

Upon seeing Mrithuri, Vara beat heavy wings, hopped to the top of the
Gage's head, turned into the soft breeze, and took off laboriously. The vulture circled, climbing the air like a drunk staggering up a staircase until it
had enough height to glide down and land on the back of Mrithuri's chair.
It landed facing in the wrong direction and made a waddling production of
turning around.

Ümmühan walked out between the Wizards, Ata Akhimah and Tsering-la.
Nizhvashiti drifted in their wake, the ragged edge of its robes sweeping above
the beautifully painted tiles, with starlight showing in between.

The Gage abruptly remembered one of the objects hidden in his secret heart—or rather, his secret compartment. Because, abruptly, it rustled inside him. A tickle, as if he had swallowed a moth.

"That one," said the pen, in a voice that rang clearly out of his body. "I belong to that one."

Everyone looked at the Gage. The Gage was glad his surface showed nothing but their own reflections in return. He knew who the pen meant, though. Who else *could* it want to be with?

He opened the little drawer in his chest and pulled free the shining thing within.

It caught the light inside it as it had before, black-red and translucent, glowing like the deep heart of a fire. "Ümmühan," he said. "I have someone here who wants to speak with you."

He hadn't met her before, but the Dead Man had told him the broad outlines of what had transpired since he'd been gone. She came toward him, light on her feet despite her years and the walking stick. Her garments were a swirl of translucent colors.

"Hello, Gage," she said. "I've heard so much about your kind. What is that in your hand?"

"My name is Heartsblood," said the pen. "Put me in your hand, Poetess, and we will write some true things before you die."

She didn't step back, but she did stand up straighter. "My."

The Gage was aware of Kyrlmyrandal looming over his shoulder. The dragon seemed inclined to be silent and observe, a demeanor the Gage found congenial. She almost startled him when she spoke. "Of course you would want this one, you vain thing."

"I am meant for the hand of a genius," the pen said. It vibrated slightly in the Gage's hand. Impatience.

Gingerly, Ümmühan reached out, her hand not quite touching the pen, as if she felt for heat before grasping a pan.

"It's cursed," the Gage warned.

"Words written with me will never die," said the pen. "I will make them true, and history. It is my nature."

"Cursed?" said Ümmühan, her fingertips hovering.

"Soaked in dragon-poison," said the Gage. "It will probably make your hair and teeth fall out. Give you tumors the size of melons. That sort of thing."

"Oh, is that all? At my age, hair and teeth are already deciduous. You make words true, Heartsblood? Do you write in the stuff by which you are named?"

"That is why I must only be wielded by the best. By poets worthy of remembrance. By those great-souled enough to see and record the nuances of things. By those brave enough to speak the truth. I choose you, Poetess Ümmühan."

"Flatterer," said Ümmühan. "I will put you in a lead box. You will poison no one but me. And I am old; it will not matter. I will be gone before you know it."

"You will live forever," said the pen. "Get me a golden box, though."

"I'm sure we can come to some sort of arrangement." She lifted the pen from the Gage's hand and made it vanish inside the layers of gauze she wore. "A pleasure to finally meet you, Gage. A pleasure to meet you, Kyrlmyrandal. Now let's get on with saving the world."

As she turned away, the shuffling about and finding of places concluded. Ümmühan settled in between Mrithuri and Golbahar. The Dead Man switched chairs to be beside the Gage. Once there, he managed to stop fidgeting.

Mrithuri cleared her throat. "I've gathered you here because we need to get our allegiances clear, and we need to bring this thing to an ending. Most of you know that, now that we have secured Sarathai-lae—"

"For the time being," said Himadra.

Mrithuri arched her eyebrows at him.

"The would-be usurper is still on the loose," he said. "And so are those damned sorcerers."

"Yes," she said. "I have not forgotten. We have planned to send an expedition east, to the Sea of Storms."

"To the Origin of Storms," Kyrlmyrandal amended.

"I see," said Mrithuri, "that being acclaimed an empress does nothing to stem interruptions."

"No lord can command the tide," said Golbahar.

Mrithuri laughed. "Fair enough, and I have you here because I value your opinions. Ata Akhimah, what did you and Tsering-la discover on your reconnaissance?"

Akhimah ran a hand over her hair, which was growing long enough to form a fuzzy halo around her head. "The way is blocked. Or never was, perhaps. Who can unmake a dragon-gate?"

That last, the Gage thought, was directed at Kyrlmyrandal.

The dragon said, "The Alchemical Emperor, probably. Or the cloistered order of practitioners of the Science of Building that he struck a bargain with and did not destroy. Or a beast that comes from Between Places." She cleared her throat. "Or a dragon, of course."

"The cloistered . . . Do you mean the walking cities?" the Gage asked.

"They're not geomancers," said Kyrlmyrandal. "Those cities were built for him by Wizards of Messaline. I believe they're some sort of joint stock corporation now. It's all an ugly business."

"Our grandfather ruined everything he touched." Mrithuri heaved a sigh. "And there's so much to put right again."

"He built a great many things as well," said Ata Akhimah, as if reluctantly. "Sarath-Sahal. The Peacock Throne. Cities and palaces."

"Isn't empire the root of the problem?" said the Gage.

He hadn't intended to say so. But now everyone was looking at him.

"I remember someone else who thought the same thing," Ümmühan said.

"What happened to him?" Mrithuri asked.

"He died. But I wrote it all down." The old woman shook her head, her lined face wincing. "It's the same thing over and over. A king rises to power by wit or magic or strength or arms. He makes a peace that lasts exactly as long as he does. His children squabble. Maybe the next king is a terrible administrator. Maybe the kingdom fails. Vultures nibble at the corners. Brigands." She looked at Kyrlmyrandal. "'Joint stock companies.'"

"What you need," said the Gage, "is a constitution."

Kyrlmyrandal laughed in the back of her throat.

"What's a constitution?" Mrithuri said.

As best he could, remembering Kyrlmyrandal's words, he explained.

Himadra listened, the knuckle he was chewing on buried in his mustache. When the Gage was done, he shook his head and said, "I've been thinking about this since you mentioned it last. So you have the army, and the people give their fealty to a . . . to a contract?"

"Yes," Tsering-la said.

"It's a nice idea, but it only works until somebody like Sekira comes along. A contract doesn't have much charisma, and people throw their promises out the window whenever they're infatuated. One charismatic strongman, and it'll all fall down. Then you're back to empires and the lot of us fighting over scraps again."

Ümmühan turned her head slightly sideways. She looked at Himadra, then she turned to the Gage and looked at him for a long time. She reached inside her silks, removed Heartsblood, and looked down on it as it lay diagonally across her open palm. "But what if the fealty lasted? That's worth being poisoned for."

"Shit," said Sayeh, closing her eyes and shaking her head in the least regal manner imaginable. "We can't imagine a better system, because we are trapped inside the paradigms of this one."

"We've imagined what could happen if we worked together," Himadra said, softening. "That isn't nothing."

"Will you forbid it, my rajni?" Ümmühan asked Sayeh, impishly. As if she were plotting a surprise party.

"No," said Sayeh.

"We have a more immediate problem," said Ata Akhimah. "More closely related to Sekira. And the beast and its sorcerers."

Everyone turned to her.

She folded her arms over her dirt-stained white blouse and said, "When Tsering-la and I rode out to see if we could find the dragon-gate . . . as you know, we failed, but I found something else. The beast has been holding our rains back all season."

"More drought?" asked Mrithuri.

Ata Akhimah shook her head. "I can feel what it is doing. I can feel it in my bones. It is going to use all that energy, which has been held in abeyance. As with the eruption that destroyed Ansh-Sahal—"

"No," said Sayeh.

The Wizard kept talking. "The beast is summoning a storm. A storm to end all storms. A storm that will wash Sarath-Sahal into the river and thence into the sea."

There was a long silence. Himadra broke it. "I'm not going to say it's a pity Anuraja was rejected by the Peacock Throne. But if somebody was sitting on the damned thing, at least we'd be able to fight the weather."

The Gage looked from face to face. All the royalty seemed to know without question something he did not understand. He was spared, however, because Golbahar said, "Excuse me?"

"The Peacock Throne," said Hnarisha, "is supposed to guide the weather, make the earth bloom. If a true emperor sits on it."

"Ansh-Sahal used to be richer in the old days," Sayeh said. "So did Chandranath. We didn't starve for water and grain in the dry season as we do now."

Nobody reminded her that Ansh-Sahal was no more.

"I suppose you want to try to sit on it?" Mrithuri asked Himadra. "I'd even swear you fealty if you tried. That takes some balls."

Himadra laughed, but not as if he found it funny. "I couldn't climb the stairs."

"Right," said Mrithuri. "No convenient dynastic rescue. So what's next? How long do you think it will be before the storm breaks?"

"Weeks," said Ata Akhimah. "Less, perhaps."

"Why now?" asked Tsering-la, then answered his own question. "The suffering from the wars is lessened. You three"—he pointed to Sayeh, Mrithuri, and Himadra—"insist on working together. The beast needs other food now."

"Yes," Kyrlmyrandal said.

"We were told to seek the Mother of Exiles." The Dead Man looked at Kyrlmyrandal. "That seems to have been sound advice. We were also told, as you have reminded us, to seek the Origin of Storms."

"I know where it is," said Kyrlmyrandal.

"We all know where the Sea of Storms is," Mrithuri said, grumpily.

"Are they the same thing, then?"

Nothing, the Gage reflected, was so capable of sounding arch as a dragon. Except for possibly a talking pen.

"We were also told—by the cloistered sisters of Sarathai-tia—that if we came to Sarathai-lae, there would be a path east," said Ata Akhimah. "But the path is closed, or perhaps never existed."

Kyrlmyrandal said, "What do you know about the Broken Places?"

"Not much," said Tsering-la. "They exist. They move around. They are the link between two places that may not be topologically speaking contiguous, but which have the same sky."

Kyrlmyrandal said, "The dragon-gates take you through the Broken Places. From what I have heard of your nuns"—her huge head nodded over Mrithuri—"their cloisters are in the Broken Places, too."

"Yes," said Nizhvashiti.

Kyrlmyrandal said, "The nuns are the heirs of those who studied Vastu Shastra. I do not know if it was the Alchemical Emperor who built them a cage in his walls, which they then expanded. Or if they infiltrated his palace to remind him that they were not defeated. But they are what remains of your empire's geomancers."

"I had figured out some of that," Mrithuri said. "So can the door that would take us to the Origin of Storms be repaired, then? Do you know how?"

"That," said Kyrlmyrandal, "is a complicated question, and in answer I will tell you a story."

Of course she would, the Gage thought. Dragons lived forever. They had plenty of time for in-depth explanations.

She settled herself, stretching as if to ease some discomfort. Her scales rustled on the tiles.

She said, "Haven't you ever wondered why there are so many suns? So many skies? So many worlds all stitched together?"

"That's the way it is," the Dead Man said.

Ata Akhimah rolled her eyes at him. "*I* have wondered."

"How can one place be in Erem, and another place, that does not touch the first at all through the true world, also be Erem?"

Nizhvashiti wafted forward. The Gage smelled dry leaves and resin on the warm wind that followed. "Remember when I told you that Sarath-Sahal had a moon once and that the Other One tore it from the sky and cast it into the sea out west, and it destroyed everything where it fell?"

"That's not what happened," Kyrlmyrandal interrupted.

The Gage turned to her. "Aren't you the one that told me stories shape reality?"

"They shape perception. Reality is whatever still exists when you strip all the stories away."

Nizhvashiti's dry laugh was like a bone rattle. "I suppose you do know what happened."

"Well," Kyrlmyrandal said. "I was there. It wasn't a moon that fell. It was us. It was dragons. We broke the world. The Broken Places are our fault. And it's probably our fault that the beasts can get in. We shattered your reality, and when we stitched it back together, the pieces didn't quite fit."

The silence that followed was general. It went on for long moments and was only broken eventually by Ümmühan's quiet, experimental cough. "So each kingdom, with its gods, is a different world?"

"The same world," Kyrlmyrandal said, "but different realities. Oh, this is so hard to explain without math."

"Show me the math," said Ata Akhimah and Tsering-la, in unison.

Kyrlmyrandal turned toward them. That flick of the tongue and curl of the upper lip might be a dragon smiling. "After the council."

"So the point of this explanation," said Golbahar, "is that you can or cannot fix the door?"

"I cannot," said Kyrlmyrandal. "Your Alchemical Emperor used his throne to stitch up any number of burrows through reality. Like wormholes through the pages of a book. He made the Lotus Kingdoms very stable, in a way. It would be hard for new gods, not the Mother and her Daughters, to gain a foothold here. Especially when the Mother is manifest and physical at all times in the land." She pointed with her nose and one wing-wrist toward the distant river. "This is why the beast and its minions needed to call up Deep, the volcano goddess. I mean, yes, to create war and the misery the beast feeds on. But also because she is an aspect of the Mother, and making her physically manifest as well weakens the metaphysical strength of the Mother.

"Meanwhile, the more the beast feeds, the stronger it becomes. Both in the Broken Places, which none of us would enjoy entering now that the beast is waxing in power, and at the edges of the world. It might be best that the door is closed, because otherwise it might serve as a path for the beast to manifest right beside this very large population of humans, once it becomes strong enough to break through into our world physically."

"So if you can't fix the door, what can you do to get us there?" said Golbahar, who had a remarkable facility for following a thread through digressions.

"I know how to reach the Origin of Storms without using the doors," said Kyrlmyrandal.

"But?"

"But I can't . . ." She extended one ragged wing, daylight showing through the rents in the red-streaked, bleached membrane. ". . . fly."

"Hm," said Mrithuri. "What if we could mend you?"

"Mend," Kyrlmyrandal said. "How would you go about that?"

"Ata Akhimah," Mrithuri said. "Could you mend a wing? Like imping feathers—" She pointed at Guang Bao.

"It would hurt," the Wizard said, dubiously.

There was silence. Kyrlmyrandal turned her long neck and touched her muzzle to the gigantic scar. She turned back to them. "What is pain?"

The Gage was no Wizard, but he knew their ways as only a servant that seems inhuman and implacable can. His moment of realization came as a physical sensation of lightness and awe. The Peacock Throne was more than a symbol. It was a tool, of course. A tool in the hands of the rightful emperor. A way to hold Sarath-Sahal together despite differences in language, culture, and geography.

He also felt Kyrlmyrandal's comment on pain in his core. Indeed, what was a little more?

He said, "Not to go over ground we've trodden, but I think you might be on to something with the Peacock Throne, Lord Himadra. When the ansha—the Godmade—and I visited Ansh-Sahal . . . Pardon, Sayeh Rajni. You may not wish to hear this."

Sayeh reached out with her left hand and Mrithuri caught it in her right. The squeeze they gave one another looked hard enough to be painful.

"Go on," said Sayeh.

"The sorcerer—Ravana, the brother, if siblings is what they are—you know that we saw him there?"

Sayeh nodded.

"He had built a throne of corpses, Your Abundance. A mockery of the Peacock Throne."

"Nizhvashiti told us," Mrithuri said gently.

The Gage folded his arms across his cuirass gingerly so as not to clatter. "I can only guess it is intended to subvert the power of the real throne and turn it to the beast's use. If the Peacock Throne has metaphorical and geomantic power, then so must the parody throne, or why else build it?"

"Oh," Sayeh said.

"I blessed as many of the dead as I could," Nizhvashiti whispered. "That might limit the effectiveness."

"It would be better if we had an emperor," said Tsering-la. "If someone were on the real throne, using its abilities . . . Maybe that person could even release the volcano goddess and make Ansh-Sahal habitable again."

Sayeh and Mrithuri looked at each other, the Gage noticed. And he saw that Himadra noticed too.

Himadra said, "Do you have something to share with us, Your Abundances?"

They dropped hands as if scalded. The Dead Man's posture was stiff, his expression masklike above his veil.

"I've asked Sayeh to marry me," said Mrithuri. "We'll solemnize it as soon as possible."

"Congratulations," Himadra said. "Then you are ruler of three of the four kingdoms, Mrithuri Empress."

"That was not—"

"Hear me out," he interrupted, nodding slowly. "Earlier today, you asked me if I would swear fealty to you. I told you I would think about it. But now I offer you a bargain."

Mrithuri watched him. She had taken a breath, and now she held it. She did not speak.

"Attempt the throne," Himadra said. "If you will promise that you will do that, I will swear fealty. And we can work out the details in this— 'constitution'—that the poetess will pen as to how that works, and how heirs are selected, and how power is shared."

"So you'll swear fealty if I do something that will get me killed?"

"Will it?" he asked. "Won't that make you ruler of all Sahal-Sarat? Empress in truth, not just in name?"

"But not emperor."

"Technicalities," he said. "Call yourself 'Emperor' if you like. There's plenty of precedent for woman-kings."

Sayeh looked at Mrithuri. "We seem to be looking to the north for all sorts of legal precedents lately."

"Yes, but I find the prospect of whether they will impress a giant hunk of precious stones and metal much more terrifying than the idea of using them to sell my reign to a bunch of nobles who would already like a good excuse to not also be at war during a famine. Besides, I still need an heir of my body—and Sayeh can't provide that. Sorry, Sayeh—"

Sayeh shrugged. "It's only true."

Mrithuri turned to the Gage. "We sent you to the Mother of Exiles to fetch the Carbuncle. Did you succeed?"

"No," he said at the same moment the dragon said, "Yes."

"You said," he said, "that you could not give it to me."

"And that was true. I also said that I would accompany you." The dragon touched her head between the horns with the wrist joint of her wing. "You know where a Carbuncle comes from?"

"The brain of a serpent," said Ata Akhimah promptly. Then, "Oh. You'd have to die, then?"

A dragon nodding is a massive undertaking.

Ata Akhimah put her hand to her mouth. "A stone. In a skull."

"Oh," said the Gage, and covered the mirror of his face with one enormous clinking palm.

"Well," said Mrithuri, "I'm not about to try for that even if I thought

I could get away with it. The natural science of your people is very confusing."

"We are not," said Kyrlmyrandal, "from around here."

"No, but you seem very well versed in our history, for a giant flying lizard who has spent Mother knows how long in a ruined city in the middle of a blasted plain."

Kyrlmyrandal laughed. It rattled the tiles under the Gage's backside.

Mrithuri asked, "So you think this beast is taking advantage of Anuraja—and I suppose the rest of us—squabbling to strengthen itself and burst through into our world?"

"Yes."

"What happens if it does?"

"In that case? The pile of corpses in Sayeh Rajni's city is just an overture."

Mrithuri sighed. "And this is all my ancestor's fault, in a fashion, isn't it? He stitched Sarath-Sahal into an empire, but the Alchemical Emperor did it by killing and driving off mages. Purging them. Making himself the sole power in the land. It's why all the Wizards come from somewhere else and why Jharni the Eyeless One went to Messaline to learn and practice. And that . . . left us open to exploitation. Metaphysically speaking."

"Yes," said Kyrlmyrandal.

"What are we going to do with these armies?" Himadra asked abruptly.

Mrithuri shifted in her chair. "Is Sekira vanquished for good?"

"If we can be rid of the sorcerers," said the Dead Man, "I don't think he'll be able to bring much power to bear."

Hnarisha had been quiet through most of the conversation, bent over his notebook. He looked up now, glancing at Marnor before he spoke. Marnor nodded.

Hnarisha said, "We need to get a move on. Not only is our esteemed dragon companion poisonous on long exposure, but there's no way in a Rasan hell we can feed all of these soldiers for long."

Himadra said, "You're telling me."

23

RELEASED AT LAST FROM THE WILD DISCOMFORT OF THE COUNCIL, THE DEAD Man walked toward the stables. He had nothing better in mind than escape, and the brown horse beckoned him. There, he thought, was a reliably uncomplicated companion. And one that wouldn't ask him if everything was all right.

Everything was not all right. But there was nothing he could do about it, and it was his own damn fault to begin with.

He was surprised when he walked into the stables and found a woman holding a toddler. The boy was dressed in princely silks, and she was supporting him so he could see over the top of a stall half-door. "See?" she said. "Button is right here. She's got all the hay she could want and a nice soft pile of sand to sleep in."

"Don't let me startle you," the Dead Man said softly, from the doorway.

She jumped anyway, of course. She spun around and the toddler began crying. It must be Prince Drupada, and the woman must be his nurse.

So much for a quiet escape to the stables.

"I'm sorry," he said, and waited for her to soothe the child before he came closer. The sight of woman and child did nothing to make him feel less lonely. He looked past them and saw a pony in the box they had been looking into. Drupada's pony, probably.

"Sorry," said the woman, straightening up. "He was worried about Button."

"That speaks well of him," said the Dead Man. "And of you for bringing him out here. I was coming to check on my own horse."

"I was a stable hand in Ansh-Sahal," the woman said. "Honestly, I'd rather be doing that than nursemaiding." She smoothed the boy's hair. "Ungrateful of me, because I would probably be dead if I hadn't been kidnapped. But I don't think it would be good for him to suffer more upheaval. I'm Iri. You must be the Uthman mercenary I've heard so much about."

He bowed, because it seemed the thing to do, and walked inside the stable. It was a light and airy space, with high windows under the eaves that gave good light.

"Which horse is yours?" she asked.

"I'm not sure which stall he's in," the Dead Man said. He walked down the aisle, peering over half-doors. "A brown gelding with a head like a warhammer."

"Oh," she said. "I think I saw him down here." She led him around a corner, into a side aisle. "What's his name?"

"I haven't had a chance to ask," the Dead Man admitted. "He's only been mine for a day or two. I'm not giving him back, though."

There was another woman in the aisle, standing beside another stall door. This one, the Dead Man recognized at once. It was the poetess Üm-mühan, who also must have come there directly after the council. The Dead Man's horse leaned over the half-door, his blunt-faced head stretched toward the poetess. She was offering him something flat and yellow on her out-stretched palm.

The horse licked it up and made it vanish.

"What's that?" the Dead Man asked curiously.

Apparently, it was his day to make unsuspecting women jump. The haz-ards of having been raised to be a killer. And sneaky, also.

"Sorry," he said.

"Oh, it's fine. They're bananas," she said, recovering herself. She held one out so he could see: a cream-colored wheel of fruit inside a dark gold rind. "Many horses love them."

"That one certainly seems to," Iri said.

"Is he yours?" Ümmühan asked. "I hope you don't mind the treats."

"I think we've adopted each other," the Dead Man said, remembering the impish bow from that evening. "And no, if he likes bananas, he can have bananas. He had a rough night."

"I think we all did," said Iri.

The brown horse lipped up another piece of fruit. The Dead Man ac-cepted a slice from Ümmühan and walked up to the stall door. There was a little plaque on it inscribed with a name. *Plug.*

"Now, that's unfair," he said. "Here, have a treat."

The horse whisked it up, touching his hand so lightly that the soft lip and whiskers only tickled. Whatever they called him, the gelding had been groomed until he shone. His legs were wrapped in bandages. From the strong smell of mint, the Dead Man could only assume there was liniment under them.

A slice along the animal's shoulder had been treated with a wound cream, as had some dings on his forelegs. They were all shallow and long since done bleeding. He was surprisingly unharmed for how long they had spent in the thick of battle.

"We got lucky," he said, scratching the gelding on his chest. The horse sighed.

"They're known for it," said Ümmühan.

"They?" the Dead Man asked, still scratching.

"That horse is of the line of Bansh," Ümmühan said. "You may have heard of her. She's a constellation now. They've all got a lighter color. Some are pale as cream, and blue-eyed to boot. The Qersnyk folk used to consider it an ill omen, and breed to prevent it."

"And now?"

"Bansh came from heaven to carry a Khagan and returned there to bear him home. The cream color is not considered unlucky anymore."

"I've heard of her," said Iri. "There was a stallion, right? Her get? He was cream-colored. Supposedly a lot of famous Qersnyk horses came from him. He belonged to the mother of the current Khagan."

The Dead Man looked down at the coffee-with-a-hint-of-cream hair his fingers were buried in. "This horse is dark."

The poetess smiled. "He's smoke-colored. He would be dark as coal without her heritage. A true black. He doesn't look like a steppe-horse, though—his ancestors must have come over the Steles of the Sky generations ago and bred with the locals."

The Dead Man said, "I had no idea you knew so much about horses."

"I lived on the steppe for many years. You learn. I was younger then." Ümmühan raised a hand to her face. "We were all so much younger then."

The Dead Man nodded inside his veil. Already, he knew the feeling, and he could only imagine it was going to get worse.

"Do you want to meet the horse?" asked Iri. Price Drupada, who had been peeking at the big gelding through his hair, shook his head violently and buried his face in Iri's shoulder. "Oh, well," she said.

"Here," said Ümmühan. "If the prince doesn't want the last banana bit, you should have it."

She put it in Iri's hand, and Iri held it out with her left hand, keeping her body between Drupada and the big horse. The prince peeked through his hair, and squeaked with delight when Plug took it.

Plug! Well, at least they hadn't named him "Dogfood."

"I could use a lucky horse," the Dead Man said, still feeling a little bit sorry for himself.

"I'd say you're both fortunate to have found each other." Ümmühan had drawn an embroidered handkerchief from her pocket. Fastidiously, she wiped away the banana slime.

"So they're auspicious. Do they have other magic powers?"

"Probably not," said Ümmühan. "Bansh could fly, and her colt too, but I haven't heard that he passed it down to his descendants. You might only get that if both parents are heavenly horses. But her line is said to be surefooted and loyal."

"It seems you haven't been appreciated here, buddy," the Dead Man said. He stepped away from the stall. The smoke-colored horse nickered softly. "Somebody spent some time teaching him, though. He's got manners, and he knows some tricks, and he dealt with a wild fight with courage. He must have changed hands, or perhaps his owner was a man-at-arms who died somehow. I wonder how old he is."

"I stole a look at his teeth," said Ümmühan. "I'd say about fifteen years. He's got some life left in him."

"You and me both, old fellow." The Dead Man gave his new friend one more scratch under the jowls.

MRITHURI DISMISSED MOST OF THE OTHERS. SHE STAYED IN HER CHAIR AND watched them leave until the only ones left were herself, the Gage, and Kyrl-myrandal. It was peaceful sitting there quietly with those two gigantic creatures. Not for long, she knew, because Ata Akhimah would be coming back soon with her needle and thread—or whatever one used to sew up dragon wings.

But for now, she would take the respite of company that did not *need* anything from her immediately. No decisions, no actions that would cost people their lives or lands—

"I was wondering," the Gage said, "if you would mind if we ran an experiment."

Mrithuri burst out laughing and buried her face in her hands. She felt the pressure of the Gage's attention and perhaps that of the dragon as well. It still took a moment before she could bring herself under control. When she looked up again, still choking on a painful giggle, she had the distinct impression that the featureless mirrored head was staring at her.

"I am sorry, Empress," said the Gage. "I don't understand what is so funny."

She waved a hand in the air. "Everything. Nothing. Just a chain of thought that broke in a funny place. What sort of experiment are we considering here?"

"Kyrlmyrandal," said the Gage, "wondered what would happen if one of your bearded vultures were to eat a dragon bone."

"Hmm," said Mrithuri. "Do we have a dragon bone?"

The Gage tapped his chest. "Safely insulated."

"Will it poison the bird?"

"It might," said Kyrlmyrandal. "But I rather think that it would, in this case, impart some . . . dragonish qualities to it. It might become more intelligent, for example. Perhaps even able to talk."

"That would have been convenient when I was traveling," said the Gage. "If Vara—"

"Vara?"

"Sorry," he said. "I named the bird, because I forgot to ask if it had a name before I left. And I needed something to call it."

"Of course."

"If Vara could talk, you could have communicated with me. And told me its name."

The Gage couldn't grin, but sometimes she could swear she heard him grinning. Mrithuri thought about it.

"Can I see the bone?"

What he showed her looked like a lump of metal studded with peridot crystals. "Is it safe to touch?"

"For a little while," said Kyrlmyrandal.

She picked the bone off the Gage's palm. It was like picking a nut off a tray, his hand—his gauntlet—was so large. She weighed it in her hand, imagining swallowing it. Nothing for one of her vultures, of course; they ate chunks of bone much larger than this. "You're confident it's safe?"

"Nothing is safe," replied Kyrlmyrandal. "I would say that the risks to his well-being are lower than those he survived flying across a continent with the Gage. But I myself am about to fly across a continent and pick a fight with a being that thrives on entropy and pain, so perhaps my judgment is not to be trusted."

"Hmph," said Mrithuri. She unfastened the brooch that held her drape to her shoulder and stabbed the side of her finger with it. When a drop of blood welled, she rubbed it on the bit of dragonbone.

Vara stretched out his neck and took it willingly. He turned the rock in his beak curiously. It wasn't any bigger than stones he would swallow for his gizzard, she thought, even if it turned out to be entirely indigestible.

This was probably a terrible idea, and if the bird died of poison, she would never forgive herself. What was she doing, trusting a dragon?

The Mother of Exiles, though. Someone whose aid she had been commanded to seek by the Wizard-Prince of Messaline.

There was a moment when she could have snatched the dragonbone back, and using her special connection to her familiar, she probably could have gotten it away from him and even kept all her fingers.

Then Vara tossed his head back and gulped, and the rock was gone.

They waited what seemed a long time. Mrithuri felt her heart pounding in her chest as if she'd taken a jolt of snake venom.

Nothing happened.

"Well, that's that," Mrithuri said, as Ata Akhimah emerged from the palace again, lugging a leatherworking kit that looked heavy. Tsering-la walked at her heels, his surgical bag in his hand.

"I CAN'T JUST SEW THE EDGES TOGETHER," ATA AKHIMAH SAID.

Tsering-la was down by the dragon's tail, inspecting the trailing edge of the wing membrane. Mrithuri had caused a brazier to be brought out on which they could boil water to follow Tsering-la's purification ritual. Then the empress had retired to her chambers to rest.

Ata Akhimah wished she were also sleeping.

She said, "I would have to roll the hems so the silk didn't rip through the holes. It would pull the wing askew, make the flight surface smaller if I did that. You wouldn't be able to extend the wing completely or fly straight."

"I see," said Kyrlmyrandal. She had lain down flat on her stomach, the more-damaged wing spanning the tiles. The Gage held the wingtip out from the body, his weight an anchor. From the trembling of the dragon's shoulder muscles, Akhimah suspected that the full reach made her old joints ache. It was going to be a hell of a thing for her to fly to the Sea of Storms, if this alone hurt her so badly.

She didn't complain about it, and Akhimah didn't ask.

Kyrlmyrandal said, "So how do you propose to repair it?"

Akhimah held up a piece of glove leather, the lightest and most supple in the palace's stores. "I'll fill the gaps in with this."

"It will be heavier, then, that wing."

"Yes," said Ata Akhimah. "Do you think you can compensate?"

"I will have to start out slowly," the dragon said. "Yes. I think as I grow stronger, I will be able to compensate." She sighed. "I won't be able to see where I am flying."

"Sayeh Rajni can be your eyes," Ata Akhimah said.

"Sayeh Rajni needs to stay in Sarathai-tia, and marry the empress."

Akhimah looked over at Tsering-la. He walked toward her, apparently unwilling to yell his comments the length of a dragonwing. When he was close enough to speak softly, he said, "Himadra?"

"He's a man," said Akhimah. "And he's fragile."

"That first thing doesn't matter," said the dragon. "They all have it, the ability to look into another creature's mind and share thoughts. You lot have just decided, for some reason, that gender determines ability." She snorted. "The second thing... you're all fragile, little humans. It seems to me that Himadra is also brave. If he will do it, I will accept his guidance."

"May I come with you on the test flight?" Akhimah asked.

"You might want a parachute," the dragon said.

"A what?" asked Akhimah.

The dragon sighed. Then she explained about parachutes, and Akhimah was delighted. She wished they were ready for the test flight now. But they had more than a night's work ahead before that was possible. So they might as well get started.

"I'm sorry for the pain," she said to Kyrlmyrandal, as Tsering-la went to get the tools out of the boiling water.

"Life is pain," said the dragon. "Fortunately, it's also very interesting."

24

HIMADRA COULD NOT REMEMBER WHEN HE HAD BEEN SO NERVOUS AND EX-
cited. Like a bridegroom, though he had no direct knowledge to back up
that metaphor.

His brothers had not seen him since they were small. And they were of
the age to violently reject things they did not understand. They would, he
thought, recoil from him at first. People so often did, and he had never hes-
itated to use it to gain an advantage.

The object there wasn't advantage, though. It was connection.

Very well, then. He could be charming. He would be charming.

Himadra shifted restlessly in his wheeled chair. What was taking so
long? The tea would be cold by the time they got there!

"What if they don't like me?" he asked, and realized too late that he had
said it out loud. It didn't really matter, because the only other person in the
room was Farkhad.

Farkhad laughed. "They're children. Be kind and not too indulgent, and
they will come around."

"Easy for you to say." Farkhad had a wife, several sons, and probably too
many daughters for anyone's comfort.

Farkhad put one gentle hand on Himadra's shoulder, the kind of cautious contact that felt safe to him. Most lords would not permit such liber-
ties from their lieutenants, but Farkhad was also a friend.

"You can't be a worse foster parent than Anuraja."

Farkhad had a point. Himadra might even have told him so, but someone
scratched on the door.

Himadra realized that he was holding his breath. He waved Farkhad
toward the door, and Farkhad went. When he opened it, there were two
well-grown boys on the other side.

Himadra swallowed around a painful lump and managed to speak without squeaking. "Prince Vivaan," he said. "Prince Rayesh. Come in."

Farkhad bowed them into the room. Himadra knew him well enough to
see his expressionless composure hid the sparkle of amusement. The more
deadpan Farkhad became, the more he was laughing on the inside.

The boys looked solemn and scared.

"Don't worry," Himadra said. "I won't harm you. Just make yourselves at
home. There is tea. Help yourselves to food."

"No servants?" said the younger boy.

"No servants right now," Himadra said. "Just family. This is Farkhad. Farkhad is my lieutenant, and like a cousin to me. He is my most trusted. I am, of course, your brother Himadra. I don't expect you to remember me."

"I think I do," Vivaan said. "A little. Shall we be seated, raja?"

He should not be surprised. Anuraja cowed everyone. And he could tell already—from the boy's posture, from the sideways flick of his eyes—that he was going to have to work at re-educating Rayesh. The lad had had no foundation at all before he was snatched away to this snakepit. Well, he was young yet. There was hope.

"Yes," he said, "please sit. And please call me 'brother.' Or use my name."

"Brother." Vivaan smiled tightly. Rayesh stayed a step behind him, keeping the bulk of his brother's body between himself and the adults in the room.

Both boys found their places. They held themselves so tightly in check that Himadra found his own teeth gritting. He forced himself to relax before he broke his own jaw. By the Mother, even with Anuraja dead, he still had the power to inconvenience Himadra beyond all reason.

It took a little urging to get them to serve themselves, but at last everyone had a plate and a cup before him. Himadra indulged himself with some sticky pastries and a milk sweet. They were riding to the edge of the world tomorrow. A little cane syrup would not kill him.

The boys nibbled nervously while he dispatched the first pastry—orange and lemon flavored—and rinsed the stickiness from his fingertips with rose-water before picking up his tea. He waited for a moment when nobody had food in his mouth and said, "The empress informs me that you have been told about the war and the thing we are facing."

Rayesh's face lit up, which was not the result Himadra had been expecting. "There's a monster!" he said. "And there's a dragon in the courtyard, a real dragon. It's white. It's *enormous*! We had to go on a boat! And then we came back, but we were going to sail to Sarathai-tia!"

"You still might, if you like," said Himadra. "But for right now, I will need you to stay here."

"You're leaving, yo . . . I mean, you're leaving, brother?" Vivaan wasn't eating the pastry. He was just crumbling it up between his fingers, which were sticky and spotted with flakes of dough.

"I shall," Himadra said. "I hope to come back very soon. Once the danger is dealt with. Do you not like pastry?"

Vivaan's smile was tight. "The . . . the empress also bribed us with sweets."

"Hm," said Himadra. "Did it work?"

"We never get to do anything fun," Rayesh said, pouting. "Nazia said you were going to ride the dragon."

"If everything works out according to plan," Himadra answered. "That doesn't always happen."

"Hmph," said Rayesh. "*I* want to ride a dragon."

"Well," said Himadra. "Why don't you ask her?"

"Nazia?"

"No, the dragon. She's her own person, after all. Once her wings are repaired. She'll probably need some practice. Maybe she will take you around."

"You'd let me do that?"

"I'd let both of you do that," Himadra said, with a spike of fear in his breast. These two, along with Drupada, were the only posterity his entire family had or was likely to have.

"Why are we staying behind?" Vivaan asked.

Himadra sensed it was an important question. He took a moment to think through how best to answer it. "Because the only other heir to any of the kingdoms is Drupada, and he's a three-year-old."

"Oh," Vivaan said, his eyes showing white around the irises. "So we'll be responsible. In your absence."

"I won't leave it on you alone," Himadra said.

Rayesh said, "I'm glad the Lord Chancellor is dead. He was mean."

"He was also stealing," Himadra said. "Lady Golbahar will stay with you to help you practice administration. And Farkhad here. And most of the army."

"Nazia?" Rayesh asked hopefully.

Himadra barely knew who the girl was—she'd been all but silent in their one meeting. But Sayeh obviously valued her, and he'd heard how she'd rescued both of them. "I will see if Sayeh Rajni and Tsering-la can spare her."

Vivaan said, "Practice administration?"

Himadra smiled. "You're fifteen. I was only a few years older than you when I inherited Chandranath. The Empress was around the same age when she inherited Sarathai-tia. I am guessing Anuraja didn't give you much authority."

"None," said Rayesh.

Vivaan put a hand on his brother's arm.

Himadra said, "You will listen to your advisors?"

"Marnor, the new Lord Chancellor?"

"What do you think of him?"

Vivaan sipped his tea. "I like him?" he said. Then shook his head. "It's not about liking, is it?"

"No," agreed Himadra.

"I think he's honest," Vivaan said. "Or if he isn't, he's too clever to get caught. I think he pretends to be less clever than he is. I think he keeps his own counsel."

"I heard his books were accurate," Himadra said. "I'm still going to ask the empress to put Farkhad over him, and General Pranaj."

"Whose wards will we be?" Vivaan's expression was serious, his tone dry.

Himadra suddenly wanted to hug him. "Mine."

"While you are away?"

The size of the gamble made his heart race. But it might pay off—in loyalty from the boys, and in confidence they desperately needed. He said, "Your own."

"You will come back, though?" Rayesh asked. He kept his eyes down. He worried at a hangnail on his thumb.

"If I live," Himadra answered, "I will take care of you."

Vivaan looked at him, his face expressionless, his eyes wide. Himadra thought he'd pushed too far, too fast. The boy sprang to his feet, then arrested himself mid-lunge. "Brother—"

Himadra hid his self-deprecating wince, "Yes, brother?"

"May . . . may I embrace you?"

Himadra smiled. "You must be very gentle."

THE WIZARDS SEWED FOR THREE DAYS. MRITHURI SPENT THAT TIME DECIDING who would come to Sarathai-tia on the back of a dragon. Assuming the dragon could fly when they were finished mending. Assuming she didn't eat them all once she was mended.

She didn't seem like the eating-people sort of dragon. But one never really knew, did one? Until one either was—or was not—eaten.

Himadra had agreed. Sayeh, along with her son, from whom she would not be parted. And the Dead Man. The Gage would run along the ground below. Both Wizards would come to Sarathai-tia. All four of those latter would go on with the dragon to the Origin of Storms.

Mrithuri tried not think that she was sending Serhan into mortal peril—to fight a terrible storm and an otherworldly monster—while she was staying behind to become a bigamist. She thought of Anuraja clutching his chest and tumbling down the steps of the Peacock Throne. Before the Dead Man left, she realized, she *was* going to have to divorce him. If she wanted her marriage to Sayeh to be at all legitimate. If she wanted a chance to survive that ascent herself, with some pretense at being a valid empress. Emperor. Whatever.

She could keep nothing for herself, in the end. The crown would eat everything that was hers alone and leave her only with duty.

Except, she admitted with whimsy, a little self-pity.

Hnarisha was staying behind to run things there in Sarathai-lae, and with him Golbahar. Nazia and Himadra's second-in-command would have charge of Himadra's brothers, who would—Himadra insisted—be titularly "in charge." Mrithuri supposed it was kinder to ease the lads into rulership than experiencing the change in role as she had, by having it fall on her head from on high.

Ümmühan would also stay behind, working on her "constitution."

Nizhvashiti would come back to Sarathai-tia. It would be officiating Mrithuri's third wedding ceremony in one season. And to think she, Mrithuri, had once mocked Anuraja for having had five wives.

Pranaj would remain in Sarathai-lae, in command of the army, and begin demustering the bulk of them. The men of Sarathai-tia would caravan home with Druja the caravan master, and they would bring along various animals, familiars, and chattels. Excluding Vara and Guang Bao, who would travel with the dragon. But including the Dead Man's newly obtained horse, because it couldn't ride a dragon and he insisted it not be left behind.

Finally, the plans were accomplished. The logistics were in place. And Mrithuri could no longer put off the conversation she needed to have with the Dead Man.

It had been a long while since she rode a horse, but she still remembered the theory. And she was feeling restless and as if she wanted to be away from everyone else's needs and demands. Riding out to review the troops would be a fine excuse, and she would of course bring her personal guards along: Syama and the Dead Man.

That latter would probably appreciate a chance to spend some time with his new horse friend, anyway.

Mrithuri referred the making of arrangements for her ride to Lady Golbahar. When she put the princeling's armor on again and walked out to the stable, she found the Dead Man already mounted. His horse was certainly not much to look at, but Mrithuri appreciated the way the gelding eyed Syama and stamped a little but refrained from further dramatics. Most horses found the bear-dog more upsetting; the brown gelding was obviously battle-hardened, and he had a big shoulder on him.

Looks weren't everything.

The mare that had been saddled for Mrithuri, for example, looked gorgeous and was extremely dubious about the entire situation. She sidled and scuffled on the cobblestones, tail swishing, ears on a swivel. The lad holding her danced after her, trying to soothe her with low tones.

"Down," Mrithuri said. Syama gave her a disappointed look but dropped to the ground, her elbows not touching the cobbles. Mrithuri rolled her eyes at the bear-dog, then stepped past the stable lad and offered the mare a flat palm. She found a peaceful place inside herself—or carved one out of the tumult of her own concealed emotions, more accurately—and tried to radiate calm and harmony to the mare. A slow breath in, a slow breath out—

The mare stopped dead in her tracks.

Mrithuri was aware of men and women around the courtyard watching her. And the Dead Man as well, but he was less likely to judge her as an unfit ruler forever if she failed to soothe the mare.

"Your Magnanimity," said the stable lad nervously.

"Shh," said the Dead Man. "Let her work."

The mare whuffed. Her muzzle was pale, her face showing the remains of what had once been a dramatic blaze now vanishing into the gray of her coat. She was a pearl-and-smoke dapple whose powerful neck was draped by a silver, flowing mane. She had been groomed until her pale hide reflected mirrored iridescence. Her ears, pricked upright with worry and focus, were finely modeled. She was bigger than the Dead Man's big gelding by a hand.

Somebody in the stable had gone to some effort to find Mrithuri a horse fit for an emperor. This had probably been one of Anuraja's war horses.

Well, then she belonged to Mrithuri now.

She stamped, iron shoe striking sparks on the cobblestone, staring at Syama with a threat implied. Mrithuri kept her hand extended, breathed quietly, looked to one side. Long moments passed before the mare blew out through her nostrils, scrubbed the side of her face against her knee, then touched her muzzle to Mrithuri's palm. Warm breath and whiskers tickled.

"What's her name?" Mrithuri asked the lad.

"Rainbow, Your Magnanimity ," the boy replied, his tone gone honestly respectful. "There's a block right over here."

When she had mounted, she rode Rainbow in a gentle circle and was pleased to find the horse sensitive and responsive. Every step she took was lightning-quick but there was no sense of jerkiness in her movement. Mrithuri turned her to face the Dead Man, whose brown seemed to have dozed off while they waited. The gelding stood with his ears relaxed and eyelids drooping, one hind hoof cocked.

"Got a difference in attitude here," the Dead Man said, and nudged the brown to wake him up. He brought the horse around beside hers and a step behind.

It occurred to her that there she was, riding out among her army with only him and Syama to protect her—and no one among her people had tried to gainsay her or even argue. Was this what ruling meant?

Was this self-determination?

Her nerves thrilled; the gray mare danced. Mrithuri calmed herself for the horse's sake.

"Do you have your pistols?" she asked the Dead Man.

"I don't take a step from my bed without them these days," he answered.

She called Syama, and they were off.

Considering the unpredictability of a brand-new mount and a giant predator at heel, it went well. Rainbow lowered her head once or twice and nipped the air above Syama's quarters when the bear-dog strayed too close to the horse's line of travel, and she threatened to cow-kick the Dead Man's gelding once when he tried to edge in front of her, but that was no more than you would expect from a mare of war.

And then they were in the streets, just the three of them and the horses. People drawn by the ring of horseshoes came out to stand in the doorways and watch them pass. She saw wonder on some of the faces, curiosity on others. A child waved shyly. Mrithuri waved in return, and the next she knew, she was returning waves all around. Behind them built a wall of cheering. The Dead Man kept his face front, hands low on the gelding's mane. But she could see around his eyes that he was smiling.

It buoyed her. *Is this it?* she wondered. *I fought off an army that was mostly their own people. Do they love me now?*

The logic of ruling baffled her.

The Dead Man's expression was mostly hidden behind his veil, of course, but what she could see of his face was determinedly impassive. He no doubt knew why she had summoned him and gone to such lengths to ensure both their privacy and the unimpeachable correctness of the circumstances under which they met. They were chaperoned by all Sarathai-lae.

"What's the gelding's name?" she asked, as they approached the gates of the city.

"Plug." His chuckle was fabric-muffled.

"That's terrible!" she cried. Big muscles tensed under her until she stilled herself and breathed in and out slowly, quietly, once more. "You must change it," she said more carefully, as they passed between the towers and onto the fertile plateau above the river.

"I don't know," he said. "I enjoy the reminder that things may be more than they appear."

There was the army camp in the distance. In a moment, they would be out of earshot of the guards and she could say what she needed to say, where here they had the privacy of public regard. She glanced over her shoulder; the horses were walking fast. Eager to be out of the stable walls.

She drew one deep breath. She owed this man honesty.

"I committed the cardinal sin," Mrithuri said. "Of imagining that I was special. Of imagining that we were special."

"Weren't we?" he said, amused. But he must have seen her expression, because his next words were soft. "This is not easy for me, either."

"You'll be leaving, I imagine?"

"If we live," he agreed. "It's not that I want to."

"No," she said. "It would be harder if you stayed." Her voice shook; she wasn't fooling herself, let alone Serhan. "Where will you go?"

"I'll go where the work takes me, I suppose," he said. "Perhaps back to Messaline."

"Is there a woman there?"

It just slipped out. As soon as she asked, she knew she did not really want to know.

His eyes crinkled. She could not tell if he was grinning or holding back tears.

"If there ever is, I will tell her that I married a queen far away, and so my hand will never be hers."

She snorted. Rainbow snorted back. The mare's stride was lengthening, becoming fluid, losing its nervous mince. Mrithuri said, "Don't your people believe in polygamy?"

He shrugged. "I was given one wife, and to be truthful I never wanted another while I had her. It always seemed like a lot of work and potential for dramatics." He kept his eyes on the horizon, his form in the saddle excruciatingly correct. "I think you and Sayeh will do well together."

"It's convenient."

"I hope someday—" Emotion cracked his voice. "I hope someday it is more than that. You deserve better. Both of you. I hope you will choose to make a real alliance with her."

"I already chose. I chose to think you would not betray me," Mrithuri said. The pain in her breast was so great that the words came past it in a whisper.

"I did not betray you. I will not betray you. Nor can I let you betray yourself."

Her anger made the mare snort and prance. Syama glanced back at them with a frown that was the beginning of a snarl. Mrithuri wondered what she herself would do next. She didn't know. She couldn't predict her own actions in this moment.

Was she too much a queen to show that anger, or was she empress enough to let it flare? "I trusted you not to hurt me. I chose that trust. I worked for that trust. And you set me aside."

"It was the wrong trust," the Dead Man said. "You should have trusted me to do what was best for you, instead."

"And who decides what's best for me? You? Do you own me? Am I a pet, a child, to be decided for?" Apparently, she was at least that much an empress after all.

Very well, then. Very well. She might be alone, but she would rule.

"You decide," he said. "You decided when you told me that you were first a rajni and only a woman after that. Now you are more than a rajni. And you decide still."

Mrithuri's eyes blurred. She wanted to scream. She wanted to hurl herself at him. But the mare of war demanded her full attention, overriding grief, overriding fury. And there were watchers on the wall above. So they argued in even tones, with straight necks and quiet hands upon the reins. The storm raged inside her; the surface was serene. "So now I have to decide to set you aside in turn."

He nodded, eyes on the horizon.

She said, "I divorce thee."

They were the hardest words she had ever said. And she had to do them without any help at all from her serpents, or from her heart.

"I hear you." He turned toward her.

She set her shoulders inside the armor. "I hate this."

He glanced sidelong. "And I—Mrithuri, beware!"

As he shouted, Syama growled. The gray mare reared; Mrithuri dropped the reins and grabbed the pommel to keep from sliding out of the saddle. Something dark surged toward her and she threw herself alongside the mare's neck. A pistol shot whistled past so close, she could fool herself she felt the wind of its passing.

"Shit!"

Mrithuri didn't know if it was her that yelled or the Dead Man. Her hair had been coiled and pinned for riding. Something yanked savagely at the braid. She swiped at it with a gloved hand and made contact with a warm and struggling body. Wings beat around her. She was the center of a whirl of shapes, erratic flickerings her eye couldn't follow.

Rainbow came down hard, her body swelling with the horrible shriek of an angry horse. She kicked out. Mrithuri's face smacked into the mare's neck. She kept her grip on the saddle with one slipping hand.

She grabbed at the creature in her hair. Something stabbed her fingers. She clutched it anyway and ripped it free, blood oozing. One of those damned birds, horrible things. The beak jabbed at her hand again. She hurled it to the ground; the screaming mare stepped on it.

Something crunched as Rainbow pawed and tore. Mrithuri wiped blood from her nose and looked around. The gelding had something in his teeth. Syama was lunging and chomping, snap-shaking and dropping, over and over again. The Dead Man had drawn his curved sword and wove it in a complicated arc above them. Rainbow kicked out with her hind feet, and when she landed, she charged forward, right into the wall of birds.

"Go," the Dead Man yelled. "Ride!"

Mrithuri grabbed after the loop of the reins. She pulled the mare around in a circle, assessing. The camp was closer than the city. When they were pointed in roughly the right direction, she shoved her hands forward and kicked Rainbow in the ribs as hard as she could.

It broke through the mare's fury, and she snorted and began to run. Not an easy canter but a flat gallop, the charge and rush of hooves. Mrithuri hunkered low and clung, blood crawling back across her cheeks in the wind. She turned her head and strained her eyes in their sockets to see behind her. A second thunder of hooves just behind her was reassuring, and the heavy panting and pad of enormous paws as Syama caught up and passed them, raising her voice in a deep bass moan of warning.

Through Rainbow's bobbing ears, Mrithuri saw sentries scurrying, alerted by gunfire, the bear-dog, the thunder of charging hooves. Dozens of black birds swarmed them, the flock trailing like a ragged plume. Mrithuri hid her face in Rainbow's mane, loosed the reins, and held on for dear life. If they fell now, she might be killed. She had to trust the mare.

They were among the tents in moments. Mrithuri pulled her horse down, reined the shuddering mare around. Though she snorted with emotion, Rainbow was not even breathing heavily. Mrithuri panted for both.

A forest of bows rose around them; a flight of arrows rose from the bows. Black birds fell by the dozens, pinned to earth as the arrows bore them down. The rest of the flock veered off and blew away in shifting formation, a murmuration of death.

"I hate those things," the Dead Man said, reining in beside her. Syama trotted up, blood-smeared and grinning. She, at least, appeared to be having an excellent time.

Mrithuri watched the flock go. "The Wizards will want the dead birds."

"They won't have time to do much with them before we go."

"That felt personal."

"Well." The Dead Man didn't look up from reloading his gun. "I'd say that we have some evidence now that the beast must be pretty unhappy with what you've accomplished so far."

"Hmph," Mrithuri said. Pranaj was coming toward them through the troops. She tried to smooth her hair and wound up smearing blood through it.

"Keep it up," the Dead Man said.

25

THE DEAD MAN STOOD IN HIS NEW RED COAT, HIS VEIL TUCKED UNDER THE collar so it wouldn't blow around, and watched as Kyrlmyrandal, with Ata Akhimah harnessed to her back, unfolded her mended wings. They were a flourish of streaked red against the chalk white of her body, and they spanned the entire courtyard and more.

"Hm," she said. "A bit of a logistical problem. Why don't I meet you all on the boulevard?"

The dragon began to evacuate the palace the same way she had gotten in, climbing over one long block of residences, the bathhouse, a colonnade, and the wall beyond like a man stepping meticulously around a child's block castle. The Wizard on her back clutched the traces and laughed uproariously. The Dead Man shrugged and began walking. He did want to see her fly. And his poor horse deserved the rest of the night off after the demon birds, so it was shank's mare down to the foreyard of the city gates.

He was pleased but not surprised when the Gage fell in next to him. The Gage had obtained a fresh robe somewhere. It looked as if it might have started life as a particularly understated bedspread, a pattern of lines of interlocking beige triangles on ivory, now folded over itself, seamed, and with a hood attached.

Just as well, the Dead Man thought. The old one had been worn down to barely more than warp threads sagging across holes, and just enough material between to make it wearable.

"Well," said the Gage, "I suppose it'll be time to move on again if we survive this."

"Yeah," said the Dead Man, feeling in his pockets for a cheroot. He stuck it between his teeth. The Gage reached out and snapped his fingers to make a spark. He puffed deeply, drawing the flame into the weed. "Unless you want to stay in Sarathai-tia, I mean. I'm sure Her Magnanimity wouldn't mind having an invincible automaton at the throne-side."

The Gage rattled when he shrugged. "You're not staying."

"How did you know?" The Dead Man drew in smoke and felt it bring with it settling calm.

"We've been friends for a while. And it would be awkward for you."

"You *could* stay. We're not married."

A creak of a laugh was the Gage's only answer. They passed under the palace gate and out onto that broad and indefensible boulevard. It was a dragon wide, if barely.

The Dead Man sighed out smoke and followed the length of the dragon tail. It seemed like half the rest of the palace was following too—the other Wizard, the nobility, and any of the plainer sort that could sneak away from their duties. Even Sayeh was there on the horse she had captured from her kidnapper. Not Mrithuri, who had gone to bed after they made it back to the palace. Not Hnarisha, who was guarding her. Not Himadra, and the Dead Man didn't know where he was. But he and the Gage managed to keep a little private space around themselves, and they could both speak in low voices.

The Dead Man said, "Here's to you for forgiving my actions, old friend."

The road creaked under the weight of the Gage. "You forgive mine, too. Hell, you don't even care."

The walk out of the city was longer on foot than on horse. This time, the people leaning out of doors and peeking from windows were staring at the dragon, though, and not the empress.

The Dead Man decided he'd had enough of his smoke. He knocked the ember off with his thumbnail and tucked the remainder away again. They went on in silence for several blocks before he said, "I don't want you to feel like you have to sacrifice yourself to keep me from being alone just because I do not want to live on an ex-lover's suffrage."

"You are alone," said the Gage, "because you make choices that keep you isolated. What would happen if you chose someone who didn't have prior commitments?"

"You'd lose your traveling companion," said the Dead Man, humorously. Then he sighed. "I wouldn't go into it knowing how it would end, and not knowing would make me uncomfortable."

"So you keep your armor up because you already lost more than one person should ever have to." The Gage sighed like a steam engine. They walked a while in silence again, before he said, "This way, you never have to let anyone inside your guard. You never have to risk another loss."

Ahead, Kyrlmyrandal climbed over the gate on her way out of Sarathai-lae. Men within the towers gaped or ducked away.

Ridiculously, the Dead Man thought of Iri holding Drupada up to see the horses. He'd had daughters, once. "Says a person who literally replaced his body with a metal armature because he was tired of being hurt by the world!"

"I'm not saying," said the Gage, patiently, "that you are unique. Or that you and I don't have a great deal in common. We wouldn't be friends if we didn't. Did you break your own heart?"

The Dead Man thought about it. "No. And I think I managed not to break hers, either, though she's not happy. We live in the wrong kind of romance for there to have ever been a different ending."

"The kind with swords," the Gage agreed. "And not the kind with kisses."

Their part of the procession passed under the gate arches, giving the Dead Man a distinct sense of following in his own footsteps. It was easy to track the dragon; she towered above the plain. Even outside the walls, she kept walking.

Toward the bluff over the river, he realized. He looked at the Gage. The Gage didn't turn to him; the Gage just began to run.

The Dead Man followed. The Gage wasn't really putting on his engine. The Dead Man could keep up if he pushed himself. His feet struck the earth, which jumped under the Gage's stride. People ahead of them turned at the ringing blows the Gage's footfalls made.

Ahead, the white wings with their ruby streaks and their wedge-shaped and lenticular patches spread again. They were still a little crooked, as if one shoulder were scarred in some manner to restrict a full reach. That was the wing that dragged when she walked.

The Dead Man ran full-out, feeling like a puppy scampering after the Gage. Kyrlmyrandal began to rush away from them, also running, a hopping ferretlike gait that should have been comical but was absolutely terrifying, even headed in the opposite direction. She leaped, her long body stretching out, the wings thrown wide—and fell like a diver from the cliff edge. Her tail snaked away like the lash of whip, close enough to touch and then gone.

She screamed. It vibrated his chest like an elephant's rumble. Ata Akhimah screamed too, much higher.

The Dead Man managed to stop himself in time to keep from tipping over the cliff edge. His hand clutched in the air before him. He could not have said whether he was grasping after the vanished dragon or making the sign of the pen. From below rose an enormous snap and a flapping sound so slow and vast it might have been a sonorously pounded drum, the heartbeat of a very mountain.

Kyrlmyrandal beat her mended wings and rose, turning her long glide into an ascent, rising and rising, turning into sky. The high light of the Heavenly River glittered on her pale hide, iridescent as fish scales. She rose into the night, glistening.

ONLY THE GOGGLES KEPT ATA AKHIMAH FROM BEING BLINDED BY THE WIND. Only the harness kept her from being ripped from the dragon's back. As Kyrlmyrandal dove from the top of the bluff, Akhimah clutched the release that would free her from the harness (she hoped) if something went wrong, grateful for the "parachute" strapped to her back, uncertain if it would work if she needed it. At least it was a nice idea.

They fell—into a huge swooping glide that took the Wizard's breath away. She shrieked in joy and heard the dragon bugling—an enormous, animal sound that vibrated the body under her like the membrane of a drum. The swoop extended, the wings pumped, and much to Akhimah's disbelief, they rose. They were flying!

She had a job to do, she reminded herself, trying not to grin. If her lips parted, the wind got inside her mouth and stretched her face quite painfully.

Anxiously, Akhimah turned from side to side in the lead-foil-lined leather saddle. She wasn't sure how much it would protect her from the dragon's toxic emanations, but Kyrlmyrandal seemed to think it would help enough to make a difference. A larger howdah, lined with lead foil, was under construction. It would serve to carry all the dragon's would-be passengers. They would limit their exposure on the trip as much as possible. They would have to fly in short stints at first, anyway, until Kyrlmyrandal regained her condition. She would leave them alone between legs: distance was a protection from the poison.

Akhimah tried not to think of how often the dragon's blood had gotten on her gloves over the last few days. She would think about it later, if she survived. If the beast was defeated.

Leaning and squinting, Ata Akhimah tried to assess the structural integrity of her repairs. The leather would stretch, eventually; sooner or later it would need to be replaced or resewn. None of them, she was sure, were looking forward to that.

But for now it seemed to be holding.

Enjoy it, she told herself. *Worry if something goes wrong.*

The sensation was amazing. Once the air was under them, once the gigantic wings were fully spread, once they were rising on a warm upcurrent, Akhimah could see abruptly how the air was a fluid. How it worked like water to hold the dragon up, and how her wings were like fins swimming through it. Akhimah felt herself at the fringes of a whole new world of natural philosophy. If they survived this, she promised herself, they would do such science that her name would live forever.

One might even be able to build a flying machine.

Why not? There were ships that went on the water. Why *not* ships that went on the air?

The land spread out below them like a tapestry, like a map drawing. Tiny houses, tiny armies, tiny palaces. Even the hills seemed small and far away, and she could see across the shore to where the Arid Sea disappeared on the horizon.

If it's all bits stitched together, she wondered, *how can I see so far?*

She couldn't ask Kyrlmyrandal now. The dragon's ears were at the end of a long neck, far ahead, and even if she shouted, it seemed impossible that

Kyrlmyrandal could hear her. When they were flying east, there would be members of the royal family to relay words to the dragon through that special connection they could forge. For now . . . She had a mirror to flash light if she were in distress. Unallayed curiosity didn't count as distress, though. Even to a Wizard.

Akhimah clung to the harness straps and looked down, peering past the beating wings, trying to identify landmarks. She was surprised to realize that from this far up, there was no sense of vertigo. Just the scope of a wide land. They were so high that she could make out the smudge of mountains on the northern horizon. Not the Steles of the Sky; merely the lesser mountains of Chandranath.

They had been up long enough, she thought, and the stitches were still holding. It was time to head down, allow the dragon to rest, and inspect the repairs.

And tomorrow, now that they were certain she could fly, and that the repairs wouldn't tear right out of her wings under strain, Himadra's brothers could fly with her.

26

Maybe the Mother was guiding their path, Sayeh thought, as the Godmade had suggested. Mrithuri could have found worse ways to cement her popularity among the people of Sarathai-lae than—as they saw it—executing a corrupt tax collector before departing to go fight demons on the back of a dragon she had tamed by treating its injuries. She also kept her troops from pillaging and her dragon from eating all the livestock in the vicinity. And she was young and pretty, which never hurt, and had brought the majority of their sons back alive from a war she hadn't even started.

That Mrithuri had nothing to do with Kyrlmyrandal's behavior didn't matter to how her people saw the outcome. It was a sad fact of politics that truth mattered less to a ruler's popularity than appearances. And Sayeh was more or less certain the people of Sarathai-lae thought of Kyrlmyrandal as a monster rather than a person. If you hadn't talked to her, it would be an easy mistake to make.

Sitting on her long back as she rowed into the clouds on powerful wings, feeling the little skip on the air that her stiff wing caused, Sayeh found it easy to forget as well. She laughed with exhilaration, forgetting all decorum. Strapped into the howdah beside her, Drupada laughed as well, shrieking with giggles as only a toddler could.

He wasn't the least bit frightened, as if in his young experience a dragon were no more terrifying than a pony. It even started to make up for leaving his new best friend Hathi behind. Toddler and elephant had formed an inseparable bond almost immediately.

It was probably best that they were staying in Sarathai-tia. Otherwise, both elderly elephant and young child would be inconsolable. Mrithuri had wanted Sayeh to leave her son in Sarathai-lae. While Sayeh could see the sense of it, her heart rebelled even from letting him out of her sight to sleep. She had been waking a dozen times a night just to slip into the nursery attached to her chamber and watch him in his crib.

It didn't matter what the empress wanted. If the empress expected Sayeh to marry her, she would just have to accept the fact that Drupada would come to Sarathai-tia with her. He would be as safe there as he could ever be in Sarathai-lae. If they were all going to die fighting the beast that had destroyed her city, Sayeh was by the Mother and the Good Daughter going to die by her child's side and not leagues and leagues away from him. She wasn't leaving him alone again until he became a teenager who couldn't stand her.

Eventually, Mrithuri had relented. She'd never stood a chance, really. Sayeh was older and far more stubborn.

She looked around—at Himadra, at the Dead Man, at Mrithuri, at Ata Akhimah and Tsering-la, at Nizhvashiti. Somewhere below them was the Gage, who would catch up when they paused to let Kyrlmyrandal rest. Sometimes when Sayeh peered out the side of the howdah, she could just make out the faint glint of his metal body against the landscape far below. Or see the cloud of dust kicked up behind him.

Vara and Guang Bao sported in the clouds beside them, sometimes landing on the dragon's horns. They seemed to amuse the dragon, though beside her they were like butterflies resting on the hair of a man.

Traveling on dragon-back was by far the most pleasant mode Sayeh had tried. Better even than a sedan chair—and far, far swifter.

Surrounded by this strange new family she'd fallen in among—and their even-stranger retainers—the wind slipping in through the sides of the howdah to steal her breath, the ground spread out below her like a sand table for planning battles, Sayeh felt a weird peace.

All the planning, all the worrying, all the waiting, all the wondering—it was nearly over now. They were moving toward destiny. Flying into it on the back of a dragon.

It was out of her hands now. The decisions were made, their course set. There was nothing left but to see it through.

She should be afraid. She should be terrified. She was going to fight an existential war with a plan born of desperation. If you could even call what they had a plan. She should be shivering in her sandals—and with more than the wind of flight. Instead, a strange kind of serenity infused her.

It reminded her of her wedding day, decades before. There was nothing left to be afraid of; nothing to escape. Nothing but whatever, inevitably, would follow.

The biggest fight of her life. And she was the person with the least to do, the least control over outcomes. She would not sit upon the Peacock Throne. She would not fly to war at the Origin of Storms.

She would wait, and wrap bandages, and do such things as that. Warlords like Himadra would never understand that waiting was the hardest way to be brave.

"My bones ache," said Himadra, rubbing his hands together. "Is it because of the flying, do you think?"

"It's because the air pressure is lower up here. And because the air pressure is lower near *that*," said Kyrlmyrandal, her voice booming as she made herself heard above the wind. Himadra leaned forward to peer in the direction her long neck twisted. What he saw caught painfully in his throat.

A wall of char-gray clouds, piled along the eastern horizon—stretching as far as his eye could see—rotating so fast that he could watch them spin. "What on earth is that?"

"The beast's storm," whispered Nizhvashiti. "In the least, that is the vanguard of it. There will be worse behind, and more."

"We'll have to go north to continue east, then turn south, once we leave Sarathai-tia," Kyrlmyrandal said. "There's no flying through that. We'll go over the Bitter Sea."

"Over Ansh-Sahal," said Sayeh.

"Yes," said the dragon.

FLYING IN A HOWDAH ON DRAGON-BACK ALMOST DID NOT SEEM LIKE TRAVEL-ing. The world went by beneath, the work of the wings went on, the river of heaven wheeled overhead. But it somehow bothered Mrithuri to sit in relative comfort, bundled in more furs and blankets than she had ever needed in her life, and traverse in a few days that which had taken weeks on her elephant.

What did feel like travel was the long breaks when the dragon took herself off to give the humans respite from her poisonous aura and to rest her wings. During these times, the humans pitched a pavilion and ate and rested. Maybe that was the problem; there was too much time to think. Too much time to worry. Too much time for Mrithuri to grieve both what she had lost and what she was still likely to lose. No servants to pitch the tent, either, or to light the fire or cook the food—the Dead Man had to teach her and Sayeh how to help. The Wizards were better pupils than the queens.

It was good for her to have practical skills, to understand what was entailed in the tasks of living. She knew that; she believed it. But when Serhan placed his hands over hers to show her how to bend a knot—

It caused pain.

She should talk with Nizhvashiti about wisdom, keeping a quiet mind, and attaining serenity. She should, but she didn't. Maybe Tsering-la would be less intimidating. She had heard the Wizards of Tsarepheth had disciplines to soothe the mind.

Maybe he would teach some of them to her. Maybe she wouldn't feel ashamed for admitting to him that she needed help. Maybe.

She was still thinking about needing help rather than asking for it when Kyrlmyrandal banked to change the angle of the howdah's windows and Sarathai-tia hove into view above a curving horizon. The sky was clear overhead despite the monster storm visible to the east. The Heavenly River gleamed overhead and the city looked like a toy beside the bend in the earthly river far below. Mrithuri caught her breath at the golden turrets, the spiral high street, the walls that sparkled along their edges with dragonglass.

The city looked like a lotus blossom on its artificial hill. She hadn't realized the likeness until she saw it from above.

Something else occurred to her that never had before, so stunning she put her hand to her mouth. Sayeh noticed and leaned close. "What is it, Your Magnanimity?"

Mrithuri shook her head. But Sayeh deserved to know. Sayeh, of all people, deserved to know.

Reluctantly, she murmured, "The kind of power that could raise up a mountain on a river plain, say—"

Sayeh too kept her voice low. "Yes?"

"Could awaken a volcano also, don't you think?"

"Oh," said Sayeh. "The throne."

Mrithuri nodded. "I know now why Anuraja so badly wanted to control it. There's a lot of power in that thing."

Sayeh dropped her voice even lower, trusting the rush of wind to keep their privacy. "You're not going to trust Himadra, are you?"

Mrithuri shook her head. Her hair, braided and wrapped in silk to protect it from the wind, flopped against her shoulder. "That depends on what you mean by 'trust.' Will he die to save his brothers from a beast? I think so. And if we all get through this, I have every confidence that he'll try to negotiate or bluff every advantage he can out of me. Out of us."

"What are you going to do about it?" Sayeh asked.

"You want him punished?"

"Yes," Sayeh said.

She looked down and drew a deep breath, held it, let it out.

"But what would that accomplish? And he also cared for my people when they came to him for help."

Sayeh bit her lip and shook her head, eyes still trained out the window.

Mrithuri said, "I thought we might set up more trade routes. Maybe find a way to raise revenues with more Chandranathi pottery. I can send the rain north, if I survive the throne."

"You will," said Sayeh, patting her arm.

Did either of them believe it? It didn't matter. She had to try. "If they have enough to eat, there's less incentive to raid."

"Hmh," said Sayeh. "He'll try to run us."

Mrithuri smiled. "Aren't you going to try to run him?"

Kyrlmyrandal spiraled lower, her wingtip pointed unerringly at the city. She was too large to land inside it, and Sarathai-tia did not have Sarathai-lae's broad avenues and spacious courtyards. They would have to set down on the plain and walk to the gates. Except for Vara, Mrithuri's familiars were left behind to follow by caravan, even poor Syama. But Sayeh had brought Guang Bao, and the birds could be dispatched to let Yavashuri know they were arriving.

A plume of dust appeared on the horizon. Below it, the distant glitter of light on metal. The Gage would be with them in a moment.

Sayeh said, "Do you think those sorcerers have studied the Science of Building as well as necromancy?"

Mrithuri glanced over at Nizhvashiti, who sat in the back corner of the howdah like a statue carved of dark wood. No answers there.

She said, "I think that what Kyrlmyrandal said about the Alchemical Emperor stitching the Empire of Sarath-Sahal out of broken pieces is interesting. As interesting as the idea that the beast is pushing its way into our world from between those pieces. Maybe the beast's power isn't too different from our ancestor's."

"Maybe our ancestor borrowed some of his power from the beast."

"Did you hear about the walking cities the Gage found?"

Sayeh nodded. "My Wizard told me."

"It seems like the emperor sourced magic from anywhere he could to build his empire. Like a sorcerer, rather than a Wizard: he sacrificed others to get his strength. Dragonglass in the rafters, nuns in the cloisters. And he did it without caring who was damaged in the process."

"That's how empires get built," Sayeh said. "Conquerors don't count the cost."

"We might be paying that price now," Mrithuri said. "Lock a beast out and it wants back in?"

Sayeh put a hand on her arm. Sayeh's laugh sounded forced—she who could maintain any political façade and make it seem spontaneous and genuine. "Like a cat."

"There's a crosswind picking up," Kyrlmyrandal boomed. "Hold on. This might be a little bumpy."

Mrithuri closed her eyes, though she knew by now it was unwise to do so if she wanted to keep her stomach settled. They were so close now, within sight of the palace. Surely, she would be able to reach her familiars now.

Reaching out, she felt Kyrlmyrandal's mind, and she felt the cheerful thoughts of Vara, returned to his home range at last. Further, further. As if she balanced on a tightrope. And then, the whisper of contact. As if a feather brushed the back of her hands. There were her birds.

She felt the lack of Syama like a pang. The bear-dog had slunk away, betrayed and flat-eared, when Mrithuri had mounted the dragon without her. She would be following with the caravan. But now, so close, the bearded vultures on their perches were within Mrithuri's range.

She had no sooner touched their minds than she knew something was wrong. Most of them were in the mews, where they should have been. But one was somewhere else. Somewhere that felt twisting, and strange. And he was not alone. Yavashuri was there beside him.

Her eyes opened as if she had been slapped. "Kyrlmyrandal?"

"I hear you," the dragon said. Her voice made the howdah shudder.

"Fly over the tower, would you? Close enough to see the banners?" She pulled her goggles up and leaned toward the window, peering down. The blind dolphin was there, a pale curve on blue, stirred in the wind of the oncoming storm. But beside it, and not below, there flew another banner. A red tiger on a green field.

"Partha," she snarled. "Oh, he'll regret that decision. Set us down close to the gates, Kyrlmyrandal. Ata Akhimah, do we still have that imperial banner?"

"I've been using it as a blanket," Tsering-la admitted. "Is there a problem?"

"Yes," she said. "I think one of my lordlings has made an attempt at a coup. Take us down, please."

Kyrlmyrandal had been right about the crosswind. They landed on the plain beside a Gage still dripping wet from having forded the river. He caught each of them as they slithered down the dragon's side, not bothering with the ladder. Nizhvashiti lifted Himadra carefully and floated to the earth with him.

"So much for royal dignity," said Mrithuri. She turned her gaze on the Gage as he set Tsering-la gently on his feet. "Your departure may be delayed a little, Gage. Will you be my army?"

When the Dead Man entered the city of Sarathai-tia for a second time, it was with a good deal more fuss and pomp than on the first occasion. The number of guardsmen that came to meet them was far more than an honor guard required, and they were not men he recognized. There was a veneer of civility about it, however. They brought horses—not too close to the dragon!—and so Mrithuri and her party rode into the city in style.

The people, at least, turned out to stare and cheer. Mrithuri rode near the head of the procession and waved left and right in a regal fashion. The Gage walked before her in the role of a standard-bearer, holding a pole from which flapped her new imperial banner. It was an excuse, of course.

He was a defender.

The Dead Man stayed to her left and behind her, parallel with Ata Akhimah on the right. Their mission was not to keep the populace entertained. Their mission was to keep the empress alive until she could be delivered safely to her palace along with her bride-to-be, who rode beside her. They would stay at her side until whatever mischief Lord Partha had managed was righted.

Then they would turn around and ride back out again.

Himadra, much to his evident disgust, was carried up in a litter. In the absence of his specially trained horse, he would just as soon have stayed with the dragon until it was time for them to fly on to the Sea of Storms. But he was meant to pledge fealty to Mrithuri, and that was best done in front of the Dharasaaba and the rest of the court.

The Dead Man was glad that they could leave immediately to go fight another war. It was better than being expected to stick around for the wedding.

THE GAGE LED HIS LITTLE PROCESSION INTO THE PALACE, STEPPING CAREFULLY again, constantly aware of the vulnerability of the humans and structures around him. He could cripple one of these fragile creatures for life merely by stepping on its foot accidentally. How had he ever survived being one of them for thirty years or so?

He thought perhaps he hadn't been terrified the whole time. He thought he hadn't had any real understanding of how delicate they all were. How soft and easily ruined.

He would miss them all when they were gone.

But for now, his job was to keep them alive for as long as possible. And to get Mrithuri onto her throne, and any pretenders disposed of.

He wasn't worried. If a Gage wasn't enough to do the job, he was confident that Lord Partha had not anticipated that there would be a dragon.

Ritu the acrobat met them just within the gate, grinning widely. Her hair was in a plain braid over her shoulder, the silver strands catching sparkles. She wore a simple tunic and trousers of undyed cotton and tan leather sandals with thin, woven straps. And a sword strapped to her hip.

Her family surrounded her, and they all wore swords as well. They outnumbered the guards, who were looking at one another as if they had not at all expected this.

She stood aside as they dismounted, taking the Dead Man's reins herself. "My son wants to know about Golbahar," she said under her breath.

The Gage had no problem hearing her.

"She's safe. She's in charge of things down in Sarathai-lae," the Dead Man murmured back. "You could always send him down there with a message."

"I'd never get him back." She winked, then frowned. She looked at the Gage. "You saw the banner?"

The Gage felt an undeniable relief at their easy camaraderie, honed on the trail and under siege. He would, he thought, miss her and Golbahar a lot. The Dead Man probably would as well. He was comfortable with clever, pragmatic women. He said they felt like home.

Well, the Gage told himself. *You make your decisions and you live with the consequences. The motto of every soldier under orders: it is what it is.*

The Dead Man had taught him that.

"We did. Where's Yavashuri?"

"In the cloisters. Partha put a warrant out for her."

"And not for you?" the Gage asked.

"We are just entertainers." As she said this, her cousins, sons, nieces, and the rest of the troupe closed in around Mrithuri, Sayeh, and Himadra. "Not worthy of notice, I suppose."

They lifted Himadra's litter onto their shoulders, leaving the bearers startled to find they'd been relieved of the burden. They formed a cordon around Mrithuri before the guards even knew they had been finessed. The Gage, with the banner still falling against his shoulder, stepped sideways to put the royal cousins within the orbit of his reach.

"Hey," said one of the guards, reaching for the Gage's arm. "We have orders—"

The Gage brushed him aside as gently as possible. The man slid across the cobblestones for twice his own length before he came to a halt. He groaned and clutched his arm.

The other guardsmen stepped away rapidly.

Ritu smirked but hid it quickly. "How long are you staying?"

"A meal and a swearing of fealty, and then I'm headed east again to pick a fight," the Dead Man said. "You're on your own for the wedding and the coronation, though."

"Wedding?" She looked at Himadra, and quickly looked away again.

"No," the Gage said. He nodded to Sayeh.

Ritu gaped, then looked at him in wonder. "I'd better tell the kitchen staff immediately."

"Get rid of the horse first," he suggested. "Let's go take back the throne room. Can you send somebody to let Yavashuri know it's safe to come out?"

"Delighted," Ritu said, passing reins to a stable lad.

He nodded sharply to the others, and they all moved toward the Hall of the Empty Throne. Ritu's family surrounded the empress and her cousins and began their tumbling performance as if in procession: silks flashing, trousers fluttering, swords a bright dance, and sashes trailing like banners as they tumbled and wove.

The guards couldn't get close: the acrobats' blades wove a wall that the guards were not quite ready to wade into and start a skirmish without someone there to order it directly. So the empress and her people departed, leaving guardsmen in disarray while Ritu giggled behind her hand.

✳   ✳   ✳

ANOTHER THRONE-ROOM CONFRONTATION, MRITHURI THOUGHT. HOW DROLL.

It was a short walk from the main door to the hall. She made a point of stopping just inside and slipping off her sandals, leaving them by the door. This was her house, and she meant to make sure everybody knew it.

Ritu joined her inside the door. Mrithuri reached out again, feeling for the bearded vulture in the twisting spaces. It was still there.

The grilles between the palace proper and the cloisters started beside the great door. Mrithuri looked through the filigree. No eyes met hers, but she was certain the nuns could hear her. "I'm back," she said. "I have a plan."

Her words echoed into silence. But as she turned away to face the door into the Hall of the Empty Throne, her retainers arrayed around her, she heard singing start within the walls. The eerie harmonies of plainchant rose and layered over their own echoes.

She smiled. "Let's go arrest somebody."

When she started forward, Wizards, acrobats, Dead Man, cousins, and the Gage all stepped with her. The Godmade drifted. The great carved doors flew open before them and the acrobats spilled in like an army with banners. A dancing army, their swords once again revealed. They moved in unison and in counterpoint as if there were music guiding them.

There was music: the song of the nuns. Mrithuri felt like a hero in a story striding across the blue and green stone flags, dressed in her plain white tunic and trousers, her bare feet slapping the floor.

There was someone in her chair. Not the throne but the chair of estate at the bottom of it. There were guards around the foot of the dais—more men she didn't know.

"Lord Partha," she said, as her people parted around her like petals strewn on the surface of the pool. She found herself with a clear path to the front, and she took it. The Gage and the Dead Man and two Wizards were right behind her. The Godmade floated like a dread cloud in her wake. They would not let her come to harm.

She missed Syama fiercely, all the same.

He didn't answer. She said, "You're in my chair."

"Lady Mrithuri," he answered.

She shook her head. The Gage stepped forward, the banner still clutched in his metal gauntlet. The stones groaned under his steps.

"Empress," he boomed, and though his voice wasn't loud, she thought she heard the roof settle.

Partha tried to stare at the metal man impassively, but Mrithuri saw the tremble along his jaw. She'd already won, she realized. It was just a matter of giving Partha a way out, because she didn't *really* want to have to kill him. The Dead Man would do it without hesitating, but it would cause more problems than it was worth, in the long run, and she didn't want to have to pacify a rogue duchy while she was trying to fight off an evil demigod.

She said, "Where are *my* guards?"

Partha lifted his chin, his lips compressing. He probably thought he looked regal. Mrithuri wanted to knock the smirk off his face. His guards clustered together, hands on swords.

"Don't," she said, and put out a hand as if she were holding the Gage back. It was, of course, beyond her power to do so, if the Gage decided otherwise. "Don't, Partha. Give me a reason to spare you. Tell me my men are alive, just detained. Let me excuse your treason as mere caution for the good of the realm. There will be a fine. Your children will come to court to be fostered with Lord Himadra's brothers and Sayeh Rajni's son."

Himadra mumbled under his breath. She ignored him.

"Hostages," Partha said.

She sighed. "Well, don't you think you deserve it?"

He stared, and she stared right back. She lifted her chin. Her eyes weren't even kohled, and she felt the lack of makeup as if she were shorn of armor and weapons—but at last he let out one big breath and dropped his gaze.

He stood, and stepped aside. "They're down by the cisterns. Under guard. What sort of palace doesn't have dungeons in it?"

"My great-grandfather shipped his enemies off to the dragonglass mines," she said, climbing to take back her chair. "Or just executed them. You should be grateful we don't do that anymore."

27

HIMADRA BORROWED MRITHURI'S FOOTMEN TO HELP HIM BATHE. AFTERWARD, before his clean clothes were even unpacked and made ready, Himadra fell into a doze on the couch in the chamber he'd been given. It was exhausting to travel without his men, who knew his needs and how to take care of them.

"Your Competence?" said someone hesitantly.

Himadra dragged himself back from the comfortable edge of dreams. The rare moment when nothing had hurt receded. He pushed himself carefully upright and rubbed sleep from his eyes. "Make me beautiful," he said, and grinned. "Or do your best, at least."

Beard braided, hair combed and oiled in ringlets, dressed in embroidered robes, he emerged from the process as close to pretty as he was likely to manage. He even hung a carnelian droplet from his earring and stuffed several of his fingers into rings.

Two stout young men brought a shield. He walked the few painful steps gingerly and settled himself on it. They lifted Himadra without effort. He stilled a familiar burst of envy and concentrated on not losing his balance. It would be embarrassing to overturn all their fragile hopes of survival along with his own fragile body if he hit the floor and broke himself in several places.

He had not been to Sarathai-tia before, and enjoyed looking around as the footmen carried him through. It was more restrained than the Laeish palace, without the elaborate tile work or ornate painting, but the carved sweetwood lattices and floors flagged with massy semiprecious stones spoke of expense.

When the bearers brought him into the Hall of the Empty Throne, though, he revised his estimation. All the ostentation was in there.

Columns carved to emulate trunks rose into arches that mimicked the boughs of lofty trees. Their dizzying height supporting a forest canopy suggested by a mosaic of leaves worked in dragonglass. The "earth" below was a mossy tiling of azurite and malachite—he thought. He was no jeweler.

The whole gave the sense of some impossibly perfect grove of white trees shedding a soothing underwater light on all who gathered. There were plenty of people gathered, too. Himadra found himself confronted with a blur of people in rich silks and glittering with jewels, mirrors, and bullion. They had drawn aside to create a path for Himadra to be borne along.

And at the far end of the hall, at the destination of his path, there rose the Peacock Throne.

He had been prepared for neither the enormousness nor the enormity of it. Set upon a basalt dais, the throne was a heap of gold like a melted candle-butt, the drips encrusted with flashing gems to mimic the shimmer and colors of the eyes of a peacock's tail. Far above, the sides of the throne seemed to rise into sheltering wings and a heraldic head. The eyes of the bird, as he was brought closer, were revealed as some tawny gemstone. Each, he judged, must be as big as a big man's fist.

The thing dazzled and disgusted him in equal measure. It was so overwhelming that he almost missed the woman sitting at its base in a black, elaborately enameled chair, a bearded vulture on a perch beside it.

She wore the undyed ivory cloth that was becoming her affectation. She sat neatly, feet together, spine straight, hands upon her knees. Another woman, older, sat upon a cushion at her feet. That must be her advisor, Yavashuri.

Sayeh was not in evidence.

The Dead Man, of course, stood to Mrithuri's left at the bottom of the stairs, one hand resting on a pistol. But he winked to Himadra as Himadra was brought close.

Himadra's bearers set him down at the foot of the steps. They were gentle with the shield. Its leather-padded rim made not so much as a scrape upon the stone.

He gathered himself and kept the pain off his face as he stood. It was only for a few minutes.

"Your Competence," said Mrithuri, doing him the courtesy of speaking first.

Himadra bowed from the waist, awkwardly, as best he could. His hip was going to tell him about that later. "Your Magnanimity. Forgive me if I don't kneel."

She laughed. So that was something.

SAYEH HAD MEANT TO BE PRESENT FOR ALL THE POMP AND CEREMONY. SHE knew she needed to be seen taking the oath herself, and witnessing what Himadra and others said and did as part of their own swearing of fealty. She knew the rote forms as they were used in Ansh-Sahal, but they would be different in Sarathai-tia—as the language was different, as the accents and customs were strange.

She had been on her way to the Hall of the Empty Throne—already yearning for Drupada, left behind with a nurse who was not Iri, and under the watchful eye of Guang Bao—when she was intercepted by Tsering-la.

So well trained to disaster had she become that his determined stride filled her with apprehension. She put a hand against the wall to steady her-self. A rushing sound filled her ears, overwhelming the rising and falling chants of the nuns immured somewhere deep within the palace walls.

"It's good news, Rajni," he said as soon as he saw her expression.

Sayeh felt weak and foolish. She had betrayed how damaged she was.

The Wizard closed the distance between them. "Rajni, are you well? Do you need some wine or water? Or tea?"

She managed a smile that stretched her face awkwardly. "A chair? The game leg still cramps sometimes."

Of course he knew she was lying. But he still fetched the chair. There were several along the length of the corridor, hallway furniture put there largely to be ignored. The nearest one was heavy for an unathletic man his size. He looked humorous enough wrestling it that her equilibrium was a little restored by the time he got back to her.

She settled herself gratefully. "Good news, you say?"

"Some of our people are here."

She stared at him blankly.

"Refugees," he added. "From Ansh-Sahal."

Sayeh could not lunge back to her feet quickly enough. She pushed her-self up with the arms of her chair, wishing pride hadn't driven her to forgo her walking stick. Maybe she could get one made that would double as a war club.

Tsering-la held out one hand, doubled in a fist for her to lean on. She did, more heavily that she would have liked, and together they all but trotted down the corridor.

"Who's here?" she asked, less out of breath than she would have been a few months previously. All this walking from one end of the fallen empire to another had been good for her. Once her leg had healed enough for it not to be torture, anyway. If they all survived the coming storm, maybe she *would* let Tsering-la and the others rebreak her leg and set it straight again, although even the anticipation of so much pain nauseated her.

No, she thought. She would do it. Worse in the short run, risky, but if it worked, so much better.

"The abbess is the one I think you would most like to talk to."

Sayeh's free hand went to her mouth. "The abbess is alive? How many others?"

"Here in Tia?" He shook his head. "She said a few hundred. Some of her acolytes are taking a census of the survivors. Here, here we are."

He opened the door to one of the receiving rooms. Sayeh walked past him, struggling to keep her breath level and not to limp.

When she saw the abbess, her eyes stung.

The old woman rose from her cushion, which lay beside a latticed wall that opened into the cloisters. She seemed to have aged a decade: her face was drawn taut over her cheekbones in a manner that made Sayeh think of Nizhvashiti. Sayeh wondered if the abbess were staying with her sister nuns or merely drawing comfort from their plainsong. A low table was already set with tea and cakes—obviously untouched.

Sayeh lowered herself to the cushion opposite, thrilled that she could manage it without assistance, now. Behind her, Tsering-la shut the door. "Please, sit," Sayeh said to the abbess, and beckoned the Wizard over.

The abbess smiled, lowered herself cautiously, and began to pour the tea. "I am glad to see you survived."

"I am glad to see you took your own advice." Sayeh accepted the cup into her own hand.

The abbess handed a cup to Tsering-la, who had settled quietly at the end of the table.

"We did not manage to evacuate everyone." The abbess shook her head and sipped her tea. "It happened too quickly."

Sayeh thought of lithe young dancers and their celebration of the Mother. She pinched the bridge of her nose. So much beauty, so much ceremony had been lost in catastrophe and war. No one had had the energy for art, for worship. For anything except survival.

"How did you get away?"

The abbess's wavering voice was soft. She had not sounded like an old woman when last they met, but she sounded like an old woman now. "We took to the Between Places in our cloisters, but the way south—to Sarathai-tia—was closed."

Closed, thought Sayeh. *Like the path from Sarathai-lae to the Origin of Storms.* "What did you do?"

"We turned around. We emerged along the road north of Ansh-Sahal. Soldiers blocked the roads south and west, and said no one was to leave the city."

By the pain, Sayeh realized she was gritting her teeth. "That was in contravention of my orders."

The abbess smiled. She pulled a worn shawl around her shoulders though there in the south and the valley, the night was balmy. "Based on our last conversation, I assumed so. We gambled and went northeast into the foothills of the Steles of the Sky. There were a lot of other refugees with us. After a few days, some of them continued on toward Song, and toward Rasa. We turned back west until we found a dragon-gate that brought us to the trade road along the banks of the Mother."

"And the Mother brought you here."

"We have been walking a long time," said the abbess. "There are children, the elderly"—she laughed in self-knowledge—"the sick and the halt."

"Children," said Sayeh. "Did you by any chance find the children of a woman named Jagati? She was a palace nurse."

"I will have them asked after," the abbess said. Her eyes went to her hands. "I do not know for how much longer we can travel, Rajni."

"You will stay here," said Sayeh. "I have made a deal with the empress. My people are her people now."

"Oh," said the abbess. "How do you feel about that, daughter?"

"Dutiful," said Sayeh, with a sigh. "And complicated. More pleased now that I have seen you and know that many of our people are still alive. We will make them a new home. We will send word to Rasa and Song that they have a place to return to."

"What about the empress?"

Sayeh glanced toward the lattices. There was no one behind them. Still, she lowered her tone. "She's young. Arrogant. Impatient. But she's a good woman and she could become a good empress. Better by far than Anuraja, may he rot in peace."

"And how is Ümmühan?"

"Alive. Wicked. She stayed in Sarathai-lae. She is writing some kind of sacred document that will somehow enforce a better government through divine grace, or something. I don't pretend to understand it."

The abbess hid her smile behind her teacup. When she lowered the cup again, it was gone. Surely her cheeks and brow had not been so furrowed before? She said, "Do you want to know what I witnessed?"

Cold formed in Sayeh's belly as if she had swallowed ice. It rose along her spine, chilled her throat, and both made her feel faint and gave her a splitting headache. "You saw what happened."

"I saw some of it," the abbess said. "And while I was waiting for you, I spoke with your Godmade about what it witnessed later. After the city fell."

Sayeh stared into her teacup. "A goddess with senile dementia."

"A goddess—or a piece of a goddess—summoned and bound. Cut off from her wider awareness. Not forming memories."

"The Bad Daughter." It was an effort of will just to say the name. To push past the fear of attracting her attention. Some things were abomination to the point that even speaking of their existence could make you feel unclean.

"Perhaps." The abbess's mouth pinched. "What I saw, though, was a woman with a storm of hair rising out of the Bitter Sea, riding a wave the same color as her gown. A vast plume of white-yellow cloud rose up behind her like a cape, like wings. It discolored and occluded the Heavenly River and cast a shadow over the sea, which boiled and bubbled like a foul soup-pot beneath it. Everything stank of rot when she approached the shore."

"And then what happened?" Sayeh asked.

The abbess closed her eyes. "And then we ran. The shock wave struck before the boiling, poisoned air."

Sayeh covered the old woman's hand with her own. "The temple still stands."

"Yes," said the abbess. "The Godmade told me. And told me it did what it could to preserve the library."

"Are there things in the books we can use tonight or tomorrow?"

The abbess shrugged. "There are a lot of things in those books. Is there a way in which we could retrieve them?"

"Perhaps not before the end of the world," said Sayeh. "What do you know about beasts in the Between Places?"

The abbess touched her face. "There are books on beasts in my library. In what was my library."

"How do we get them?" Sayeh asked.

The abbess shook her head. "Maybe the Godmade can go back? Maybe the poison gas has faded?"

"Hmm," said Sayeh. "Dragons and Gages can go a lot of places that the rest of us can't. How much else might have survived?"

"If the way weren't blocked, you could get there through the temple."

". . . really," said Tsering-la, so suddenly that Sayeh jumped. She had forgotten he was standing silently behind her.

The abbess looked to Sayeh for permission. Sayeh gave it with a wave, and the abbess nodded. "It was not built as deep as the cloisters here. But we had our ways."

"Well," said the Wizard, "we do have to fly right past it to go around the storm. We could have a look along the way."

HAVING FEALTY SWORN TO ONE WAS A BORING, ELABORATE, AND REPETITIVE process. At least there was a limited number of people who needed to do it, since she wasn't going to make those vassals who had already sworn to her as rajni swear to her as empress as well. Not with time so limited and the sky above growing hazy and dark as day. Not with Partha waiting his trial and punishment between Mrithuri's freed guards at one side of the hall. Not with the Dead Man and the Gage watching everyone who approached her with suspicion, in readiness for a swift intervention.

As if Yavashuri knew what Mrithuri was thinking, the old woman put her hand on Mrithuri's foot. Old! Mrithuri shook her head. Yavashuri wasn't much older than the Dead Man, and the Dead Man wasn't much older than Sayeh. Ümmühan . . . Ümmühan was old.

Mrithuri had been looking at other adults through the eyes of a child, she realized.

But Sayeh had not appeared, and that made Mrithuri worry. It made her worry, and she could not show her worry. She had to keep her face as smooth and unmoving as an ivory mask. The implacable face of the Mother.

She had never thought she would miss the heavy, awkward gold masks she had despised. But here she was, struggling to keep a serene expression through oaths delivered by refugees from Ansh-Sahal and people like Ritu's acrobat family, newly attached to her court—and proving to be her most loyal retainers. She was to be their empress. She held the responsibility for their lives and well-being whether she wanted it or not. It was only common courtesy that she stay awake.

At long last it was done. Mrithuri rose from the chair of estate to make her way from the room, gravely missing Syama's constant company. Her peripheral vision caught on the glitter of the Peacock Throne behind her, and she turned and stopped, staring up at it—a towering edifice of gold and death. She was afraid of it. She was afraid that it would kill her as it had killed Anuraja—if it hadn't just been his own heart failing. The room wobbled slightly as she contemplated the rail-less stair and the height.

She couldn't let herself be seen to be afraid. Her people were here behind her, watching. They needed to see confidence.

And if she died on the throne . . .

If she died on the throne, she wouldn't have to worry about any of it anymore.

Mrithuri picked Vara up from his perch onto her own ungloved hand. She must be tired, because he seemed impossibly heavy. She walked around behind the throne, to the royal entrance where Yavashuri, having gone first, awaited her. Ritu's people fell in around her, a cavorting guard. Their antics made her smile a little.

The Gage and the Dead Man did not follow.

28

When the Dead Man walked out to rejoin Kyrlmyrandal where she waited, he was surprised to find Sayeh standing there beside a dogcart drawn by a pony, accompanied by a groom and a couple of guardsmen. "I thought you were staying here."

"I am." Her mouth slanted. "I have to get married. But it will be growing cold in the north, in the mountains, already." She reached under the cover on the cart, which was barely more than a barrow, and pulled out a bundle of red cloth. "Our mistress would not like it if you froze."

The wind was picking up, fluttering his veil. The air smelled incongruously like the sea. The first few droplets of rain spattered earth baked dry in the drought.

The Dead Man knew a peace offering when he saw one. He had an inkling how much of the courage of women rested upon keeping a straight face and a level tone. He took the coat—thick felted red wool, quilted to a silk lining with some warm, fluffy stuffing between the layers. "Thank you."

"I'd rather things were different."

He tucked the coat through the straps on his duffel. "It is what it is."

The soldier's lament. Or maybe it was a kind of prayer.

"Stay safe," he said.

"You've got the dangerous job."

"I'm not so sure." He stepped toward the dragon. "You have another customer."

She followed the line of his gaze. Tsering-la was approaching. She pulled another coat out of her cart: this one black and embroidered around the skirt with yellow chrysanthemums. She must have had every woman in the palace who could pinch a needle sewing through the whole of the day.

The Dead Man climbed the steps of the howdah. Inside, he was surprised to find the Gage seated on the floor at the back. "How did you get up here without breaking the ladder?"

"Kyrlmyrandal gave me a lift. She says the next part of the journey won't be as amenable to me following along on the ground. There are mountains and an ocean or two. And just possibly some teleportation."

The floor shivered against the Dead Man's feet as the dragon underneath it chuckled.

* * *

THE GAGE WASN'T AFRAID TO MOVE. IT WASN'T FEAR TO KNOW THAT ANY SHIFT of his enormous weight on a flying creature's back, in a fragile wooden structure, could be disastrous. So he wasn't afraid to move. But he still sat very still.

It was a quieter trip when they left Sarathai-tia again, headed north and east toward what had once been Ansh-Sahal. There was no toddler in their company, and no enormous birds.

And now their numbers were reduced to just the Gage, two Wizards, the Dead Man, Nizhvashiti, and Himadra. And, of course, Kyrlmyrandal.

Himadra sat up front behind a pane of thick, bubbled glass set in the front wall of the howdah. He alone among them was the dragon's eyes now. As he'd taken the place, he'd said, "And thus, my unmanliness is complete."

It didn't seem to bother him too much. Perhaps it was fun to share sensations with a dragon.

In truth, the Gage was envious. The Gage sat straight behind him, all the way in the back, where his weight would rest on the dragon's shoulders. The other four entertained themselves how they could. The Dead Man slept, mostly.

They would have to go north and then east and then south, skirting the edges of the storm. When they reached Ansh-Sahal, the dragon and her fragile cargo would stay high in the air. Nizhvashiti would descend to see if it was safe for the rest of them, and if it was not, the Godmade would bring back whatever books on beasts it could find in the library.

They would then proceed on to the Origin of Storms, and Tsering-la and Ata Akhimah would cram in as much information as they could along the way.

They had not discussed the dangers of it, but they all knew that the time for taking it slow and limiting their exposure to the dragon-poison was over. They would fly straight through, as fast as Kyrlmyrandal's wings could bear them. She knew of dragon-gates that were not on Tsering-la's map. They would use one, if it was open.

As the Gage sat and watched and waited, Tsering-la got up and walked to the front of the howdah. He pitched his voice to carry and said, "Kyrlmyrandal."

"You don't have to shout," she answered. "I can hear whatever Himadra can hear, after all."

"Sorry." He paused. "Is it the beast that is closing dragon-gates, do you think? Or the sorcerers? They do have a tendency to appear and disappear in a most . . . dragon-gate-ish fashion."

She seemed to think it over for a long time. When she answered, it gave the Gage no comfort. "I'm not sure there's much difference between the two anymore."

✴   ✴   ✴

As Sayeh had predicted, the air grew colder. The beat of the dragon's wings wore on. Clouds enveloped them in chill moisture. Tsering-la wrapped lines of yellow Wizardry around the pillars of the howdah. They radiated a gentle heat, enough to keep hands and feet from freezing. The wind, when it came, came from behind them, hurling Kyrlmyrandal ever faster through the sky, buffeting them all. Akhimah worried about the strength of her repairs in this environment. Would silk and sinew and kidskin hold? She'd brought more; she could mend anew if it were needed.

If a wing didn't tear clean through and send them all tumbling from the sky, to be dashed on whatever lay below.

Lashings of rain surrounded the howdah, blowing in through the windows even when the Dead Man and Tsering-la tacked the curtains down. Akhimah tied herself into her seat with her harness loops. She saw the others doing the same. She locked her arms around her neck to keep her head from being snapped to the left and right. It helped a little.

Himadra had just lain down on the padded floor and tied himself in place there.

The Gage clung to what Akhimah at first assumed were iron loops in the floor. Only when they climbed so high she gasped for breath and stuffed her gloved hands into her armpits did the sky lighten enough that she could see what the Gage had done. He had broken out the floorboards of the howdah in one small place and made a hole in one of the cartilaginous scale-spikes that rose from the dragon's spine. It was that to which he clung.

Akhimah's throat tightened. Her head ached with the lack of air; her lungs strained. She understood that they had to get above the storm. She unhooked her harness and stood. Tugging the curtain aside, looking down, she could see the long white bands stretching like a curved road behind and before. They seemed fluffy and welcoming, not at all like the tumbling maelstrom they had just flown through. To the north, rising out of the endless plain of white, she saw glimpses of the ragged, impossibly tall peaks of the Steles of the Sky.

The mere act of standing, even leaning on the window, left her dizzy, her lungs burning. She sagged. Ice formed on her lashes. The curtain slid out of her hand.

Someone was beside her. Tsering-la, hands gentle, guiding her to the bench again. He seemed to be handling the thin air much better than she was—but he was from the mountains, she supposed. "Breathe slowly," he told her. "If you can help it, don't gasp."

She tried. The Dead Man, she could see, leaned in the corner. Himadra still lay in his padded nest. Black dots swirled in from the corners of her vision—

A cold hand touched her hair, pressed the curls down, touched her scalp. It felt as stiff and hard as a bundle of twigs, but her breathing eased. She drew in a breath and it felt as if it filled her up, rather than being comprised of emptiness. The ache in her chest lessened. Her vision returned.

She turned her head and saw Nizhvashiti looming over her. Unlike all the rest of them apart from the Gage, the Godmade was not wearing a new coat. It stood erect and pillarlike, woodenly stiff. Its pupilless eyes stared ahead, one glassy and one golden.

But its touch was gentle.

"Ansh-Sahal is just beyond the northern edge of the storm," it said. "Not too much farther now."

THEY HAD COVERED THE DISTANCE IN AN IMPOSSIBLY SHORT TIME, AND NOW they circled over a choppy sea on a cushion of evil-smelling air. Evil-smelling but apparently not poisonous, because Nizhvashiti had checked and returned and declared the site safe for the rest of them to descend, as long as they didn't linger. The Dead Man was just happy to have air that he could breathe without a priest's blessing again.

They'd come past the margin of the clouds, which meant they could clearly see the blasted land beneath. Tsering-la leaned out the window so long that his goggles indented the skin around his eyes, his hand pressed to his mouth like a man fighting nausea. The Dead Man looked too but did not feel the need to look so long.

He saw toppled buildings, cracked pillars, great trees uprooted and blown away from the water. A blanket of snow mercifully hid worse details.

"Does it usually snow here?" he asked Tsering-la. Sayeh Rajni had said it was colder in the north, and these were the foothills of the Steles of the Sky— foothills that stretched hundreds of leagues, as befitted the mightiest mountains in the world—but he had had an idea of Ansh-Sahal as an arid place.

"Not like this," Tsering-la said. "But the sea is still steaming. And I have never known it to be this cold here. This feels like the mountains. The haze must block the warmth of the sun."

Of course, the Dead Man thought. The steam would rise, meet cold air in the heights, and freeze—then fall again to blanket the ruined city.

Following Tsering-la's pointing finger, he saw the Bitter Sea. A cliff rimmed it. At the base of the cliff was a narrow beach, and as Kyrlmyrandal swerved lower, the Dead Man saw the border between land and sea looked like a heap of enormous shards of glass, a wall of frozen pikes.

"What is that?" he asked.

"Sea ice," Kyrlmyrandal answered. "The waves shatter it and stack it against the shore."

"This must be what a Rasan hell looks like," said the Gage.

"Several of them," Tsering-la agreed.

Guided by Himadra, they came down among the ruins, on the heaved flagstones of the road before the gates of the ruined abbey. Himadra stayed behind as the Wizards, the Dead Man, and Nizhvashiti descended. Kyrlmyrandal helped the Gage down with a claw—even she seemed to find him heavy, though she put him down lightly enough. When she set him on the road, he adjusted his rumpled robes and said, "Let me go first. There is broken dragonglass and bodies all over the inside."

The Dead Man fell in right behind him. No one else seemed inclined to argue. Nizhvashiti floated alongside the Dead Man, bony hands folded, only the hem of its robes disturbing the snow in its passage.

Kyrlmyrandal remained behind.

They walked through gates fallen askew on twisted hinges. The Dead Man had enough experience of battlefields to know which of the outlines under the drifts were likely bodies. He did not point them out. He put his hands in the pockets of the warm coat and took care to step exactly where the Gage had stepped. The others followed behind him, single file, matching his own erratically spaced footsteps. Shards of dragonglass poked up from the snow here and there. The Dead Man had no doubt there were many more underneath it.

To have someone stabbed in the foot and poisoned by dragonglass was absolutely what they all needed.

The air stank of brimstone and rotten eggs. It made the Dead Man feel lightheaded in a different way than altitude. It was colder there than in the howdah. It was not as cold as crossing the mountains had been. But it was cold enough that the ceaseless wind tore shreds of vapor from their noses when they breathed. The Dead Man was glad of his veil.

No one spoke. They walked forward into a silence that felt hallowed and also apocalyptic.

There were more bodies once they were inside, these not hidden by snow. But at least this roof—miraculously mostly intact—was stone and wood, not dragonglass. The Gage and Nizhvashiti led them unerringly to the library, Tsering-la's witchlights illuminating the way.

As meticulously as a human handling a butterfly, the Gage grasped the doorhandle between two fingers and slid the door open.

Warm air rolled out, ruffling their clothes, fluttering the edges of the Dead Man's veil. The Gage stopped dead, a wall of brass and homespun blocking the doorway.

"Hello, Deep," he said.

THE GODDESS IN HER BLUE-GREEN ROBES AND ROPES OF DIAMONDS SAT IN A chair at a table in the center of the library, facing the door. She held one of her cheroots in her left hand, well away from the book she was reading with her right. The vermilioned part of her hair was pointed right at the Gage.

She heard his voice—how could she have missed it?—and looked up with a slow smile. Her diamonds sparkled, catching the yellow light that Tsering-la had summoned. She had, the Gage realized, been reading in near-dark, with only what haze-dimmed light from the Cauled Sun filtered through the windows to illuminate the page.

"Hello, Gage," she said. "Hello, ansha. I'm glad you came back. I was lonely. And you brought friends."

She did not stand. She waved them in, grandly, setting her smoke on the rim of a metal plate.

The Gage let his companions pass, then stood, himself, on the threshold. "What are you reading?"

She held the book up to display the title. Nizhvashiti could probably read it in the dimness, with its inhuman eyes. The Gage didn't think the rest of his companions would be able to, so he said, "*A Brief History of Time.* How is it?"

"Brief," she said. "But I think it's somebody else's cosmology. Still, it's interesting to read about other places and times."

"It is," said the Gage. "My friends want to look at the books and maybe borrow a few."

"It's not my library," Deep said. She dog-eared her page, making the Gage shudder, and closed the book.

"I thought you might have left by now," said the Gage, as Nizhvashiti and the Wizards began to fan out toward the shelves.

"I can't seem to work up the ambition." Her eyes half-lidded, she stared at the ember on the end of her cheroot. She yawned like a panther, shielding the gape of her mouth with the back of her hand. Her teeth glittered glassy and black. "Maybe I'll take a nap."

The Gage understood that volcanos spent a lot of time sleeping.

From just to his left inside the door, Ata Akhimah murmured, "Like the Mother Wyrm."

Deep had put her forehead down on her fists. The ash from her cheroot drooped precariously. The smoke tangled through the wild coils of her hair.

"Mother Wyrm?" the Gage whispered.

"A beast of the Mother River. Anuraja's sorcerer bound it and used it to attack Sarathai-tia. Sayeh Rajni managed to free it and send it on its way. A kindness it apparently remembers: you might have seen it attack one of the men who kidnapped her."

"Ah," said the Gage. "A pity Sayeh Rajni is not here now."

Snow blew along the corridor behind them, swirling around the Gage's ankles. It did not pass the door into the library.

Nizhvashiti drifted toward the reading table. "Do you *want* to leave?"

Her brow furrowed. Her lips pursed. "I have nowhere else to be."

The Gage noticed that this was not what the ansha had asked.

Nizhvashiti obviously did too. It pushed the hood back from its bald head with its thumbs and seemed to waver in a wind the Gage could not feel. "What do you know about the Alchemical Emperor?"

Deep's hand came up, clutching the book she had been reading. She raised it beside her head, ready to hurl it—and then looked at the book, looked around herself at the shelves, and sighed. "Right. Library."

The Gage moved into the room so he could get his metal body between the seething goddess and his friends.

She set the book down on the table again. "Are you his creature?"

"The Alchemical Emperor is dead," said Nizhvashiti. "I am the Good Daughter's creature. As we established when last we met. That made you angry."

"Mmm," Deep said around her cigarette. "It did make me angry."

"Talking about the Alchemical Emperor makes you angry too."

"I don't like being told what to do."

"And he made you do things?"

The goddess didn't answer. Nizhvashiti persisted: "Who is making you do things now?"

The book hadn't flown through the air, but this time, Deep's twist of a beedi did. It sailed across the room, directly at Nizhvashiti. The Godmade's hand came up amidst a flare of sparks. For a moment, the Gage thought the butt had struck it in the face, but the hand came down again and the cigar was between its fingers. Nizhvashiti inclined its head, took a long puff, then offered the beedi back to the goddess on the full extension of a tree-limb arm.

Looking up at Nizhvashiti's face, Deep accepted the return of her smoke. The floor trembled under their feet. The battered abbey groaned and dust filtered down. The Gage wondered if it were a reaction or a threat.

"And if I tell you that, what's in it for me?"

Nizhvashiti gestured, a broad sweep of the arm, the wrist leading. "They used you, didn't they? All these dead, all these sacrifices. And yet none of them yours to keep. Nothing to assuage your hunger. Nothing to soothe your appetite. No worship and no sacrifice. They took what should have been yours, O Deep, and used it to usurp the power of the Peacock Throne and lock the rains away."

The smoke rising from Deep's cigar trembled on the air. Or maybe that was just the earth under their feet once more. The Dead Man looked about apprehensively. Ata Akhimah placed a hand on his arm.

"What's in it for me?" Deep repeated.

The Gage stepped forward. Just one step. Closer to Deep and Nizh-vashiti, farther from the more-fragile others. His joints creaked as if he had been immobile for an age.

"We'll help you get even," he said.

Deep stared at him. She took a drag and blew the smoke out on her words. "That's no good to me. Their kind and their witchery"—she pointed at the back of the room—"why should I trust any of you? Bind me to raise up a throne. Chain me to knock down a city. Nothing ever comes back to me but more mind control."

"We'll help you get even," Nizhvashiti echoed. "And we'll help you get free. Are you ready?"

"What's to stop me from just destroying all of you once you free me? If you can free me?"

"Nothing. But you lose our assistance."

Nizhvashiti raised one fingertip to its face and tapped the chime of its eye. The sound pealed through the library and through the abbey beyond. Pages rustled and scrolls rattled in their racks.

Deep looked up. The air shimmered as if she were surrounded by sunlit dust motes. There was no sunlight—there was never any sunlight in the Lotus Kingdoms—but to the Gage it seemed as if a cloud of fine particles swirled in a sudden gust before being blown away.

Deep blinked thoughtfully. She turned her head from side to side like someone who has just taken a bad fall and is assessing the damage. Her movements were meticulous, experimental. She drew in one breath, then another. A plume of smoke drifted from her nostrils although she had not lifted her cigar. She smiled.

The earth bounced under the Gage's feet, a blow as hard as if somebody had struck his soles with a mallet. Around him, the humans staggered. The room seemed to leap around Nizhvashiti's floating, motionless form. Even the Gage staggered a step.

Books rattled in their shelves; scrolls fell from their racks. Pages fluttered.

Deep surged to her feet, "Oh, I didn't mean the books!"

It would be poor form to point out that she had been engaged in turning down the page-corners just a few moments before. It was the privilege of goddesses to be as inconsistent and hypocritical as any human.

The Gage took a step forward, as softly as he was able. "Are you going to take your anger out on us? Or on those sorcerers and the beast they work for?"

"You're more convenient," the goddess said. But she sighed a big sigh, blew out another puff of smoke, and unclenched her fists one finger at a time. She bowed her head to massage her scalp. A rain of ash fell like dandruff from her hair. When she looked up again, she was smiling. "You know of course that a temperate and precise response is . . . not my style. Nor is . . ." She paused.

"Targeted destruction?" the Gage offered, keeping his tone light.

"Depends," she replied, "on the size of the target. But I do tend to go in more for 'wanton' and 'wholesale.'"

"Save us for after," the Gage suggested. "Just in case it's convenient to have a little help with those sorcerers."

Deep looked up at him through her lashes. A threat rather than flirtation—or possibly both. "Are you betting I'll be tired or bored by then?"

The Gage let his armor rattle as he shrugged. "If one puts off a reckoning for long enough, the end of the world might intervene and render any consequences academic."

As the Dead Man was the person least suited to either facing down volcano goddesses *or* sorting through ancient texts to find the ones most useful for fighting interplanar intruders, the experience in the abbey had been an opportunity for him to feel not particularly useful.

Once Deep had vanished into a smoking hole in the floor, the Wizards, the Godmade, and the Gage had fanned out around the room, inspecting shelves and racks. The Dead Man had been left with nothing to do except peering down that bottomless-seeming hole and wondering what he had gotten himself into. It might not actually be bottomless: the annealed walls, which at first glowed a glassy scarlet, curved away toward the ocean. The heat curled his eyebrows. The fumes stung his eyes and—even through his veil—burned his lungs.

He leaned away quickly.

At least he was good at carrying things.

The Dead Man's pulse didn't stop racing until they were back aboard Kyrlmyrandal with their cargo of books, most written in languages he couldn't read. He hoped the Wizards hadn't picked up so much vellum and paper that it would overweight the dragon. He supposed if she could carry the Gage, the odds were good that she would be all right.

His burden transferred, the Dead Man climbed aboard and settled himself on the front bench alongside Himadra. The Lord of Chandranath appeared to have been taking advantage of their absence and Kyrlmyrandal's immobility to nap. He was still rubbing sleep from his eyes when the Dead Man sat down.

"It went all right?"

"I feel like I've wandered into a legend," the Dead Man admitted. "Here we are, trading with gods and pursuing monsters. I'm a simple mercenary. I'm over my head."

Himadra snorted. "At least you're taller than me."

"I can't be the eyes of a dragon, though." The Dead Man reached for his gun, patted the reassuring heft of it. "This is all I bring to the party."

"Take it from a tactician. Sometimes, a single bullet in the right place is worth more than ten armies in the wrong one." Himadra leaned forward, peering through the window as Kyrlmyrandal rose to her feet. She navigated toward the cliff edge hesitantly, her neck extended and her whiskers sweeping the ground.

"What's it like?" the Dead Man asked, a moment before they fell into flight. "Sharing experiences with a dragon?"

29

WHILE THE STORM RAGED OVER THE COUNTRY, SAYEH RAJNI ALLOWED HER-self to be dressed for her second wedding. She had been given a royal apart-ment of her own, with one glazed window between a pair of shuttered ones. She was high up; she could watch the water fall.

She might have seen the Mother River—called Brightest, called Giver of Honey—under other circumstances. Now, she could see only grayness, the flicker of lightning, and sheets of water running down the panes. She stood very still while women she had not previously met draped her in red and green silk, hung her with jewels. She sat very still on a tuffet while those same women gilded her eyelids and blackened her lashes and vermilioned her lips and the part of her hair.

The wind howled outside, rattling the closed shutters, blowing the rain so hard that the inside of the louvers glistened. The edges of the dragon-glass panes glowed in faint shades of green and turquoise, picking out the pattern of a leafy tree painstakingly leaded into the window. In the dark of the storm, there was no light to hide it.

Drupada had been taken away to his nursery. Sayeh already missed him.

She sipped tea while they gilded her toenails. Not too much tea, since she would disarray her elaborate pleats if she tried to use a chamber pot. She tried not to listen to the storm, to its howling. To its uncanny resemblance to voices.

Familiar voices. The voices of her own women in Ansh-Sahal, all dead now, probably. The voices of her parents, her husband. Her grandfather, crying out in pain. Jagati, wailing in grief for the children she had been torn away from.

The women dressing Sayeh glanced nervously at the windows: it wasn't just an old bride's nerves making the storm seem strange.

Sayeh laid a soothing hand on the head of the nearest one while she slipped a sandal on Sayeh's hennaed and gilded foot. The woman smiled up at her shyly. Sayeh missed her own people. She missed Nazia and Ümmühan like a spike in her heart. She missed Jagati and her women of the bedcham-ber from Ansh-Sahal.

These were her women now. She had better get to know them. She had better make herself a place of strength, a place from which she could defend and advocate for the refugees from Ansh-Sahal. She must make a place for herself so she could make a place for them.

Nobody would be going home to Ansh-Sahal.

The other sandal was laced. Sayeh took deep breaths, her belly full of butterflies. She held out her hands, painted with henna and draped with rings and chains, and let the women help her to her feet.

Thunder cracked, painfully loud. A gust of wind and rain slashed into the room, splashing Sayeh's face and spotting her gown. For a moment, Sayeh thought with horror that the dragonglass window had fractured into deadly shards. But the woman—Szavitri was her name—who had smiled at Sayeh pulled her away from the flood of wind and water, and the other lady-in-waiting—Aarushi—ran to catch the shutter that had broken open. She was soaked in seconds, her hair and drape in soggy, wind-whipped disarray. She snatched at the clattering shutter while trying to keep her fingers from being smashed.

With great dexterity she managed it, though Sayeh cried out with fear when it seemed the shutter, like a sail in the wind, would drag the lady's substantial self right out of the window frame. She held on where a slighter woman might not have and, bracing her feet in the puddles, hauled it closed.

"A rope!" she called.

The other lady hastened to her, untying the silk cord of her belt. Together they bound the shutters to each other by their knobs, already making the knots fast by the time a guard burst in from the hallway, one hand on his sword.

The two women turned in surprise. The one who had smiled raised a hand to hair, ineffectually patting at frayed strands.

The guard drew up short. "Just the window?"

"Just the wind," the lady confirmed. "Oh, dear, we aren't fit to be seen—"

"Don't worry," Sayeh said. "I can make my own way down."

"Rajni!" they protested as one.

Sayeh waved them aside with a smile. "Fix your hair and dresses, Szavitri, Aarushi. This isn't my first wedding, and I won't let them start without you."

Besides, she thought, she could use a few minutes alone. Strange how she had gone from being a person who had spent every hour enfolded by others to one who craved silence and introspection. She had spent her whole life being looked at, being a performance of a royal woman. Being the serene ideal that people could imagine as they wished, like an idol of the Mother. The past months had forced her to become more resourceful, more willing to use people's expectations to accomplish her own goals. And she had found friends, too—people she trusted in crisis beyond the few loyal retainers who had guarded her family in Ansh-Sahal.

It turned out you really never were too old to change.

There were people in the halls of the palace. They drew aside for Sayeh as she approached. She heard them murmuring, wondering where the bride's entourage was.

They'd be there soon enough. For now, she could walk the halls alone.

She paused outside the Hall of the Empty Throne—not the royal door behind the Peacock Throne and not the Grand Door at the far end, but by one of the side entrances that let into the little curtained grottos between the carved trunks of the stone trees. Music came from within: the milling of feet, the scuff of cushions, the chatter of voices.

Sayeh drew the curtain aslant with her fingertips, creating a narrow gap. Within was a wall of light, color, scent, drama. She watched forked lightning crack above the dragonglass ceiling and flinched. The people within seemed to take the violence of the storm in stride. Perhaps the Hall had stood for a hundred years. Perhaps it was the work of the Alchemical Emperor.

It was still a sky full of suspended—and poisoned—daggers. And Mrithuri's entire court was standing around underneath it—in the midst of a tremendous storm.

And where was the empress herself? Sayeh stood on tiptoe in her sandals and peeked over the crowd. No one had yet assumed the chair of estate at the front of the hall. Was Mrithuri—no, there, a ripple of ivory silk. A slight woman with an enormous bird upon her fist—the biggest bearded vulture that Sayeh had ever seen. Mrithuri was talking to some nobleman whose name Sayeh could not remember but about whom she had a vague unpleasant association.

Well, Sayeh thought, it was nearly time to get this over.

She let the curtain fall closed. By the time she returned to the Grand Door, the women assigned to her had arrived—hair hastily tidied, drapes hastily changed. Thunder rattled again through the building.

"Oh, I hope that isn't an ill omen," said the woman who had nearly been dragged off her feet by the swinging shutters.

"It's ill will," Sayeh said, surprised at how calm she sounded. There were puddles on the flagstones here and there—water seeping under doors from the outside. They were on the top of a small mountain, and still the court-yards were flooding. "What we do today will oppose it."

She sounded glib, certain. The confidence she was able to project surprised her. But it soothed the women. They rearranged her clothing hastily while a few latecomers slipped past them into the hall. One man winked; Sayeh decided arbitrarily to like him.

The smiling woman slipped inside the hall, then bustled out again. "Your music should begin soon. Then the doors will open."

"My music?" Sayeh asked. But barely had the words escaped her when she heard the familiar strains of a Sahali zither, and the notes of a song called "Across the Bitter Sea."

It was a lament for a lover gone away, and it was one of the oldest songs of Ansh-Sahal.

Perhaps not a wedding tune. But these were strange days, and perhaps it would become a wedding tune after this. Royalty had a way of making innovations fashionable.

The Grand Door—really two doors—swung open. A long aisle lined by courtiers stretched before her. At the end of it stood Mrithuri and the abbess of Ansh-Sahal.

Sayeh started forward. There was her bride; there was her objective. She only had to get through this wedding with a better result for both parties than the last one she had attended in this hall. A sense of dread filled her at the idea of Mrithuri ascending the steps of the throne. Sayeh remembered too clearly the thumps Anuraja had made as his body slid back down them.

And she liked Mrithuri. She cared for her.

She wouldn't mind being married to her, she thought. If she lived.

She *had* to live. If she didn't, it was up to Sayeh and Himadra to save the world. And Sayeh didn't think they could do it without the power of the Peacock Throne. If Mrithuri fell, could Sayeh make herself face the climb?

She made herself walk forward, timing her stride to the music. It was not precisely a processional. She had to sway more than march. That was fine; this was not precisely the most traditional of nuptials.

For now. They might set a trend on that front, also.

Eyes and whispers followed Sayeh, and marigold blossoms fell around her. The lightning danced above, so bright she thought she could see her bones through her hand. The disembodied voices rose, wordlessly crying.

She kept her chin up, her eyes forward. She walked.

She stopped at the foot of the dais, beside the abbess. The abbess winked at her.

Mrithuri placed her familiar on its perch—truly, the bird was enormous—and came down the low basalt stairs. The throne rose behind her, glittering with what Sayeh could only see as menace. Sayeh tried to focus on the woman and not the backdrop.

The ceremony was brief, formal, traditional. The abbess invoked the Mother and her Daughter. She bound their hands together and anointed them with slaked turmeric and river water. They placed the wedding jewelry on one another's arms. Sayeh stroked the peacock on Mrithuri's slender biceps.

Mrithuri rolled her eyes and smiled.

She bestowed a coronet upon Sayeh and made her Consort. There had been a little discussion beforehand about titles, and that had been the one they all deemed least confusing, in the end. Empress and Consort. Simple.

Thunder rolled over the abbess's voice and Mrithuri's voice when they spoke. Sayeh had to strain to hear them. She had to strain to make herself heard when her own turn to speak came. She was trembling with the exhilaration and the terror of the storm. Lightning came so fast now, it flickered like the most brilliant imaginable candlelight—continual, but not constant. The wind howled now not with human voices, but with the voice of a beast in agony.

The beast, Sayeh thought. *If it feeds on war, then are weddings a weapon against it?*

"You are married in the sight of the Mother," the abbess said. "Give her a kiss, Your Magnanimity."

Mrithuri did. The sound of the wind rose to a roar and the cheers of those assembled rose over it. How many of them were dissembling?

Sayeh didn't mind kissing the Empress. It was a brief kiss, with a thousand pairs of eyes upon them, but it was soft and tender and Mrithuri's lips were chapped but, under the roughness, silky as rose petals. *I suppose,* Sayeh thought, *I could get used to that.*

Mrithuri led her to the chair of estate that had until that moment been Mrithuri's, and saw her seated upon it. Sayeh forced her hands to lie open in her lap when they wanted to clench on the chair arms.

The moment of truth was upon them. The moment of destruction, perhaps. Mrithuri gave her a look of such intensity that Sayeh almost froze. She summoned all her strength and gave her new wife a brave, tight smile.

The whole court held its breath below them.

"You'll do this," she murmured. She imagined her words were lost in the storm. She touched her lips, where the sensation of the kiss still lingered.

But Mrithuri said, "Your faith in me is touching." It might have been sarcasm, but Sayeh thought she detected a sparkle of humor in the tension behind the words.

"Before you go—"

"Don't you dare remind me of what happened to the last guy."

Sayeh said, "—Who's the bird?"

Mrithuri looked over at it. "That's Vara. You've met before."

"Vara? But—"

"He's growing."

Mrithuri faced the stair.

30

W**HAT WAS IT LIKE,** H**IMADRA TRIED TO DECIDE, AS** K**YRLMYRANDAL FELL INTO**
the sky? He couldn't say. He couldn't find the words to describe what he was
experiencing, even to himself. It wasn't like anything. It was like flight, and
there was no metaphor for the shared sensation of air tautening, solidifying
under wings, the push of the updraft off the ocean, the way forward speed
converted to rising force.

There were also no metaphors for the pain the dragon felt as her arthritic
joints were stretched and flexed, as muscles stiff and atrophied from long
disuse were forced to work and strain. She was stronger than she had been;
their careful flight from Sarathai-lae had conditioned her and made her able
to do this. But it was a supreme effort, a constant exertion of will, and even
when she rested on a thermal, there was discomfort in her weight pulling on
her wings. When she stood, there was discomfort in resting her weight on
her legs, so it wasn't so very different.

Himadra was familiar. Familiar with overcoming pain, familiar with
"doing it anyway," familiar with the price that was later paid. Familiar with
the sense of there being no position that wasn't in some manner uncomfortable. In a strange sort of way, sharing Kyrlmyrandal's pain made him feel
at home. They had so much in common. Enduring her hurt made him less
aware of his own.

They flew on.

The vastness of the Mother Storm was a wall to the south now as they
circumnavigated it. The mountains were a wall to the north. They threaded
a narrow canyon in the sky, buffeted by crosswinds, chilled by frost. The
dragon herself was warm; that heat radiated through the howdah and was
contained by it, and that and the shelter of the wood and canvas walls
breaking the wind made the situation bearable.

Behind him, papers rustled. Wizards read. Ata Akhimah became un-
pleasantly airsick and had to lie down until her stomach settled. The Mother
Storm walked on legs of lightning south and west; the dragon bore them
east into a place where the sky changed and a red sun and a blue sun wheeled
in opposition to one another. Here there was no night, no Heavenly River.

Himadra had heard that the sky changed between kingdoms, of course,
but he had never seen it. It struck him like a blow on the chest as he watched
the stars vanish behind a moving line in the sky, as if somebody wiped them

away as the dragon passed under. They were no longer within sight of the Mother. They were a very long way from home.

"Takes some getting used to, doesn't it?" the Dead Man said. Himadra jumped; he hadn't heard the mercenary come up behind him. For a guy who wore a bright red coat, the Dead Man was pretty sneaky.

"It's unsettling," Himadra admitted. "Where are we?"

"I haven't seen this one before." The Dead Man settled himself on the bench, respectful of Himadra's personal space. "Song, I guess? They're sup-posed to have two suns."

"Must make it hard to sleep." Himadra yawned, as if the word itself re-minded him of how long he had been awake. "No Heavenly River."

"Still got that storm." The Dead Man nodded in its direction.

"It reminds me of something," said the Gage. He had not risen from his place directly over Kyrlmyrandal's shoulders, where his weight would affect her balance the least. "The storm, I mean."

Himadra leaned forward to peer out the side. A vast boil of cloud, stretch-ing from horizon to horizon, was lit from beneath and within by actinic flashes, and from the west and east by opposed suns that stained its white hammerheaded towers in shades of peach and violet. "I thought storm clouds would be dark."

"They're dark underneath," Kyrlmyrandal said, her words rising up from her chest and larynx through the floor, vibrating the bodies of the riders. "Because they block the light. What does it remind you of, metal man?"

Himadra had a curious sensation that she was asking because she knew and wanted the words out in the open.

The Gage said, "What did you call it, Lord Himadra? The Mother Storm?"

"It just seemed like the right thing to call it."

The Gage shrugged, clanking. "You are a priest of your Mother, after all. Priests know things."

Nizhvashiti whispered, "I asked the Good Daughter to mitigate the storm before it reached settled lands. I have no sense that I was heard. I *know* I was not answered."

The Gage said, "It reminds me of the walking cities, writ large. The ones the Alchemical Emperor caused to be built to harvest dragonglass. The ones still operated by debt-slaves from Messaline."

"It's all one thing," said Nizhvashiti. "What the Alchemical Emperor did echoes in what the beast does now. Like that throne of corpses in Ansh-Sahal."

"Mother," Ata Akhimah said. Then she laughed, but not as if she found anything funny. "I don't know why I said that. I worshipped Kaalha the Kind when I still found gods worth believing in."

The Gage touched his mirrored face. "Me too."

Tsering-la craned out the window, watching the cloudless sky and the mountains off the north wing of the dragon. Ata Akhimah rose to her feet, pressing a hand against her stomach. She sat on the bench and scooched over to look out the window beside him.

He shook his head. "What worries me is what becomes of that power now."

The Wizards leaned against the sill beside each other.

Himadra said, "What do you mean?"

Ata Akhimah looked over at him. "The strength of the storms. The rains that have not come. It can't be held in forever. Eventually it must be unleashed."

"Unleashed." Himadra pointed to the south, to the direction she was not looking.

But it was Tsering-la who answered. "Snapped loose. Like when the stuck earth finally breaks, and the mountain surges, stone snaps, chasms gape beneath one's feet and slam shut again."

Himadra felt nauseated himself as he understood. "Except a storm. Except all the storms of the whole rainy season. Turned loose all at once."

"Yes," Tsering-la said. "Except the mother of all storms."

They dropped in altitude, and desert-bred Akhimah felt intense relief as the air grew warmer. Tsering-la let his warming spell lapse and fell almost instantly into a deep sleep, exhausted. Akhimah tried to make him eat before he dozed, but the only result was that he dropped off while chewing.

They flew so fast that Akhimah watched the massive Steles of the Sky drop away to foothills in the space of an hour or so. Plains stretched before them, and then the most peculiar terrain she had ever seen—towers of limestone draped with greenery, white pillars reaching toward the sky. That too passed into hill and plain again, and then out of the blue haze before them she began to see the deeper blue of the ocean, stretching toward a horizon she could not even imagine.

Kyrlmyrandal did not pause. Her wings beat with heavy regularity. The storm to the south faded away. Now only ocean stretched in that direction. They turned that way and flew on as the suns reeled over them. A long curve of land hove into view ahead. They turned southeast and saw that it broke, eventually, into a profuse chain of islands. A vast archipelago, streaming east, it seemed, into eternity.

The sky above had become a blue entirely transparent, a single sun white as a diamond burning there. The sea below was a darker blue but just as transparent. Ata Akhimah had no idea how deep it might be, but the water was so clear that she could see the ripples of sand on the bottom, even from their height in the air.

"Is that . . . ?" she pointed to the archipelago.

"The Banner Islands," Nizhvashiti whispered. "And this is the Sea of Storms."

"And there is our landfall," said Kyrlmyrandal.

Himadra leaned forward, his hands on the sill of the forward window, his face pressed to the crystal. "Do you see it?" he asked.

"I do," said the dragon.

Akhimah pulled her goggles up from around her neck and leaned out the window. Ahead, past Kyrlmyrandal's pale shoulder and the leading edge of her wing, rose a rugged green island. It was far from the others—the chain nearly vanishing to the south—and seemed quite different in character. The water in that direction was greener, perhaps shallower. Here it was a deep true blue, and through its clarity Akhimah could see the slopes of the island stretching down into the sea.

The whole island seemed to be a jungle except for its silver-gray beaches. It was big—well, she wasn't much judge of islands, but it seemed big to her— and at its center rose a mountain, tall enough to be snowcapped even in these tropical climes.

Around Akhimah, the others rushed to the windows—except the Gage, who stayed right where he was. They looked down on the picture of a pristine tropical paradise—except for an enormous, sustained rumble that reached them as they flew closer. Akhimah caught her breath as a swath of the mountain's glacier cut loose from the rest, plummeting down the slope in a cloud of steam and sparkling snowdust. Trees snapped under the weight of the slide, and the stone where it had been jumped and shuddered. A chthonic glow seeped from the depths of a crevasse that opened in the exposed face of the mountain. A thick billow of smoke roped from the peak, bursting forth heavy and black and seething with lightning.

"The Origin of Storms," said Kyrlmyrandal.

Akhimah squeezed the window frame until her fingers hurt. "I think Deep beat us here."

"CAN YOU EVEN LAND ON THAT?" THE DEAD MAN WAVED TO THE STEEP slopes and heavy jungles, remembering too late that Kyrlmyrandal could not see him. "I mean, it doesn't look like there's room for something the size of you."

"There's a beach," Kyrlmyrandal answered. "And there was a temple on the far side, a few hundred years ago."

The Dead Man sucked his lip behind his veil. "Barely enough time to mention."

The dragon laughed, which shook the howdah. Her passengers grabbed at seat edges and window frames—except the Gage, who clung fast to her shoulder spines until she got herself under control. She stabilized herself and banked left, groaning a little.

"Are your stitches pulling?" Akhimah worried.

"No more than usual," Kyrlmyrandal said. "I am flying again. Do not fret so."

They spun through the air like a leaf spiraling from a tree. The dragon might be showing off a little. Funny how everything had its pride. The Dead Man hung on to his seat and allowed himself to be glad that they'd only been eating dried fruit, jerky, and sips of cold tea and water for some time now.

Days, maybe? It was hard to tell when the sky kept changing.

They came around the island. The Dead Man heard satisfaction in Kyrlmyrandal's voice when she said, "There's the clearing. Keep looking at it, Himadra. I'm going to land in the water but I want to be close enough to shore not to thrash us into a reef."

The Dead Man realized that a drawback of Himadra serving as Kyrlmyrandal's eyes was that he could not see directly under the dragon or anywhere the howdah or her body blocked his line of sight. Also, the Lord of Chandranath looked as exhausted as Mrithuri after a long session with her vultures. He'd slept along the way, when they were flying in a straight line through open air. But there probably wasn't enough rest in the world to let him keep doing what he had been doing indefinitely.

The Dead Man just barely kept himself from crying out with delight— and a little fear—at the thrill of their descent. Apprehension at what they might face at the bottom kept him silent. Tsering-la and Ata Akhimah seemed to have no such reservations. The Wizards were both giggling.

Enjoy life now, the Dead Man thought, *for tomorrow we get skewered.*

Except it was today that they faced skewering. No lack of skewering in sight. Unless they were first roasted.

The temple the dragon had mentioned was there, off her left shoulder. An enormous vine-hung ziggurat. It seemed they descended beside it forever, and yet they fell in a rush. And then the water was coming up at them—

The Dead Man put a hand out, risking royal displeasure, and braced himself between Himadra and the crystal of the forward window like a woman restraining a child in a carriage. Himadra grunted as his chest made contact with the Dead Man's arm, but the Dead Man didn't feel anything break, and Himadra was able to lift his hands and push himself back onto the bench again.

"Thanks," he said.

"Don't mention it."

They had landed in a bay or lagoon so placid it seemed like a lake, not a finger of the ocean. Kyrlmyrandal stood knee-deep in water, the only disturbance the spreading ripples she had caused. The air smelled of salt, sand, and something too-sweet and tropical. Like overripe bananas or smashed papaya.

The dragon folded her uneven wings and walked up the beach toward the land.

The ziggurat was even bigger than the Dead Man had imagined when they were swooping past. It rose as tall as the mount upon which stood Sarathaitia. It sloped back into the jungle, making itself part of the mountainside. Perhaps it was carved from the very basalt cliff and not a freestanding structure at all. Before it stretched an incongruous lawn, trimmed close and dotted with flowering trees—jacaranda and plumeria. The Dead Man had expected ash over everything, but though he looked up into a sky seething with columns of poisonous smoke, the air around him remained fresh and pure.

There was soft sand, and after the sand there was grass clipped into a velvety lawn. Amidst the lawn stood trees twisted into fantastical shapes, loops and arches, branches that bent down to touch the earth before surging skyward again.

"Well, this is inconvenient," Kyrlmyrandal said as her passengers other than Himadra disembarked or were lifted down.

"What in particular?" The Dead Man walked toward the nearest tree. One limb coiled out from the trunk in a spiral he could crawl through—

"Stop!" the dragon said.

He stopped. Then turned around to look at her. "What?"

"Beware the trees. If you move through the loops, they can have unexpected properties."

"Oh," he said. "Is that what you are finding inconvenient?"

The dragon sighed. "I could use them—if Nizhvashiti's chime had not returned me to my true form."

"Pity we couldn't stop off in your city," said the Gage. "You could have walked through the transformation door again."

"And poisoned all your friends. And then been unable to carry them."

"A small matter."

"What do the trees do?" asked Ata Akhimah.

"Various things," said the dragon. "If you crawl through that spiral, it makes you more youthful by a decade for each ring."

"Tempting," said the Dead Man. "What's the catch?"

"It makes your mind more youthful by a decade, also." The dragon snaked her enormous head around and grinned at him. "Right now, I'd be willing to trade a half millennium or so to fight better. Not such an easy trade for you."

"Mmm," said the Dead Man. "I see your point. But I suppose the sorcerers might have a use for it." He turned to the Gage. "We ought to come back here when this is over. Take a nice vacation. Lie on the beach."

"Corrode in the salt water," the Gage replied.

The Dead Man turned, looking for the rest of the party. Nizhvashiti was sweeping up the lawn toward the temple in a stately fashion, Tsering-la following.

Ata Akhimah cleared her throat. "I guess it's time to go."

31

It felt like the longest stair Mrithuri had ever seen, and she was at the bottom looking up. She tried to focus on the chair at the top, but the gold and jewels in the foreground and the swirl of lightning and green-black clouds and the rainwater sheeting the glass roof in the background pulled at her gaze and attention.

She had counted the stairs. She knew there were exactly fifty, and she knew that the pitch was steep. Right now, contemplating them, contemplating the lack of railing, contemplating the distance to the top, the throne seemed as distant as the horizon—as if she could walk and walk and walk, and never get there.

She took a breath. Another.

In the hall, no one spoke. There was no music—neither from the singing of the nuns nor within the hall. Just the thunder and the creak of the ceiling under the torrent of rain. She had to make herself do this. She *had* to. She had to take up this tool, and master it, and use it to fight the beast that would otherwise destroy her.

And she could not be seen to hesitate too long before the stairs—but every blink brought her the image of Anuraja clutching his chest and thumping down them.

"You can do this," Sayeh whispered, and gave her hand a squeeze.

Mrithuri looked down at her gratefully and smiled. In that moment, when she felt strong enough to begin—a single drop of water fell on the back of her neck. And then another.

Mrithuri said, "The roof is leaking."

"Go," said Sayeh. "*Go.*"

Mrithuri picked her foot up and set it on the bottom stair. A jolt zipped through her as if she were pricked by static. Her foot felt as if the stair gripped it. No turning back now.

She rose another step. Two, that was two. She should count them. Two steps accomplished. Forty-eight more to go.

She felt as if she leaned into a current. As if a strong wind or the flow of the Mother River pushed against her. She leaned forward, wishing for railings. Water splashed her bare ankles. The drip she had stepped away from had become a narrow stream.

Climbing stairs should not be this hard, thought Mrithuri. Another step, one more. Three. She was glad she had spent so much time traveling. It had hardened her body, made her fit. Still, this was a supreme effort. She took another step. Her breath quickened. Her heart raced as if she struggled against a mighty gale with all the strength she had. As if she were dragging the whole kingdom up the stair behind her. Tendons creaked, muscles burned.

Water pattered on the basalt dais. The wind of mighty wingbeats stirred Mrithuri's garments as Vara bated on his perch. Something cracked overhead. The howl of the wind, the rumble of thunder came suddenly louder, no longer muffled by the intervening roof. A sensation like the sharpness from crossing a wool rug and touching a silk curtain started in her feet, ascended her legs. Her left foot prickled with pins and needles. She could not feel the pressure of the step against the sole.

This did not help her balance at all.

Mrithuri risked a glance over her shoulder. Sayeh had arisen, snatched up the hooded vulture. Her wings buffeted Sayeh's face as Mrithuri's Consort retreated away from the cascade of rain, away from the dangling dragonglass panes as a section of roof collapsed inward and more peeled away, flying into the rage of the storm.

Wind tugged Mrithuri's hair. Rain splashed her and slicked the steep stairs underfoot. She squinted down at their shining surfaces, placing each foot carefully. She had to climb.

Each step came with more effort than the last. Sparks flew around her feet now, something she was sure she hadn't seen when Anuraja climbed. A foxfire halo rose from the steps. She thought nervously that she was standing in water, on a gold-clad stair, while lightning forked across the open sky above. It didn't matter if she was the rightful empress or not. Lightning could still kill her even if the chair did not.

Doubt would not help her. Nothing would help her except determination to get to the top.

There was nothing else. There was only the steps, the rain, the chair. The whirl of aurora rising around her, green-gauze light like the Mother's heavenly veils. She leaned forward, feeling as if she had grown unbearably heavy. Feeling the weight of the world, the weight of the throne as if it rested on her shoulders.

How could there be so many stairs?

A tremendous sound from above, a noise like the Dead Man's Scholar-God tearing up the paper the world was written on. Mrithuri looked up into the eyes of the storm. Voices cried out to her from within it—the voices of loved ones, and the voices of those she feared. She could almost see the hundred misty hands with which it shredded off the roof and hurled the pieces away. She could feel its attention and see the will behind it.

She took another step. One more step. And then one more. She had always been climbing this stair. The stair was longer than it had been when
she began. The stair reached to the horizon. To the edge of the world and
back again.

Her numb foot slipped in the water. Her arms pinwheeled as she fought
for balance, fought not to tumble down the steps. She did not fall back into
the sickening space behind her.

She pitched forward instead.

Her forearms slammed into the steps. Blood ran from torn skin, pud-
dling in the rain, too diluted to feel sticky. Her eyes stung with water. Her
lashes stuck together. She had bitten her tongue. She had managed to avoid
smashing her face into the stair. But barely.

Fine, she thought. *If I can't walk up, I will go up like Syama.*

She had run up stairs on all fours as a child, until adults forced her to
behave as a royal princess should. She could do it now. If her arms weren't
broken.

She tested her weight against the palms. She pushed herself to hands and
feet. She looked up and regretted it. She could barely see the throne through
the rain.

It was so far. She was so tired. She was so alone—

No.

She was who she was, and she would climb and keep climbing. Until
whatever was sending the rain drowned her, or until her heart gave out and
she fell.

That throne was the power she needed to fight this thing. She would
reach it, or she would die trying.

She picked up her foot and lifted it, pushing through the water, through
the numbing tingle of the sparks that flew. Sweat and rain and blood stung
her eyes. There was glass in her hair. She lifted her opposite hand and raised
it to the next step. One at a time, not scrambling like a child.

Crawling like a weary old woman, all her dignity forgotten.

She would never have managed this if she had not given up the snakebite,
she knew. Worthy of the throne or not, she *would* have died of a burst heart
from pressing upward, pressing on. But she was better now, stronger. And
as the palace came apart around her, she was climbing closer to the storm.

Mrithuri had no idea for how long she climbed. She just did one thing,
and then the next thing, and thought no further ahead than the thing after
that. She climbed, and climbed, and climbed. So intent was she on the
pattern, the repetition, that when she raised her numb hand, prickling as if
with needles, and there was no next stair to clutch, she fell forward again.
Her elbow struck the landing, and she cried aloud in pain.

The agony was almost incapacitating. It gave her the impetus to shove her feet up the last few steps so she could fall to her side and curl up around it, though.

Something enormous laughed in the back of her mind. *Weak little thing. Unworthy scrap. What makes you think you could stand against something like me?*

You die here, pretender queen.

Mrithuri was too busy breathing in gasps that seemed half rainwater to reply. Her courage withered with the surge of pain. She clutched her elbow. She couldn't move her other fingers. *Well,* she thought. *It might be broken now.*

Doesn't matter.

Get up.

Her drape had come loose from crawling over it. The loose end trailed behind her down the stairs. There was a scarf still sodden at her neck, and in her blouse and slip she sat for long enough to tie her arm to her chest and over her shoulder. The tightness helped the pain.

Even the thought of standing left her dizzy.

On three limbs, through the shards of glass and the rubble, she crawled.

There was the throne, atop its towering pedestal. And she was atop the pedestal too. She put her good hand on the seat, got her feet under her, and heaved herself to a half-crouch. She wobbled but clutched the armrest. She turned—and the elevation dizzied her again. She'd lost track of events in the Hall of the Empty Throne.

Now she saw the whole of the space below her swept with water and tumbled with broken glass. The green darkness of the storm filled the hall. Mrithuri stared through swags of rain like trying to see through a wall of broken bottles. She heard weeping above the thunder and the torrent, and the screams and moans of someone more injured than she.

Mrithuri took a deep breath. It was full of flying water, and she doubled over coughing, clinging to the throne to keep from falling once more.

You'll die if you try, the beast whispered.

"Fuck you," Mrithuri said. Lightning rattled in answer, cracks and flashes coming endlessly. There was no rubble on the throne, at least.

She sat down on the chair.

DROPS OF WATER SPLASHED SAYEH'S FACE, AND BY INSTINCT, SHE BEGAN TO RUN. Not toward the main doors of the great hall but behind the throne, toward the exit reserved for royalty. Vara flapped, gouging her arm as it fought for balance. The remembered horror of collapsing roofs and people in peril seized her and shoved her forward.

She had to get to Drupada as fast as she could. She pelted up the stairs toward the royal apartments, so full of panic, she did not even notice the pain in her bad leg until she was running down the hallway toward her rooms. This part of the palace was intact, unharmed.

She burst through the door and found her son tucked into his little bed, the covers pulled over his head. A nurse sat beside him, her hand on his shoulder.

Sayeh stood there foolishly, dripping blood and rainwater, Vara mantled on her arm. The nurse looked up at her with concern. "He was afraid of the thunder."

"It's fine," said Sayeh. "You did well."

A perch intended for Guang Bao stood beside the door. Guang Bao himself was probably still in Sayeh's own bedchamber, on the other side of the connecting door. She bundled Vara onto it and found a cloth to wind around her scratched arm.

"Mommy!" Drupada cried, sitting up. Sayeh went to him and crouched beside the bed to kiss his forehead.

"Go back to sleep, sweetheart," she told him. "Mommy won't be far."

"Stay with me," he demanded. "I don't like the thunder."

She ruffled his hair with sticky fingers. Her heart broke. "Mommy has to go chase the thunderstorm away."

THE STRENGTH OF THE PEACOCK THRONE FLOODED MRITHURI'S BODY LIKE the shock of plunging into cold water on a hot day, like the rush of falling through the sky with her vultures, like the icy burn of snakebite through her veins. She forgot her arm, forgot the blood running down her body from her contused and lacerated forearms. Forgot the glass in her hair. Forgot anything but the hum of the throne around her, the veil of green light that swirled up to surround her like a mystic dust devil. Dragonglass green, green as the storm clouds in the sky. Green as the eyes of the beast looking down at her.

It's all one thing.

I will stop you, Mrithuri answered.

The beast smiled with teeth of lightning. *You can try.*

It was an animal's howl she heard now, and not just the howl of the wind or the howl of trapped voices. An animal's howl, hurt and lost and enraged. Paw in the trap, canny enough to wait and try to kill the trapper. But in too much pain not to scream.

What did my ancestor stitch into the world when he stitched the world together?

Whatever it was, these were the consequences.

Let me help you, she offered. *Let me set you free.* She didn't know if she could. She didn't know if there was a way to do it without unravelling everything.

Maybe what was needed was to unravel everything. But that, too, would harm untold innocents. *We've inherited the sins of our fathers,* she said to the beast. *We've inherited their misdeeds.*

The beast slashed at her, its claws fury and hate. She parried with a shield of desperation.

Belatedly, Mrithuri realized she was sitting on the Peacock Throne, and that she wasn't dead. A bit of an anticlimax, but the war had found them. There would be time to marvel at her achievements later. Unless there wasn't.

The chair was not cold and hard, as she had anticipated. It seemed instead made to fit her, to be molded to her form. Almost a part of her body, as if she could sense the deep roots stretching into the earth, the nerves running through the palace and from the palace through the whole land. Through the many lands of Sarath-Sahal, from sea to sea, north to the mountains. Down into the belly of the world and up upon the bosom of the air. The land felt to her as if it were her own body. The whole atmosphere, her own breath.

The storm, a punch in the diaphragm. Her physical body wheezed and strained with the pressure. The shattered palace was a physical pain as real as her broken arm. But it was one, she realized, that she could do something about. Because in the strength of the throne, in its reach—was not just the capability to sense. There was the capability to act, as well.

That capability began right there, in the rain-swept Hall of the Empty Throne, a throne that was empty no longer. It began when she reached out into her sense of the palace, of its structure, and found that with the aid of the throne she could manipulate it. It was not so different from speaking to Syama, or Hathi, or riding inside the mind of one of her familiar vultures.

She reached out and tried to lift the roof back into place.

The wreckage covering the floor of the hall grated, stone and metal on glass. Some of the people trapped under the fallen structure whimpered or cried out as the weight came off them. Some would never make a sound again.

Sayeh. Yavashuri.

If they were hurt, she could not help them now.

The rubble shifted, lifted. Rose in the air. Mrithuri flexed the fingers on her good hand as if she were stretching into a glove. That was what it felt like—as if the bones of her fingers extended into the bones of the palace. As if her mind and nerves and muscles were the mind and nerves and muscles of the city, of the land. As if she stretched her tendons to crack the stones of the palace back into place.

Triumph flooded her, dizzying exhilaration. She was doing this! She could make this happen.

She was the empress, and she could make *so many things happen.* Even when the weight of the uncanny storm seemed to press her breathless. Even with her head swimming with exhaustion, she could find the broken things and fix them *now.*

The bits of the fallen roof were halfway back into position when an opposing force grabbed her and shoved like a wrestler trying to force her arm down.

The beast had noticed what she was doing. The beast did not approve.

Mrithuri gritted her teeth and shoved back. She was going to put these stones and this glass back where they belonged. She was going to repair her palace. No beast from the crevices of time could defeat her. No monster that fed on sadism and suffering would stop her from healing her land. Not with this power in her hands. She was herself. She would not give in.

She was so incredibly tired. It felt like she had put her shoulder under Hathi's foreleg and was trying to lift the elephant with the strength of her back and legs. It was as if she pushed with all her might against something enormous and muscular and resilient and entirely unyielding. She had to press this thing up; it was beyond her physical capabilities to press this thing up.

The wind howled through the broken palace. The hot rain lashed her face, indistinguishable from the tears of effort. It was so warm, that rain. Like bathwater, like a puddle in the sun. Like blood.

The beast was enormous. Green-eyed, staring down at her malevolently from the storm—

Green-eyed. Where was the strength from the dragonglass going? Not just to her, through the throne. No, it was being drained away. Used. Sucked up by the beast and turned against her.

Well, there was plenty of dragonglass in the city of Sarathai-tia. It topped the defensive walls in big shards. It was worked into glazed windows.

And with the throne, Mrithuri could tap into its might. She just had to get it away from the beast.

She feinted, shoving hard to lift the fallen ceiling. When the beast blocked her, she let go—oh, the people underneath! Less-injured survivors were dragging the more-injured clear—and lunged for those other sources of energy. The beast could not block her in time. She had them—she caught the falling rubble a handspan above the injured as they scrambled, dragged each other, ran. Screams of fear cut through the roar of the beast, of the wind.

With her new strength, she hurled a dagger of banishment at the heart of the storm. There was an eye, a serene center around which the monster whirled. There was a place there where the storm's power was strongest, though it felt so calm. If she could disrupt that center—

The beast feinted toward her load of broken stone and deadly glass. So many of the people it had wounded would be ill. Some would die. *Mother, where is Sayeh? Where is Yavashuri?*

Some others—herself? Her loved ones?—would sicken from the dragonglass dust. Some of those might die as well.

There was nothing Mrithuri could do about that now. She took the feint, absorbed the power of the blow. And felt a moment of distraction, as if the beast's attention were drawn away. To some other threat, or at least to some task that was not destroying this city and the people in it.

Mrithuri took advantage of the distraction. She used that strength, and all the other strength she had collected, to strike hard at the source of the storm.

The wind shrieked with a voice like a wounded god. The lightning shattered the sky, limning clouds as bulbous and green as round crystals of malachite. Mrithuri thrust harder, as if she were leaning on a knife. She visualized the stiletto she wore in the serpent-shaped torc around her neck. She imagined it in her hands. She imagined pressing it to the bosom of her foe and leaning against it until it *popped*.

A silence fell, so quiet after the rage of the storm that it was stunning. Mrithuri clutched the armrest with her good hand, gasping a full deep breath for the first time in what felt like a thousand years. Rain still tumbled through the broken ceiling. The storm had not relented—but the will that had been driving it had broken, and Mrithuri thought it already seemed less fierce.

When Ümmühan makes a song out of this, she thought, *I will look up and see the stars in a cloudless sky, their light falling down all around me.*

The broken arm didn't pain her. The places where she had lacerated her forearms on the steps were neither bruised nor bloody.

She had not succeeded in healing the palace. But it seemed, in the effort, she had healed herself.

She set the shattered remnants of the ceiling down carefully, avoiding the dead on the floor, avoiding the living still stumbling away from the scene of destruction. They splashed through puddles to their mid-calf. All that water would be poisoned too. And would flow into the cisterns—

An unhealthy sense that she had been there before made her head ache. She rubbed her temples.

Mrithuri checked with the throne. Its strength was exhausted, as wasted as her own. Any repairs would wait until later. The rain would fall in. The rain was falling in, but now it was natural rain, without the venomous green will behind it.

But . . . she could keep the poison out of the water, at least. That poison was energy the throne could use. She could mop it up and save it for later. She could pull the poison out of the dust in the air as well, and out of the wounds of people the glass had injured. She could feel it in her own cuts. She could draw it into the throne and store it.

Or use it to get her safely down the steps to the floor—

No. That was the kind of temptation that had led her into trouble with the serpents. She would collect the power and she would wait. She would wait, and when she had recovered herself a little, she would descend. Under her own recognizance, if she had to regally slide down on her imperial bum.

Mrithuri's resolve to sit in the damn rain and rest until she felt like she could stand up without toppling over lasted exactly until she saw Sayeh at the bottom of the stair, with a group of others, picking through rubble, searching for the dead. Her chest clenched with fear. She was down the stairs before she thought it through, in her underwear with that cold strength running through. Her soaked drape was trapped under a heap of stone and glass. She used the water to sweep the steps clear of shards before setting each foot down.

When she got to the bottom, Mrithuri could only tell that Sayeh was crying because she sobbed out loud. Any tears were invisible in the rain. She touched the other woman's arm—her wife's arm!—as gently as she could with shaking hands.

Sayeh whirled.

"Drupada?" Mrithuri asked gently.

Sayeh stared at Mrithuri blindly for a moment before pulling herself together. "No." One more sob got out, and then the rajni was all business again. "No, he's in our chambers. Scared. Didn't want me to leave again but I thought you might need help."

"I did," said Mrithuri.

Sayeh's voice almost got away from her again, but she leveled it with a visible effort. "But I can't find the abbess. And there might be others under there."

Mrithuri started to tell her not to worry, that she had been careful. Then she stopped herself. How frightened Sayeh must be, who had lived through the fall of Ansh-Sahal. Her arm was streaked with blood from deep gouges that Mrithuri recognized as the marks left by a terrified bearded vulture.

"You need to get those washed out with wine," Mrithuri said. "Vulture claws are filthy. Thank you for rescuing Vara."

Sayeh smiled weakly. "It looked like you took one hell of a fall."

Mrithuri looked down at the arm still strapped across her chest. The fingers wiggled. The pain was gone. Sheepishly, she untied it. "The throne healed me."

She looked down. "Not anyone else, though. The water is getting deeper. You get that arm tended to, O wife. I will lift these girders up again and be sure there is no one left under them."

"You look exhausted—"

"Lives may be at stake," Mrithuri said. "The worst that happens to me is that I faint."

Sayeh nodded. She turned away, then turned back again. "Did we win? Is it defeated?"

"No," Mrithuri said. "I tried to help it. It's stuck. It can't get out, so it's trying to get in. Our ancestor did something I don't really understand. Something to stitch up power. To put it in the throne. It made a mess in the long run. Maybe he even *made* the thing, by accident or on purpose, as part of making Sarath-Sahal. But it doesn't want help. It wants revenge."

"Women's lot in life," Sayeh said tiredly. "Cleaning up after men."

"I don't think I cleaned anything up. I think I made it worse," Mrithuri said. "Now go get your arm fixed. I'll take care of this here."

32

A RAIN OF HAIR-FINE THREADS OF GLASS AND OBSIDIAN TEARDROPS HISSED from the sky, smacking Ata Akhimah painfully on the head in the moments before Kyrlmyrandal spread her wings over everyone. Everyone except Himadra, who was still ensconced in the howdah, that was. The translucent shade was a relief, filtering the light of that searing pale sun. Akhimah only realized her head was aching when the pain eased.

She scooped up a piece of obsidian and turned it in her hand. Smooth, glossy black, transparent, the size of a finger joint and shaped like a perfect teardrop with a tiny rough spot at the pointed end. It had formed with the filaments attached, she realized, and they had broken off in flight.

It was still warm to the touch. Akhimah slipped it into her pocket. She'd make an earring when they got back to Sarathai-tia.

They were *going* to get back to Sarathai-tia. She was walking along in the shadow of a dragon's wings, like a Wizard of old. Like someone out of a storybook. And like heroes out of a storybook, they were going to face a monster from another world. And defeat it, by the blessing of the Good Daughter and the Mother River and Kaalha the Merciful and the Scholar-God and the six hundred godlets of Rasa and by every other deity or demigod one of their number had ever worshipped along the way. By the gods of the dragons, too, if dragons had any gods.

The obsidian droplets pattered on Kyrlmyrandal's wings like rain on a roof, but droplets of rain didn't click and chink against one another as they slid to the ground. Maybe ice would. But this wasn't ice. It was glass, of a kind—the same glass from which Tsering-la's surgical tools had been crafted.

It crunched underfoot.

"Be careful of that stuff," Tsering-la said, a moment before Akhimah would have mentioned it. "It can cut up sandals and even boots, and cut your feet inside them. Right through the straw or leather."

Picking their way, almost mincing along (*Ferocious warriors, we*, Akhimah thought) they advanced toward the mountain and the monolithic temple. Crystalline planes glittered in the black rock. The mountain was an overwhelming surge of jungled cliff, green and looming as a monstrous wave. Akhimah had the same sense of alienation she'd felt when she first came to

Sarathai-tia: this was a land so foreign to her experience that she felt disoriented and estranged.

Brightly colored birds zoomed through the trees. Some kind of black ape vaulted from branch to branch, swinging on arms as long as the animal was tall. Lizards scuttled up the warm stone of the temple.

"There will be snakes," she said.

Nizhvashiti's laugh was itself like the rustle of snakes in dry leaves. "It's the insects you have to watch out for. Everything in these islands stings, bites, or spits venom."

"You've been here before?" Akhimah asked.

Nizhvashiti gestured to itself. "This is where I learned to do what I have done."

"So where do we go now? Other than the eruption"—the Dead Man craned his head back—"I don't see any indication of enemy action."

The heady scent of flowers and fruit and rich green jungle was overlaid by something bitter and stony—a tang of sulfur and hot rocks. She said, "If a huge lava flow comes down here and buries this whole cove, we're going to be sorry."

"So are they." Kyrlmyrandal pointed with her neck at two figures exiting the temple. A man and a woman, Akhimah thought. Both looking somewhat the worse for wear, with torn clothing and dirty faces.

It was several moments before she recognized the smaller of two, limping and with one arm bound across her chest. It was Chaeri.

The traitor's spring-coiled hair stood out around her, frizzed and greasy, matted. All the auburn highlights in its darkness were dulled. Her once-rounded cheeks looked gaunt; her eyes were sunken. Ground-in sand stained her threadbare clothing, as if she had been sleeping on the beach. Her nails were broken, her hands sunburned and raw.

The man walking beside her was Sekira, the erstwhile general and would-be usurper of Mrithuri's throne. He didn't look quite as lean and shopworn as Chaeri, but then he couldn't have been in the beast's power for as long. His irises were rimmed with white. He stood his ground, his thumb hooked into his sash near the hilt of his sword.

Chaeri's face tilted up. Her expression warmed and she took two quick steps toward the Gage as they approached, seeming all but oblivious to the dragon.

"The answer is still no," said the Gage.

Chaeri's step faltered. She turned to Akhimah and held her free hand out in front of her—not as if reaching toward the Wizard but as if, had she two hands, she would be clasping them in supplication. "Please, Akhimah! Please get us off this island! Please take us home!"

Akhimah raised both her hands to ward the woman off, feeling the twinge in the one that had been broken when Chaeri made her escape from Sarathai-tia. "Maybe," she said. "What can you do for us if we rescue you?"

Sekira looked like he wanted to turn his head and spit in the grass, but he didn't. He just leaned away warily.

"Oh!" said Chaeri. "They forced me to work for them, Ata. They have threatened my life, told me they would feed me to a monster. You know I never would have betrayed Mrithuri Rajni otherwise—"

"Of course not," said the Dead Man in a tone so flat that Akhimah could have missed the sarcasm if she hadn't by this point spent half a year with him. "You would never harbor resentment, nor act out of pettiness or greed."

Chaeri stared at him. Her eyes looked less enormous without the habitual rings of kohl. It made her expression of wide-eyed innocence seem far more calculated.

Or maybe that was just Akhimah's experience talking. "Stop stalling us," she said, and stepped forward, ready to push past.

"Please just take us away," Chaeri said, snatching at her sleeve. "Please, we can all leave, before the mountain explodes. They will just kill us, they don't care—"

Tsering-la must have insinuated a shield of light between Chaeri and Akhimah, because Chaeri's fingers slid away from Akhimah in a shower of yellow sparks.

Sekira grasped the hilt of his blade and tugged. The pale light of Tsering-la's sorcery surrounded the sheath, however, leaving Sekira to stare down in dismay when the blade would not come free.

"I don't trust you with that thing," Tsering-la said. "Where are the sorcerers?"

Sekira yanked the hilt again, the tendons in his forearm flexing. He pulled so hard, he staggered in a circle and barely caught himself before he fell.

"If I were going to kill you," the Gage said tiredly, "I would have done it then. We don't care about you, but we'll probably take you with us when we leave. If you tell us where the beast is, and its sorcerers."

Mutely, Chaeri pointed up to the highest reaches of the temple with a beringed finger. The ring, Akhimah noticed, was adorned with a coral-colored stone.

"God and Her Prophet," the Dead Man said. "That's going to be a lot of stairs."

"I'll fly us," said the dragon.

"This is easier." Nizhvashiti spread its arms. It lifted off the grass like a leaf gusted up in the wind, like a tattered raven, and all the rest of them—even Kyrlmyrandal, Chaeri, and Sekira—rose with it. Himadra whooped loudly, his voice echoing within the howdah.

"What the hell is this?" Sekira demanded.

"A miracle," the Godmade said.

They rose in a stately fashion. Ata Akhimah felt as if a great hand cupped and lifted her. It was nothing to the exhilaration of flying on dragon-back, but the sensation had its own joy even as her heart hammered with apprehension at what they might find at the clifftop. Gray-barked trees clung to the rocks, reached out all around them. The enormous boughs hung with vines, dripped with exotic flowers, buzzed with nectar-seeking moths and bees and birds like darting jewels.

The rain of glass seemed to have passed. Kyrlmyrandal kept her wings spread over them like an enormous parasol nonetheless. As they rose, Akhimah saw what she could not have seen as they descended—that the overhang of enormous trees sheltered a flat tabletop of a plateau, carved with ancient-looking symbols.

The dragon stepped forward onto it. Nizhvashiti whisked the rest of them along beside her.

Here, there was no litter of obsidian underfoot—just the black stone, marked with runes that Akhimah, for all her education, did not recognize.

"Is that Eremite?" she asked Tsering-la, in what was meant to be an undertone.

"I don't think so. It doesn't hurt my eyes to look at," he said.

"It's kyPrylerie," said Kyrlmyrandal. "Draconic, you would say."

"What does it say?" asked the Dead Man.

"It's a long inscription," the dragon answered. "Even if I made our friend Himadra stare at it until the sun set, we would be here all night while I tried to explain the translation. The simple answer is that this is a dragon-gate, like the ones you are familiar with. But bigger, and rather than just joining two of the worlds, it cuts across them all."

"So where's the beast?" the Gage asked.

A chorus of voices came from among the arched, buttressed roots of the great smooth-boled trees, from the cliff at the back of the plateau, from near the edge behind Akhimah with nothing but air beneath.

"We're all around you," said Ravani, and Ravana, and Chaeri, and Sekira. Each spoke as one.

HIMADRA COULD SEE ONLY THE FOREST TO THE FRONT AND SIDES, AS THE structure of the howdah blocked his vision behind and below. He leaned forward against the harness straps and managed to make out the form of a gaudily dressed man within the forest shade.

"Take us up," he told Kyrlmyrandal immediately.

"Would you abandon your allies?"

"I would keep us from getting trapped on the ground!"

The dragon didn't argue further. She turned in her length like a whip and dove off the cliff while Himadra was still orienting himself. Somehow she managed not to sweep the others off the mountain with her.

She beat hard, gaining altitude, and when they came back around, she banked so Himadra could see what was going on. It looked like Tsering-la had thrown up a shield around himself, Ata Akhimah, and the Dead Man. Nizhvashiti and the Gage stood closer to the wood. Himadra could only assume that was what they had wanted.

They probably didn't need a Wizard's protection, even from sorcerers.

Kyrlmyrandal hung back so the wind of her immense wings wouldn't sweep anyone from the plateau. She let her head droop on its long neck to improve Himadra's field of vision. He almost would rather she hadn't.

Around the edge of the plateau, Chaeri, Sekira, and the two sorcerers were wrapped in a kind of spiderweb of pale jade-colored light. It stretched between them, the same variegated shades as dragonglass, as a storm that might birth a whirlwind. The four of them moved in choreographed unison. They raised their hands, and the glow swirled, stretched into a vortex, a rising gyre. Up and up, making Himadra regret his comparison to funnel clouds. It had a rotation as it reached into the plume of smoke above, and began to draw the rank stuff down.

The Gage lunged toward Ravani. Trees jumped and shuddered with each stride. Rock dust sifted down from above, mingling with the drifting ash. Ravani did not raise a hand or even look at him. Her eyes were turned toward the sky.

The Gage struck those filaments of serpentine-colored light and bounced back. He did not fall: he rebounded, sliding across the stone with a horrific scraping sound, shedding sparks until he fetched up against Tsering's shield.

The cone of green light kept climbing. It was taking on a form now—a sort of body, perhaps. Not a humanoid body but one that had a head and arms and blazing green eyes. A storm of lightning and smoke stood around the head like wind-lashed hair. The gyre of light trailed off into a long lashing tail like a cobra's, rooted on the plateau where the others stood. The four traitors marked the boundaries of its origin.

The figure dwarfed the dragon. The people at its root might have been specks—ants, weevils. It towered into the volcano's column of smoke and beyond, wrapping the billows around itself, taking more solid form from the pillar of ash and gas.

"Maybe them letting Deep go wasn't such a good idea," Himadra said. "She doesn't seem to be slowing this thing down any. She might even be feeding it."

"I guess we'll see," Kyrlmyrandal said.

"Can you breathe fire?" Himadra asked.

"At my age," the dragon answered, "I can barely breathe oxygen."

The monstrous entity seemed to gather itself. It looked around, storm-face grinning, teeth of lightning jagged in a face like nothing Himadra had seen. The glaring green eyes fastened on Kyrlmyrandal, and in that moment she seemed as slight and darting as a dragonfly. A hand snaked toward her, a filmy wrap of sickly light around a billow of black clouds.

"Duck!" Himadra yelled.

The dragon folded her wings and dropped like a stone. An ivory arrow plunged toward the startlingly blue sea. Himadra wrapped his forearms around his neck for support, praying. When she broke her dive, it was going to hurt.

The world spun around them: blue sky, bluer water. Black tower of smoke, jade-and-charcoal monster. Blinding white sun and emerald mountainside—and the pale dragon falling like a javelin toward the sea.

The clawed hand of the beast snatched through the air, swiped, missed them. It lunged again. Himadra saw the sea coming. He imagined broken bones, perhaps his own death from the shock of Kyrlmyrandal opening her wings. The sky whistled around them—

Her path began to curve. Himadra felt the air catch in her membranes. She was no longer diving. Now she was bending on a long parabolic arc, rising softly as she eased her wings open bit by bit. She was trying to save him. Save him and elude the massive fist punching down.

Himadra wanted to close his eyes. He couldn't, because Kyrlmyrandal was using them. She sideslipped and rose, and the huge hand missed them and plunged into the ocean beneath the spot where, an instant before, they had been.

The glass-clear water boiled at its touch.

"Shit," Himadra said, looking sideways at the plume of hissing steam. "Keep flying!"

"Eyes front!" Kyrlmyrandal answered. "I'm doing my best here!"

THE GAGE PICKED HIMSELF UP, HIS BRASS HIDE SCRAPED ON BASALT SO LONG bright gouges streaked his sandstorm-antiqued shell. His robe hung in tatters, ripped by sliding across rough stone. In every meaningful way, he was undamaged.

"Well," he said. "That was unsurprising."

The shape of the beast towered over them. He saw Kyrlmyrandal like a distant dart, shimmering in the brilliant light, a tiny figure dusted with scales that glittered. He saw Ata Akhimah with one hand on Tsering-la's shoulder as he raised his hands to keep a shield up around them. He saw the Dead Man right behind them, looking at the sky with a disgusted headshake.

He saw the wraps of sorcery that united Ravana, Ravani, Sekira, and

Chaeri. He saw the rent in the sky above them, wrought about with twists of smoke, hidden from casual sight by the foul black breath of the volcano.

He reported dryly, "Punching the sorcerers doesn't work."

"It wants to make us fight each other," Nizhvashiti said. "The fight itself is the point. It gets stronger when we battle."

"I haven't got a way to stop it," the Gage answered. "How about you?"

"Maybe?" Nizhvashiti folded itself into a cross-legged pose, the red-brown soles of its feet upturned upon its thighs. A normal-enough manner in which to sit—except the Godmade did it in midair, lifting its legs off the ground rather than lowering its backside. "Pardon me, I need to call someone."

It closed its pupilless, mismatched eyes.

"We're in the middle of a fight here, if you hadn't noticed!" the Gage protested.

Nizhvashiti just sat there on the air, weightless as a cloud, and did not respond.

AKHIMAH KEPT ONE HAND ON TSERING-LA'S NECK, MAINTAINING SKIN-TO-SKIN contact, giving her life force to him. It was his Wizardry keeping them alive, immediately. And he could use her strength in ways she could not, because that was the special and powerful gift of the Wizards of Rasa.

But while he was doing that, perhaps she could find a way to strike out, to break the sorcery binding the beast's thralls together. To send the beast back where it came from.

Kyrlmyrandal seemed to be distracting it, from the glimpses Akhimah got. In the meantime—if ever there were a time to be throwing pillars of energy around, Ata Akhimah believed she had found it.

She clenched her free hand—somewhere, Jharni was wincing in despair—and summoned one, aiming for Chaeri. Not, Akhimah told herself, because she was petty. But because Chaeri was the one least likely to be able to defend herself.

And maybe a little because she was petty.

She smiled to herself as she twisted sparks out of the heavens and threw them down. The attack burst on the stone plateau like a cannon shell, shattering directly where Chaeri stood, flashing up in a rising, incendiary torrent—

—that parted around her as if she were a needle thrust into the heart of a candleflame. The inferno raged and roared. It did not touch her.

Chaeri put one hand out as if to stroke the sparks. They bent away from her. She looked directly at Akhimah and laughed. "I never liked you."

Akhimah's gut twisted. She wished Jharni had deigned to come herself, to fight beside them. But perhaps you didn't get to be a Wizard-Prince by going looking for pissing contests with angry demigods. Angry demigods supplied themselves quite liberally enough in the history of the world without any need to send out search parties to find them.

The Eyeless One wouldn't have left them on their own if she didn't think they could handle it, would she? After all, she lived in the world too—and in the Between Places the beast was inhabiting.

The stone bucked under their feet. Akhimah and Tsering-la grabbed at one another. The Dead Man had probably been a cat in a past life; he rode the motion like a sailor riding the deck of a pitching ship. The massive shoulders of the mountain overhead seemed to shrug as the entire island jumped with the force of an internal explosion. The bruised column of smoke disfiguring the crystalline sky glowed violently from within, like a cracked old ember enlivened by a breath of air.

Akhimah felt the heat on her face even from this distance, as if she looked upward at the sun.

It was just her ill luck that there were people—was Deep *people*, strictly speaking?—in the neighborhood who were even better than she was at throwing around pillars of energy.

Tsering-la looked over his shoulder. He touched the jade-and-pearl collar at his throat as if for reassurance. Expressionless, he said, "Well, this is officially out of control."

The Dead Man sighed. "I should have known better than to bring a gun to a god fight."

Chaeri was still laughing. Laughing—and growing in size. Her aspect changed as she became taller and taller, broader and more broad. Her hair writhed about her like snakes. A belt of skulls appeared about her hips, above the rags of her trousers. Akhimah remembered the impression she had had of Deep, that the goddess was just the closest in a long line of women standing one behind the other. That if she squinted, she would see their arms in various poses.

A multitude of shadowy arms seemed to emerge from the shoulders of the being who had been Chaeri. The multitude of hands held a multitude of weapons. Her skin grew glossy, translucent—as if she were carved of amber. The column of power Akhimah had thrown dwindled into a twist that the transformed woman held on her palm. Those webs of oil-green light still bound her to the others, but now they seemed to pull strength into her, pulsing like the proboscis of some feeding insect.

The ground shook again, but it wasn't the mountain this time. The Gage stumped up beside them, stopping on the other side of Tsering-la's shield.

Tsering-la extended the shield around him.

The Gage pointed to the figure that had been Chaeri. "Is that what I think it is?"

"A possession?" said the Dead Man. "It seems likely."

"The Bad Daughter," the Gage said.

"I might guess so," said Akhimah. "It's not, by rights, my mythology."

It wasn't the religion of any of them—except Nizhvashiti, who appeared to be floating in midair, meditating.

How ironic.

Nevertheless, Akhimah felt they were looking up at a goddess. A great and awful goddess, as unforgiving as the sea. Her face, impassive, burned like the sun. Her gigantic hands were magnificently formed. The part of her hair blazed with light. The sun burned in her crown, and heat rolled off her.

She dropped that captured lightning and dusted her hand off on another of the dozen or so now surrounding her. She had an arrow in one of them, a bow in another. She fitted the one to the string of the other and turned within the towering form of the beast that now surrounded them all.

She faced out over the ocean, toward where Kyrlmyrandal twisted and dodged, evading the beast's clutch.

She drew the string back to her ear.

33

THIS TIME, THERE WAS NO STRUGGLE AS MRITHURI CLIMBED THE STEPS OF HER throne. This time, the structure welcomed her, supported her. As if she had earned her place and now things might be easy. As if the pointless opposition might be behind her.

She knew better than to believe that. The rain was still falling through the shattered roof. Though the will behind the storm was, well, not broken, but focused elsewhere, perhaps, there was still baked earth outside. Dry soil that wouldn't absorb water quickly. Mrithuri could feel the ghost of that water as if it pooled on her skin. The throne and her connection to the throne gave her an intimate awareness that they were on the verge of floods. And not the seasonal, useful floods of the Mother.

These would be dangerous floods: trees uprooted, sewage unleashed, boats overturned, houses washed away. And Mrithuri needed to solve it, because she was the empress now.

She wanted to put her face in her hands and sob at the ridiculousness of it all. Instead, she put her butt on the throne and pulled the power of the land up around her.

First things first. Her people waited for her below. She would raise the roof, repair the hall, and give them access to retrieve the dead and injured who had been crushed beneath the roof beams.

It was easy, without the beast fighting her. So easy it should have worried her, perhaps. It felt effortless, lifting the roof back into place, healing the broken stone, setting the cracked panes of dragonglass back into place. She could not grow them back together as seamlessly as the stone, and some were powdered into oblivion—but she could clean the poisoned dust away and make new glass to patch the gaps with. The poisonous, powerful powdered glass she sealed within the stones. It was too deadly to do anything else with.

She tried not to think about the bodies. There was nothing she could do to fix those. Even the Alchemical Emperor had been unable to reverse death.

When the roof was healed and the rain no longer sheeted over her, over the throne, and down the steps in a river, she reached out and felt the water, ankle-deep over the tiles. She put her will into it, humped it up like a wave, and swept it from the hall, out the door, down the street. She thrust the city gates open and let the water flow out onto the flooded plain at the bottom of the mountain.

Nobody would be traveling by foot anytime soon.

With the roof reassembled, Mrithuri felt even stronger. The strength of the dragonglass flowed into her, sweeping away pain and tiredness. It was a better drug than the snakebite had ever been.

She reached out into the storm, into the earth surrounding the palace, into the whole flooded infrastructure of Sarath-Sahal. Here were rice terraces with broken dikes in need of healing. There were cattle enmeshed in a field turned to a mire. The whole land spread out in her awareness like a game board, as if she looked down on the sand table in the war room. No, as if she *were* the sand table in the war room. As if her land were her body, and her proprioception saturated it all.

What she found made her face grow wet with tears to replace the rain. The beast had wreaked such destruction, she could not compass it. Houses, families, livestock, crops swept away. Hillsides collapsed in the torrents of rain; rivers in flood; people stranded in trees and other trees uprooted and blown over.

Mrithuri could repair the damage to the land. She could even help some of the plants and crops and grasses—the ones still rooted were part of the earth and part of her domain. She could fix houses and raise barns that had fallen. She could coax rivers back within their banks.

But restoring lost lives—human or animal—was beyond her power. As it had been beyond the power of her great-grandfather before her. *All this strength,* she thought. *All this ability and no way to use it for the things that mattered most.*

Below her, workers had rescued the remaining injured and were now carrying the bodies away. She felt their footsteps on the floor. She heard the lamentations of the nuns within the cloisters. She felt . . . a pressure there, a swelling. The taut sensation of a finger within a too-tight ring, blood trapped beyond it.

Something was trying to get in.

Mrithuri could feel her way into the cloisters now. If the whole land were like her body, the palace was its chambered heart.

She brought her will and attention back from the far-flung reaches of Sarath-Sahal, here to the metaphorical center of the empire her ancestor had constructed. She recognized her enemy. It had not been so long. The taste of it was still on her tongue.

The beast was there, oozing from the Between Places, creeping into the cloisters like rising water. Mrithuri felt the nuns joining forces, their songs echoing like a heartbeat within the walls and down the strange, otherwise corridors of the space between spaces where they worshipped, worked, and lived.

She felt the abbess of Ansh-Sahal awaken, injured and confused. She had not been killed by the falling roof, but Mrithuri could sense the damage in her body. She would not walk again.

The abbess should rest, should heal. But she, too, felt the plainsong. She felt the resonance of it. She raised her wounded voice and sang.

You should not, said the empress. *You must rest.*

I choose this, the abbess answered.

The song was her life, Mrithuri understood. She was giving her life to her sisters in the cloisters, to make them strong. She would give it all before she was done.

Some of the rain on Mrithuri's cheeks was salty.

Mrithuri sensed those sisters as individuals and as a collective. She felt them clutch one another's hands, hold tight in a ring, summon all their strength to chink up the cracks the beast crept through. The monster felt slippery. Incohesive. Mrithuri only touched it with her mind, and still it felt cold and gelatinous and as if it, like the land, were made up of many parts stitched together.

There was strength in the throne, and she remembered how to use it. She pushed the beast away.

It was like pushing fog, like giving a hard shove to a bag full of jelly. It flowed around her, over her head, between her fingers. Suffocating and enormous, it filled the space around her like wet mud sliding into a grave. Her heart clenched with terror; the beat raced in her ears. She wobbled on the throne, lightheaded.

If she fell, she would fall all the way. All the way to the ground.

She'd lie where all the other shattered bodies had lain. And there would be no one to fight the monster.

The throne had power, yes. The skylights above had power to give it. There had been more in Ansh-Sahal, before the dragonglass canopies there were shattered. The beast had been quietly chipping away at their defenses for a long time—and they had been too ignorant to know.

If her great-grandfather had not been so greedy. If he had not been so secretive. So power-hungry—

She might not be empress. But she also might not be fighting a creature that was oozing into her house from the cracks between time.

The nuns found her awareness threaded through their cloisters and reached out with their own. They offered her strength, leaning against her as she leaned against the metaphorical door. The throne offered her strength as well, though it was wounded. Mrithuri pushed as hard as she could, hands clenched on the chair arms, eyes shut tight, half-aware that she was uttering little grunting sounds.

Not enough. It wasn't enough.

She thought of sorcerers and Wizards, and how they made sacrifices for power. What had Akhimah said? That sorcerers sacrificed someone else . . . but Wizards sacrificed themselves?

Mrithuri thought, *Oh. Maybe that is what I'm here for.*

Her serpent torc was at her throat, in the place where it always lived. She grasped the head that hung in the hollow of her throat between her collarbones. She grasped it in her fist and with a gentle twist, she drew the flexible, razor-edged blade forth.

It wouldn't hurt much, not with a blade so sharp. She placed the edge against the back of her wrist and drew it across the skin.

Skin parted and blood beaded, then flowed. She opened her eyes to watch it, realizing that she'd cut the tail on the blind dolphin tattooed on her arm. The liquid spilling across her skin was warm, only sticky at the edges where it began to dry. Most of it flowed like water. And like water it ran from her flesh onto the arm of the throne.

The throne seemed hungry.

It had an awareness, Mrithuri realized. Maybe not an intelligence, but a mind, of sorts. It was awake and observing. And now it was leaning toward her, soaking up the strength she gave it. Seeming to swell with radiance, casting a shocking glow.

It hurt her eyes. She closed them again.

The sound of screams echoed through the throne room where singing had been a moment before. Something had broken through into the cloisters. Something dark and watchful, formless, dimly alight with a sinister green aurora. Something pushing through the cracks in the world, shoving them wider. Pushing hard.

Hurting the women who tried to hold the way against it. Harming people who it was Mrithuri's responsibility to protect.

No.

There was so much power in her, and she was so clumsy with it. She did not know how to use it, how to force the beast back without harming her own women, the priestesses who protected her palace with their chants and invocations. The guardians of the ways.

She had the power, and she did not know how to use it.

But perhaps the nuns did.

They had skills and strengths she could not imagine. They were, she realized, also making sacrifices for power: locking themselves away from the world, never leaving their strange and winding cloisters. Perhaps in driving them there, the Alchemical Emperor had only made them stronger.

Yes, they would be able to use it. So Mrithuri had to figure out how to get it to them.

How did you share magic with somebody? How did you do what the abbess was doing, with her flickering, dying strength?

Mrithuri imagined her hand reaching out but felt nothing. No responding clasp. Just the tug of sensation as the women in their cloister drew what little power they could from their surroundings and frantically sandbagged—as if the beast were a rising flood of filthy water and they stood along the river banks.

They were being driven back, and the beast was seeping in. It had tried tearing the roof off and failed. Now it came through the basement.

Of course, Mrithuri thought.

She mustered the strength of the Peacock Throne, and her own strength as well. And she sent them back into the palace. Into the roots and foundations of the place. Shoring it up, feeding it, filling its reservoirs. *Find it,* she prayed. *Find it.*

The cloistered sisters found it just as the brilliant light that was—that *had been*—the abbess of Ansh-Sahal guttered and failed. They grabbed at it and began at once to use it. She felt them digging in, fighting as if pushing an opposing force uphill. She reached into the throne, into the roots of the palace . . . into herself, until she clutched the arms of the chair and felt the world wheel beneath her.

The walls of the palace shuddered. The mountain bucked beneath her seat. She felt the sacred space the nuns held open, and felt it begin to buckle with the pressure of the beast's rage.

Her great-grandfather had pushed the beast back once. Could she be less than him?

No. She would be more. She would find her strength not in subjugating others but in allying with them. She stood on the shoulders of giants. Flawed giants. She was flawed herself.

She would be a giant too, and she would do what she could to repair those flaws which came within her span of control.

The nuns rallied. Mrithuri gave them more. She barely felt her body, but she knew it was sliding back into the throne, her head slumping onto her chest. She would just nod off for a moment. Sayeh would be fine without her. Sayeh could be empress just as well as Mrithuri could, if not better.

Sayeh had an heir of her own body, that mystical thing that was needed to hold this empire together. Mrithuri understood its importance now. It was for this that the blood mattered. Because her great-grandfather had built the world that way.

"*Mrithuri!*"

The Hall of the Throne, Empty no longer, was an acoustically peculiar space. The Alchemical Emperor had designed it so whispers carried to his perch on the heights, and so that his own words, spoken from the throne, could be heard by all. The voice that snapped Mrithuri back into awareness was Sayeh's. It was Sayeh's limping step, rushing up the long, precarious stair, that made her open her eyes.

Her Consort bent over her, hands on her wrists, chafing them, trying to rub awareness back into her. "Oh, thank the Mother," Sayeh said. "You fainted—"

"It's trying to break in," Mrithuri whispered, every word an effort. "Don't worry about me. You'll do fine . . ."

"Don't be ridiculous," Sayeh snapped. She tried to pull Mrithuri from the throne, but the seat was deep and there was no place for Sayeh to brace herself, with her back to the steeply descending stair.

"Stop," Mrithuri said. She paddled at her wife's hands. There was no strength in her. "The beast can't get in."

"You can't die!" said Sayeh. "It's eating your life—use the river, Mrithuri. *Use the river.*"

Of course. The Mother was right there, washing the roots of the palace in her milk-white abundance. Flowing from her source deep in the Steles of the Sky, deep in far Tsarepheth, where she had a different name and a different character—a wild youth, not a nurturing mother—but was fundamentally the same. The same water bound the whole land together, from the Bitter Sea to the Arid, from the Steles of the Sky to the Sea of Storms.

The Mother was right there, and Mrithuri—called Her Abundance, called Her Magnanimity, called Empress of Sarath-Sahal—was her priestess and her daughter. She had strengths that her great-grandfather could never have called on. She was the goddess incarnate, and that power was hers to use.

She reached into the river. She reached into the earth. The earth she had healed, the river she had strengthened. She imagined the coolness, the softness of the silty water on her skin. She thought of the dolphins who swam within its embrace, the lotuses that floated on the surface. All the creatures within it, even the Mother Wyrm. She thought of the roots it fed and the banks those roots supported. She thought of the crops nurtured by the flood, and the people those crops nourished.

Sayeh's hands were on her arms. In the blood she had let as her sacrifice. The shapes on Mrithuri's arms seemed limned with a pale cool light. Her tattoos: Bull, Tiger, Peacock; Dolphin, Elephant, Vulture.

Strength, ferocity, confidence.

Speed, steadfastness, wisdom.

The qualities of a rajni. The qualities of an empress. And her link to the spirits of this land. These *lands. Her* lands.

Not in the sense of ownership but in the sense of guardianship. These lands were hers to warden.

As she was Syama's.

The women in the cloister were hers to guard as well. Or, in this case, hers to give the tools to guard themselves—and her.

"Hold me," she told Sayeh.

Sayeh's hands tightened on her wrists. "I've got you. Just don't throw me down the stairs."

Mrithuri smiled tightly. Then she opened the gates within herself and let the river flow through.

MRITHURI'S HANDS CLENCHED ON THE ARMS OF THE THRONE AS SAYEH PRESSED down on her wrists. She thought to be careful, to protect Mrithuri from her own strength—but it was all she could do to hold the empress on to the throne. Mrithuri's head went back. Light streamed from under her closed eyelids. Her mouth opened and light fountained from her lips like a scream. There was no scream.

The sound that came from Mrithuri was no human sound. It was not even an animal sound. It was the thunder of rapids, the rush of floodwater. The sound swept over Sayeh. She thought it would push her legs out from under her, but it only felt cool. Cool and soft, like wading in the gentle shallows of the river.

The light coursed down the pedestal as if it were heavier than air. It flooded like cold smoke through the throne room, rising, rising, sloshing in waves, pouring out the doors. Filling the palace. Probably flooding out to fill the city as well.

From somewhere distant, Sayeh heard singing. There had been singing all along, she realized. There in Sarathai-tia, there was always singing. But it echoed more now. It resonated. It seemed to be no longer distant, a thread of sound from the depths of the palace. It was close, and strong, and all around them.

Sayeh knew the chants. She'd heard them enough, and they were not so distant from the plainsongs of her own city. She felt them now in her bones, the rhythm calling her, the syllables resonating in the empty spaces inside her lungs and abdomen. Inside the network of her bones. Inside the river within her body, the one of blood flowing along its tributaries to the heart, as the Mother River flowed down to the sea.

Sayeh, too, began to sing.

Sayeh, too, was swept into the river. She felt the priestesses all around her, like a line of women linking arms, holding hands, leaning on one another. Creating a barrier that would not be broken. And through them all, from the river, from Mrithuri, flowed the strength of the world.

And the strength of the world was vast.

It filled up the palace. It filled up the Between Places and the city beyond. It swept into every corridor and room and seeped into every crevice. It filled the people and it filled their homes, and it made a wall—a sort of field—that the beast could not enter. There was no path into the Between Places when the cracks between them were filled. There was no path into the kingdom when the Between Places were knit together.

The light brightened, intensified, seeped into the golden walls. Flowed down to the cisterns and filled them up, saturating the water. Flowed into the cloisters and spackled up the cracks where monsters could get in. Sayeh felt it happen through the song, through her one-wittedness with the women in their cloisters, though the river that swept through them all.

She opened her eyes and saw that light curl up the vaults of the roof, soak into the tiles of the floor. She watched it saturate, puddle, soak in, and dim.

Like the floodwater the beast had meant to use to destroy them, but the opposite in result.

Sayeh stood for a moment, panting, trembling. Drained and yet full of well-being, as if she had played a difficult game as hard as she could and was now allowed to rest. She was still bent over Mrithuri, holding her wrists against the throne.

Gently, she opened her hands and straightened. Mrithuri breathed still. She looked asleep, slumped in a royal chair too large for her like a child collapsed in her father's seat. She wore a blouse and underskirt. Her drape was strewn down the stairs, wrinkled under Sayeh's feet. A slow trickle of blood still oozed from her arm.

Sayeh pulled a scarf from around her neck and began to bind the wound up. The empress's eyelids fluttered.

"And stay out," Mrithuri said weakly, with an even weaker laugh. "Please tell me that's the only problem that needs me today."

"That's what I came to tell you," Sayeh said. "Vara—Well, you had better come and see."

Mrithuri blinked at Sayeh, seeming dizzied. "Vara?"

"I heard flapping. I thought maybe Kyrlmyrandal was back, but . . . it was Vara. He hasn't stopped growing," Sayeh said. "He's in the courtyard where the dragon was before."

"Oh," said Mrithuri. She was still breathing like a sprinter who had overreached herself, wheezing on each inhale.

Sayeh petted the empress's arm beside the improvised bandage. The blood was drying. "We've driven the beast back, though."

Mrithuri sat up. "We've made it angry. And chased it back to the Sea of Storms."

Sayeh put her fist against her stomach, as if to quell the sinking feeling there. "Oh."

"They need us," Mrithuri gasped. "They need us right now."

"We have no way to get there."

Mrithuri pushed herself to her feet. Sayeh caught her as she staggered. Somehow, neither one of them fell down the stairs.

Mrithuri said, "Kyrlmyrandal left us a way. Left you a way."

"What do you mean?"

"You go," Mrithuri said. "I need to stay on the throne. I can fight from there. I am the Alchemical Empress."

She stopped.

"What?" asked Sayeh.

"How big is Vara now? Could she carry two?"

"Unless one of them was the Gage, I'd reckon. But you just said—"

Mrithuri brushed it aside with a gesture. "Not me. Is . . . Do you know what happened to Yavashuri?"

Her voice cracked.

"She's not among the dead or crippled." Sayeh put a hand to her mouth but would not sob. "The abbess is dead."

Mrithuri nodded somberly. "I felt it. Send a page to find Yavashuri, and send her to me. And get somebody to rig up a harness for the bird. A harness that can carry two."

34

THEY WERE DOING AS WELL AS COULD BE EXPECTED, HIMADRA THOUGHT. Staying ahead of the monster. Keeping it distracted from the people on the ground. Winding it in spirals around the stem of smoke and light that connected it to the mountain, to the portal that had allowed it to escape the Broken Place from which it hied.

"Come on, Himadra," he muttered to himself. "You're supposed to be the great tactician. *Think*."

Mostly, he was leaning forward to peer out the window, eyes watering with the glare and the fumes from the volcano, squinting as Kyrlmyrandal banked. His eyes weren't made for this. She should have adopted an eagle. One of Mrithuri's bearded vultures.

She dodged and twisted, throwing him against the straps of his harness as one of the avatar's clawed hands swooshed past. The edges of Himadra's vision redded out. Deep in his thigh he felt something important snap. He was familiar enough with broken bones to know what it was. That the pain was familiar didn't make it any less intense.

He felt Kyrlmyrandal's apology through their link. He threw himself into the contact more deeply in order to escape the pain. The wind tossed them, the updraft from the volcano's heat an unexpected advantage. They climbed like a cannonball fired directly up. The beast swiped again, missing as they sailed up, up, beyond its reach—

It grew taller.

Himadra had a good view as the amorphous, twisting form whipped around, stretched up—then suddenly staggered as if hit by something invisible. It doubled up as if punched, and when it straightened again, it seemed . . . denser. Thicker. More muscular.

More wracked with lightning within its cloud-shaped body. More greenly lit from within.

"I think something made it angry," he said to Kyrlmyrandal as it billowed upward again.

She sideslipped out of the updraft. He felt the air fall away from beneath her wings as if they had stepped off a cliff, and what had been firm under them was firm no longer. Himadra leaned over to peer out the side window. Something big uncoiled from where the beast's feet would have been. A glistening woman, enormous, many-armed like a goddess, her skin irides-cent as mother of pearl and golden as citrines. She raised two of her arms.

"A bow," Himadra gasped. "She's got a bow!"

Kyrlmyrandal dropped on a wingtip spiral, falling like a leaf rotating around its stem. Himadra groaned and pressed both hands to his thigh, trying to hold the snapped bone immobile. At least the padding around his hips was—so far—keeping him from breaking his pelvis.

The arrow missed them by less than the span of Himadra's arms. It was as big as a tree. A smallish ornamental tree, maybe, not a forest giant.

But a tree all the same.

IN MOMENTS OF CONFUSION, QUANTIFY YOUR ASSETS AND YOUR LIABILITIES.

The Dead Man had more of the latter than the former. Between him and his allies and the cliff stood a confused-looking Sekira, anchoring that film of greenish light. Also wrapped up in the light was the towering goddess-form that had been Chaeri, now nocking a second massive arrow to her incomprehensibly large bow.

The Dead Man did not have any resources that could debilitate even a minor enfleshed deity.

Between them and the jungle, beyond the apparently entranced Nizh-vashiti, were the two sorcerers. They too were wrapped up in filmy webs of green light. That light seemed to serve as a protection, much as Tsering-la's shields. The Gage had rebounded from it ferociously.

Anything that could toss an enormous metal man as heavy as a statue across a small plateau was not something the Dead Man wanted to run headfirst into.

Still, he wondered . . . why were the sorcerers on that side of the plateau? Why didn't they move forward? What were they guarding?

He turned to the Wizards. Everybody in this group knew more about magic than he did. "Tsering-la."

"Brilliant idea?" the little man asked.

"Maybe. Kyrlmyrandal said this plateau was a dragon-gate. Can you use it to get us back . . . behind those sorcerers? Farther up the mountain?"

"Closer to the volcano?" Ata Akhimah asked.

The Gage said, "It's all a volcano."

"Hmm," said Tsering-la. "You know, maybe. There was some informa-tion about this place in those books from Ansh-Sahal."

Akhimah, head craned back to track the aim of the Bad Daughter's bow, rubbed her hands on her sleeves. "Not enough to seal the gate, though."

"We'd need somebody more attuned to Vastu Shastra than we are," said Tsering-la.

"I'll run right back and kidnap a nun," the Dead Man replied.

Akhimah said, "Well, get us up there. It's better than standing around, feeling outclassed."

"They're coming toward us," the Gage reported. "If we can figure out how to go—"

"One moment," Tsering answered. "It's not easy doing two things at once."

The Dead Man leveled his gun. "I'll distract them."

He had no reason to think his ball might be more effective than the Gage's fist, except that the pistol balls were lead, and lead was famously immune to magic. Tsering-la's shields could stand against cannonballs . . .

"Can things leave?" the Dead Man asked.

"Pardon?" the Wizard answered, his eyes unfocused.

"Can things go out of your bubble?"

"Yes. Almost got it—"

The Dead Man sighted on Ravana. That bottle-green coat would have made a better target without the green of the jungle behind. He braced his pistol hand with his other hand, pulled the hammer back with his thumb, and squeezed the trigger. The wheel spun, spitting sparks, and the pistol roared in his hand. Akhimah yelped in surprise.

He hadn't known what to expect. But Ravana rocked back, pivoting from the hips as if something had slammed into his shoulder. He clapped a hand below his left collarbone. Blood started through the fingers and the Gage said, "Kaalha's cold silver tit, you winged him."

The Dead Man was already wadding fabric around another ball and reaching for his powder horn. His head bent over the ramrod, the gun butt braced on his thigh. But he looked up when Akhimah said, "Shit."

Ravana's hand came down, and no rush of blood followed. The veil between him and Ravani glowed more intensely. The Dead Man heard someone cry out behind him. He turned his head enough to see Sekira fall to one knee as blood splashed from his shoulder.

"Bet he didn't bargain on that when he betrayed us," Akhimah said with satisfaction.

"Fucking sorcerers," the Dead Man answered, pulling the ramrod from his gun. He straightened and leveled it again. They weren't *walking*, Ravana and Ravani. But they were *coming* nonetheless.

An enormous tiger burst out of the jungle, big as a cave-cat. Big enough to ride upon. It bounded toward them, following Ravani's pointing finger.

"Shit," said the Dead Man. He swung his pistol away from the sorcerers.

Slaver flew from the tiger's jaws. Its ears were pinned; its flews pulled back in a snarl. The Dead Man tracked it with his sights, holding his fire until it was too close to miss, until he could see each pale hair on the snow-white ruff. He waited for the moment between breaths—

"It's not real," yelled Ata Akhimah, and he jerked his finger away from the trigger as it leaped, snarling, smashed itself into the barrier, and dissolved in a cascade of sparks.

"What the hell?" the Dead Man asked.

"Illusions," said the Gage. "Those fuckers."

The fuckers in question advanced. They parted to pass around Nizhvashiti. Now they were nearly to Tsering-la's defenses.

This time, the Dead Man lowered his veil. He lifted his gun to his lips and kissed it. "Scholar-God, guide my aim. Defend us from demons, and write our names on the book of Heaven in letters of gold and indigo."

He aimed at the woman. His bullet had hurt the man, before he transferred the damage to an ally. Maybe he could kill Ravani in one shot. Maybe if he did enough damage to kill Sekira, she and her brother would have no place to send the injuries.

She was close enough that he saw her smile.

The world before him ripped in half. As if someone had torn a painting handing over another painting, he saw the mountain, the beast, the sorcerers. And through a gap in that scene he saw quiet forest and moving leaves.

"Damn it!" the Dead Man said. "You spoiled my aim!"

"Don't complain," said Tsering-la with satisfaction.

"What about the Godmade?" the Dead Man asked.

"I believe in their ability to handle things for themselves," the Gage answered.

Someone grabbed the Dead Man's arm—Akhimah, he thought—and then he was tumbling through the hole in the world and into the forest beyond.

THE JUNGLE WAS EERILY SILENT, EVEN TO THE GAGE'S SENSES. UNLIKE humans, insects and birds knew better than to draw attention when incarnate gods were tearing up the land. Or even when mere humans were stampeding up their mountainside.

Mere humans . . . and a Gage.

The Gage led the charge, the others struggling through the path he forced. Vines and undergrowth barely impeded him. The steepness of the slope was harder on the others, though he stamped a staircase into earth and basalt as he climbed.

"Are the sorcerers following?" the Dead Man gasped.

"No," said Tsering. "I closed the door."

"Couldn't they just open it again?"

"Keep climbing," said the Gage.

The dragon-gate had brought them out most of the way up the peak. They were still on the windward side of the mountain—a blessing, because the shuddering underfoot and the smell of hot stone reminded them the mountain was alive.

They burst out of the jungle above the treeline and found themselves beside a path worn by long foot travel into the weathered red-black stone.

"I guess there was an easier way up," panted the Dead Man.

"Don't look back," the Gage answered.

Of course, everyone did.

Here above the trees, they had a clear line of sight to the horizon. In the direction they had been going, the plume of the volcano's eruption rose beyond a crevassed wall of ice—still perhaps an hour's hard climb above. Bad enough, but the sky behind was full of monsters. The beast—a clawed and muscular outline full of roiling smoke and lightning—rose beside the avatar of the Bad Daughter. Her eyes glared like suns beneath the white sun in her crown; when her gaze swept in this direction, the Gage could feel the heat on his metal hide. The humans winced and shielded their faces.

Below, the Gage could make out a glimpse of the plateau the four of them had fled. The black stone was mostly overshadowed by trees. He could not see Nizhvashiti.

Kyrlmyrandal, however, was a pale missile hurtling through the blistering sky. The snap of her red-streaked wings, the agility of her flight, made him wonder what she must have been like in her prime of youth and physical power.

"Iashti," Akhimah prayed, "let my stitches hold."

The beast swiped at the dragon. The dragon twisted out of the way, her long body contorting into a spiral. The Gage knew how enormous she was, but the smoke-wraith beast looked like a big man fighting a hummingbird.

As she straightened, the dread goddess let fly another arrow. Kyrlmyrandal, still recovering, wheeled sideways—

At first the Gage thought it had taken her in the wing. Then he realized the wreckage tumbling from the sky was pieces of the howdah.

"Himadra—" the Dead Man said.

"Beyond our help," said the Gage.

"He might yet live," said Akhimah, not explaining why she thought so. "Come on. Keep climbing. *Climb!*"

They followed the path higher, now at a stagger, now at a run. Stones scattered from beneath their feet. The Gage held himself back so as not to abandon the others. They skirted below the ice until the path led them to a place where the earth fell away and the glacier caved into a massive bowl, as if someone had scooped a gigantic handful of mountain away. Somebody the size of the beast towering in the sky, perhaps.

The Gage put out his arm to prevent any chance of the others running past him. At the bottom of the pit, far below, was a vast crack, and from the crack flowed a long, ropy thread of lava. It pushed along the edge of the tumble of rocks and boulders from the collapsed mountainside, mowing down ancient forest giants. Though lush, the trees hissed, popped with steam, and burst into flames. Below, the ocean was boiling.

The Gage felt he'd seen enough boiling oceans for one functionally immortal lifetime. "End of the road. What next?"

"I'm an idiot." Ata Akhimah was looking back over her shoulder. "Those aren't the sorcerers. Down there, I mean. That's why they didn't chase us."

"What?" said Tsering-la. He pressed a fist into his side, wheezing from the run up the mountain. "Of course. They're illusionists. They left copies of themselves here as a distraction. But then where are *they*?"

The Gage wished he could sigh. At the rim of the crater, he raised his metal hands to his metal forehead. "They're in Ansh-Sahal. They're on the throne they built there."

The Dead Man had put his hands on his knees and was bent over, panting. He'd fixed his veil at some point. The Gage was not sure when.

"Shit," said Tsering-la. "I bet that's why they were trying to keep us away from the top of the mountain."

"What do you mean?" The Dead Man looked up.

"There's a dragon-gate on the edge of the cliff," said the Wizard. "What do you want to bet where it leads?"

"On the edge of the cliff," the Dead Man said. "You mean, in the open air, half a mile straight up over a volcano?"

"It's not a volcano," said Tsering-la. "It's just a vent."

"Oh," said the Dead Man. "So if we jump into it, we'll only be *somewhat* dead?"

"We're already somewhat dead," said the Gage. "Tsering-la, can you open the door?"

"Yes," said the Wizard.

THE SECOND ARROW STRUCK THE HOWDAH. IT BURST INTO SPLINTERS— Himadra had once seen a cannonball go through the gates of a fort—and came apart all around him. At first, he thought he too would be hurled into space, thrown from the dragon's shoulder's. But the engineers (Ata Akhimah, of course it was the Aezin Wizard) who had designed the structure had planned for its destruction, and when Himadra pulled his hand away from his eyes he found himself blinded by the rush of wind but still harnessed to the dragon. The padded platform on which he sat was a saddle now, not a bench—but the straps of his harness held him to it, and more straps held it to the dragon.

A flutter of papers turning in the air around him alerted him that the Library of Ansh-Sahal had not been so lucky.

He pulled his goggles up from around his neck, blinking to clear the tears once his eyes were protected. His hat was long gone, his jacket ripped back from his arms and full of air. He was too busy holding on for dear life either to shed it or pull it closed around him.

It came to Himadra that as much as Kyrlmyrandal was relying on his vision, he was privy to all her other senses. He could feel the air in her wings, scent the smoke and salt that filled her nostrils. And something else—a sense like currents in water but with the prickle of static on her skin.

"What's that?" he asked, as the prickle intensified to near-numbness.

"Magic," she answered. "Currents of power in the world. It's how I get around, usually."

"Something's about to—"

"—happen." She wheeled back to the mountain. Without the howdah, with his hair whipping in the wind and the cold numbing the pain of his broken bone, Himadra had a much better field of vision. He had to squint to see through the filmy outlines of the translucent monsters, but what he saw when he did so terrified him.

The beast lifted its foot—and tore that foot free. It stomped into the ocean with one island-spanning stride and a splash, and seemed to elongate as it stretched into the sky. A banner of smoke, its second leg, still connected it to the portal. Himadra yelled out loud as that leg lengthened, pulled slender—and snapped free as well.

"Oh, this is bad," said Kyrlmyrandal.

"You think?" Himadra replied.

She beat hard, spiraling into the thermal again, rising and rising. Himadra could barely see the ground—but he saw the plateau of the dragon-gate, and he saw the form of the goddess turn away from tracking them and lower her bow. His relief was short-lived, because she turned toward something in the haze of green light on the ground. A dark figure in dark robes. One who was just . . . sitting there.

"She's going to kill the priest."

"The priest is already dead."

Whether that was true of not, the Daughter tried. He saw her pick up one vast bare foot, aim like a woman at a centipede, and *stomp* with all the force of her mountainous body.

Her foot slid to the side. She staggered and had to hop to keep from falling off the mountainside. The small shape of the priest was unmoved.

With a roar, the Bad Daughter brought two of her hands around. They wielded a double-bladed axe as big as a ship's sails.

That blow fell, true and irresistible—and somehow Nizhvashiti, unmoving, resisted it. The Godmade stayed in the same posture, as near as

Himadra could tell—it was like trying to tell how an ant was sitting, from this height—and the blade just . . . turned aside.

It cracked into the basalt plateau, though, and sliced a massive gouge in the rock. And through the symbols.

The beast staggered. The beast roared. It threw back its head; its nebulous body swelled as if with a great influx of breath. The sound that issued forth was beyond deafening. It could not be heard. It could only be experienced.

It had ripped free of the volcano. Now it firmed itself and, with one mighty heave, yanked free the last smoky tendrils tethering it to the portal.

"I guess it's in the world, then," said Himadra.

"All the way," the dragon answered.

"Do we stay here and fight the evil goddess, or do we follow the alien monster?"

"I don't *know*," said Kyrlmyrandal, in a tone that made Himadra wonder if she had ever felt that helplessness before. "What's the ansha doing?"

Nizhvashiti was rising to its feet, Himadra saw. It spread its arms wide as if to receive the Bad Daughter's next blow. There was no way he should have heard its whispery voice—he and Kyrlmyrandal were a mile in the air. But he heard it nevertheless.

"Sister," it said. "Dear sister. Won't you embrace me? Can't bygones be bygones? Can we not live as a family again?"

The avatar of the goddess roared in fury, a sound indistinguishable from the roar of the volcano. She whirled a dozen arms with a dozen weapons over her head, a blur of motion that made them seem half-real.

"Fuck your mother," the Bad Daughter said, and brought all her weapons to bear.

A glint of gold showed high on the mountainside. The Gage, at a dead run along a cliff path below the snowcap. For a moment, Himadra dared hope he had some plan to intervene.

Nizhvashiti stood its ground. Its ragged robes whipped in the wind. It raised one hand to its face and tapped the chime in its eye socket.

The sound that rang forth was clear and crystalline as a glass bell. It went on and on. It rang across the water and the water seemed clearer. It rang across the sky and the sky seemed bluer. It rang across the plateau and swept images of Ravana and Ravani away, blew them from the places where they stood like smoke.

The Bad Daughter was thrust back as if someone had caught her multitudes of blows and parried, hurling her a step down the mountainside. Nizhvashiti looked up at her. She looked down at Nizhvashiti.

"I'm real, sister," the Bad Daughter said, tenderly. Her voice changed, became less the voice of a goddess and more the voice of a woman. "You're not the one I need to destroy, ansha. But I will go through you to get to Mrithuri. One bad sister deserves another."

"Well, it was worth a try," said Nizhvashiti.

The Godmade dropped its arms to its sides, squared its feet . . and began in turn to grow.

35

A CHIME THE DEAD MAN HAD HEARD BEFORE SHIVERED THROUGH THE AIR, rolled across the mountain, rang across the sea. A wave of . . . clarity went with it, as if the air had become more transparent. Suddenly he, too, could see the dragon-gate hanging before them. About an arm's length from the cliff edge, and wide enough for two Gages side by side . . . or a good-sized wagon. Or an ice-drake if it folded its wings.

No sweat. Just a long step through a shivery, immaterial frame.

If only it weren't two thousand feet in the air. If only whatever was on the other side were more than a guess and a prismatic blur.

The Dead Man made the sign of the pen. He had not come this far in his God's service—possibly, he thought, at his God's behest—to fail one final leap of faith.

He looked at the Wizards, at the Gage. "Well?"

"I'll go last," said Tsering-la, which was a kind of courage of its own. "I can keep it open, maybe, if someone tries to bar the way."

The Dead Man tugged his veil up his nose. "I'll go first."

He holstered his pistol, made sure both it and its partner were tied down, and drew his sword. There were downsides to jumping blade-first through a hole in the universe. But the Dead Man's tactical assessment supported his conclusion that those drawbacks were currently outweighed by the benefits.

"Don't look down," he told himself. "The first step is a doozy."

The Gage patted him on the back so gently it felt like a human touch. "Go."

The Dead Man went. One step, two. Running. Pebbles scattered from his boot at the cliff edge. He did not hear them fall into the seethe of lava. It was too far down. He was gone through the shimmer in the air before they struck bottom.

On the other side, he fell.

Fear clutched him. And then it was over; his boots struck earth, he absorbed the impact with knees and ankles that protested that they were way too old for this shit. He'd dropped most of his own height. No time to baby complaining joints, though. He lunged out of the way. Faster than he had needed to: the Gage waited a polite several seconds before following.

The ground shuddered when the Gage struck. The Dead Man, expecting it, didn't turn. His attention was on the horizon.

And what a horizon.

The ruined temple had been isolated, away from other habitations, bordered by that terrible sea. Here, the Dead Man stood in the midst of rubble that stretched to the sharp slopes of the naked red hills. Tumbled pillars, shattered walls.

The air reeked like rotten eggs and burned in his nostrils. He coughed, half-expecting to keep coughing until he expired on the spot, but after a short protest, his body seemed to settle in and accept the raw sensation in his chest, though not happily.

Two smaller thuds let him know that Akhimah and Tsering had made it through safely. He turned to the Gage, who had come up beside him with a stealth unsettling in a massive metal monster. "Which way?"

"To the palace," the Gage said.

Tsering-la made a sound in his throat. When the Dead Man turned to him, the Wizard had a hand to his mouth. Of course, this had been his home.

"Hey," the Dead Man said.

Tsering-la looked at him. "I thought myself prepared."

"No one could be ready for something like this." The Dead Man stroked the Wizard's arm. "I know from experience. Come on. It's best if you keep walking."

Keep walking. And never stop.

Tsering-la took a breath, then another. He looked around, nostrils flared, eyes showing their whites. He steadied himself like a horse coming down from a spook, bit his lower lip, and at last pointed. "It's hard to tell. But I think the palace was that way."

Snow mixed with ash all around them. The Dead Man helped the Wizard balance, guiding him by one elbow. Ata Akhimah walked on the other side. The Gage led, heaving aside rubble as necessary. Through his grip on Tsering-la's sleeve, the Dead Man felt it each time the Wizard flinched.

It wasn't far, but the walk seemed long. The Dead Man was aware of every uncomfortable breath, of feeling faintly disoriented and headachy—from the destruction, from the poor quality of the air. From the grief that poked him uncomfortably, like the rubble under the soles of his boots.

He was not usually an angry man. But he was angry now. Angry at all the destruction. Not just *this* destruction. All of it. The destruction of Asitaneh in his youth; the destruction of this city now. And all the many times between he had seen houses, people, livestock, livelihoods—just obliterated because of some warlord's ambition, some Wizard's megalomania. His children, his wife, his home, his duty—all of it swept away, not even a footnote to history.

History was not kind to ordinary people. They got lucky and lived in peace, or they got unlucky and war found them. There had been thousands of people in this city when some godling with a grudge had summoned up a weapon beyond human comprehension to wipe it from the earth. Ordinary people doing ordinary things.

People, not bothering anybody except their spouses and their business rivals, their illicit lovers, their parents and children. People who might have lived and died in peace rather than choking on poisoned air or having the flesh boiled from their bones. People who could do no more about it than he had been able to do when his own home fell.

Just because some ambitious villain felt it was important enough to do murder on a grand scale in order to change out which ass occupied a particular fancy chair.

The Dead Man knew he wasn't angry about Ansh-Sahal. Not really. Or not *only* about Ansh-Sahal. He had been unable to save Asitaneh. That inutile, incandescent fury still lived inside him. He had kept it from eating him alive or driving him to some futile attempt at vengeance that would only have resulted in more destruction.

But as they entered the courtyard of what had been a palace and he saw the heap—the plinth—of bodies the Gage and Nizhvashiti had both described, he realized that there *was* something he could do about this. This thing in front of him, this desecration. Right now.

These were not people who had followed his God. That didn't matter. They had been people, and they had not deserved what happened to them.

The Dead Man had seen horrors in his life. This rivaled any of them— and contained most. Bodies heaped together, stacked precipitously into a spire that did indeed resemble the Peacock Throne. A spire shaped like the sweep of a peacock's tail, the fall of a woman's columned dress. They were undeniably dead—his nose told him so even before his eyes did—but they twitched and struggled, and they all seemed lit from within by a crackled, patchy orange-pink radiance. It was the color of sunlight through eyelids, and it crawled over the pile of the dead like the mottled glow closest to low embers. In places where the flesh had broken, veins of cracked padparadscha sapphire showed through.

"I hope *these* ones don't get up and fight," said Tsering-la.

The Dead Man snorted. There was a degree of existential horror, once surpassed, after which one could do nothing but laugh.

"What are you talking about?" said the Gage.

The Dead Man didn't have time to recount the experience of fighting a deathless corpse in a basement. "I'll explain later."

"Fucking hell," said Tsering-la. "I knew some of those people."

"Some of the dead aren't glowing or . . . twitching. Why's that?"

He had never expected to find himself in the situation where that was the obvious question, rather than the opposite. He also hadn't expected the Gage to answer, but the metal man said, "I think those are the ones Nizhvashiti blessed."

"Good job, priest," said Akhimah. She pointed. "There's our sorcerer."

"Which one?" the Dead Man asked.

"I'll see to them in whatever order they prefer," the Gage answered, stepping forward.

The Dead Man fell in behind. He craned his head back. This unhallowed mockery could not be any taller than the real Peacock Throne, but somehow it seemed to stretch to an indistinct height. When he blinked and shaded his eyes, though, he could see that someone sat upon it. A figure that blurred into a series of half-seen shapes stretching out behind it, as the many arms of the manifested goddess had at the Origin of Storms.

Ravana—he thought. Perhaps. But a Ravana stretched and altered, crowned in a horrible orange light. Something swirled around him—a vortex of dark flecks like a thick swarm of insects. It concealed and revealed him by segments—an arm, a shoulder, a hand. He wore a brilliantly colored coat with a furry collar. He sat upon a tiger pelt spread over the heaving bodies beneath. His feet were planted on the heads of two unfortunates immured in the terrible throne. His arms rested along bowed spines. A long braid draped his shoulder, thick as a wrist.

"What a pity," he said, in a chorus of anharmonic voices. "For you to have come so far, to such a terrible place, and all in vain."

"Great," said the Gage. "I was just thinking that what we needed was a Villain Speech."

The column of the dead twitched, humped, elongated. A thick tendril split from each side. It stretched upward. The base divided. One half wrenched free and slammed forward, bent like the knee of a man about to stand from an obeisance.

It wobbled.

It rose.

"Well, that's not good," the Dead Man said.

The worst was the sound. You couldn't call it screaming, because there was so little air behind it. A whispered keening slipped from a thousand mutilated throats at once. It rose and fell in waves, each step punctuated by sibilant cries as the shifting weight of the abomination forced air in and out of the lungs of those trapped within. It shambled forward as if finding its balance.

"They're dead," the Dead Man told himself. "They can't feel pain."

The Gage tilted toward him slightly. "Are you sure about that?"

Ata Akhimah rubbed her hands together. "What if that's an illusion too?"

"What if it isn't? Hit it now, while it's still off-balance." Tsering-la suited action to words. Yellow light streaked from his fingertips. It found a crevice between bodies aligned like muscle fibers, penetrated, and expanded catastrophically.

The Dead Man assumed that was the plan, anyway. What actually happened was a brief, sharp expansion—and then a contraction, just as sharp, as the bodies recovered from cavitation.

"Recovered" was perhaps not the correct word. Bones snapped. Limbs tore. There might have been a limp, the suggestion of a stagger before the structural corpses knit themselves together again. The abomination lurched forward, hands reaching out, each finger a dead person. The sorcerer's throne was its head, staying miraculously oriented as the monstrosity slouched forward. Like the head of a bird on a swaying branch, and just as disconcerting.

This was worse than being strangled by somebody's intestines, the Dead Man thought. He sheathed his sword, snatched a pistol out. Cocked and leveled it. He aimed not for the abomination but for the sorcerer in his chair.

"Gods, that must smell," said the Gage, striding forward. "Sitting up there."

"I can assure you it does," said the Dead Man. "And I'm not even on top of it."

The Dead Man felt his pistol leap against his hand. He knew he hit. He felt it in the part of himself that knew the shot was good before the ball ever left the gun. He squinted—and saw no response. No lurch, no clutch at a chest. Not even a wave of the hand.

"This is not going well."

"Stay back," said Ata Akhimah, and channeled her power.

A hissing column of sparks erupted between the abomination's misshapen feet. It licked upward, bathing one side of the monstrous giant in lightning. Flesh sizzled, bodies contracted. The smell of roasting, rotten meat made the Dead Man's gorge want to rise.

High above, the sorcerer laughed, voices layered as if by echoes, strangely resonant. The thing stumped forward again, burned bones cracking.

No time to reload, and the Dead Man might as well save his other gun. He put the fired one in its holster and dragged his sword out again. He hoped he wasn't about to ruin the temper on a second blade.

A great hand grabbed at Ata Akhimah. The Dead Man saw it coming and stepped in front. His hip led his shoulder, his shoulder led his wrist, his wrist led his sword. The sword passed through the neck on the "thumb," and the poor victim's head rolled away. The Dead Man only kept his feet because of fifty years of footwork. Lopping off heads was supposed to be considerably harder.

Most things yank their hand back when you hack off a piece of it, but not this squelching horror. The grab kept coming. The Dead Man braced his hilt with a cupped hand, aiming for a staring eye in the palm. If he could wedge his blade against the back of the skull, maybe that would keep the hand from closing on him—

A wall of yellow light knocked the hand aside.

The Gage lunged past, accelerating toward the abomination, pistons driving, flagstones shattering under his feet. He struck the thing's leading leg head-on, not slowing, charging through flames and into the rotting pillar of flesh, arms pinwheeling.

It exploded around him. The abomination fell to a knee, the sorcerer shouting curses in his chair. It grabbed at the Gage with the hand the Dead Man had injured—or "injured"—and swept him up. The Gage's arms burst out from his sides. The fist around him shredded into a dreadful spray that splashed—among other things—Tsering-la's shield, leaving the rest of them standing in the one clean patch among the rubble.

The Gage fell.

He didn't hit the ground, because the abomination's other arm swung around like a club and knocked him flying. The Gage sailed away like a kicked bladder. It was seconds before the Dead Man heard him hit, a tremendous clang of stone and metal that was painful even at a distance.

The abomination pulled itself together—literally, shattered bits reknitting to the whole. One arm was shorter than the other. The whole creature seemed a tiny bit smaller.

That was all.

It straightened, wearing the sorcerer like a crown.

THE GOOD DAUGHTER WAS A GREAT AND TERRIBLE GODDESS, AND HIMADRA had never been so reminded of it as in this moment—astride a dragon's back, watching her apotheosis.

Nizhvashiti's gaunt form straightened. It reached out its arms like someone stretching to greet awakening. By the time it completed the gesture, it was the size of Kyrlmyrandal. By the time it—she—took her first step forward, she was as big as the avatar of her sister.

Her wrap was full of stars. Her face was as bright as silver. Her sandals wound calves like graceful pillars. Her eyes were two calm pools of water, featureless and alight.

She reached out and grasped her sister's shoulder. When the sister turned, the Good Daughter punched her in the face.

The beast swung back and roared. Its roar was the deep rumble of a landslide, the shudder of earthquakes cracking the ground. It reached out a hand clawed in lightning on an arm that elongated fantastically. It swiped at the God that had been Nizhvashiti.

The goddess danced, her drapes swirling around her. She moved with the lightness of a gazelle, the power of a warrior. Like a lithe tiger she swept beneath the blow, her backward bend as graceful as a dancer's. She cart-wheeled, a trail of stars weaving behind her. When she rose again, the trail had formed itself into a sword for her right hand.

The beast swiped at her again, hunching like a twisted funnel cloud. The Bad Daughter too reached out. She found a shaft of sunlight streaming through the smoke and broke it off with a gesture like a child snapping off a branch. She twirled it in her unnumbered hands. She lunged, stamping her foot, and what extended from her hands was a burning spear.

The Good Daughter parried, riposted to keep the beast at bay, gave a step under a flurry of blows. Each parry rang with a sound like a crystal bell. They layered over one another, sustained, until the fusillade became atonal music.

Now it was two against one, and she was driven back another step, then another.

The basalt plateau was small by comparison to the gods that stood astride it. Himadra wondered what would happen when the Good Daughter ran out of room to retreat.

Perhaps she would just step out onto the air.

Far above, Himadra sat alone on the back of a dragon, the warm wind playing in his hair, and felt as helpless—as small and fragile as he ever had in this world, this lifetime.

And he felt, through Kyrlmyrandal, enormous, world-spanning, pro-foundly free.

The pain from his thigh was old and familiar—and distanced, one more pain among all the ancient dragon's aches and hurts—as he cast himself more and more into Kyrlmyrandal's sensations. He was not good at this, not experienced. Not like the women, who had learned the skill from youth. If there were dangers, he didn't know them. Could he lose himself inside the dragon's mind? Would his body die if he went too far into the link with her?

How did you dispel a god incarnate? How did you jam a beast back into the crevices between the worlds?

He said, "We need to go help the Godmade."

The dragon rumbled. "You are hurt. You are fragile."

Would losing himself be so bad? He had heirs to carry on. If he could save the world for them. If he died there. Then he died in the best way he could imagine.

"You avoided me before. *Can* you breathe fire?"

The dragon paused. Perhaps he had surprised her. "You know, I haven't tried in a very long time."

"It probably wouldn't do much against a beast made of captured volcano anyway."

"It might," Kyrlmyrandal said. "Dragonfire is not so much a chemical process as a metaphor. We, after all, come from somewhere else as well."

"Well," Himadra said. "I'm not doing anything else right now."

Kyrlmyrandal said, "Then hold on, and by the Vast Black keep your eyes open." She bent herself into a dive, folded her wings, and dropped like a cannonball.

Kyrlmyrandal had begun her dive from so high in the thermal that the struggling figures below looked like whittled twig dolls. The wind was so sharp, it hurt. Himadra would have buried his face in his arms and shut his eyes, but the dragon needed them. At least he had the goggles. Ata Akhimah came in handy, sometimes.

A thin trickle of smoke drifted from Kyrlmyrandal's nostrils. It smelled stagnant and odd as it whipped past Himadra, like the cinders of a wet campfire. She snorted as if clearing the pipes. A modestly stronger but intermittent trickle followed.

"Are you sure this is going to work?"

The words were ripped from him by the wind, but because they were linked, the dragon heard them in her mind.

"I'm trying to work up to it. Let me concentrate."

Himadra thought about arguing. Then he thought about the impudence of arguing with a gigantic beast as old as the world. He laughed to himself and set his eyes and intention forward, as if he were riding his horse at a jump. There was the beast, twisting itself in the column of smoke. There was the Bad Daughter. There was the goddess that had risen from Nizhvashiti.

None of them paid any attention to Kyrlmyrandal falling like a falcon from the sky.

"Steady," she told him. The body underneath him expanded—a huge, held breath. The beast and the Bad Daughter hammered at the other god— the beast swinging fists as if taking blows at an anvil, the Bad Daughter twirling and thrusting with her incandescent spear that left bright-edged black streaks behind it like the afterimages of an Uncauled Sun. The Good Daughter's star-forged sword was a blur, moving so fast it could have been a thousand bright swords held in a thousand black hands.

Whatever happened, Himadra thought, he had witnessed Nizhvashiti's exaltation. And it was beautiful.

Something alerted the beast before they were upon it. It could have been as slight as the rush of air through Kyrlmyrandal's wings. Or maybe, like the Gage, it could see without eyes. It turned. Himadra thought he saw its eyes narrow. He was probably imagining things.

They were going to plow right into it. It was only smoke, but it was smoke solid enough to batter the Good Daughter's blade aside. Its arm began to swing, sweeping incredibly fast across a gigantic distance. Himadra could already see that it would intersect their path.

"Eyes open!" the dragon reminded him, which was the first moment he knew that they were closed. He blinked them open again. The enormous arm seemed inches away.

Kyrlmyrandal snapped her wings wide, flipped sideways like a bat despite the sudden sharp pain that made Himadra gasp, and spat her held breath right in the Beast's surprised face. A gale of reeking smoke blew from her broken-fanged mouth, spittle like embers sparkling among it. She coughed, and a single fat ball of fire issued lazily forth.

They whipped past with a horrible flapping sound like a torn sail in the wind. Himadra unwisely jerked his head around and realized that a rib had cracked in his chest. His vision swam with the pain. But he saw the beast try to bat the pathetic ball of fire into the ocean—

—and then grasp its arm and bellow in pain. The fireball burned into its smoky substance, lighting it purple and green from within. Kyrlmyrandal banked and rose, struggling hard to gain altitude.

"You have to land," Himadra said. "One patch has started to tear free in your wing."

"If I land," said the dragon, "I'll never get off the ground again."

"What are you going to do, burp at him again?"

"He didn't like it last time," she answered, flapping frantically up the column of rising air. "And every little bit helps, don't you think?"

36

THE RAIN PLASTERED MRITHURI'S BLOUSE AND UNDERSKIRT TO HER BODY. Water sheeted over her feet as she splashed across the courtyard, but at least it was warm. She felt as if cold had seeped into her soul, not just her bones. She couldn't stop shaking.

And Sayeh was going to be up there on Vara's neck, soaked to the bone, probably freezing. Even as Mrithuri thought it, though, she saw the oiled silk pavilion pitched next to the rain-veiled hulk of Vara, his red-stained wings washed white again by the rain. His head was sunk between his shoulders, his red-outlined eyes half-lidded, pale blue like gigantic aquamarines. If a bird could glower, he was glowering.

One of Mrithuri's austringers stood by his head, looking both awed and worried. He was about the right size for a morsel the bird might snap down like an owl downing a mouse, though so far, Vara was restraining himself.

Feeding him was going to be a problem. Where would they get so many bones?

Sayeh, sensibly, was both warmly dressed and dry under the pavilion roof. Yavashuri stood beside her, and beside Yavashuri was the person Mrithuri had asked Yavashuri to fetch. Someone Mrithuri had never seen in the light, and never outside the cloistered halls of the priestesshood.

The head anchorite of Sarathai-tia.

The nun stood dressed all in red, veiled over her tunic and trousers. The skin around her eyes was unlined, for it had been decades since her face had been exposed to the Cauled Sun. But the hair that escaped from her veil was white as swan feathers.

The rain had died back to a drizzle, and the howl in the wind was gone. Mrithuri stepped under the awning, teeth chattering. Yavashuri frowned at her and took the shawl from around her own shoulders to drape Mrithuri.

"Fine empress you'll make, dead of a chill."

Mrithuri clutched the warm goat-hair at her neck, too cold to resist. She looked at the anchorite. "Mother, are you ready for this?"

The nun raised her palm to the brightening sky. "I have to be, don't I?"

Mrithuri looked up and realized with a clench of horror what she was seeing. The rain was pattering to a stop, the clouds burning away from a bright sky. Mrithuri had lost track of time in the storm and the fight.

The brightness beyond was not the Heavenly River. It was the Cauled Sun, cauled no longer.

The black disk that hid its face glided aside, slowly revealing the bloated inferno behind. It scorched through the clouds, raising steam from the flag-stones.

"Your Magnanimity," Yavashuri said, "you'll burn your eyes."

Hastily, Mrithuri looked down, blinking afterimages from her gaze. She stepped farther under the shelter of the pavilion. "It drowned us; now it scorches."

"The one we do not mention is breaking her chains," said the anchorite. "Let us not tarry."

A stepladder was set beside Vara, which first Sayeh and then the ancho-rite mounted. The harness had bolsters sewn onto it, cut from side-saddles, so one woman could ride on each side of Vara's neck, comfortably seated and strapped safely in. Sayeh still looked drawn as she fastened and checked her buckles.

Mrithuri stepped out into the overwhelming brightness of the sun. Her hair steamed like the flagstones. She had to shade her eyes with her hand, and she could already feel her skin contracting in the harsh light and the heat.

She reached up and touched Sayeh's toe. Their eyes met. There were so many things she wanted to express, but the words she found were "Don't widow me again so soon."

Sayeh winked, her face almost lost in the glare. "I could say the same to you. Take care of Drupada for me."

Somberly, Mrithuri nodded. She stepped back under the pavilion, flanked by Yavashuri and the austringer. When Vara opened his wings, their shade was a blessing.

A brief blessing, because the wings stroked down, and with two mighty flaps Vara leaped to the top of Sarathai-tia's highest tower. For a moment he perched there, head sliding side to side as if independent from his body, surveying the horizon. He seemed untroubled by the glare, but a raptor's eyes were adapted to the brightness of the open sky. He opened his beak and squealed, a ridiculous high-pitched sound rendered earth-shaking and skull-piercing by his size.

Mrithuri clapped her hands to her ears, pitying Sayeh and the anchorite. Vara lifted his wings again and with one enormous beat he sailed from the tower, headed east. In an instant, he was out of sight behind the walls.

Mrithuri took Yavashuri's hand. "Let's run."

The flagstones were nearly dry, and already warm from the heat of the unveiled sun. The women's feet slapped them as they dashed from the shel-ter of the pavilion into the shade of the palace entry. Inside, they did not pause, but ran to the open door to the Hall of the Throne. Mrithuri was not out of breath—until she saw within.

The light of the searing sun glittered and broke as it streamed through the dragonglass ceiling. It filled the throne room with a moving green lambency like the light at the bottom of a still pool. Radiance poured in rays between her fingers when she raised her hand.

The light through the dragonglass bathed her in renewed strength, in power. Any chill fell away from her.

She turned in awe to Yavashuri. "It has never seen such light before."

Yavashuri took back the shawl. "What will you do now?"

Mrithuri looked up at the glittering pillar of the throne. "Fight."

ATA AKHIMAH CONSIDERED HERSELF A PERSON WHO WAS, GENERALLY, PREPARED. But she had *not* been prepared to see the Gage hurled through the air to land with a terrific crunch somewhere in the rubble, too far away for her to tell what had become of him.

She expected the abomination to turn back toward her, Tsering-la, and the Dead Man. She was even more surprised—and embarrassed to feel relieved—when it wheeled and squelched unevenly away, toward where the Gage had been hurled.

"It hates him," she said. "No, I mean the *sorcerer* hates him. Why does the sorcerer hate him?"

Tsering-la shook his head. "We hate people who have harmed us, or who have something we lack, or who make us feel we're not doing what we should."

"Hmm," said the Dead Man. "Or against whom we've sinned, and so wish to justify it." It had the sound of a quotation. He put his sword away without looking, drew the gun Akhimah had made for him, and weighed it in his hand. "What do you think?"

"Give me a moment," Akhimah said. "I just had an idea."

She reached out with her Wizardry the same way she did when calling down the lightning or summoning a spark. This time, though, she didn't try to *call* anything. She just let herself *feel*. Feel for the energy running through whatever passed for nerves in the lurching monster stumbling toward where the Gage had fallen.

And there it was, as she had suspected, like pins and needles inside her mind. A bright tickle, a tingle. A sensation of power—of activation—running through the corpses. Like the power she could feel when she designed an arch, or a tool, or the Dead Man's gun.

"When I say," she told the Dead Man.

He grunted assent.

"Want a distraction?" Tsering-la asked.

"Yes." All her concentration on that flow of energy. She unclenched her jaw, told herself to breathe. "Now."

A dozen flowering witch-lanterns blinked into being around the sorcerer's throne, darting at his face, sparking against the coral-colored aura that protected him. They came from the front and the side, from above, diving like birds protecting their nest. As if they were trying to keep the monster from reaching the Gage.

The three on the ground followed, scrambling over debris and unspeakable remnants as the corpse-beast lurched on, unaffected. But the sorcerer swiped at the lanterns with his blurred hands, distracted. His aura thickened at the front and thinned behind, pushing the lights away from his face.

Akhimah took up those tickling skeins of energy and drew in one deep breath to brace herself. When she let it out again she said, "Dead Man," and gave the skeins a yank.

The construct staggered, its shorter leg buckling. The pistol went off, the report leaving Akhimah's ear ringing. A spray of bright blood surrounded the sorcerer's head as he was hurled forward by the impact—

The construct skipped a step, like a man who had stumbled, and caught itself. The sounds of crunching bone and tearing flesh turned Akhimah's stomach. Tsering used the distraction and extended his shields again, ripping part of the other leg asunder.

The sagging sorcerer straightened, pushing himself up on the corpse arms of his horrible chair. The blurred sense of possibilities around him thickened. He reached his arms up, stretched, and when he turned back, he was someone else. A woman, with the same thick braid and pugnacious jaw.

"Damn it," the Dead Man said, reloading without looking down.

"Huh," said Tsering-la. "Multiple bodies, I guess?"

"Wonder where it stores them," Akhimah replied. "And how many we're going to have to destroy."

THE GAGE PICKED HIS DENTED BODY OUT OF THE RUBBLE WHERE IT HAD landed, dust and snow powdering from his joints. He shook himself, feeling the places where bent metal scraped. When he stepped forward, his left hip grated. His left foot dragged on the stone at the beginning of its arc, a trail of sparks in its wake.

The sensation of vulnerability reminded him too much of human frailty. It made him angry.

Anger was good.

He clenched his gauntlets and went to meet the abomination lurching toward him. The air was growing noticeably warmer, the sky brighter with every step he took. Ash and mist blew off the heavens as if someone had opened a door to clear a smoky room. What had been a bright spot wore through the clouds and was revealed as a blazing sun. A sun the Gage had never seen before.

When he and Nizhvashiti had been there before, there had been no sun. Only cold and empty stars. This sun came out noon-high, hot and close. The Gage's metal body soaked the heat in. His surface would soon be scorching. And the humans would probably be prostrated with heat very fast.

But before either of those things happened, he had to deal with Ravana's unholy, ambulatory throne. It stank in the sudden heat and squelched as it shambled toward him, unbalanced on damaged legs, the male sorcerer who had piloted it a moment before now replaced by a woman.

"Die, won't you?" she yelled, her voice carrying over the ringing and screeching of the Gage's uncareful steps.

"Sorry," he called back. "No immediate plans to!" He heaved a chunk of fallen column at her. The monstrosity batted it aside. Bones snapped. Its awful hand fell limp.

The Gage stopped. He tilted his head back and pretended to look up at the creature. "You know," he said conversationally in a voice that could carry across battlefields, "you sold away far too much when you bargained with the beast to leave behind your mortality. Your name, your freedom. And what was Ravana to you? Anything? You've lost him, too."

The Gage was guessing, but he had half a century's experience as a servant of Wizards to draw on in addition to decades on his own.

"Hah! Why would anybody want to be human?" Ravani swiped at him with the monstrosity's unbroken hand.

"Don't ask me," the Gage said. "But you're the smart one, aren't you?"

She laughed angrily. The monstrosity lurched to a halt and stood facing him, turned halfway so its back wasn't to the Wizards and the Dead Man. They were running to catch up, but there was a distance to cross.

"He hates you," she said.

"I know." The Gage tugged his tattered robes straight. Clothes never seemed to last on him. "He hates me because I'm what he wanted to be, doesn't he?"

Ravani glowered at him, her pugnacious jaw set hard enough to chip teeth.

"You're trapped in those bodies."

"It's meat," Ravani said. "It rots." She kicked a heel back against her horrible throne. "He's like a caterpillar eaten away by the wasp inside. Hollow."

"And you?" the Gage asked.

She snorted. "Maybe I started that way."

The sun seared down like coals above a grill. The Gage felt the lubricant in his joints loosening. He hadn't known heat like this since he crossed the endless sand-sea deserts south of Messaline.

"You were something else once," the Gage said tenderly. "Was it better than what you are now?"

He held up a palm to keep the Dead Man and the Wizards back. The searing and unexpected heat was taking a toll on all of them, he saw. Even the Dead Man. But especially Tsering-la.

They saw his gesture and stopped running. Trusting him. Trusting whatever he was doing.

What the hell *was* he doing?

"Bought," said Ravani. "Sold, and paid for. Like everyone else. Bought like everyone in the world."

The Gage nodded. "Ravana told the masters of the walking cities to look for me, didn't he? Or was it you?"

She snorted. "You know your Eyeless One profits from the taxes on those. She's not so pure."

The Gage eyed her throne of corpses but decided she probably already knew. "Which of us are?"

"I guess we'll find out," Ravani said.

Her throne knelt. It bowed down, though somehow her chair stayed level. The genuflection brought the brow to earth, so once she stood, she had only to step down to stand on the flagstones. There was no snow anymore, and even the glistening wetness was steaming off the ground.

"Oh, screw it," she said. She stripped her gloves off, one by one. "Ravana's as good as dead. And me . . . I quit. The beast can spin its own lies and fight its own wars. I repudiate it."

The monstrous throne shuddered. Without straightening, it collapsed like an arch with the keystone pulled, slumping into a horrible pile of bodies. Ravani stepped back, as if it now disgusted her. She just looked like a woman now. The echoes of other beings, other possibilities around her faded one by one.

The Gage thought of lights flickering out in the windows of a distant city.

The Wizards and the Dead Man came up behind her, picking their way around the small mountain of dishonored dead. The Dead Man looked as if he were about to grasp Ravani's elbow, but perhaps he caught the air between the sorcerer and the Gage. His hand dropped back to his holstered gun.

A scurrying sound reached them, like the skitter of crab feet on rocks. The Gage wished he had eyes to close, or that he could not see behind himself as plainly as in front. There was an object cresting the next hill to the south of them. A thing like a storm cloud walking on legs of rain and lightning—but solid, quite solid. And coming from the direction of the poisoned desert where the dragons had fought and died. And rendered their mortal energies bound up in the fused glass they left upon the murderous plain.

"Oh, for fuck's sake," said Ata Akhimah. "What the hell is that?"

"The Many-Legged Truth," the Gage replied. "You didn't answer who sent it after me. You, was it? Or the other one?"

"You see, the thing is," Ravani finished, as if no one had spoken in between, "I can't fight the beast. It won't let me. And the beast? It *can* fight its own wars."

The Gage turned, his foot dragging an arc of sparks behind him. The grease in his joints was loose and fluid in the heat. Sparks landed in the gaps, and between two ticks of his gears, he was wreathed in a thick, greasy fire.

He began down the hill toward the walking city, which was running before a poisoned wind.

Said he, "So can I."

THE WIND WAS ENOUGH TO BEAR THE WEIGHT OF SAYEH'S ARM WHEN SHE lifted it. She was glad of the goggles Ata Akhimah had given her, and glad to have had Mrithuri's spares to offer to the anchorite. They flew side by side, shoulder to shoulder across the bearded vulture's pale neck. The naked sun burned her skin where cloth didn't cover it. She wished for a hat, not that a hat would have withstood the wind of their passage.

She was aware of Vara's mind and intention, his confusion at finding himself so vast. She felt the wind moving the surfaces of his feathers. It was not so different from riding inside Guang Bao.

The sun did not dazzle the vulture's eyes, so Sayeh closed her own.

"Hold on," shouted the anchorite. "This will be unpleasant."

Sayeh, watching with Vara's sight, did not see what happened on his back. But the sky tore open before him, as if somebody had punched a blade through paper and ripped it wide. Beyond lay cold blackness strewn with icy stars. "Hold your breath!" the anchorite called.

Sayeh, hastily, did.

At her urging, Vara plunged into the gap in the sky.

After the heat of the revealed sun, the cold struck her like a wall. She managed not to gasp. Her eyelashes tugged as rime tried to stick them together. Vara's squeal of protest sounded thin and cold, his wingbeats muffled.

There was no up, no down, no sense of gravity. The stars wheeled around them as if they fell, but Sayeh had no sense of spinning, of momentum. It was as disorienting as being tumbled by a wave. She buried freezing hands in her armpits and tried not to lick her lips.

How long could she hold her breath? How bad would it be if she didn't? Vara was breathing, but she could feel the cold, thin air searing even his nostrils. Sayeh went lightheaded.

The cold stars spun.

37

Kyrlmyrandal wheeled at the apex of her thermal. For a moment, Himadra knew what it felt like to be a thunderhead, spilling off the top of the updraft, swept sideways in the wind. He held himself stiffly upright, grateful now for the cold that numbed him, pressing his arm against the stabbing ache in his chest for support.

From what he could see from there, the Good Daughter seemed briefly to be gaining ground. While the beast was distracted—clawing gobbets out of its own self and hurling the dragonfire-touched stuff into the ocean—she was holding her own, winning back a step or two. He supposed he shouldn't be surprised the fight was in such close equilibrium. The Good Daughter and the Bad Daughter were sisters, after all.

The Bad Daughter's incandescent spear flickered in her grasp like shafts of sunlight falling through leaves. It fell here, then there, without seeming to pass through the space between. As Kyrlmyrandal folded her wings and fell into her next pass at the beast, Himadra saw how the spear's shining point scored the basalt plateau where it missed the Good Daughter, leaving smoking gouges behind.

The Good Daughter danced and parried, blades in four or six or a dozen hands, her impassive face with its shining eyes the image of Nizhvashiti's. Himadra could just make out the tiny form of the Godmade inside her, its hands resting on crossed legs, its head bowed motionless. Each of the goddesses had come into the world through a physical avatar, but while the Bad Daughter had apparently subsumed and remade Chaeri's body into her own enormous form, the Good Daughter seemed to be reaching *through* her ansha.

Himadra's chest stabbed with every breath. Wetness bubbled into his mouth. He knew without wiping at it that it was blood.

The beast loomed large beneath them. It turned, eyes like cinders burning deep in ash, and one arm as long and gray as a stormfront hurtled toward them.

The dragon's ribs swelled as she drew in a huge breath.

"I hope you have a plan!" Himadra yelled, and blood blew back on his goggles. He didn't try to wipe it away, knowing that would only make it worse. The wind drew each droplet into a hairlike streak.

Kyrlmyrandal's answer was to backwing suddenly, with a force that rocked Himadra against the belts. Something small in his wrist snapped, and his left thumb too. He screamed out loud at the tearing sensation in Kyrlmyrandal's wing, a pain that overwhelmed his own. More blood blew into the wind and was whipped sideways this time. Kyrlmyrandal hung in the sky, starting to sideslip as her torn wing luffed.

She threw her held breath out like a singer exhaling from the diaphragm. He felt her body collapse, constrict from back to front, even with the wooden saddle isolating him. The heat from the blue-white flames leaping from her jaws washed back and sizzled his beard. His skin drew tight. He shielded his face with his broken hand.

Kyrlmyrandal's flames seared down, met the beast's arm, and consumed the entire thing. It bellowed again, a sound Himadra thought would render him deaf for hours. His ears rang as if he had stood too close to a cannon. He held on to straps with his right hand as Kyrlmyrandal spiraled down and away toward the water. She did not beat her wings. Himadra could feel, through her, the wind rippling the edges of the tear. She fell like a leaf, controlling the limping glide, slipping back and forth as the ocean rose up to meet them. The beast turned, raging, its remaining limb clawing toward them. Kyrlmyrandal dodged the blow at the cost of altitude, jarring Himadra against the straps once again. He was too lost in her pain and his own to know if the jolt did any more damage, but it sure hurt.

The beast splashed in pursuit. Kyrlmyrandal arrowed toward the mountain, still high enough to clear the peak, but Himadra imagined that even if she could survive a flight through the volcano's seething ash cloud, it would cook him alive.

Well, if that was the cost of defeating the beast, he would take it. It would be quicker than waiting for his lungs to fill with blood.

A little faith here, Kyrlmyrandal said inside his head, but he thought she sounded worried.

Then the sky in front of them tore open.

VARA FELL OUT OF DARKNESS INTO BLINDING, ENDLESS BLUE. THE HEAT OF AN Uncauled Sun whisked away the frost riming Sayeh's lashes and rimming her nose. Her lips cracked and bled. She looked over at the anchorite. The old woman shaded her eyes with her hands. She had pulled her veil aside, and her peach-smooth face was split with a wondering grin. "I always wondered if I could do that," she said happily.

Her smile melted. "Oh. That's bad."

Sayeh followed the line of her gaze. Off to Sayeh's side of the great bird's neck, a smoking island loomed, molten rock plunging down a cliff into the steaming ocean like the opposite of a waterfall. Titanic figures battled on the mountain's flank, one with swords flashing and parrying the blindingly bright spear of the other.

Above them, but rapidly descending, was a speck Sayeh recognized as Kyrlmyrandal. And beyond her was a towering blackness, a twisted thing of smoke and lightning so huge, it seemed to swallow the horizon.

"Oh," Sayeh agreed. "What are we going to do?"

A BEARDED VULTURE HALF AS BIG AS THE DRAGON BURST THROUGH THE RIP IN the sky. The tear healed behind it. Himadra caught a glimpse of two figures on its back. Surely, Mrithuri could not have come *there*.

Kyrlmyrandal fluttered downward like a shot hawk, and Himadra kept his eyes open and prayed. The Good Daughter's blades danced and wove, deflecting the point of her sister's spear into the mountainside, into the beach, into the sea. The Good Daughter seemed to be bleeding now, if gods bled—a line on her cheek dripped light, and light ran down her shoulder and the length of one arm. The Bad Daughter seemed untouched, and she was laughing. The sound rolled over Himadra like the sound of a storm beating a hollow roof. It took the heart right out of him.

What did it matter? His body was failing. Kyrlmyrandal was falling from the sky. Even if they made it down and survived the landing, they were out of the fight. It was done—

The clamor of the goddesses in combat grew over the roar of the volcano and the roar of the beast. The beast splashed back toward the island, each step like a tidal wave, pursuing Kyrlmyrandal. Its single arm lashed out and fell short of Kyrlmyrandal but missed the vulture by almost no margin at all. Enormous feathers spiraled toward the water. The bird squealed and beat higher.

Suddenly, Sayeh was in Kyrlmyrandal's awareness beside Himadra. He felt her gasp, her body contracting as she assimilated both his and Kyrlmyrandal's pain.

"Ah," Kyrlmyrandal said. "I thought feeding him dragonbones would be interesting."

"You're hurt," Sayeh said unnecessarily. "No, never mind. The anchorite can open dragon-gates."

"The Good Daughter is losing," Himadra said as her sister's spear-tip pierced her thigh. "Can you open the door they're standing on? Send them back where they came from?"

In the brief pause, he could only assume that Sayeh was conferring with the anchorite. She said, "It's already open. I suppose that's how they got into the world in the first place. She also says there's another small door just above the place where the lava is coming from—"

"Where does that go?"

"Ansh-Sahal," Kyrlmyrandal said. "Our friends went through it not long since."

"You didn't tell me that!" Himadra gasped. It was hard to breathe. Filling his lungs might as well have been stabbing himself in the chest. Things bubbled and shifted inside him.

"The anchorite thinks she can make it big enough to trap the beast back in the Between Places. If we can decoy it there," said Sayeh. "No, I'm sorry. She's not sure she can, but says she's willing to try."

Kyrlmyrandal had found the updraft alongside the volcano's plume. Himadra understood now what she had meant when she said to trust her. Her damaged wing had enough lift to keep her in the air, even climbing a little, as long as she balanced on the hot, rising air. It hurt, but what was pain?

"What are the downsides?" Himadra asked.

"She says——" There was a pause where Himadra could only assume she was asking the anchorite his question and receiving an answer. "She says the beast is powerful and might damage the Between Places and things that intersect them."

Like the cloisters and the dragon-gates. Probably other things, too.

A warm breeze that reeked of brimstone tickled in his hair. No rush of wind now: they were rising with it, part of the thermal.

Sayeh continued. "And it might just tear through the other side of the door."

"Where our friends are."

"You're the warlord." Her mental tone was full of complicated emotion. Resentment, resignation. She'd never forgive him, but she was willing to respect his skill.

It was probably more than he deserved.

"It might give the Good Daughter a fighting chance."

Kyrlmyrandal spiraled behind the column of ash. When she emerged, the beast was that much closer. It noticed the god-battle still in progress on the shoulder of the mountain. The Good Daughter, gleaming with silvery starlight, had rallied. Step by step she beat her sister back. The beast swung around and reached its clawed hand toward her.

Kyrlmyrandal bellowed, a warning that stunned Himadra's already-ringing ears. The Good Daughter parried with a sword like the hook of a quarter-moon. But the distraction was enough.

Her sister stepped inside her guard and grasped her wrist as she was off balance. With a twist of her hip and a dropped head, the Bad Daughter hurled the Good over her shoulders and into the mountainside.

Trees splintered; the mountain shuddered. A gout of lava sprayed from the open vent. Himadra saw the shimmer of the dragon-gate the anchorite meant to open as a pale silhouette against red-black fountains.

The Good Daughter dragged herself back, trying to sit upright. Could a god be stunned? She struggled; that much was obvious. And her sister and the beast bore down.

"Do it," Himadra said.

Kyrlmyrandal folded her tattered wings and fell from the rising column of air like a stone. The beast reached back, winding up to slam its remaining fist into the fallen goddess. The dragon zipped past its chest, slashing a stream of blue-white flame behind her. Himadra knew it was foolish, but he bent as close to her as saddle and harness would allow, as if lying along the neck of a horse as it charged through trees.

Now there was a wind.

They plunged toward the cliff face, toward the caved-in place where the volcano vented. Their path—their dive—seemed as if it would plunge them directly into the glowing spray. That would be a faster death than a collapsed lung too.

Himadra gritted his teeth and held on. They skimmed over the shining doorway, the beast's clutching arm snatching after Kyrlmyrandal's tail. The lava fountained—and again the hot air caught them, sent them up like a seed puff on a child's breath. A child's breath, if that breath were searing. Himadra's skin stung and contracted as if from the burn of a too-close fire.

One of the figures on the vulture's neck pointed toward the mountain, and behind them the door tore open wide. A cold wind ripped the veil of heat away, so bitter and unexpected that Himadra yelled out loud—a reflex he regretted, because the pain made him cough and the coughing filled his mouth with blood.

Kyrlmyrandal sailed out over the cliff edge, into the plume of steam from the lava pouring into the sea. It billowed around them. She turned on her good wing, rising. Himadra saw the beast's legs and lashing tail as it vanished through the rent in reality.

"I think I'm done." Kyrlmyrandal sank rapidly, wobbling on her downward trajectory. "This wing has given what it had."

"We'll do what we can," Sayeh answered.

Himadra didn't answer. He saw the ocean rushing up at them, the silvery sands of the beach. The long combers rolling over shallow water—

They hit with a splash that threw rainbows into the air. The dragon found her footing, folded her wings—as best she could—and breasted toward the shore. Her long body didn't drag only because it was floating until the last few steps. She crawled a little way above the high-tide mark and let herself collapse into the warm sand with a sigh. Her tail still dangled in the water.

Himadra fought with his harness one-handed. The cracked thumb was swollen stiff, and moving the wrist brought sharp tears to his eyes. Somehow he pushed leather through buckles, helped as the sun warmed and softened it.

After some time, Kyrlmyrandal recovered herself enough to raise one fore-foot and lift him gently down between thumb and finger without stabbing him with her talons.

"We're alive," gasped Himadra, sprawling on the warm sand. The sun would begin to bother him soon. But for now it was a blessing. Lying flat on his back, his thigh straight, his pelvis cradled by the beach, he almost felt he could draw a full breath.

"Who'd have thought it?" the dragon said.

The mountain jumped. The sand under his back shuddered. He didn't know if it was the goddesses still at war, or the volcano. Either way, there was nothing he could do about it.

"It might not be for long," he cautioned.

Kyrlmyrandal snorted. "Let's enjoy it while it lasts." She craned her long neck up at the cliff. "I don't think I can climb that."

Himadra closed his eyes. "We did what we could. It's somebody else's problem now."

38

THE THRONE HELD MRITHURI LIKE AN EMBRACE. ITS POWER RAN THROUGH her, filled her up. The snakebite had only been a foretaste of true strength, true clarity. This—this was what she had been born for.

This was what she had been made for.

She basked in it for a moment, knowing the urgency of action but feeling no anxiety about it. She would be in time. She was the empress in truth now.

Then, as she had before but more deliberately this time and with greater knowledge, she reached out into the veins and flesh and nerves of Sarath-Sahal, of Sahal-Sarat.

She felt the gods moving in the land. Far to the east, outside what should have been her reach, two titanic forces struggled, and the hot and furious one was on the verge of overwhelming the one that was dutiful and stern. She felt them because of their link to her kingdoms, because their strength was tributary to the strength that underlay the Mother River, and the Mother River underlay the land. She felt something else, too—a web of constraints, of bindings. Of taps that fed the strength and flow of the throne, that fed her strength in turn. Not just the dragonglass and the light it caught and focused, but the Mother itself—called Abundant, called Milk of the Earth—was bound to the yoke of the throne.

Mrithuri could feel other things, too—the beast like a wound that itched and festered, the dragon-gates like stitches that bound the layers of a quilt together. The Between Places, the cloisters, the wreakings that kept the world from flying apart. The awareness of the Mother of Exiles, Kyrlmyrandal, threaded through everything. And a half-familiar sense of another sentience out there, observing but restrained from intervening. This, Mrithuri understood, must be Jharni, the Eyeless One. Wizard-Prince of Messaline, Princess of Sarath-Sahal, exile from same. And now, Mrithuri could see, prevented by the very bonds that held the Lotus Kingdoms together from intervening personally in their fate. Or even from ever returning home. She was exiled, entirely.

Had her father, the Alchemical Emperor, truly been so afraid of what she might do to his creation?

He must.

The Wizard-Prince of Messaline had done what she could. It was up to Mrithuri and her cousins now.

There was one presence, Mrithuri realized, that she could not sense anywhere in the land. It was the Mother herself. Not just the river and its power but the goddess who personified it. The strength and the freedom and the will of the water, of the fertile and giving land. The nurturing presence to whom Mrithuri prayed and ministered was nowhere to be felt. Her power was there for Mrithuri's taking.

Her presence, her will, were nowhere to be found.

Where is she? Mrithuri asked the throne. And the throne through all its tendrils and roots and connections asked the land.

And the land answered with a fearful shiver.

But from beyond it came a reply of sorts, two words, strained as if spoken under great duress. The voice of the Eyeless One. *Ask Deep.*

Well, then. Where was she?

Where wasn't she? The goddess of the volcano dwelled in Ansh-Sahal, still, and she dwelled far out to the east, in the Sea of Storms. She rested at the roots of the Cold Fire, in the headwaters of the wild Tsarethi that became, when it left the mountains, the Mother River.

Mrithuri spoke her name. "Deep. Come, and treat with me."

Mrithuri stood over a dream landscape, all of Sarath-Sahal spread out before her like topography on the sand table in her war room. As she watched, the earth cracked, and a woman in a low-cut dress the color of aquamarines rose out of the revealed inferno. Updrafts lashed her hair and hems. Flames licked around her soot-dark feet.

"You want my help," Deep said.

"I do."

The volcano goddess fingered the diamonds at her throat. "I don't love your family any better than that beast or those sorcerers. I was thinking of letting them fight it out and then cleaning up whatever is left over. Besides, what makes you so certain I can defeat them?"

"I'm not," said Mrithuri. "But I know *we* have to try."

"Will you force me to intervene? You have your filthy throne."

"Mine is the hand that holds the knife," Mrithuri admitted. "And I will. If I have to. But I'd rather we came to an accommodation."

The goddess put a hand against her chin. "Will you feed me virgins?"

"How do you feel about calves?"

Deep sighed a smoke ring. "I suppose your vassals *did* break one binding on me. Are they fat calves?"

"The fattest. And we'll fight beside you. I'm not asking you to do anything we won't do ourselves."

Deep frowned, sucking thoughtfully on her cheroot. When she spoke at last, each word was a curl of smoke. "That is one difference between you and your great-grandfather. And you and those sorcerers. But still you hold my chain."

"The throne holds your chain."

"And you hold the throne."

"I was told to ask you something," said Mrithuri, trying to feel like an equal to this transcendent and terrifying being. "Where is the Mother?"

Deep stared at her. Deliberately, the goddess took a long drag on her twisted cigarette. Then, as if her self-control had finally broken, she threw her head back and laughed as if she could not believe, could not internalize the fact of Mrithuri's naiveté. It was a mocking laugh, and it went on for a long time.

Mrithuri's spirit shriveled. She held on to the strength of the throne that filled her, the heady sensation of knowing and feeling the land. She *was* the empress. She had every right to ask this question. The throne gave her that right.

"Wow," said Deep. "They really did raise you lot in the dark. Kid, who the hell do you think I am?"

THE EARTH SHOOK UNDER THE DEAD MAN'S FEET AS THE GAGE RAN PAST HIM, limping heavily, kicking snow out of the way and scraping sparks with the arc of one twisted leg. Behind him, the monstrosity that the sorcerers had ridden into battle slumped, an obscene mockery of a sleeping child. Ravani stood beside it in her bottle-green coat lined in tiger fur, hands on her hips and head cocked to one side as if she didn't quite believe what she was seeing.

The Dead Man leveled his remaining pistol at her.

"Don't shoot," she said, raising her hands. "I'm just here as a spectator. Your boss is breaking a lot of bonds, and I'm just as happy to be free of them."

He wasn't inclined to be forgiving. But—to be honest—he had bigger things on his mind. Like the three massive structures gliding down the slope of the far hill on rows and rows of mechanical legs, taut sails outlining their frames.

Knuckling his eyes in disbelief, Tsering-la came up beside the Dead Man. "How in the six hundred hells are we supposed to fight those?"

"Cannons?" said Ata Akhimah.

The Dead Man looked at her sidelong. "You got one in your pocket?"

It wasn't even halfway funny, and they didn't laugh. They just stood there, watching what was now several cities run over the landscape toward them on their hundreds of enormous, insectile, openwork legs. "When they get a little closer," Tsering-la said.

Ata Akhimah nodded. "I might be able to take one." She didn't sound confident.

"Well," said Tsering-la. "Let's see."

Marigold light streaked from his hands, forming a shimmering plate in front of the rightmost city. The Dead Man had seen cannonballs bounce off those shields.

The city ran right through it, legs glittering weirdly green and iron-bright as they cycled and spun. The shield shattered like a pane of poured glass.

Tsering-la wiped blood from his nose onto the back of his glove. "Nope."

Akhimah grunted. She scrubbed her hands against her trouser legs and squared her shoulders. The Dead Man saw no other sign of her Wizardry, but thick, soft-looking sparks coiled up one leg of the city on the left, crackling like lightning. The leg seized, joints welded, and with each rippling step the city took, it pawed in midair.

She sighed. "Maybe if I do a whole row?"

As she spoke, the Gage reached the middle of the three. He grabbed a leading leg and swung up it hand over hand, using the gaps in the armature as handholds.

"Is that dragonbone?" Ata Akhimah asked.

"Explains why the magic wouldn't work, then," Tsering said. "Not much Wizardry works on dragonglass or dragonbone."

"So what happens next?" the Dead Man asked.

The Gage was nearly to the top of the leg he was climbing. The Wizards looked at one another.

"I think we run away," said Tsering-la.

"Great idea."

The Dead Man jumped in his boots at Ravani's voice so close. She had walked up beside them, and now she stood there nonchalantly, arms folded.

"I'll start." She snapped her fingers and vanished.

An instant later, the sky tore open and a gigantic, howling, amorphous figure toppled through. The beast, the Dead Man dimly recognized, a monumental gray billowing form with eyes that crackled lightning.

The earth jumped and split. The Dead Man fell against Ata Akhimah. Reflexively, she caught his elbow. They both dropped to their knees. His trousers tore and blood trickled. He didn't want to think about what filth lurked on the cobblestones. They helped each other up, staggering as the ground rose and fell in waves.

The earth between the Dead Man, Akhimah, and Tsering-la and the walking cities ripped apart like . . . like soft wax bent between giant hands, like a pastry cracked in half. The brittle top broke, and the softer insides stretched and pulled.

"There's our retreat," said the Dead Man.

They pulled each other around to face the beast as it humped and shifted, rising. It was all the way back where they had come through the dragon-gate; it must have followed them. It was just simply so enormous that ten minutes' walk for humans was for it a single stride.

It turned slowly and seemed to notice them, and to notice the walking cities. Snow swept up its legs into the vortex of its body, combining with ash and what might be a mist of water. Steam rose from its surface as the merciless Uncauled Sun beat down.

Tsering-la dropped his new coat on the ground. The white hemp shirt underneath was transparent with sweat. The Dead Man's head swam from heat. He wished he had time to strip as well, but his reload supplies were in his coat pockets and his weapons were belted over it.

The Dead Man leveled his gun. He remembered standing in the snow of a mountain pass, the enormousness of an ice-drake attacking the caravan. How useless his pistol had been.

It was even more useless now, he reckoned. But he had nothing else to try. The beast was misshapen, one arm gone almost to the shoulder. Something *could* hurt it, then.

Probably not a little pistol in a Dead Man's hand.

The beast threw back its head and laughed. A hollow, booming sound. A sound like glaciers cracking. It rolled across the land, each beat striking the Dead Man in the chest like a blow. The ground trembled.

"It's been an honor," Tsering-la said, and raised his hands.

Ata Akhimah just took one deep breath and held it, a shimmer like a heat mirage surrounding her. The Dead Man had a sense that if he touched her, she would jolt him with electricity.

Laughing, still laughing—

—the beast turned away. It turned its back on all of them, and its face toward the Uncauled Sun, and strode south as fast as a stormfront. With a clattering rumble of uncountable legs and a snap of giant sails, the walking cities tacked away from the ruined palace of Ansh-Sahal, the heap of corpses and the melting snow, and turned to follow.

"Oh, shit," said Ata Akhimah. "It's headed toward Sarathai-tia."

THE LEGS OF THE WALKING CITY CHURNED ALL AROUND THE GAGE AS HE swung higher. He'd climbed into one of these before, under worse conditions. This was comparatively easy. His metal body had no muscles to tire, no ligaments to feel strain. The jerky motion of the leg swung him like a pendulum, and he let each swing toss him higher.

Before long, he was in the undercarriage of the thing. Before, he had seen it in a clogging sandstorm. Now the bright sun streamed down on every side, and even in the shadows of its belly he could clearly make out the rows of crankshafts that drove the legs along. Propulsion came from the wind.

These cities were abominations, run on debt slavery, poisoning those who worked within. They had been built of the corpses of dragons and existed to collect dragonglass and dragonbone in the wastelands, and the very materials they prospected for poisoned them. Helpless people from Messaline toiled within, people as innocent as anybody ever was, which was to say, *somewhat.* That was why he hadn't destroyed the Many-Legged Truth the last time he encountered it.

But now he could see plainly how to cripple it. How to render this thing unusable without harming its passengers.

And if the people inside had to walk to Song or Rasa afterward, well. It wouldn't be any worse for them than staying inside while their hair fell out and their jaws rotted. If the Lotus Empire didn't fall, maybe Mrithuri could send them food and water.

He reached the top of the leg and saw the swiftly rotating crankshaft. One shaft operated the whole rank of legs, so they rippled along like a horizontal centipede's, automatically rising and falling.

The Gage swung his lower body out, locked his legs around the crankshaft, and let go of the churning leg. He reached up with his hands and caught a tooth on the big gear that the shaft locked into. Then he just— held on.

The crankshaft turned. His lower body dropped and pulled his hands down. The gear twisted out of alignment, dragged by the force of the very machine it turned.

The Gage snatched his gauntlets away as metal ground on metal and orange-white sparks shot in a long phoenix tail from the undercarriage. The city lurched, and the whole front line of legs seized—some lifted, some dragging. The legs behind continued pushing it forward. The seized legs began to buckle, and the Gage decided that now was an excellent time to jump ship.

Mrithuri looked into Deep's pellucid eyes and knew the truth of everything. Knew where the power in her throne came from and its connection to the land. Knew what the Alchemical Emperor had done, how he had raised his throne and built his empire.

And knew it was her duty to repair it.

It's not fair. I just got this strength. I shouldn't have to!

But she did. The original sin wasn't hers. But the restoration couldn't be performed by anyone else. She could make Deep do as she wanted. She could keep this power, this intoxicating rush. It made her confident; it made her feel like an empress in truth instead of a fraud. It was the proof of her Divine Right. She *could* keep it.

Or she could return it to the divinity to whom it rightfully belonged.

"I see," she said. "Yes, of course. The path of justice is easier when somebody else forces you onto it; did you know that?"

Deep smiled. "A good daughter is dutiful no matter the price. A good Mother makes the decision that is fairest for everyone, and does not ask unreasonable sacrifices of her children. Or herself. And if there is an unfair price to be paid, she pays it. You are not the Daughter, daughter. You are your people's Mother now."

For the last time, Mrithuri gathered up all the strength that ran through Sahal-Sarat into her hands. She cupped them, let the power brim and trickle through her fingers.

She spread them wide and loosed the flood.

ATA AKHIMAH YELPED AT THE HORRIBLE RENDING OF METAL. THE CENTRAL walking city toppled forward, as if it tripped over its own legs, and fell. The crash happened slowly, in stages rather than all at once, and by the time it was over, the second city was tumbling forward in the same manner as the first.

The beast had begun to turn back at the sound. Now it rounded.

The earth before it split, bulged, and shattered, a long chasm running out from the split in the earth that had formed before. A woman in a peacock-blue gown rose up from the crack, standing with bare feet on a pillar of molten stone.

Her back was to them. She faced the beast as it rose up over them like a whirlwind, like a thunderhead. Blazing eyes glared down.

It spoke, which was a thing Ata Akhimah had somehow never imagined.

"You," it said. "My creatures bound you once. Do you think I cannot do the same?"

Deep hooked her thumbs through her belt. "It is true," she said. "You have done that to me. But I am not what I once was. And what I am, I am."

She tossed her hair. In the distance, the third city began to collapse. The beast roared in fury. "I will be avenged!"

"It's time to heal," she said, and with a gesture of her delicate hand she reached out and pulled the enormous figure down into her arms. It struggled as it fell in on itself, but the struggles were like those of a toddler. As if Sayeh scooped up her son and held him when he didn't want to be restrained.

The goddess sighed as the beast kicked out. It swung a gigantic arm that was too short to reach her. She tucked it under her elbow. "I know you've been badly treated," she said. "But let's put you back in your own home, shall we?"

The remaining cities had ground to a halt, their sails hanging slack with no wind in them. The beast wailed in rage. The goddess looked down at the wreck of the Many-Legged Truth and its sisters and shook her head theatrically. "You don't belong here. You need to go home now. Scoot! Back to the Lion Sun with all of you."

She waved her free hand over them. As it passed each one, that city vanished with a sound like a popped bladder, and no more fanfare than that.

She turned over her shoulder, her hair falling like ash-streaked blackness beside her face, and she winked one bright eye at Ata Akhimah and the others. "You've done well, children. It's also time you went home."

She snapped the fingers on her free hand. Ata Akhimah felt a rush of air, and then she was standing in the golden courtyard of Mrithuri's palace. She staggered slightly under the blazing sun, as if the spin of the world beneath her feet had altered slightly.

The Gage, the Dead Man, and Tsering-la stood beside her. Tsering-la stooped to pick up his discarded coat, which lay neatly folded at his feet.

"Wow," the Gage said. He was holding what looked like a·bent clockwork gear as big as a wagon-wheel in his hands. He set it down carefully. "I was not expecting that."

The flagstones baked Akhimah's feet inside her boots. She pointed at the sun. "That's still a problem," she said.

Tsering-la ran a finger under his jade collar, raising it from the sweat. "Let's go inside and see what we can do about it."

Mrithuri swam through a dream, still enmeshed in the awareness of the throne though she had given up the ability to direct its power. It swept her along like the current of the Mother, a white and formless light like the light that was all the river dolphins saw through their sealed eyelids. She tumbled in it. The current bore her. And it bore her toward the Origin of Storms.

She saw the dragon on the beach, the broken body of Himadra on the sand. She saw Vara, and would have reached into his mind. But the river bore her past, tumbling, tumbling, tumbling. To where Chaeri stood, wrapped in the coils of her spiraling hair, the light twisted around her ankles like ropes dragging her down. Tears streamed down Chaeri's face. She reached out her hand to Mrithuri. "Save me, save me. Forgive me. I am so sorry, Your Abundance! I am so sorry! I was wrong!"

Mrithuri reached out her hand. She swam downward through the light. Chaeri reached up toward her, receding, pleading. Their fingertips touched. Mrithuri felt everything—the grief, the anger, the resentment. The undeniable but poisoned love.

All of it. All at once.

"Forgive me!" Chaeri whimpered.

"I cannot forgive you," said Mrithuri. "Because if I do, you will just find a way to harm me again."

Lost in the light, she drew back her hand.

39

FORGETTING PROPRIETY, SAYEH REACHED ACROSS VARA'S NECK AND GROPED for the anchorite's hand. The old woman clasped her and squeezed in return. Her skin felt papery and soft but her grip was firm.

Sayeh's other senses were subsumed in those of the bearded vulture. His keen eyesight; his unmatchable sense of smell. He still felt some adolescent awkwardness in his newly grown body. But the updrafts were strong and the flying wasn't complicated—so far.

It was good that Sayeh wasn't using her own eyes to see with, because even closed as they were, they stung with hot tears. The Bad Daughter was beating her sister back, step by step up the mountainside. Trees snapped under their enormous feet. Ancient basalt outcrops cracked and crumbled. Avalanches rumbled down the slopes to plunge into the sea.

The warring goddesses parried and lunged, thrust and countered. Their many arms were seen and half-seen, weapons too numerous to count blurring into one another. The sound of their combat lifted on the wind, strange and attenuated. They sounded, the two of them, like an entire battle.

"What . . ." Sayeh began, but she didn't even know how to form the question.

"They fight," said the anchorite, "in all the worlds at once."

"The Good Daughter is losing. What happens then?"

The anchorite's voice was just barely audible above the wind. "I would guess . . . her sister burns everything."

KYRLMYRANDAL COCKED HER WING OVER HIMADRA'S FACE TO SHADE HIM BEfore the sun could start to burn. He would have laughed at being treated like a child or a pet in need of care, but he supposed from Kyrlmyrandal's perspective, nearly everything that wasn't a god was the moral equivalent of a child or a pet. Also, he couldn't laugh, because when he tried, his chest felt stabbed and fresh blood filled his mouth. Because he was lying on his back, he had to swallow it. And if he swallowed too much, it would make him sick, and he didn't even want to think about that.

He just wanted to die in peace, soon, without too much more pain. The sand was warm and comfortable, and his body felt so heavy—

Something darkened the filtered light that fell through Kyrlmyrandal's wing. He opened his eyes, only then realizing he had closed them.

Nizhvashiti stood over him, black robes fluttering in the wind, bare scalp reflecting the sun. It seemed darkly transparent, like a piece of obsidian held up to the sun.

"Did you win, then?" Himadra asked. He yawned. It was so hard to focus his eyes.

"*She* is still fighting." The Godmade crouched beside him, more fluidly than he had seen it move before. Its feet seemed to hover a finger's depth above the sand. "But She sent me to care for you."

"I'm so tired," he said. "I'm thirsty. It hurts."

"You are bleeding inside. I can ease your path back to the Mother if you wish. Or I can help you stay."

"Ansha." He blinked, fought his eyes open again. It hurt to breathe. It hurt to speak. He *could* rest, he thought. Let someone else sort it out. Go and see . . . his father, his mother, all the friends lost in long years of hunger and war. He could come back to the world as a new being, in the fullness of time. Someone with different challenges. Different tasks. Maybe he had learned enough to earn that.

Or he could stay and get to know his brothers. Help them grow into men. Heal what he could of the damage Anuraja had done to them. And to him.

It seemed much harder than falling asleep.

Virtue, he thought, was not accrued by doing what was easy. And he owed it to Sayeh, didn't he? To stay and help keep her son safe.

"Is the world going to end?" he asked.

"Not the world," said Nizhvashiti. "Maybe Sarath-Sahal. If She cannot defeat her sister."

"I'll stay," Himadra said, before he could doubt himself. He doubted himself anyway.

Nizhvashiti laid a hand upon his brow.

It felt like a cool breeze, like something that wasn't really there. The pain eased, and the thirst.

The tiredness didn't change at all.

"Your bones will be a little stronger, Lord Himadra," said Nizhvashiti. "A gift from Her, for the service you have done. And because you have two boys to raise, if they survive."

He sat up, because he was going to fall asleep if he didn't. "Is there nothing we can do to help Her?"

Nizhvashiti shook its head. "She is doing what she can. And Mrithuri has freed the Mother from a binding she was under, to do the bidding of the Peacock Throne. Perhaps she will be moved to protect the Kingdoms, if my patron fails."

"Maybe not," Kyrlmyrandal said. "But there is something *I* can give. I am not out of strength yet."

Nizhvashiti looked up at the dragon, blind eyes glittering. "You are older than the world, Kyrlmyrandal. That is a great deal to give up."

"It's our fault the world got broken in the first place. And it's the waste of our wars that was used to wreck it further. Besides—" She laughed. "—Mrithuri needs a daughter, and I can give her one. That's the real secret of the royal line, isn't it, Nizhvashiti? Not that the women can talk to beasts. But that the women carry the spark within them that kept the Mother real and present in the world, even when the Alchemical Emperor bound her away? That it is they, as the Mother's priestesses, who will stay her wrath now that Mrithuri has freed her? And all of the three living young heirs of the house are male."

"Excuse me," said Himadra. "But what are you talking about?"

The dragon tipped her head sideways over him, as if to acknowledge that she knew much more than she ever told.

"What he left for his daughters and granddaughters was not a gift," said Nizhvashiti. "It was a burden, because he thought less of them."

"They will make it their strength," Kyrlmyrandal said. "Now take *my* strength for the one you serve. Take my immortality and this dragonshape of mine. And take the Carbuncle for Mrithuri. But you must return it to the eldest of my folk when she has had her child. There must be a new Mother of Exiles when I am gone."

Nizhvashiti bowed from the waist. As Himadra stood, marveling at how easy it was to just put his feet under him and rise, it reached out one immaterial hand and pressed it through the dragon's lowered head, into her enormous skull.

The dragon winced. The Godmade grimaced. A wind that Himadra could not feel blew from the dragon, ruffling the Godmade's robes. The Godmade grew . . . brighter, more solid.

Far above them, Himadra heard a goddess laugh.

When Nizhvashiti drew its hand back, a red-orange stone the size of a fist was clutched in the dark, twiggy fingers.

The dragon gave an enormous sigh and laid her head upon the sand. Her eyelids fluttered once, then drooped.

Nizhvashiti gave the sun-radiant stone to Himadra. He enfolded it in both hands. It was as warm as blood. The brilliant carnelian color was streaked in his vision by tears.

The dragon lay still. Himadra stuck the gem inside his coat and touched the warm skin of her cheek with his hand. It was soft as fine muslin, sparkling with tiny scales.

Nizhvashiti drifted along Kyrlmyrandal's extended neck until it came to the shoulder. Waves that could have been carved from aquamarine rippled beneath its feet.

It reached out, with both hands into the body of the dragon this time. When it drew back, it brought with it other hands clutched in its own, long arms with crepey skin, the teardrop muscles of a pair of shoulders. A head crowned with white hair.

Kyrlmyrandal the woman stepped out of the body of Kyrlmyrandal the dragon and into the calf-deep sea. She let go of Nizhvashiti's insubstantial hands and turned back to lay a hand upon herself.

"That's unsettling," she said. She dusted her hands down herself and shook her head. "Well. I guess I had better get used to being small."

"And brief," said Nizhvashiti.

"I GAVE AWAY THE POWER," MRITHURI SAID, AS THE WIZARDS, THE GAGE, AND the Dead Man came into the empty throne room.

Her whole body ached with exhaustion. Her thoughts swam. She had dragged herself down the steps of the throne and now sat on the dais, on the torn cushion salvaged from her chair of estate. The chair itself had been crushed by falling debris.

"I gave it back to the person it belonged to."

"What does that mean?" the Dead Man asked.

She looked up at him, vision blurring. "It means I can't do anything about the sun."

Tsering-la nodded. Then he sat down on the green and blue flagstones in the brilliant, dappled light, put his hands over his face, and cried.

"CAN WE DISTRACT HER?" SAYEH ASKED. "CAN YOU . . . DO WHAT YOU DID before?"

The Good Daughter was climbing the glacier now, feet nimble on snow and ice, skipping over crevasses as if they were cracks between cobblestones. A whirl of snow came up around her as she spun, glittering like the sequined skirts of a dancer. A sudden glow suffused her and she laughed, defending herself more nimbly—as if a tired arm found more strength all of a sudden. She beat a few steps back down the mountain, pushing the Bad Daughter sideways.

But the Bad Daughter was inexorable, like a glacier herself. She would not retreat, and even strengthened, the Good Daughter could not quite pierce her guard.

At least she wasn't losing ground anymore, whatever had just happened.

"I will try," said the anchorite doubtfully. "There is no door where they are, and I am tired. Even if I managed to make one, the Good Daughter would reach it first."

"No," Sayeh said. "Don't do it. Too many risks. Would a dragon-gate even hold a goddess? I had something else in mind."

With her mind, she asked Vara a question that wasn't in words. The vulture responded with doubt, his head moving from side to side as he surveyed the mountain, the glacier, the dueling gods. He was not confident in his own estranged body, in the strength and dexterity of his wings.

Can you try? Sayeh asked without words.

He answered with action.

Folding his wings, Vara toppled from the sky like a felled tree, plunging toward the battling gods. Sayeh shrieked aloud and so did the anchorite, their voices raised in equal parts fear, surprise, and delight.

It was like nothing Sayeh had ever experienced, hurtling from the sky toward the seething mountain. The Good Daughter teetered on the lip of the crater now. Plumes of ash lit with crackling lightning towered behind her. The Bad Daughter drew her spear of light back for one more blow—

Vara plummeted between them, falling so fast that the sulfuric fumes barely had time to sting Sayeh's eyes. His claws raked toward the Bad Daughter. Then they were past, and he opened his wings with a snap that sent Sayeh and the anchorite rocking back against the straps that held them in the saddle. Vara skimmed over the glacier for a moment, his angle of descent almost matched to the angle of the mountain's slope. Then they passed over a sudden drop, and an updraft caught them and threw them skyward once again.

The pommel struck Sayeh right between the legs. "Shit!" she yelped, then looked apologetically at the anchorite.

The anchorite was laughing so hard, tears streamed back her cheeks from beneath her goggles.

Vara turned on a wingtip, and Sayeh craned her head around to see what happened next.

The Bad Daughter reeled for a moment, ducking away from the unexpected assault. The Good Daughter recovered first, advancing, all her swords at play. But her sister parried, and the shining shaft of her spears sparked off the blades. It was too fast. *They* were too fast, because the spear was reflected in all the Bad Daughter's reflected hands. They glittered. They danced. They fought the Good Daughter to a standstill once more.

"Oh, no," Sayeh whispered. The anchorite squeezed her hand all the harder. Sayeh was surprised to discover they were still clinging together.

The Good Daughter smiled.

She stepped forward and impaled herself on her sister's spears of light. The shafts collapsed inward on one another, as if someone folded a mirror, as if all the possible worlds fell in that one act into a single eventuality. A single *inevitability.*

Sayeh heard herself howl. In grief, in despair—she did not know the answer.

The Good Daughter walked up the spear, step by step, immobilizing it with her own body. And when she reached her sister's hands, she lifted her sword and slashed it through the Bad Daughter's neck.

Sayeh's free hand flew to her mouth, and whatever happened next was lost in a blaze of light like the sun.

THE TERRIBLE FLASH OF LIGHT CAME AND WENT, AND THEN THERE WERE NO more sounds of battle. Himadra didn't know what had happened—but the world was still here. He was walking through the water. Feeling it wash his calves and ankles. Under his bare feet, feeling the sand. He held his boots up high to keep the leather from getting soaked with salt water.

He wasn't any taller. He assumed he wasn't any better looking. But he was walking on his own. And he didn't feel any pain.

A woman walked beside him, tall and white-eyed, dark of skin. Her face was lined around the lips. The sun cast a halo through the whiteness of her hair.

They came around the headland where the cliff reached down to the water. There was still sand to support them. He saw darting fish beneath the waves, and what looked like white trees made of bone, blossoming in every imaginable color. A writhing, many-armed sea creature the size of his fist jetted away. It was the bluest thing he had ever seen.

He looked up at Kyrlmyrandal—at what was left of Kyrlmyrandal—in wonder.

"Octopus," she said, succinctly.

Ahead, he saw the cove where they had landed, the twisted trees and the towering temple. He wanted nothing in the world so much as to lie down on that soft grass.

A vulture the size of an elephant rested beside the shore, ruffling its pale crest in the wind. Some sort of apparatus harnessed its neck and shoulders. Two women stood by its feet.

One was Sayeh Rajni. The other wore the clothes of a priestess.

Himadra raised his hands to hail them. Sayeh sighed visibly—he couldn't hear it over the ocean—and stepped forward to meet them. "I think we are what remains," she said. "You're walking."

"There was a miracle."

"Several." She pointed up the beach. There were two figures there. Nizhvashiti, cross-legged and unmoving, its strange mismatched eyes open wide. And laid out on the grass, a pretty young woman with spiral curls. He'd seen her, he thought. Riding with Ravani that once.

"The missing handmaiden?" he guessed. He remembered Ata Akhimah mentioning it.

"Mrithuri will want her body back," Sayeh said.

"What about Nizhvashiti?" He walked up, touched the Godmade lightly on the cheek. It felt like polished wood, like lacquered leather. There was no sense of life within.

Carry me into the temple, a voice said. *I have much to meditate on.*

"The transformation is complete," Sayeh said, with a catch in her voice.

Himadra just felt numb. It was beautiful that Sayeh still had it in her to grieve. But then, she had always been a better person than he was.

Himadra held out his hand and laid the red jewel in Sayeh's palm. "For your wife. From Kyrlmyrandal."

She looked at him. Then at Kyrlmyrandal. "Is this what I think it is?"

Kyrlmyrandal's creased face smiled. "I'm not a dragon anymore."

Himadra said, "Can I call you a Wizard now, then?"

She pursed her lips. "I'm only human. So . . . I suppose you can. Oh, tell the Gage something from me. Tell him it means 'the breaker' or 'the broken' or 'the thing that binds.'"

"Tell him what does?"

She shrugged. "He'll know."

Himadra nodded. It didn't hurt. He might become reckless now. "You're not coming back with us?"

She tossed back her long pale hair. "There's only so much room on that vulture," she said. "And the first thing *I'm* going to do is go climb through that magic tree arch a couple of times and see if it makes my hips stop hurting quite so much."

40

WHEN THE GAGE'S REPAIRS WERE COMPLETE, HE EMBRACED ATA AKHIMAH very gently in thanks, because he thought she, of all the mechanics and all the Wizards he had known, would appreciate it. She grinned at him and threatened him with a wrench. "Don't get any ideas. I can put a dent in that shine."

"You'd just have to polish it out again," he said, and went to find the Dead Man.

The Dead Man was with the empress in her stellar, which the Gage supposed was also a solar now—now that the Uncauled Sun burned in a sky as blue and pale as aquamarine. It was hot, but it wasn't *too* hot. The Mother, Mrithuri explained, had taken pity on them and made the Sun smaller, or perhaps moved it farther away. Despite her grief over her daughters.

Mrithuri sat on cushions cross-legged, her belly bare between her undyed blouse and the waistband of her wrap, the Queenly Tiger winking in her navel. Syama lay with her great head upon the empress's knee.

The daughter inside Mrithuri was not yet showing. The Gage didn't know if she had told the Dead Man. The Gage only knew about it because she had entrusted the Carbuncle to him, to pass on to the eldest of the dragons.

He would have to seek Kyrlmyrandal as the first step of the quest, because none of them had the least idea where to start looking. It had been Nizhvashiti's promise to get it to the next Mother of Exiles. As the Godmade was indisposed, he guessed it fell to him to get it back to the prior owner.

Sayeh was also in the room, lolling on cushions, and three small children played beside her, watched over by a grinning nurse. Not Iri; Iri had gone back to Chandranath with Himadra, to be one of his horsemasters.

One of the children was Drupada; the other two were orphans of some beloved servant, rescued from Ansh-Sahal.

Ümmühan and Yavashuri sat beneath the windows. Lady Golbahar, who had arrived with the caravan and Syama and a certain elephant—among others. She combed the poetess's long, gray hair. Hnarisha had been left behind in Sarathai-lae, seeing to administration. The latticed door to the cloisters stood open and a cool breeze emerged from the depths. Far away, the Gage could hear the nuns singing.

He paused within the doorframe until the empress waved him to come in. Sayeh bent to whisper to the nurse, and the children were bundled up despite complaints and whisked away. Syama lifted her head from Mrithuri's knee and watched them go, sad-eyed.

Or perhaps the Gage was imagining that he knew the bear-dog's emotions. She did always look as if she were frowning.

Mrithuri stretched her leg out with a gasp and a sigh. "We're talking about my illustrious ancestor. And all the trouble he caused."

"He sinned," said the Dead Man. "And the problem with sins is that somebody always gets left with the cleanup. And it's nearly never the original sinner. It's their spouse or their grandchild."

"Great-grandchild." Mrithuri sighed.

"Injustice gets passed along the generations." He looked down at his tea. "It's Sarath-Sahal's good fortune that it came to such an exceptional pair of women in its time of need."

"I'm not unlike other women," Mrithuri said. "And neither is Sayeh."

"It's a good selling point," Yavashuri argued. "The mythology of royalty—"

"Nonsense." Mrithuri spoke as an empress, and Syama tensed but did not rise. "I am the Daughter and the Mother in my person. And in that I am exactly like all other women, because all women are unique."

The Gage saw the Dead Man look away, the pinch at the corner of his eyes.

"Well," said Yavashuri, "in any case, we still have some work to do. But we've sent a draft of Ümmühan's document up to Lord Himadra for review, so once that is out of the way, we can begin moving forward."

"Kyrlmyrandal sent a message for the Gage," said Mrithuri. She held it out to the Gage, a sheet of parchment folded into its own envelope. "All the way from the Banner Isles."

He took it, a scrap light as a leaf in his hand. He broke the red wax seal. Inside, there was one sentence.

You know where to find the door.

He did. He knew the door she meant. The door that would turn him back into the human being he had been.

Maybe someday he would go there, if he could figure out a way to leave again in mortal flesh without rotting of the dragon-poison.

He folded it into his hands. "Do we know where she sent it from? That would be a place to start looking."

"Ata Akhimah might be able to tell you," said Mrithuri. "She has ways of tracing things."

"I'll ask." The Gage paused, but no one else seemed inclined to speak. "To return to the previous topic for a moment, the other problem with inherited sins is that once you *notice* an immoral thing, you are constrained to either try to fix it or sustain a moral hurt yourself by allowing it to persist. So a lot of people will conveniently fail to notice the problem. And often, correcting one injustice leads to a series of other injustices. There's no way out. It's like mortality."

"There's a way out," said Sayeh. "But it's not a human way. You have to give up too much."

Nobody said anything, but the Gage knew they were all thinking about Nizhvashiti.

It was only later, when the palace slept and he walked the battlements alone, that he realized they might also have been thinking about him.

Of course, he noticed the Dead Man coming up beside him. He slowed, to make it easier on his old friend.

They walked in peace a little, until the Dead Man said, "It was a strange thing, being saved because somebody else's god worked a miracle."

The Gage stepped carefully on the golden stones. "Is your faith tested?"

"No," said the Dead Man. "But I might be ready to admit it's not the only one."

The Gage chuckled. "We could leave tomorrow. Druja is heading east, it turns out."

"Go out by the same means we came in? It has some poetry to it. Not sure how we'll get my horse through the desert without him."

"Eh," said the Gage. "If he got tired, I could carry him. It wasn't a pleasant trip on the way in, as you recall."

The Dead Man snorted. "This one might be better. Anyway, my memory is impaired, as I intend to be very drunk soon."

"Don't drink too much," the Gage said. "Your horse would prefer you not vomit all over his withers."

MRITHURI CROUCHED ON HER THRONE ALL IN IVORY, LIKE A VULTURE. HER bare arms rippled under the lines of her tattoos. Sayeh stood at the bottom and looked up at her. "Come down."

The hall was empty. Sayeh had sent everyone away. Everyone except Syama, of course, who lay across the foot of the throne's tall stair.

"Come up," Mrithuri countered.

"Your chair would eat me."

"So sit in my lap."

It was an effort, and Sayeh smiled. "All right," she said. "But if I die, you have to feel bad about it."

She climbed, hitching her bad leg a little. It was an effort, and by the end of it, Mrithuri stood and helped her up the last few steps. She aided Sayeh in sitting down at the foot of the throne, and then perched herself upon it. "I can still feel everything, you know," she said. "I just can't use it anymore."

"Well." Sayeh rested her back against Mrithuri's shin. "At least we'll have some warning of problems."

Mrithuri sighed. "Why do I never feel the things I am meant to feel?"

"Empress, no one does."

Mrithuri's voice dropped to a whisper. "I knew there would be grief. I knew it with the writing on my bones, as Serhan would say. I knew I ought to make different choices. I knew it was a cobra's bargain. And yet I did what I did."

Sayeh thought of saying *You are young, my wife, and this pain too will pass.* But that would be cruel. So instead she said, "You don't eat *ought to.* You only eat *did.*"

Mrithuri snorted.

"You could ask them to stay." Sayeh put a hand on her ankle. "I wouldn't mind much."

Mrithuri flexed her hands on the arms of the chair and said nothing.

Outside the caravan was assembling. The Dead Man's hammerheaded magic horse was tacked up and waiting for him. The Gage was loading crates into the wagons.

Sayeh knew Mrithuri would let them go.

THE DEAD MAN PUT ON HIS OLD, FADED RED COAT. HE BUCKLED HIS GUNS ON over it, and the sword Mrithuri had given him. He laid the new coat, the one Mrithuri had also given him, on the bed.

He turned away and picked his bag up with one hand.

He stopped, as if the threshold were a wall too high to step over. Something pierced him, and he thought of a line of scripture. *The word for family is written in the flesh and in the bone.*

He turned back. He folded the coat and slid it into the bag. There was not too much to carry in there, after all.

MRITHURI SAT ON HER THRONE, AND WITH THE EYES OF THE MOTHER SHE watched the oxen and the horses draw wagons down the road that led to the gates of Sarathai-tia. The Gage glittered in the light of the Uncauled Sun. A slim figure in red, wearing a blue scarf as a veil, rode beside him.

She could watch them all the way to the Sea of Storms, if it suited her.

If she did, she thought, it would just be another kind of addiction.

She stood so abruptly that she woke her wife, who had drowsed sitting there with her back against Mrithuri's knee. Sayeh scrambled to her feet. "What's wrong?"

"Nothing," said Mrithuri. "I need to do something."

"I can do it for you—"

"Take Syama for a walk," Mrithuri said kindly. "Your leg is stiff, and she needs the exercise."

Sayeh might have argued, but she wasn't fast enough to chase Mrithuri down the stairs. Syama sulked too, when Mrithuri left her. It would be fine. Mrithuri could not be responsible for everyone's feelings all the time.

When she entered the library, the person she was looking for was already there. She had expected it: she had cheated with the throne.

"Ümmühan, may I borrow your pen?"

Ümmühan looked up from what she was doing.

"Bring it back quickly," Ümmühan said, with a significant glance at Mrithuri's midsection. "You have a long life ahead of you yet, young woman. And so does your child."

"Yes," said Mrithuri. "But I want to write something down and I need it to be remembered."

Without breaking her gaze, the poetess slid a book out from under her parchments and scrolls. Mrithuri knew it at once. It was the book of lineages of the royal family that Ata Akhimah had . . . corrected.

Mrithuri smiled and sat down cross-legged opposite the poetess. She sought through the book for a blank page. With infinite care, she lined it. She uncapped the lustrous pen and thought.

With infinite care, she wrote *Mrithuri Maharajni, first of her name, Empress of the Peacock Throne.*

"Is that all?" the pen in her hand said, startling her so that she jumped. It was a good thing it was a magic pen, because if she'd had an inkpot, she would have upset it.

"I—"

"You're the empress of everything that lies between the seas, and you fought a goddess and a demon both and won. Surely, you can do better than false modesty!"

Mrithuri looked to Ümmühan for support, but Ümmühan was laughing silently.

"Fine," Mrithuri said.

The entry went on long enough that she had to sand the page and wait, blow the sand away, and go on to the next page before she was done. When she couldn't think of anything else to write, she looked at Heartsblood, admiring the shimmers deep in its red-black shape. "Satisfied?"

The pen gave a happy little sigh.

Mrithuri shook her head. She gave Heartsblood back to Ümmühan and let the book lie open, drying naturally, so as not to disturb the sheen rising to the surface of the ink.

There was yet a satisfying amount of space to be filled.

AUTHOR'S NOTE

Well, we made it.

This was a novel written, in large part, during a plague year. It was a difficult time in the United States, marked by civil unrest, social upheaval, and a great deal of grief, loss, and fear. It was a strange experience, writing this book about, among other things, stewardship and taking responsibility while all around us leaders were failing to take existential threats seriously.

Sometimes writing a novel can feel like chipping away at a mountain.

Anyway, I am inexpressibly happy and relieved to have finished it, and not to have left the friends of Mrithuri, Sayeh, the Gage, and the Dead Man hanging in suspense as to what becomes of them. I could not have done it without the support of my dear friends in various online fora, who kept me sane and helped me through the isolation we all suffered this past year. Alex, Devin, Aliette, Max, Fran, Sarah, Sara, Camille, Karen, Kevin, Amanda, Jamie, Ghis, Mia, Emmy, Celia, Chelsea, Jodi, Amal, Arkady, Viv, Deanna, Ryan, Fade, Liz, Liz, John, Stella, Marissa, Ginger, Cat, Tochi, Clarissa, Sheila, Stephanie, Laura, Yanni—thank you all.

My dear friend Asha's comments were the spark for the Eternal Sky books, which these build upon: thank you too to her. Thank you again to Shveta and Ritu, who helped me with world-building and advice early on in developing this world.

My esteemed editor, Beth Meacham, retired last year, and this will be the last book we work on together. It's been a fifteen-year relationship, and I am full of complicated feelings that something that has been so central to my professional life is changing. She is one of the best in the business. Thank you to her and to her assistant, Rachel Bass, and to my new editor, Melissa Singer, and to everybody in the production department at Tor Books.

My amazing copyeditors, Deanna Hoak and Richard Shealy, make me look good, and bless them for it. I'm also extremely grateful to my agent, Jennifer Jackson, and her assistant, Michael Curry, who help me keep the lights on in more ways than one.

I also want to thank my spouse, Scott Lynch, for keeping the food and coffee coming during the most difficult parts of writing this, and for telling me relentlessly that I *was* good enough to get this hydra in a headlock and wrestle it down. I'd like to thank my mother, Karen, and her spouse, Beth, for everything they do, including picking up Chinese food and enabling me with fountain pens. Heartsblood owes its existence to my mom.

I want to thank my father, Steve, for all the weird archaeology links. I'm pretty sure the inspiration for Nizhvashiti was originally his fault.

Last but not least, thank you to those on Patreon who have opted in to being recognized in these acknowledgments: Emily Gladstone Cole, Thalia C., Patrick Nielsen Hayden, Phil Margolies, DF, Jack Gulick, Blake Ellis, Tiff, Christa Dickson, Tom B., Noah Richards, Grey Walker, Adam De-Coninck, Besha Grey, Paul Stansel, Emilie, Umar, Karen Robinson, John Appel, Jodi Davis, Kari Blackmoore, Valerie DeBill, Paul Keelan, David Lars Chamberlain, Dave Diehl, M. Reppy, E.E.Yore, Alexis Elder, Brigid Cain-O'Connor, Jessie Roy, Heather K., Brooks Moses, Margaret N. Oliver, Max Kaehn, Kim Mullen-Kuehl, Sara Hiat, D. Franklin, Vickie R., Stephanie Gibson, Kyle K., Jack Vickery, Persephone, Marla Carew, Brad Roberts, Jenna Kass, Curtis Frye, Siobhan Kelly-Martens, George Hetrick, NegCol, BC Brugger, Deirdre Culhane, Kevin J. Maroney, Anne Lyle, Jesslyn Hendrix, James Gotaas, Harriet Culver, Edmund Schweppe, Cathy B. Lannom, Olen Thorn, Graeme Wiliams, Kelly Brennan, John Goodrich, Helen Housand, Jon Singer, Dilvish the Damned (Hey, how's Black doing?), Christina Zola Peck, Aimee Kuzenski, Beth Coughlin, crystalbrier, dyslogorrhea, Pierre, Richard Taylor, Marzie Kaifer, Wendy Lindstocking, Amanda Miller, Michael Carychao, cosmii, Mike Harknett, Chris Dwan, Edward Hanlon, Thomas Lumley, Ann Rhodes, Sarah, Karl Dandenell, Tegan M., Bonnie Shackleford, and Jenny D.